INCANDESCENTLY

INCANDESCENTLY

a collection of modern
Pride and Prejudice stories

McKinley James

CONTENTS

To the one and only Jane Austen, for writing some of the most beloved novels of all time, and to the JAFF community for loving them so hard we had to create more.

"You may only call me Mrs. Darcy when you are completely, and perfectly, and incandescently happy."

-PRIDE AND PREJUDICE, 2005 FILM

A TURN OF EVENTS

"I'M sure he'll turn up, Elle."

Elizabeth Bennet paused her room-scan for her date to look at her best friend and roommate, Jane. Jane was the sweetest soul on the planet, but at the moment Elle didn't share her optimism. The party at the big house on Netherfield Street just off Meryton U's campus had been going strong for an hour, and Grant had not only not shown up, he hadn't even bothered to text her. Good thing she'd decided to meet him there instead of letting him pick her up.

"I don't know whether to be pissed or worried," she sighed. "It's possible he forgot, or maybe something happened, but if not, he should have the decency to let me know he's not coming."

Jane's bluebell eyes radiated sympathy, and she squeezed Elle's hand. "As much as I don't want to think he stood you up, the chances of something so terrible happening that he couldn't even send you a message are slim."

Just in case, Elle pulled her phone from the pocket of her tan corduroy skirt, double checking for any messages. There were none.

"I'm sorry, hon."

"You know," Elle huffed, "I'm not. I like him, but not enough to be hurt if he's ghosting me. Oh, here comes Chase."

Jane instantly perked up as her newly-minted boyfriend, the handsome and affable Chase Bingley, approached them through the thickening crowd. He grinned at both of them, but the joy in his expression was all for Jane.

"I should be done with host duties for a while," he said. "Ricky can handle it."

"What about Liam?" Elle asked.

Chase lifted an amused brow and glanced at the corner where they'd set up food and drink tables in the dining room. William Darcy, second-year Publishing grad student, wealthy Pemberley Publishing heir apparent, and perpetual thorn in her side, was leaning against the wall brooding into a clear plastic cup while Chase's sister, Carrie, tried to get his attention by twirling her hair and babbling at him.

The sight of him—tall frame and lean build in jeans and a turquoise t-shirt, raven-black hair waving around his face, eyes she knew to be a deep green sulking behind stylish square-framed glasses—had her foolish heart doing a slow roll. Heat flushed in her cheeks when he looked up, seemed to be looking directly at her. Why did he have to be so good-looking? Especially when he only thought she was *decent*-looking.

She didn't care, she reminded herself. He was an arrogant prick.

Since she'd met him at her grad school orientation a little over a month before, his disdainful attitude had quickly put her off any romantic notions and, for the most part, kept them at bay. Every now and then she weakened enough to admit she was attracted to him, but it was simple enough to curb those feelings into contempt when she recalled the rude comment about her she'd overheard him utter.

She was brought out of her trance when Chase spoke. "Darcy organized everything. He gets a break from hosting."

He held out a hand to Jane. "Shall we, m'lady?"

Jane blushed and put her hand in his. Elle watched them join the throng of people dancing in the living room, content to watch Chase twirl Jane, her curly honey-blonde hair and flowy dress swirling around them.

She thought about hitting up the snacks, but not wanting to endure what she'd coined the Darcy Stare, she decided to find her friend Charlotte, the third of their four roommates, instead. She edged around the dancers, passed the line for the first floor powder room, and eventually poked her head into the den.

She didn't find Charlotte, but there among the packed bodies, on the far side of the room next to a pile of jackets, she found the roommate she hadn't been looking for—blatantly playing tongue hockey with Grant Wickham.

Elle did a double take—though if she was being honest, she wasn't that surprised—before ducking back into the hall, taking a breath. She didn't think Lacy had seen her, thankfully, but Grant might have, so she began making her way back to the dining room. She'd almost made it to the living room when she felt a hand at her elbow.

"Hey, E. Sorry I'm late." Grant looked down at her with the smile she'd once thought charming, not even a hint of sheepishness in his manner. "And Lacy, she just came on to me—I think she's had a little too much to drink, ya know?"

She returned his smile with one of her own—one with all the warmth of a polar ice cap. "Yeah, and you looked like you were having a real hard time fighting her off."

He shrugged without missing a beat. "I didn't want to embarrass the lady. I'm sorry if you're jealous."

She scoffed. "No you're not. If you didn't want to go on another date with me, Grant, you could've just told me. I'm a big girl."

"I had a good time, E." He used his grip on her to tug her a little closer. "And you know I like you—"

"I'm just gonna stop you right there," she said, halting him with a hand on his chest. "Before you say something else you don't mean. We're done here."

He shrugged again. "So no hard feelings?"

"None whatsoever. Go have fun with Lacy."

She yanked her arm from his grip as she turned away, but didn't get very far when she met the solid wall that was Liam Darcy.

"Elle. Would you like to dance?"

Flustered, she responded automatically. "Sure."

He took her hand and pulled her toward the dance floor, sparing a scathing look for Grant. She looked over her shoulder as Liam led her away in time to see Grant's smug smile vanish. It may have been small of her, but she felt a tug of satisfaction. She didn't look back again.

It wasn't until they were among the dance crowd she realized what she'd gotten herself into. She thought about making an excuse when the music changed to a lilting male-female duet accompanied by soft guitar and piano melodies, but when he pulled her into a swaying rhythm with ease, she supposed dancing with him wouldn't be too painful.

His arm came around her waist and he nudged her a little closer when she put her other hand on his shoulder. As the song swelled with melodic violin his eyes tracked around the room—probably making sure Grant was gone—before landing on her face. She met his gaze as they swayed, and she found herself leaning into him. She could have sworn his eyes shifted to her lips, and the thought drew her own eyes to his mouth, which was much closer than she'd anticipated.

She didn't jolt, but her intake of breath had him holding her closer so she was pressed against him. To calm her thundering heart she leaned her head in the crook of his shoulder. She felt him sigh; whether it was the emotion of the music, or the surprising calm of his presence, her eyes fluttered shut and she let him lead. It was odd, but it felt natural to be there with him, that way.

When he leaned his head against hers, his breath tickling her hair, her eyes shot open. Remembering who she was with, she abruptly tilted her head up at him. "Thank you for coming to my rescue," she sputtered. "I know you hate dancing."

He seemed a little startled, but then he actually smiled at her. "It depends on my partner. But you're welcome." He paused as he turned her. "May I ask what happened?"

"Grant was supposed to meet me here, but he didn't show—or at least I thought he didn't. Imagine my surprise when I caught him shamelessly making out with Lacy. And he had the gall to blame her, like he was just an innocent bystander." She sighed, watching the other dancers around them. "My own fault. I knew he was a bit of a player and I went out with him anyway."

"I'm sorry. He doesn't deserve you."

A half-laugh escaped her. "No, he doesn't. Don't worry, I'm not upset, my pride is just a little bruised."

"Good. He's not worth it."

Her eyes whipped back to his, searching. "You don't like him, do you? Which is odd, considering you used to be friends."

He stiffened. "Grant is good at making friends, just not very good at keeping them."

Though she couldn't argue, as the exchange from a few minutes before leapt back to her mind, she frowned. "Then, as his former friend, you might understand how his past struggles influence his current actions."

"Why are you so concerned about him?" His frown deepened as he studied her. "Are you trying to understand why he treats women so badly?"

"No, just trying to understand you better."

"Me? And how's that going?"

"I'm not sure," she admitted. "I never know what to expect from you. You keep throwing me off."

"I could say the same of you. Maybe now isn't the best time to dive into the past."

"Fair enough."

The song faded into another, and they stepped back from each other, the spell broken.

"Thank you for the dance," he said stiffly, before turning on his heels, leaving her on the dance floor to wonder at him.

⸱ ⸱ ⸱ ⸳ ⸳

SHE PASSED the next hour chatting with Charlotte, dancing some with Ricky Fitzwilliams and Chase, snacking on some truly delectable meatballs, and nursing a beer. She didn't spot Liam, but she did spot Grant leaving with Lacy. She laughed with Charlotte and pretended not to notice.

Unfortunately, her episode with Grant wasn't the end of the theatrics for the night.

Colin Huntsford caught her alone, during a moment where both Jane and Charlotte were dancing.

"Elizabeth!" His enthusiasm nearly bowled her over.

"Colin."

"Fine evening, isn't it?" he asked, then continued talking before she could make a reply. He droned on about one of his classes, and she did her best to tune him out, silently amused by the way he waved his hands around when he talked. When she couldn't stand it anymore, she interrupted him.

"You know what, I'm thirsty, I'm gonna go get a drink."

"Oh! Of course," he said. "You must be parched. Allow me."

"Oh, that's...not necessary," she protested to his retreating back. Then she shrugged, moving to the other side of the room. At least she'd gotten rid of him.

Her relief, however, only lasted so long.

"Elizabeth!"

The familiar exclamation had her closing her eyes in annoyance.

"There you are!"

She turned around just as he thrust a very full plastic cup at her. Unfortunately, Colin hadn't quite stopped his forward motion, and a good portion of the liquid sloshed over the brim, directly onto her shirt.

He immediately started apologizing profusely.

"Oh, Elizabeth! I'm terribly sorry!" He said, reaching for her shirt.

She swatted his hand away. "It's fine, I can—"

"Oh, no! Let me—"

"Colin." To Elle's immense relief, Charlotte appeared out of thin air and took the cup Colin was still waving around from his hand. "Elle knows what to do, why don't you come with me?"

She gave Elle a knowing look from under chestnut brown bangs as she steered him away, and Elle mouthed "thank you," before looking down to survey the damage. She could only be grateful she was wearing a black top, thus avoiding a potential stain. She pulled at the fabric and sighed.

Jane stepped up to her with a napkin, Chase just behind. "Here."

"Oh, thank you."

"We saw, but I don't think anyone else was paying much attention."

"Do you need anything?" Chase asked her.

"No, I'll be fine, thanks, as long as Colin doesn't come back."

"Charlotte can handle him," Jane assured her.

"I think I'll just go wash up in the kitchen. Go enjoy the party."

"Are you sure?"

"Yeah, get outta here you crazy kids."

Jane squeezed her hand in comfort before she and Chase joined a group of friends that included Carrie. Though Elle was sure Carrie was smirking at her, she was too fed up to care.

Wiping at the spill with the napkin, she made a beeline to the kitchen. Pushing open the swinging door, she stopped almost as soon as she entered.

Great. You again, she thought.

Liam stood leaning against the counter near the sink, a drink in his hand and a frown on his face. He eyed her with a look she couldn't quite read—the good old Darcy Stare—as she rounded the island, tossed the napkin in the trash, and ripped a paper towel from its stand.

"Spill something?" he asked as she let the paper towel absorb moisture. She spared him a glance, and could have sworn he was smirking at her, as though he suspected she was drunk.

"*No,*" she said dryly, "Colin Huntsford insisted on getting me a drink —without asking me what I wanted, I might add—then promptly dumped half its contents on me."

He snorted. "That guy's got two left feet."

"He's harmless, really. I just wish he'd take a hint."

"What did you want?"

"Huh?" She tossed her paper towel, grabbed another. Turned on the faucet.

"To drink."

"Oh." She wetted the towel, began dabbing at fabric. "I guess I would've asked for a beer, but the way this night is going I could probably use a rum and coke."

To her surprise, the corners of his mouth turned up in a small smile. "Coming right up." He set down his drink and had left the kitchen before she realized what he was about.

She shrugged to herself—at least it would get him out of her hair for a minute or two. And she could be reasonably certain neat-as-a-pin-Darcy wouldn't spill anything on her.

Satisfied she'd gotten most of the stickiness out of her shirt, she considered how best to wring it out. She squeezed out some drops into the sink, but her shirt was so soaked it seemed hopeless. Eventually she decided it would be simpler to take it off first. She thought of the line for the powder room down the hall and sighed. Maybe she could sneak upstairs and use a private bathroom.

She turned and headed toward the kitchen stairs.

"What are you doing?"

Damn. Almost made it.

She turned to face Liam as he walked toward her, took the drink he held out.

"I was going to try and find a private bathroom. I need to wring this shirt out but I'd rather not strip down in the kitchen."

"Oh." His eyes flicked over her as he adjusted his glasses, and he cleared his throat. "I think I can help with that."

"There's no need, I can find one," she insisted.

"Yes, but even after that you'd still be wearing a damp shirt. I could toss that in the dryer for you, loan you a shirt while it quick-drys," he offered.

She wanted to decline on principle, but decided it would be stupid, especially since she didn't want to wear a damp shirt the rest of the evening. Of course, she could go home, but did she really want to leave the party just to avoid him?

"Good idea. Thanks."

"No problem."

He led her up the stairs, and she followed him down the hall to his room. She stood just inside the door as he switched on a lamp. While he went to his dresser, dug out a dark gray t-shirt, she took a sip of her drink —of course it was mixed perfectly.

"Thanks," she said when he handed her the crisply folded shirt.

"Bathroom's right here." He turned on the light to an ensuite bath as she set her drink on the dresser.

"You have your own bathroom?"

He shrugged, but smiled, pulling a towel from under the vanity and laying it on the countertop. "All the bedrooms here have an ensuite."

Of course they do, she thought, but she only gave him a thin smile as she went into the bathroom, closed the door. It was clean, she noticed as she unbuttoned her shirt, pulled it off. She couldn't say she was surprised, but she had to admit she appreciated it wasn't covered in grime, toothpaste, and little shaven hairs like other guys' bathrooms she'd seen.

She ran the shirt under the water a little, then wrung it out as much as she could, shook it out. She used her hands to rinse her skin where some stickiness had soaked through, then used the towel he'd provided to dry herself. The front of one of her bra cups was a little damp where some moisture had gotten through; she did her best to dry it, but overall it wasn't damp enough to concern her.

Finally, she tugged the gray tee over her head; it hit her thighs, a few inches above the hem of her skirt. Sighing at herself in the mirror, she experimented with tucking the front of it in to her skirt, decided it looked less stupid than before. Not that it mattered—Liam Darcy wouldn't care what she looked like. Even so, she met her reflection's hazel eyes and finger-combed her hair a little before re-opening the door.

"Where's the laundry room?"

"I'll take care of it." He held out a hand. She frowned, but handed him her shirt and the towel.

When he left, she scanned the room.

It was tidy, as she'd expected, the queen-size bed made with soft-looking pillows and dark blue sheets, a laptop and miscellany organized on a surprisingly simple three-drawer desk, books tucked neatly on various shelves and stacked on his nightstand. There was a comfy-looking chair in one corner, and another door near the bathroom she assumed was a closet.

He didn't have much on the walls, but she couldn't help smiling at the posters—some baseball, some rock bands, and video game posters just like any other college guy. His were framed, of course, and none of them were crooked.

When she walked to the dresser to pick up her drink, she noticed the framed photographs on its top next to the rather large TV and the latest Playstation model.

In one, he was clearly younger, maybe in high school, standing with a slightly younger girl, a man, and a woman—his family, most likely. What stunned her was how happy he looked; she didn't think she'd ever seen him smile the way he was smiling in the picture. In the other photo, it was just him and his sister, and though they were both smiling, they didn't appear as happy.

He'd lost his parents, she remembered, and she couldn't stop the sting of pity in her heart. He may have been a jerk, but he didn't deserve that. And though she knew their aunt had taken them in, she imagined he felt he had to look after his younger sister; if there was one good thing about him she was certain of, it was that he loved his sister.

Maybe it was grief that had changed him.

Still no excuse for his behavior, she reminded herself. To distract herself from unwelcome sympathetic feelings, she carried her drink to his bookshelf. She was reading titles—and noting how many of them were published by Pemberley—when he returned.

"Should be about twenty minutes," he informed her as he shut the door and joined her.

"Okay. Thanks again."

He nodded. "What do you think?"

"Of what?"

He gestured to the shelf in front of her.

"Oh. You have quite the collection."

"Thank you." He actually smiled. "I imagine you have quite the collection yourself."

She sipped her drink, nodded. "At home I do. I only brought one box to school. Didn't want to move a bunch of books back and forth from apartments and home over the next couple years, plus there's the library."

"You seem like you really like working there," he observed. "Though if you didn't, you're probably in the wrong field of study."

He surprised a laugh out of her. "True. But I've always loved books, so

I've always been drawn to libraries. A degree in Library Science just felt like the right thing for me, and my bachelor's in Lit I think helps supplement that." She paused, but when he only looked at her, she continued. "What about you? I can't imagine the home of a publisher without books."

"Neither can I. Our family home has its own library, and I would constantly escape there as kid. Not just the room, but the books. I'm sure you know what I mean."

"Yeah." She tilted her head as she studied him. "What's going on here?"

"What do you mean?"

"You're being nice to me."

His brows lifted. "You make it sound like I'm not usually nice to you."

"Well…" Might as well have it out, she thought. "It's just, you usually act like you don't like me very much."

For a moment he could only blink at her. He opened his mouth, closed it, then finally said, "What?…"

She could only give him an arch look. "You think I don't know what you think of me? I heard you tell Chase, the day we met, that I was decent-looking, but you'd never waste your time with a scholarship case—"

"I'm so sorry, Elle," he cut her off, eyes wide with what appeared to be genuine shame. "I was wrong, and I don't know how…I'm not the most sociable of people."

"I've noticed."

He ran a hand through his hair, causing some of the dark mass to stick up a little, and despite herself a little curl of lust tingled in her belly.

"I didn't want to be at that party," he continued, meeting her eyes. "I'm introverted by nature, and, admittedly, shy on top of it. All I was really thinking about was leaving, and I was just trying to get Chase off my back. It didn't have anything to do with you, really, but it was unspeakably rude of me. I can't tell you how incredibly sorry I am."

"Okay, but what about after that? Any time we were in the same room you seemed so annoyed by our presence it was pretty clear you didn't think me or my friends worth your time; you hardly spoke, but if you did you just sounded arrogant." She threw up her hands, exasperated. "I'm an introvert, too, so I get not wanting to make small talk, but I'm aware it's not a reason to be a douche-canoe to people."

He half-laughed at the moniker. "And here I thought we'd been engaging in a battle of wits all this time."

He turned away for a moment, then turned back, edging close enough to her that she could see the green shadows of his eyes. She caught the scent of him, sweet and musky, and one curl became two.

"For the record, I don't think you or your friends aren't worth my time. Sometimes it just takes time for me to open up to people, but that doesn't make me arrogant. I also sometimes have trouble expressing myself, or things just come out wrong. Which is why I usually prefer to say nothing at all."

He fiddled with his glasses to steady himself. "I swear, I never meant any offense. And I should point out, you often willfully misunderstood me."

She shut her eyes, took a swallow of her drink to hide her temper and a creeping sense of shame.

"I suppose that was an unfair assessment," she admitted reluctantly. "I just...you...really hurt my feelings at that party. I guess I decided to counter that hurt, I'd just think of you as this..." she searched for the right word.

"Douche-canoe?" he supplied.

"That's it."

He shook his head. "I'm sorry if I ever made you feel less. That's the opposite of what I wanted. I wanted to get to know you because I..." He trailed off, took a breath. "Because I like you. A lot."

Now it was her turn for speechlessness. He *liked* her?

Her mind did quick replays of some of their interactions—how he'd often try to strike up a conversation with her at the library's checkout desk when he checked out books, or come upon her shelving materials at seemingly random moments. The couple of times they'd run into each other walking across campus, and he'd walked with her. She thought he'd been trying to find ways to criticize her, but could he have been flirting with her? Or as he'd said, simply trying to get to know her?

And the Darcy Stare—could it be he'd actually been admiring her? She wanted to doubt it, but when she glanced back at him, his posture was tense. It was not unlike what she'd seen before, but she realized what she'd thought was hauteur was instead his social awkwardness. And when she could meet his eyes again he looked so...nervous. And damn if it wasn't adorable.

She set her cup on the bookshelf, paused. "You...like me," she finally said.

"Yes." He kept watching her. "You doubt it. Doubt me."

She shook her head. "I don't know what to think."

"Then let me show you something you can't misinterpret."

With both hands he reached to cup her face, and ducked his head, pressing his lips to hers.

He was surprisingly gentle, and still that first meeting of lips made her heart pound in her ears. As he deepened the kiss, his hands beginning to roam to the back of her neck, her waist, the small of her back, she found herself reaching up to put her arms around his neck. Her body hummed as if to say *I told you*.

He ran his fingers through her long auburn waves and lifted his head enough to murmur, "Your hair is like titian silk. And your eyes…" He brushed his lips teasingly over hers, then his eyes met hers with such intensity she held her breath. "I get so lost in them. That sounds corny, but I love how the color shifts depending on what you're wearing."

And his mouth took hers again before she could think of a reply. This time he wrapped his arms around her and molded her body to his. Her hands dug into his hair, gripped his shoulders as their lips became more greedy.

He wasn't having trouble expressing himself now, she thought.

She nipped at his bottom lip and he groaned before trailing his lips down her neck. She gasped as his hand slipped under her borrowed shirt to skim the flesh just above her waist, sending tingles along her skin.

"And you look ridiculously sexy in my shirt."

She let out an involuntary moan when his thumb brushed just under the cup of her bra, and he smiled against her lips.

Her hands began to explore, moving up his back, even as she questioned how she got there. There'd been some heat when they'd danced, but she hadn't let herself imagine…

The dance. Their conversation about Grant.

There was still one thing she had to clear up.

He stopped kissing her when she went still. "What is it?"

She tried to conjure up the righteous anger she usually felt when she thought of the story Grant had told her, but any sparks she could manage were extinguished by the concern in his eyes. She swallowed.

"I need to talk to you about something," she said, pulling away from him. "I need to clear the air before there's any more…of this."

"Alright."

Away from his embrace, she again wanted to be angry at him, unsettled that all it took was a kiss from him to undo her, but she found she just couldn't be. She couldn't blame him for her feelings, not after everything they'd just discussed—and certainly not after that apology. She was afraid of how this next conversation might go, she realized, but she also felt hope begin to bloom in her heart—the one thing she hadn't allowed herself to feel when it came to Liam Darcy.

She sat on the edge of his bed. "It's about Grant."

Something flashed in his eyes. "Are you telling me you…the two of you…"

"Wh-no!" She shook her head when realization dawned. "We only went on one date, and though it did end with a goodnight kiss, that was it."

He visibly relaxed, but he spoke quietly when he asked, "Then why bring him up?"

"Because he told me something about you, you and him, and I need to know if it's true."

"Whatever it is I can pretty much guarantee it's not." When she gave him a bland look, he held up his hands. "Alright, alright. Go ahead."

"When I met Grant, he told me you'd gotten him expelled last year by setting him up to look like he'd cheated on his exams."

Liam's mouth dropped open. "Really?" he scoffed. "And what was my motive?"

"Your sister."

Now his eyes darkened. "What did he say about my sister?"

"Just that he was dating her, but you didn't think he was good enough and didn't want him around her. So you got him kicked out of school."

"And you believed him?" He shook his head. "Believe him still?"

"I...I don't know what to think anymore," she confessed. "That's why I'm asking. If it's not true, feel free to contradict it."

"I damn well am going to contradict it," Liam stated, then began pacing, pulling off his glasses. "Yes, Grant got expelled for cheating, and I am the one who reported him, but I assure you no one set him up. He actually *did* cheat on his exams—if you don't believe me you can ask Dr. Gardiner."

He kept pacing. She thought to ask more, but as the subject was a touchy one, decided she shouldn't push him. At length, he continued.

"It's also true he and Anna...dated a bit—*after* he was expelled. I wasn't aware, as I was here focusing on my second semester's studies, and she was a sophomore at Berkley, studying music. He sought her out. I didn't find out until she brought him home over spring break." He paused now, looked toward the picture on his dresser. "I knew he didn't have feelings for her. I thought he just wanted to get back at me—to break her heart to get to me. But he also wanted money."

"Money?"

He flicked Elle a glance, carefully set his glasses on the dresser before pacing again. "He told me if I gave him ten thousand dollars, he'd never go near Anna again. So I did, and he got what he wanted—my money and my pain of knowing I'd failed to protect the person who matters most to me."

She didn't want to believe it—didn't want to believe anyone was capable of such a thing. Then she remembered how eager she was to believe it when she'd been told Liam had done something cruel. She recalled how Grant had readily admitted he had no proof of Liam's set up, but had still just as readily spread the story among his friends, and to her, unprompted. It was all too apparent now that he'd used her dislike of Liam to endear her to him.

And the part about Anna—Liam had no reason to make that up. It was evident it was painful for him to recall, and even harder for him to tell her; Elle could imagine how it went down all too well, especially after the nonchalant way Grant had dismissed her earlier that evening.

"Is she...is Anna okay?"

"She's recovering still, but yes, she's better."

"I'm so sorry." Tears began to roll down her cheeks. "I let myself believe him because I was hurt by your insult, and it fed my pride to have someone confirm you were a jerk. I—"

"No, I'm the one who should be sorry." He stopped pacing to sit next to her on the bed, covered her hand with his. "I should have warned you about him. You especially, as he likes to take what I want."

She almost smiled at the comment, but couldn't. "You don't understand. I'm such a hypocrite, aren't I? Sitting here calling you a snob, when I'm the one who's been turning my nose up at you. You don't deserve that." She wiped at her eyes. "I feel like such an *idiot*, but...relieved at the same time."

"Relieved?"

"Yeah. Realizing how wrong I was sucks, but it's a relief to find out you're not an asshole because..." She looked up from their clasped hands to his eyes. "Because despite myself, I was starting to like you, and I'd hate myself for liking someone I knew was an asshole."

A slow grin spread over his face. "I guess now you're free to like me all you want."

"I guess I am."

He was just about to kiss her again when he pulled back. "I forgot about your shirt. I should go get it before I forget again."

She held his arm to keep him in place when he tried to rise, then got up herself. "Not to worry," she said as she faced him, kicked off her shoes. "Neither of us will be needing a shirt for a little while."

His eyes widened as she undid the top couple buttons of her skirt, slowly slid it down her legs. The soft cotton of the t-shirt brushed the top of her thighs as she stepped to him, braced her hands on his shoulders to balance herself as she straddled his lap.

His arms immediately came around her, and she kissed him, pouring the whirlwind of emotions she'd experienced throughout the night into the kiss as her hands gripped his shoulders. He responded in kind, and her belly quivered as he shifted back so their position on the edge of the bed was more stable.

She took the opportunity to trail her hands down his chest, until she found the hem of his shirt, lifted it. She caught the amusement in his eyes when she tugged the shirt up over his head. Her hands trailed again, this time over smooth skin and lean muscle. His hands dived under her shirt as she leaned in to nibble at his ear; she let out a gasp of pleasure when his hand closed over her breast under her bra.

She rolled her hips and he groaned. She reached for the buckle of his belt.

"Elle, wait."

She stilled, laying her hands on his shoulders instead. When she met his gaze, his eyes were dark and clouded with arousal, but his hands had rested gently on her hips.

"Is something wrong?"

His face took on a pained expression. "I just…I want to be sure you want this," he said slowly. "You've been drinking and—"

Her laugh came out as a half-sigh, and she leaned her forehead to his. "You're choosing now to be a gentleman?"

He blew out a breath. "Curse my good breeding."

"You've been drinking too," she reminded him with a smile. "And I don't know about you, but I'm not even tipsy. I promise you I'm sober, and I know exactly what I'm doing."

When she felt him sigh, she pulled back a little to meet his eyes again. "Unless…you're not sure *you* want this?"

The hands on her hips gripped a little harder. "Yes—I mean, no, I—God, I want this. I want you," he said. "I've been imagining this for weeks, but now I…I'm afraid I'll screw it up."

When she quirked a brow he let out a strained laugh of his own. "Bad choice of words. You know what I mean."

Her face softened.

"I do," she said, laying her hands on the sides of his face. She brushed her thumb over his cheek with an affection that surprised them both. "And I'd be lying if I said I wasn't nervous, too. So, we can stop right now if you want. Or, we can just take it really, really slow."

She waited as he searched her face, and in another surprising gesture, he smiled and took one of her hands from his face, turned it to press his lips to her palm. "You are…"

"Amazing?" she suggested. "Gorgeous? Obstinate?"

"Yes." And his arms were around her again. "You are all of those things."

He took her at her word, and slowly drew the t-shirt over her head, laid soft, sweet kisses on her lips, her neck. He lifted her, rolling so they lay on the bed, and Elle arched and quivered under his touch.

They gave to each other as they removed clothes, hands and lips exploring, arousing. Her heart fluttered as he whispered *Elizabeth*. When he reached for a condom in his nightstand, she took it from him; her fingers taunted him as she slid it on.

Even when she opened for him, drew him into her, he took his time. And she matched him, with achingly slow, sinuous movements, until bright waves of pleasure rolled through them both.

LATER, she lay under the covers with him, relaxed and ridiculously happy. She was curled up against him, his eyes closed as his thumb drew little circles over the hand she'd laid on his chest. The song they'd danced to was stuck in her head.

She couldn't take her eyes off his face; every line and curve of his features made her want to smile like an idiot.

"It's getting late," she murmured. "I should go soon."

"Stay," he said, shifting to face her.

"Liam, I should—"

He cut her off with his lips, pulling her against him and kissing her senseless.

"Stay," he said again.

Was it possible for hearts to glow? she wondered.

"Okay."

IN THE MORNING, he took her to breakfast at a nearby café, then walked her back to her apartment.

"You could ask me in for coffee," he suggested as she unlocked the door. "Then I wouldn't have to angle to come in."

"You had coffee at the café," she teased him. But she jerked her head to gesture him in.

Jane and Charlotte were at the kitchen table when they walked in. Ignoring the raised eyebrows and smirks of her friends, she smiled as she went to a cabinet, got out a couple mugs.

"Uh...good morning," Liam said to them. Evidently he hadn't thought about her roommates.

Jane smiled brightly. "Good morning, Liam."

"Morning." Charlotte hid a smirk with her coffee.

"Um." He searched for something else to say. "Where's the bathroom?"

Jane told him where the guest bathroom was, and when he'd shuffled out of the kitchen, Elle turned to face her very curious friends.

"What?" she said in mock innocence, bringing the mugs to the counter. She began filling them with coffee as they observed her.

"We got your text, but I gotta say I didn't believe it until now," Charlotte told her.

"I did. You look happy and…satisfied," Jane beamed.

Elle picked up her mug, turned to them, waited.

"You slept with Liam. Liam *Darcy*," said Charlotte, slightly bewildered.

"And you're both happy about it," said Jane.

Elle smiled. "Those are both true statements."

"I'm not surprised." Jane drank some of her own coffee. "I know we could all see the way he looked at you, but honey, you should've seen the way you looked at him, too."

"Major heat," Charlotte confirmed. "But still, I *am* surprised, considering your dislike of him. Or should I say former dislike."

Elle nodded, sighed as she took a seat at the table. "I was surprised myself. It's a long story, but we had a good talk, and…I realized how wrong I was about him."

"Details!"

"You'll get them," Elle assured her. "Later."

They looked like they wanted to ask more, but at the sound of approaching footsteps, they kept silent. Liam returned a few moments later.

"Ladies," he said as Elle handed him a mug. "Did you enjoy the party last night?"

"Not as much as you, I'm sure," Charlotte smirked.

Jane elbowed her, then her face went wistful. "It was wonderful, Liam, thank you. Chase and I had the best time."

"Somebody talking about me?" Chase sauntered into the room, grinning, his sandy hair damp. His eyes immediately tracked to Jane.

"I didn't know you were here," Liam said.

"I was in the shower. What about you, Darce?" Chase wiggled his eyebrows.

"Uh…" Liam fidgeted with his glasses, a habit Elle now realized was something he did when uncomfortable. "Elle and I went to breakfast."

Chase winked at Elle. "Breakfast, huh?"

Elle only smiled, sipped her coffee.

"Oh, Elle," Jane shifted in her chair. "You haven't heard from Lacy, have you?"

Elle frowned. "No. Why?"

Jane and Charlotte exchanged a look.

"She didn't come home last night," Charlotte said. "And she hasn't texted either of us. We tried calling a couple times, but no answer."

Elle's stomach dropped. "The last time I saw her...she was leaving the party with Grant." Her eyes met Liam's.

"Grant was there?" Jane asked. "I thought he ditched you."

"He did," Elle clarified. "But he still came to the party, and I saw him kissing Lacy."

"Grant Wickham?" Chase asked with a worried glance at Liam.

"The one and only." Now Elle set down her coffee, looked up at Liam. "Should we be worried? Is it possible they're just out late and that's it?"

Liam's face went grave. "I don't know. But I'll find out."

"Are we missing something, here?" Charlotte wondered.

When Elle gave Liam an understanding look, he took a deep breath. "There's something you should know about Grant," he said, and began to explain, though more briefly than the night before, his history with Grant Wickham, while Elle left the room to try Lacy on her cell.

She changed quickly into jeans and a tee as the phone rang, pulled on a flannel shirt. When she got voicemail, she began to pace, and left a message. "Lacy, please call me as soon as you get this message. It's important."

Back in the kitchen, Jane and Charlotte looked stricken.

"But he wouldn't hurt her, would he?" Jane asked Liam.

"I don't think so," he said. "At least, not the way you mean."

"She forgets to charge her phone all the time. It's possible her phone died," Charlotte pointed out. "Which may be why we can't reach her, but even when she stays out all night she's normally back by now."

"We'll find her," Liam assured them, starting to pull out his phone. When he paused, frowned, Elle narrowed her eyes.

"What is it?"

"I was just thinking. There is somewhere Grant might go, someone he might go to or who might know where he would take Lacy."

"Who?"

"Her name is Sarah Young. She helped him cheat on his exams."

Jane perked up. "And you know where she is?"

He nodded. "I do."

. . . . .

LIAM PARKED his car in the street just outside an apartment complex downtown. He and Elle got out just as Jane pulled up and parked behind them, Chase and Charlotte with her. Liam led them all to an apartment on the second floor, stopping to turn to them.

"Uh, maybe you should stand farther back," he suggested. "I don't want to freak her out with a bunch of people at her door."

So they stood back while he knocked, waited. Then all at once, the door opened with a flash of movement, and Sarah Young stood on the other side, hands on hips, glaring.

"What do *you* want?" she demanded.

"You wouldn't happen to know where Grant is, do you?" he asked calmly.

"No."

She moved to slam the door in his face, but he stopped it with his foot. "I'm not here to cause trouble, Sarah. We're looking for a friend of ours, and she was last seen with Grant leaving a party last night. We're just trying to find her."

For the first time Sarah seemed to notice the small crowd behind Liam; though her eyes narrowed, she re-opened the door a little wider.

Elle thought she detected a hint of jealous curiosity in Sarah's expression, and taking a chance, stepped forward.

"Please," she said. "We're getting worried. If you know where they might be, it would really help us."

Sarah studied her for one long moment. Then finally, she sighed. "He's not here," she confessed. "But I did get a message from him last night saying he wouldn't be by. Said he had something to do at the university."

Elle exchanged a look with Liam.

"Thank you," he said, and they headed back to the car.

. . . . . .

"WHAT ARE YOU THINKING?" Elle asked Liam when they were back on campus. His stride was purposeful as he marched toward the publishing and media building.

"I'm thinking," Liam said as he looked around, "that Grant has an idiotic revenge plan up his sleeve. Perhaps breaking and entering, preferably into Dr. Gardiner's office."

"Dr. Gardiner's office!" Jane was horrified. "But Lacy wouldn't... surely she wouldn't..."

Liam shook his head. "I hope not, but Grant can be pretty persuasive."

When they got to the main entrance, the doors were locked.

"If he got in, I doubt it was this way," Chase observed.

"A window?" Charlotte suggested. "What side is Dr. Gardiner's office on?"

They walked around the building, keeping an eye out for open or broken windows; they didn't see any until Liam pointed to a spot on the second floor, where there was clearly a hole in the windowpane, fractures ribboning out along the glass.

Elle sighed. "If they were here, they must be long gone."

But when she looked at Liam, his eyes weren't on the building, but a tree in the courtyard a stone's throw away. And under the tree...

"Lacy!" she shouted, and broke into a run. The others weren't far behind her.

The figure slumped on the ground beneath the tree stirred, moved to sit up. "Elle?"

"We were so worried about you," Elle said as she knelt and threw her arms around her friend.

"My phone died. I couldn't call you guys."

At the pain in her voice, Elle drew back, saw the threat of tears in Lacy's eyes. Gently, she plucked a couple newly fallen leaves from Lacy's light brown hair. "What happened?"

"Grant..." That was as far as she got before she burst into tears. Jane immediately moved to put an arm around her shoulders, and Charlotte sat next to her, holding her hand. Chase and Liam shared a glance, tacitly agreeing they shouldn't interfere. Finally the tears slowed enough for Lacy to continue.

"We went to a club and got drunk. After, he wanted to trash his former professor's office, for getting him expelled," she told them. "He threw a rock through the window, and tried to get me to climb up onto his shoulders. I didn't want to."

Now Jane rubbed her back, and Lacy sniffled, wiping at her nose with her jacket sleeve. "I may be irresponsible, but I'm not stupid. I told him no way in hell, but he tried lift me anyway. I struggled away, and I landed funny on my ankle." She looked down at it. "I think it's sprained. It's purple and it hurts."

She bent, pulled up the leg of her jeans for them to see. Sure enough, her ankle was swollen, and deep purple bruises marked her skin.

"Where's Grant?" Elle asked her.

Now a look of fury came into Lacy's eyes. "He left me here. I couldn't walk so he left me here—said he would go get help, but he never came back. Probably thought campus security would come along and nab me for the window. I hobbled over to this tree when I realized my phone was dead. Eventually, I fell asleep. I want to go home." She started to cry again.

"I know, honey," Jane said. "But you need to see a doctor."

She stood, but before they could help Lacy to rise, Liam stepped forward.

"I've got her," he said. He slid his arms under Lacy, instructing her to put her arms around his neck, and lifted her.

They were silent as he carried her back to the cars.

"Put her in mine," Jane offered, opening the back door. Liam set Lacy down gently on her good leg so she could slide into the car. She studied him before she got in.

"He hates you," she said to him, her eyes tired.

Liam held her gaze. "I know. Don't worry, he won't get away with hurting you."

"Thank you."

"What's the plan?" Chase asked as Charlotte slid into the back with Lacy, propping up her swollen ankle, and Jane opened the driver's door.

"Get Lacy to the infirmary," Liam said, then turned to Elle. "I was thinking of reporting some vandalism to the local police, if you'd like to come with me."

Elle only smiled. "Always."

⠂ ⠁⠄ ⠄ ⠄

LATER, after they had filed their report, and the others had returned from the infirmary with Lacy on crutches, Elle stood in her kitchen contemplating the events of the past twenty-four hours as she filled a plastic baggie with ice for Lacy's ankle.

"Are you alright?"

She glanced at Liam as he came in.

"Yeah, just...thinking," she told him. "It's been a crazy couple of days."

He nodded, but remained silent. Before Elle could ask him what was on his mind, Jane came in.

"Lacy is in bed; I convinced her to take a nap. Do you have the ice?"

"Yep." Elle closed the baggie, handed it to her. "I figured I'd make more coffee if everyone is going to hang out here for a while."

"Good idea." Jane smiled. "When Lacy's settled I'll come back and put together some snacks. Maybe we could all play some games or watch a movie. Lacy can join us when she wakes up."

"Sounds good."

When Jane was gone, Elle turned back to Liam, who, at the mention of coffee, had moved to rinse out the coffee pot, fill it. His face was set in a brooding expression, but now instead of disdain, she saw he was simply deep in thought.

"Thanks," she said, taking the pot from him. "Now it's my turn to ask if you're alright."

"I think so," he said. "I just wish there was more I could do, so he can't hurt anyone else."

"You're not responsible for his actions." Elle finished readying the coffee machine, started the brew, then turned to him. "And we appreciate everything you've already done. Thank you, for all your help. We may not have found Lacy without you, and then she'd likely be in the hands of campus security." She huffed out a breath. "I can't believe he left her there. Thank God it wasn't too chilly last night."

"It may be too much to hope he'll do time, but he'll get in big trouble, so that, at least, is satisfying."

"It is. So with that in mind, I think we owe it to ourselves to remember the past only as it gives us pleasure."

He took her hand in his. "I can do that." And he turned his green eyes to hers with such a look of warmth it made Elle's heart beat faster.

She leaned into him, brushing her lips over his, and he used his other hand to cup her face, deepen the kiss. When he pulled back he met her eyes again.

"I'm pretty sure I'm falling in love with you, Elizabeth Bennet."

"This time yesterday I would have thought the idea of you being in love with me ridiculous," she responded, her smile bright and teasing before it grew more serious. "But now it seems like the most natural thing in the world, because I'm falling in love with you, too, William Darcy."

With her heart full she kissed him again, laughing in delight, as Jane returned. Before long they were gathered with their friends in the living room, talking, laughing, simply enjoying each other's company.

As Elle took it all in, indulging in gazing at Liam from time to time, she wondered how, as Jane had once put it, she could stand so much happiness.

And as Liam turned his head, gazed back at her with his heart in his eyes, she knew.

NETHERFIELD VACATION

ONE

IF THERE WAS a truth universally acknowledged, it was that even my infamous Bennet stubbornness couldn't hold out against the sincere wishes of my most beloved sister.

I felt myself caving the moment I looked into familiar gray irises.

"Please, Em?"

Jess widened her eyes just slightly. It wasn't a practiced expression—Jess was guileless and too kindhearted to manipulate—but she certainly had the furrowed brow, pleading eyes, and subtle pout down to a T.

"Jess, you'll be hanging out with Cameron the entire time. The last thing I want to do is be left to spend my fall break putting up with Dickhead Darcy and Catty Chloe."

I was super happy for Jess, really; she'd been dating Cameron Bingley for nearly a couple months and by all accounts they were already in love. But his self-absorbed, scheming sister was bad enough—having to simultaneously fend off digs and insults from her and Cameron's aloof, stuck-up best friend, the aforementioned Dickhead, did not sound appealing in the slightest.

"Darcy's not that bad," Jess assured me. "He's just quiet, like me. And Chloe is nice."

"She's nice to *you* because of her brother, and you are nothing like Darcy."

Jess merely tilted her head, giving me that I'm-older-trust-me-on-this look. "I'm not so sure about that. I tend to be quiet and reserved, and so does he—there have been people in the past who thought I was stuck-up because of it."

"But those people didn't know you," I pointed out.

"Exactly."

I tossed up my hands. "The point is, you, Casey, and Cameron are the only ones who want me there, but you and Cameron will be too wrapped up in each other to notice anyone else."

"Oh, you're going."

Both Jess and I turned at the voice as our friend and roommate Casey entered our apartment.

"I am?" I asked, amused. "Why?"

"Because we've been invited to spend a week in a private McMansion with hot guys, meals made by a professional cook, a heated pool, and who knows what else—all for free. You'd be an idiot to pass it up."

She made a good point.

"And it's near several hiking trails," Jess reminded me. "You could walk for miles, and take tons of pictures."

"I could…" I hedged.

Casey and Jess shared a grin—they knew they'd already won the debate.

"You and I can handle Chloe." Casey tossed her mahogany hair and grinned wickedly, her hazel eyes zeroing in on me. "And don't worry about Darcy; he likes you."

It was the same thing she'd been saying since we'd met Fletcher Darcy and the Bingleys in August, when they'd transferred to Longbourn University, despite the fact Darcy had taken one look at me and declared me, "Okay, I guess, but not *that* pretty." I rolled my eyes but smiled back.

"Like hell."

.　.・ ˙ .　.

"WHAT HAPPENED TO GUYS ONLY? You know, like we do every year?"

Cameron, affable as ever, only shrugged at me as he stuffed a couple pairs of jeans in his duffel. "I'd miss Jess too much. Besides, the more the merrier as they say. And you know Jack won't mind."

I frowned. "That's all well and good, but it gave your sister leave to invite herself. You know I don't like staying in the same house with her."

I felt a little guilty at the way Cam's shoulders slumped; I know he'd tried over the years to convince Chloe I wasn't into her, but nothing he or I said ever got through to her. Occupying the same space as her just gave her more freedom to seek me out. Cam sighed and ruffled his dark blonde hair in distraction.

"I know, and I'm sorry about that. But with the other women there, she'll have them to hang out with, and they can keep her in check."

I scoffed at the hopeful look in his brown eyes. "Maybe you haven't noticed, but she's even worse when Emerson is around. Like she thinks Emerson is her rival."

"Gee, I wonder why that could be..."

I ignored his teasing smirk. "You know, you'd have a lot more room in that bag if you didn't just shove stuff in there."

In contrast to my friend, I had already tucked my belongings neatly into my own suitcase.

"Yeah, yeah." He ignored my advice. "But seriously, man, I'm not *that* oblivious. You talk to Em more than any other woman. You've got a thing for her."

There was no point in denying it, at least not to Cam.

"That doesn't mean I have any intention of doing anything about it."

"Why the hell not?"

I sighed, trying my best to put the image of a pair of sparkling sea green eyes, a raised brow, and attractively curved lips from my mind.

"Because..." I trailed off, trying to think of some excuse, even if he wouldn't buy it.

"Because?" he prompted, stopping his packing to give me his full attention.

I couldn't meet his eyes. "Because she could matter more than I bargained for."

For a moment there was only silence, and when I looked up, to my surprise, he was grinning from ear to ear.

"That's how you know, my friend."

For a moment I considered asking him what he meant, but I was afraid I already knew the answer. Instead I simply nodded, then left him to his last-minute packing flurry.

WHEN JESS, Casey, and I finally pulled to a stop in front of the giant cabin at the end of a private drive, none of us moved to get out.

"Holy shit," Casey whispered.

"McMansion my ass." I gaped at the sprawling two-story wood and glass structure surrounded by picturesque fall foliage in front of me. "This is a McChateau."

After a few more moments of silence, Jess finally pointed out we should probably get out of the car. As we were unloading our luggage, the front door opened and a beaming Cameron jogged down the front porch steps to greet us.

"Welcome to Netherfield," he said before giving Jess a quick peck hello.

Casey and I shared a look at the mention of the house's name; the fact that it had one at all was endlessly amusing to us.

"You ladies need any help?"

We all turned in the direction of the unfamiliar voice to see Darcy, all sweeping ink-dark hair, stormy blue eyes, and bored expression, walking next to an equally tall man with similar features, excepting his sandy hair. In contrast to Darcy's staring and stoic posture, he wore a wide grin.

"Jack Fletcher, Darcy's cousin." He introduced himself, shook our hands with enthusiasm.

"Fletcher?" I asked, sparing a quick glance for Darcy.

"My mother's maiden name," Darcy clarified.

"Fletcher family tradition." Jack winked at his cousin. "The firstborn is named after his or her mother's maiden name, depending on the name. I have an older brother named Murphy."

"That's...actually really cool. The tradition and the names." I smiled back at him until I glanced at Darcy again and noticed he was scowling at me. Realizing I'd inadvertently complimented him, I changed my expression to a bland stare and moved to pick up my duffel bag.

Jack beat me to it. "Let me get that."

"Thank you."

Darcy rolled his eyes at Jack but hefted the large cooler we'd brought and headed in to the house.

"Ignore him," said Jack as he picked up Casey's bag as well and we all followed. "He's broody."

"I thought that was just his default state."

"Ha." His lips quirked as he nodded. "Yeah, his moods can be hard to read sometimes, but he's one of the best men I know."

I decided not to comment on that one and let the others do the chatting as we entered the house. Cam waved us toward the stairs, carrying Jess's bag.

"I'll show you guys your rooms, and then give you a tour of the place." Cam explained as we walked. "Some of these rooms have a Jack-and-Jill bathroom. Jack and Darcy have the one on the right, and there's another across the hall. I'm in the master at the end of the hall, Chloe is in the room to the right of the master, and there's one more room to the left of the master."

He stopped in the middle of the hall, gestured to the left side, looked at us expectantly.

"Take your pick."

Casey and I shared a grin, and each moved toward a room with the shared bathroom. Which left Jess the room near Cam's...assuming she used it, that was.

Jack set my duffel down near the door to the room I chose, then left to do the same for Casey. I set my backpack down on the cozy-looking bed, took in the wingback chair in the corner, the wooden dresser near the door, and the spectacular view of the endless forest out the window. I'd definitely have to take a picture of it—maybe at sunset.

The door to what was evidently the shared bathroom opened, and Casey stepped out.

"You lay on the bed yet?" she asked. "Mine's like a freaking cloud."

"Not yet." I shook my head but smiled. Perhaps this would be a pleasant week after all.

. . . . .

UNFORTUNATELY, I was alone with Chloe for a few minutes as Cam and Jack took the girls upstairs. I'd brought their cooler to the kitchen and began unloading its contents into the fridge when she followed me in.

"I can't believe my brother invited them," she sniffed.

I thought it best to say nothing, especially since no one had invited her.

"Jess is sweet, but her sister is so weird." Chloe continued, tossing her blonde hair. "And too snarky for her own good."

I loved Emerson's biting retorts to Chloe's criticisms, but I didn't dare say so to Chloe.

"Oh, and her hair was a mess; she really should get some highlights to brighten that dull color, or change it so it's more like her sister's."

Now I frowned, thinking of the way Emerson's chestnut hair caught streaks of red in the light—and how the only real difference I'd seen between Em and Jess's hair was that Em's was longer.

"But Jess and Emerson have the same hair color," I pointed out.

Chloe looked like she wanted to argue, but thankfully Jack came down a moment later, sporting his usual grin.

"Something tells me we're going to have a very interesting vacation," he said.

Chloe only rolled her eyes. I set the emptied cooler near the door.

Jack continued, "I can already see why you and Cameron enjoy their company so much."

He winked at Chloe, who scoffed and stomped out of the kitchen. Jack annoyed Chloe to no end, something I was often grateful for.

"Jess is gorgeous, Casey is hot, and Emerson..." Jack's too-understanding eyes read me like a book, and he smiled knowingly. "Well, I bet you've got plenty of flattering adjectives to describe her."

"Shut up, Jack."

"Ooh, clever." Jack smirked.

Before either of us could say more, the others came down.

"This is the kitchen," Cam gestured widely. As Jess and Casey took in the dark green cabinets and stainless steel appliances, Emerson's eyes looked past my shoulder.

"Is that our cooler?"

I blinked when I realized she was asking me. "Yes," I pointed a thumb at the refrigerator. "I put all the stuff in the fridge."

"Oh. Thank you."

I was confused by how surprised she seemed, but didn't know what to make of it. "You're welcome," I said as Jack and I joined the group.

Cam showed the girls the dining room, the pool, the living room, the den complete with large TV and game consoles, and finally, the library. I watched Em's face as she absorbed the space. It was clear she was disappointed in the limited contents, but the room itself seemed to appeal to her.

"And here we have Fletcher's favorite room." Cam smiled as though he'd made a joke. "Despite his complaints that its contents are lacking."

I returned his smile. "You can't deny there's quite a bit of empty space on these shelves."

Still smiling, Cam shook his head. "You got me there." Then he took Jess's hand, pulling her out of the room and asking her if she wanted to go for a swim.

Em looked at Casey. "I think I might do a little exploring."

My eyes automatically watched her leave. When I looked back at the remaining members of our party, they were both observing me with knowing expressions that told me I didn't hide my interest quite as well as I thought.

"Excuse me," I said gruffly, deciding it would be best if I hid out in my room for a bit to gather my wits.

When I eventually went down, everyone was gathering for dinner. I could see Chloe left the spot next to her open for me, as she looked at me expectantly. Thankfully, it was a big round table that seated eight, so there were a few other spaces open; I took a seat between Jack and Jess.

Emerson was the last to come in, and as the two remaining seats were between Casey and Chloe, she chose the chair next to her friend. Chat over dinner was pleasant; though I mostly listened, I found it was easy to chime in now and then. I knew I had been a little grumpy about losing our guys-only trip, but I had to admit it was much more lively with the women there, and it was good to see just how happy Cam was.

I only hoped he didn't impulsively decide to move on, as he sometimes did.

After dinner we moved to the living room to play board games and watch TV. I forewent the games to write an email to my sister on my laptop. Chloe declared board games childish and went to her room to fetch nail polish to paint her toes.

She chatted incessantly to me while I tried to write my email, and I noticed that Em was watching us with an amused expression. When the game ended and the others were choosing another, Em begged off to do some reading on her e-reader, cozying up in the big chair by the window.

"An e-reader, Emma?" Chloe asked with feigned friendliness, giving me a sly look. "I wonder what you have against physical books."

At the deliberate misuse of Emerson's name, I narrowed my eyes at Chloe, while Emerson herself only raised an eyebrow at the absurdity.

"Nothing at all. In fact I have a decent personal library of physical books, and even brought one with me. It just so happens I wanted to read something I only have in e-book form—plus e-readers take up much less space when traveling."

"I bet your library is also better stocked than Cameron's," Jack joked.

"But no home library compares to the Darcy library at Pemberley," Chloe proclaimed.

"True," Cam laughed. "But the Darcys actually read their books."

"I would hope so." I gave up on my email for the time being. "My family has spent generations building the Pemberley library, but because we enjoy it. It's pointless to buy books if you don't intend to read them."

"So you would rather the library here remain mostly empty if filling the shelves meant the books would only gather dust?"

I looked at Em. "I admit the room itself would improve in atmosphere and aesthetics if the shelves were filled, but yes, I suppose I would rather it stay the way it is if it meant I didn't have to see more Netherfield books look so sad and neglected."

The corner of her mouth quirked up, and I couldn't help smiling back at her. We all resumed our activities after that, the conversation moving much as it had at dinner until we decided to call it a night. I went to bed more light of heart than I had been in a while.

TWO

I BREATHED out a sigh of relief as I hefted my backpack and headed down one of the groomed paths with my camera—alone at last.

I couldn't seem to escape Darcy that morning. First he'd been in the kitchen drinking coffee when I went down for breakfast, then he'd been in the pool when I'd thought about going for a swim. Instead I'd curled up with a book in the library; of course, an hour later, he'd holed up in the library as well.

We'd spent a reasonably pleasant hour in complete silence.

He'd muttered good morning to me at breakfast, and I'd responded, but other than that we'd managed to say absolutely nothing to each other. Despite the relief of not having to speak to him, his silent stare eventually became somewhat stifling, especially since he had been a surprisingly decent conversationalist the previous evening.

I decided it was time to take advantage of the trails and the unseasonably warm weather.

Although it was nearly mid-October, Mother Nature still had her grip on summer. The trees were slowly but surely shifting their colors toward their brilliant autumn hues, but the heat had me shedding the flannel I'd worn over my tank top, tying it around my waist.

I walked for half an hour in blissful, peaceful quiet, enjoying the scenery and the exercise. Stopping to snack on an apple I'd brought, I scanned through the pictures I'd taken with pleasure before stowing my camera. I thought about heading back but was comfortable where I was sitting on a log, so I pulled out the old paperback I'd packed for the drive.

I don't know how long I was there, so absorbed in the words and the quiet I didn't notice anyone approaching.

"Emerson?"

I jolted. "Why are you everywhere?"

I frowned at Darcy, who, instead of his usual blank stare, had the nerve to look amused.

"Jess and Casey are wondering where you are," he explained. "I offered to find you."

I checked my watch. "I suppose it's about time for lunch."

I shoved the book back in my pack and he held out his hands to me. Surprised by the gesture, I took them and let him pull me up. Though he let go of my hands when I stood, I could feel how intently he stared at me as I picked up my backpack. I did my best to ignore it, and started to walk back.

"How'd you find me?"

He shrugged, met my pace. "I saw you go off down one of the trails when I went to the kitchen for coffee. You walked farther than I thought, though."

I bristled. "I like to hike."

"So I gathered." I could hear the hint of amusement in his voice, and when I glanced at him, he was actually smiling a little. "I'm surprised you didn't take the waterfall trail."

"There's a waterfall?" I could already imagine how it would photograph.

He nodded. "About a mile from the house. It's not huge or anything, but it's beautiful, and it has a small pool. It's not that deep, but Cam and I swim in it sometimes."

"That sounds awesome. I'll definitely have to check it out."

I found myself smiling at him. What was happening? I returned my eyes to the trail in front of me.

"Does your house have a waterfall?" I teased.

"I wish, but sadly, no. The grounds have a lot of woods not unlike these, but no waterfall. There's a large lake, though, with its own little beach."

"Nice."

We were silent after that for a few minutes. I didn't mind so much, but after a while it just seemed odd to keep up the silence.

"It's your turn to say something," I told him. "You can ask me a question if you want."

"I will ask whatever you want."

"Oh, no," I wagged a finger at him. "I'm not letting you off that easy."

He hunched his shoulders a little, furrowed his brow. "I'm not very good at conversation. It doesn't come as naturally to me as it does to some, and I can't always think of anything to say."

"There's probably a reason they call it 'conversation skills,' you know." I shrugged. "Any skill requires *practice.*"

He gave a small smile of acknowledgement. "Fair enough."

I let the silence hang, determined to ensure he would be the one to break it.

"Have you been enjoying your classes this semester?" he finally asked. "You're studying photography, right?"

"I am, yes. I'm particularly enjoying my nature photography class. I've learned a lot."

He gestured to our surroundings. "Did you get any pictures out here?"

"Tons," I grinned.

"Can I see them?"

Surprised, I turned to him; he was watching me intently, and I had to wonder if he only wanted the opportunity to criticize my work. But I decided it didn't matter, and stopped to dig my camera out of my backpack. I brought up the pictures, handed it to him.

"These are nice," he said with a small smile after a few moments. "I particularly like the one with the sunlight filtering through the trees. And the one of the little bridge over the stream."

As he spoke, we approached the bridge in question, and I stopped halfway over it.

"It was just so idyllic, it called to me," I commented as I gazed up at the trees. I heard a faint click behind me, and turned to see him lowering the camera with a sheepish smile.

"Sorry," he said as he handed the camera back to me. "I couldn't help it. It was too perfect to pass up."

I only gave him an arch look, pulling up the photos to see for myself. I let out a half-laugh when I saw it; he'd framed the photo pretty well, and I looked wistful standing on the bridge, half turned toward the trees, half toward my sneaky photographer.

"I'm sorry if it's terrible," he said.

"No," I assured him as I put my camera away, suddenly a little self-conscious. "I like it."

We chatted more idly the rest of the way back; I was wary of the sudden intimacy created by his taking my picture. The moment had seemed almost quietly flirtatious, if there was such a thing.

Though it wasn't a hardship to flirt with a handsome man, I wasn't sure how to handle this side of Darcy, or how to feel about it. He'd been friendly enough since our arrival yesterday, though his arrogance had reared its head on occasion.

"You're quiet all of a sudden."

His voice brought me out of my wandering thoughts.

"I was just thinking."

"Were you thinking of anything in particular? Or anyone?"

Was he teasing me? Now that was new. I met his amused look with my own. "Perhaps."

He chuckled.

"If you must know," I continued, "I was thinking that you seem different on this vacation than you do at school. I can't figure you out."

"I don't think I'm that much of a mystery."

"Oh, but you are. For instance, you're prone to frowning or scowling on a regular basis, but this afternoon I've actually seen you smile, and you even impulsively took a picture of me." I studied him as the outline of the house came into view. "I don't know how to account for it."

He shrugged, clearly uncomfortable. "I mentioned I'm not always comfortable around strangers. I suppose over time I've become more comfortable with our little party."

"Even me?" I teased.

"Especially you. You're easy to be around."

I stopped and stared at him in confused shock. We had just breached the backyard, and apparently lunch was ready, because Chloe came rushing out to greet us—or rather, to greet Darcy. Neither of us had opportunity to say anything more to each other as we headed inside.

Though Mrs. Nicholls's chili was delicious, I found my mind drifting more than once to my unexpected afternoon companion, and the way his eyes blazed an interestingly soft blue amid the reds, rusts, and golds of the autumn leaves.

I gave myself a mental slap out of it. What the heck was I thinking?

Evidently there was more to Fletcher Darcy than I thought, but that didn't mean he was altogether pleasant. *Only time will tell*, I thought.

Later that afternoon I decided to hole up in the library for a little while. Darcy had been his usual reticent self after lunch, though he seemed more lost in thought than anything; I couldn't say I blamed him. He was probably just as disconcerted by our earlier camaraderie as I was.

As I approached the library door, I heard Cam's voice.

"Why would you think I would change my mind?"

"Because I'm your friend and I know your habits."

That was definitely Darcy's voice. Deciding I shouldn't intrude on their conversation, I moved away from the door.

"You've been seeing her for a couple months now."

I stopped when I realized they were talking about Jess.

"Yeah, and?" Cam said.

"Don't play dumb. You're positive you want to continue the relationship?"

My eyes widened in outrage. It sure sounded like Darcy was trying to convince Cam he should break things off with Jess.

Who the hell did he think he was?

"I know what you're getting at," I heard Cam say. My heart lurched for Jess just before he continued, "But I'm sure."

Even through the relief that washed over me, I could've sworn my ears were ringing as I turned and walked away. *Dickhead Darcy strikes again*, I thought. Or nearly struck—Cam apparently wasn't as easily swayed as his friend seemed to think.

I decided I wouldn't say anything to Jess; there was no reason to. I thought about venting my spleen to Casey, but I felt I'd complained about Darcy a lot to her already. This little discovery was one I would keep to myself.

Dinner was a little tense that night.

Darcy sat right next to me and I resisted the urge to glare at him. He, of course, seemed oblivious to my annoyance. Though I ate, I hardly tasted the food as I tried to deflect Darcy's conversation; the realization made me feel a little guilty, since Mrs. Nicholls had made us a fantastic meal. She'd already left for the day, so perhaps I could clean up the kitchen a little for her.

"Are you alright?" Darcy asked me.

I gritted my teeth in an attempt to keep my composure. "I'm fine," I said in the politest voice I could muster.

I refused to look at him, lest he see the anger in my eyes, but through my peripheral vision I could feel him staring at me again.

"If you say so."

What was that supposed to mean? Did he think I didn't know my own mind? To be fair, I *was* upset and doing my darndest to hide it—but couldn't he tell I wanted to be left alone? After dinner I would claim I was tired and go up to my room, I decided.

Darcy still seemed like he wanted to talk to me, so for once I was thankful when Chloe demanded his attention from the other side of the table, where Casey and Jack had been baiting her by talking about beauty standards.

"Fletcher, I'm sure you would agree with me," she was saying.

"About what?" he said reluctantly.

"Every woman should have a good hair stylist, don't you think?"

"I have literally no opinion about that." His bland tone conveyed his annoyance, and I bit my lip to keep from smirking.

"But surely your mother has one?"

"I'm sure she does, but I've never spoken to her about it. She's not overly concerned with her vanity."

"She sounds like a sensible woman," Jess said.

"She is." Darcy actually smiled at Jess, as though he hadn't tried to ruin her happiness only an hour ago. I nearly growled at him.

"I take it you're not overly concerned with vanity either?" I asked him.

He turned to me and shrugged. "Vain people annoy me."

"What about pride, then?" I challenged him. "Since vanity is a form of pride, would you consider pride to be a good thing or a bad thing?"

He thought for a moment. "Pride is all well and good if you have something to be proud of, and keep that pride in check. But if you can't keep it in check, you risk being too proud, or arrogant."

"Agreed." I slit my eyes at him. "Pride often gives people an inflated sense of self-importance."

Casey gave me a questioning look, so I pretended to smile and shook my head slightly.

"It can," Darcy responded. "The point is, I think it can be both a good thing and a bad thing."

Across the table, Chloe huffed, clearly put out she wasn't getting the attention she wanted. Cameron looked uncomfortable with the growing tension.

"Why don't we all play a card game after dinner?" he suggested.

Everyone agreed, but I dissembled.

"I'm a little tired," I said. "I want to clean up the kitchen a little for Mrs. Nicholls, then I think I'll call it an early night."

Everyone but Chloe seemed disappointed; though Casey looked skeptical, she didn't question me. When we'd finished dinner, everyone took their plates to the kitchen and put them in the sink. I assured Jess I didn't need help when she offered, and as the others went out into the living room, I began rinsing a plate.

As the kitchen was quiet, I thought everyone had gone until I heard Darcy's voice behind me.

"You don't need to clean up after everyone. Mrs. Nicholls doesn't mind. In fact, she likes having so many people to cook for."

To my annoyance and surprise, he took the plate from me, stuck it in the dishwasher.

"That may be, but with seven people staying here, I don't want her to be overwhelmed in the morning. Besides," I shrugged, rinsing off another plate, "It's the least I can do to thank Cameron for inviting us."

I held the plate out to him; when he held it, but didn't take it, studying me with a quizzical frown, I arched a brow.

"You gonna help me, or you just gonna stand there and look pretty?" I asked.

The frown quirked into a small smile and he shifted, adding the plate to the dishwasher with the other. "I suppose it's the least I can do as well."

We worked silently; it only took a minute or so, with me rinsing and him organizing. When we'd finished, I dried my hands on a kitchen towel, while he dug around in the cabinet under the sink for dishwasher detergent. I noticed a tub of disinfecting wipes in the cabinet, and began wiping down the countertops as he started the dishwasher.

After I'd stowed the wipes back under the sink, I turned to find him leaning against the center island across from me, staring at me again. The hum of the dishwasher swirling water in the background seemed to add to the intensity of his gaze, and I pursed my lips, glancing away.

"Well…" I searched for something to say. "Thanks."

"You're welcome."

When he said nothing else, I just nodded, began to turn away.

"Emerson?" He stopped me. "Would you like to go to dinner with me sometime?"

I froze. There was no way I'd heard him right.

"Excuse me?"

"Dinner—you know, two people, sitting across from each other—"

"No I know what you meant, I just don't understand why you're asking me."

He blinked, frowned. Straightened. "I would think that would be obvious," he said slowly.

I scoffed, leaning against the counter behind me and folding my arms. "Obvious why you'd ask the woman you think is 'okay, I guess, but not that pretty' on a date?"

His eyes widened, but when he opened his mouth I held up a hand. "Please, don't feel obligated to apologize. We both know you wouldn't mean it."

He narrowed his eyes, pushing off the island counter; in one step he'd surrounded me, his hands on the counter on either side of me, his tall frame looming over me. Though my pulse quickened, I tilted my head up to meet his glare with my own. I wouldn't be intimidated.

I expected his gaze to be cold and disdainful, but instead he seemed frustrated, his midnight blue eyes searching my face, unsure what he might find.

"I don't do anything I don't want to do," he finally said, the edges of his voice hard, echoing the frustration on his face. "So when I tell you I'm sorry—and I am—I sincerely mean it."

"Glad we cleared that up."

I moved to push away from him, but he didn't budge. "Why do I get the feeling you don't accept my apology?"

"You're right. Apology not accepted."

"Why?"

"Why?" I resisted the urge to scoff again, but raised my brows. "Because it wasn't a very good apology, and because you don't like me, and I don't like you."

He hadn't moved, but somehow he was closer; I realized I'd straightened as I spoke, putting me nearly eye-level with him as he bent over me. As his eyes flicked down to my mouth I was suddenly aware of his proximity, and my eyes inadvertently dropped to his lips.

And then his mouth was on mine, hard and...hungry, I thought, as his hands lifted to the back of my neck, my hair. He stepped forward, pressing against me, trapping me between his body and the counter—and frustration was still pumping off of him, clogging the air. Surprise warred with anger and reluctant attraction inside me; I brought my hands up, intending to push him' away, but instead my traitorous fingers curled against his chest.

Then just as suddenly, he broke the kiss. Still cradling my face, his voice came out husky when he spoke. "That's how much I don't like you."

He brought his lips back to mine, softer, but still demanding. At the tingle that ran through me, my eyes fluttered closed. A part of my mind registered I was probably making a mistake, but I also couldn't deny kissing him was exhilarating, even intoxicating.

My lips parted in invitation, his tongue taking the opportunity to tangle with mine. I stretched into him as his hands moved over my shoulders, down my back. As my fingers dug into his shoulders, his hands kept roaming down, over the curves of my hips; then, in one swift movement, he bent, his hands gripping the back of my thighs, and lifted me so I sat on the edge of the counter.

I gasped against his mouth, the sound muffled as his lips never left mine. He brought his arms around me, hugging me to him, and my arms automatically twined around his neck.

This is dangerous, I thought, fighting the instinct to wrap my legs around his waist. Dangerous, unfair to both of us.

With my heart pounding, I pushed against his chest, drew my head back.

"Wait, Darcy, I can't..." I took a breath, steadied my voice. "I can't do this."

He released me, pulled away slowly, but when I looked at him his expression was clearly smug. "Are you still going to claim you don't like me? Because I think I just proved otherwise."

Temper and mortification flared through me, and I brought my chin up as I slid off the countertop. "Being attracted to someone and having feelings for them are two different things," I said coldly. "If you think you can just kiss me and I'll forget your past behavior, you are sorely mistaken. So no, to answer your question, I will not go to dinner with you."

An expression of confusion and his own temper replaced his smug smile. "I don't understand you," he said. "It seemed like…"

"Like what?" I demanded. "You thought I'd just fall at your feet because the great Fletcher Darcy deigned to ask me out?"

When he opened his mouth, couldn't form words, closed it, I smirked. "You did, didn't you." I let out a half-laugh. "Well I hate to disappoint you, but I'm not an easy mark. I appreciate you're classy enough to take me to dinner first, but I don't sleep around, I don't sleep with someone I don't have feelings for, and I definitely don't sleep with guys who don't respect me."

I didn't think I'd ever seen a man blush, but pure horrified shock heightened his color.

"I never—that's not what I—I didn't expect…" he stuttered.

Then he ran a hand over his face, breathed deep. "I don't think you're an easy mark," he said with forced calm. "And my intentions behind dinner were to take you out, get to know you more. If I just wanted to get laid, I'd hit on Chloe."

Despite myself, I snorted. "Touché."

I suspected I'd been a little harsh, but I wasn't about to admit it to him, so instead I said nothing else.

"So that's it, then?" he asked bitterly. "Because I accidentally insulted you once, you're dead-set against me?"

"There's pretty much nothing you can say to convince me to enjoy your company."

"Aside from the rude comment I already apologized for, what exactly have I done to offend you so much?"

"You want a list?" I quipped.

"Apparently that might be best."

"Fine." I crossed my arms. "All you've done since we met is criticize me, you have ridiculously high expectations, you treat those of us here who aren't rich like we're mooching off the Bingleys' hospitality, and I have the sneaking suspicion you've tried to get Cameron to dump Jess."

I paused, closing the space between us again, but this time to glare up at him. "If he does, if he breaks her heart, I will blame you, and I will do my best to make your life hell. In a nutshell," I said, stepping back again, "You're conceited, arrogant, and you give absolutely no thought to other people's feelings."

The emotions on his face were so mixed I couldn't read them, but I had the sinking feeling I'd gone too far. This whole situation was too much.

I don't know how long we stared at each other, the silence pulsing with our mutual, confusing emotions, but when he finally spoke he was so quiet I wouldn't have heard him if he wasn't a breath away from me.

"I'm sorry I bothered you."

Then he turned sharply and walked briskly away.

I swallowed, my throat tightening as the tumultuousness of what just happened burst forth through hot tears. I sank to the floor and hugged my knees, folding myself and sobbing. Eventually the sensible part of me realized I couldn't stay there, having a breakdown on the kitchen floor, so I picked myself up and somehow made it to my room, where I closed myself off.

What have I done?

THREE

I HARDLY SAW Emerson at all the next day.

That wasn't a surprise—she was likely avoiding me as much as I was avoiding her. I knew she was an early riser, and it had been her habit to walk the paths in the woods around the house after breakfast, so I waited until I saw her leave to get breakfast myself.

I'd spent part of the night holed up in the library trying to distract myself with its meagre selections, but my mind inevitably kept wandering back to the argument with Emerson.

How much more oblivious could I have been? Thinking she was just waiting for me to make a move, longing for me as much as I had been for her. And all the while she'd been wishing me far away.

Once I got past the sting of her words, I started to accept some of what she'd said was right. It still hurt, perhaps because there was some truth to them, but I had to admit I admired her for setting me straight.

The older I got, the more women tried to get my attention; though Emerson had never acted that way, I'd still just assumed she'd jump at the chance to go out with me.

I always thought I'd done my best to be a decent person and support those I cared about; evidently I'd been raised with good principles, but had failed to implement them due to my...what had Em called it? Ah, yes: 'Inflated sense of self-importance.'

But I had been conceited and selfish. If I'd thought of her feelings more than my own I would have understood her more clearly, and certainly never insulted her. If I'd thought of Cam's feelings more, I would've left him to his own decisions, instead of worrying about the outcome of those decisions—he was his own man. Though she had been wrong about one thing: I was concerned how Jess would be affected if Cam broke up with her.

I spent hours looking back on how unsavory my words and actions may have seemed since I met Emerson; at some point I pulled out the bourbon for company so I could wallow properly.

Eventually thoughts of Emerson by extension led to thoughts of the… encounter.

I'd fantasized about kissing her, and more, before, but the reality of her lips on mine and her body pressed against me put all my fantasies to shame.

She was a live wire and I got too close.

By the time everyone gathered for dinner the next day, I'd analyzed the situation from every angle I could think of. I couldn't resist glancing at Emerson down the table occasionally; she was never looking at me, but she was much quieter than usual. A part of me thought she even seemed a little sad, which only made me feel more guilty.

Now, I used my frustration to push myself through a more rigorous morning swim. It helped a little, but by the time I got out, my thoughts had drifted to alluring green eyes yet again.

After I'd toweled off, pulled my t-shirt back on, I picked up the book I'd brought out (wary as I was about its ability to distract me.) I was about to sit on the lounge chair when I caught a movement out of the corner of my eye, glanced up, thought: Crap.

On the second floor terrace, Chloe strutted across in a bikini that barely covered the essentials, trailing a hand lightly along the railing. She was deliberately keeping her gaze forward, but I had no doubt she knew I was there—the strut was likely deliberate as well, as she'd want me to watch her, I knew. If I wanted to escape, I'd have to do it now—I knew from experience she was quicker than she looked.

As Chloe continued toward the stairs that led down to the patio, I dashed back into the house. Ridiculous, I thought, that I had to resort to literally running away from a woman. I turned down a hall at random, slowed my pace.

"Fletcher?"

Damn it. There was no mistaking Chloe's purring call from the living room just down the hall. I ducked into the den, closing the door behind me as quietly as I could and moving to the wall just next to the door.

"Darcy?"

I froze. This time the voice was unmistakably Emerson's.

When I glanced up, I saw she was spread out on the couch, a book in her lap.

Eyes wide, I brought a finger to my lips. At her questioning look, I opened my mouth, but before I could explain, Chloe's next "Fletcher?" could be heard on the other side of the door.

My eyes still on Emerson's, I shook my head, begging her not to say anything.

The door opened, and Chloe stepped just inside the room, the door blocking her view of me.

"Oh," she said when she saw Emerson. "Have you seen Fletcher?"

I watched Emerson's face as she responded with her customary raised brow expression, "No, sorry, I haven't seen him since breakfast."

"Are you sure?" Chloe sounded suspicious. "He likes to take a swim in the morning."

Emerson shrugged. "Then maybe he went to take a shower or something."

I couldn't see the face Chloe made, but I imagined she did, and after a few agonizing moments, the door closed. I waited several more seconds just to be sure, then let out the breath I didn't realize I'd been holding.

"Thank you."

"There's no need to thank me." Emerson granted me the teasing arch look that had haunted my dreams all week. "I had no desire to witness her fawning all over you. Though I admit it sometimes provides me with ample entertainment, I'm not in the mood right now."

"Still," I said, approaching the couch. "You saved the prey from the predator's grasp."

I was rewarded with a small smile. When she glanced down at her book, bit her lip, I took the opportunity to study her; she wore a slim green sundress and light cardigan over her petite form, and at the memory of her wrapped around me, I had to stop myself from inadvertently licking my lips.

It could only be a memory.

"Hey, um, while I've got you alone…" She looked up at me, her green eyes clouded with something like regret. "I, uh…I've been doing a lot of thinking about what happened the other night, and I realized I may have been…*was*, a little hard on you. The things I said—"

"Oh, no, you don't have to—"

"No, no. Please." She held up her hands. "I need to apologize. I said some harsh things, mostly because I was angry and upset. I was a bitch, and I meant to be. So I'm sorry."

My heart lifted and lodged in my throat. "Apology accepted. But I don't think you were a bitch."

She looked away, not meeting my gaze, and it tore at me.

"I know you think I don't respect you," I continued. "But I do. I have the highest respect for you, even more so now because of what you said to me. I owe you an apology, too."

Though her eyes were wary, she did turn them back to me.

"I—can I sit?" I asked.

Nodding, she closed her book, scooted to make room on the couch. I set down my own book on the coffee table, then sat next to her.

"I should probably start by apologizing for insulting you when we first met. Really apologize, I mean."

She turned her head away, expression unreadable.

"It didn't have anything to do with you. I was in a crappy mood. I barely even glanced at you, and I wasn't even sure who Cam was talking about. I only said what I did so he'd leave me alone." I watched her carefully, imploring her to look at me again. I needed her to believe this time that I was sincere. "That's a sorry excuse, I know; I should never have said such a thing, regardless of whether or not I thought anyone could hear me."

"So you didn't mean it?" Her voice was quiet.

"Of course I didn't mean it. You're…well, I think my actions yesterday make my attraction to you evident." I felt my face heat at the statement, and I was pleasantly surprised to see a light blush pink her cheeks.

"Speaking of which," I continue. "I should also apologize for…um, kissing you the way I did. I have no excuse for that either."

A hint of a smile graced her lips. "Well, I didn't exactly fight you off, did I?"

I cleared my throat to tamp down the memory of her mouth moving over mine; she still wouldn't look at me, and I couldn't help but wonder if the memory stirred her too.

"The point is, you were right. If I'd thought about your feelings at all, instead of just how much I wanted you, I never would've—"

"I know." She stopped me, laying a hand over mine and giving me an apologetic smile. "I kissed you back because I wanted you, too, so I get it. But physical attraction isn't enough for me, so eventually reason interceded."

"I understand." Now it was my turn to look away. "But you should know, my feelings for you are more than just physical. They're still raw, so I'm still sorting through them, but they're real—I'm sorry I did such a terrible job of showing it. I'm sorry if I made you feel less."

She squeezed my hand, and I looked back at her. "It wasn't all you. That comment you made colored my perception of you from the start; I think it hurt so much because of my initial attraction to you, because normally I wouldn't have cared. You were right when you said I deliberately misunderstood you."

Heart lightening, I turned my hand under hers, interlaced our fingers. I took a breath.

"There's one more thing I should explain. About Cameron and Jess."

She immediately stiffened, but thankfully didn't let go of my hand.

"I have nothing against your sister. She's a nice person, and by all accounts she makes Cam happy."

"He makes her happy too."

I didn't miss the edge to her voice.

"I'm glad to hear that." I stroked my thumb over the back of her hand, hoping to send calming vibes. "And believe it or not, I think they're good together. I just worry about Cam; he's thought himself in love before, and while he's definitely more into your sister than I've seen him with anyone, he has a tendency to be...impulsive."

When I paused, she only kept watching me, raised a brow.

"He doesn't usually date anyone more than a couple months. As it's been nearly a couple months now, I just wanted him to be careful, to be sure this time that he wants a long-term relationship—and to point out that if he didn't, it wouldn't be fair to lead her on. I don't want him to break Jess's heart any more than I want her to break his."

She blew out a breath. "I suppose I can understand that. I wouldn't want him to encourage her either, if he didn't intend to stick around."

"He might've intended to stick around, but left anyway if he met someone else, or if Chloe convinced him he should break up with her. But I don't think he'll do that with Jess. She might even help him listen to himself more than his sister."

"Or you." This time her raised eyebrow was accompanied by a pert smile.

"Or me," I acknowledged. "I probably shouldn't offer my opinion so readily."

"I don't think you do, really." She narrowed her eyes in thought. "I thought about it, and as far as I've seen, you really only give your opinion if asked for it. You don't say much unless you feel it's necessary. Whereas I say more than I should."

"Whose side are you on?" I teased, hoping to lighten the mood.

She shook her head, but smiled a little more. "Neither of us have behaved very well, so we could sit here and apologize to each other all day. Or, since we seem to be on good terms now, we could agree to forgive and forget."

"I can do that. Start over?"

She tipped her head. "Deal."

It was silent after that; we stared at each other for a moment before she looked down at our clasped hands, bit her lip. I opened my mouth, but couldn't think of anything to say. Her feelings didn't match mine at that moment, so I couldn't kiss her, not if we wanted to start over properly. But it didn't mean her attraction to me couldn't grow into something more.

While I wondered if I should try asking her out again, a soft knock came at the door. Emerson slipped her hand out from mine as the door opened and Jess popped her head in.

"Em? Oh, hi Fletcher." She smiled brightly at us both. "Jack suggested we all go to a corn maze this afternoon. Interested?"

"Heck yeah," said Emerson.

"Sounds fun," I agreed.

"Great! I'll let everyone know. We were thinking of leaving in an hour." Jess closed the door quietly. When she was gone, I looked back at Emerson, who had tilted her head, and was watching me with an amused expression.

"What?" I asked.

"Fletcher Darcy thinks it sounds fun to tromp around through stalks of corn?"

"Yes, he does," I said with mock offense. "He rather enjoys fall activities, actually, especially if there's apple cider."

She pursed her lips. "He might enjoy it less if he gets lost in a maze with Chloe Bingley."

Something swelled in my chest—hope maybe? She'd teased me before, but she was flirting with me now, if the look in her eyes was anything to go by.

"Then I guess I'll just have to keep you around to protect me," I said.

"I'll be sure to bring my Shield of Wit."

FOUR

WE COULDN'T all fit in one car, so we piled into two vehicles—Jess, Casey, Chloe, and I in Jess's, Cam, Jack, and Darcy in Cam's.

Jess kept glancing at me as she drove; I could tell she wanted to ask me about Darcy, but didn't dare with Chloe around. As much as Chloe irritated me, I was momentarily thankful for her presence. I hadn't talked to Jess or Casey about what happened between Darcy and I, and now that we'd sort of had a heart-to-heart, I wasn't at all sure what I felt.

That I was attracted to Fletcher Darcy, I was certain of, and I now knew and admitted he was a far better man than I thought, or had let myself believe. I'd even double checked my appearance in the mirror when I'd changed into jeans for our outing. But beyond that...

I felt a little flutter in my stomach as I thought of the way he'd rubbed the back of my hand with his thumb—a soothing gesture that had been surprisingly comforting. He was surprising. And I had a feeling he wasn't done surprising me.

I had to admit I was looking forward to it.

When we arrived, Chloe suggested we all pair off, automatically attaching herself to Darcy. He sent me a pleading look, and I countered the suggestion with the idea it would be more fun if we stuck together as a group.

Relief washed over his face as everyone agreed. Cameron went to collect some maps of the maze, and I spotted a concession stand near the farm's pumpkin patch.

"Apple cider, anyone? I'm buying."

Everyone but Chloe wanted one, so Jess came with me to help carry the cups. When I held out a cup to Darcy, he gladly used the opportunity to remove his arm from Chloe's grip and put some space between them.

Once we entered the maze, Jack and Casey led the way; Darcy made sure he was in the middle so Chloe couldn't pull him away from the group, though he couldn't stop her from sidling up to him again. I flanked his other side, and Jess and Cameron brought up the rear.

Darcy and I had fun consulting Jack and Casey about the direction we should go, and marking off numbered checkpoints on the maze's app. Eventually we reached the large circle that was the center of the maze, where there were a few activities.

Jess pulled Cameron toward a photo arch made of corn stalks and other autumn assortments.

"We lost Jess and Cam," I said, tossing my empty cider cup in a trash barrel.

Casey pulled out her phone to take a picture of the giant scarecrow in the middle of the circle, and Jack moved to pose beside it. Chloe rolled her eyes.

"I wish I'd brought my camera," I laughed.

"This is so childish," Chloe pouted, looking at Darcy, clearly expecting him to agree with her. But Darcy threw out his cider cup and held out his hand to Casey.

"Here, I'll take a picture of the two of you," he said.

Though surprised, Casey handed him her phone and went to stand beside Jack, who shifted and lifted her up in his arms. Laughing, Casey braced her arms around Jack's neck just as Darcy snapped a few shots; he snuck in one more as each turned their head to look at the other with expressions of amused flirtation.

"Oh, these are so cute!" Casey said when she took her phone back, beaming at Darcy. "Thank you, Fletcher."

"You're welcome," Darcy responded, sending a wink to his cousin while Casey was absorbed in flipping through the photos. Jack smiled mischievously, reaching out to tug me toward the scarecrow.

"Your turn." He winked at Darcy in turn.

I acquiesced, thinking he meant to pose with me, but he dropped my hand while Casey nudged Fletcher toward me. Fletcher gave me a questioning look, so I smiled and quirked a brow as if to say, *what are you going to do?*

"Fletcher, you're not going to pose in front of that ridiculous thing, are you?" Chloe asked him, gripping his arm. No one missed the sneer she sent the scarecrow—and me.

Darcy shrugged in an effort to seem casual, though I could tell he was annoyed, and moved toward me.

"Why not?" he said. "It looks like fun."

He smiled as he said the last part, in a way that mimicked his cousin's earlier mischievousness. I thought perhaps he would sweep me up in his arms the way Jack had Casey, and my heart flipped a little at the romantically corny thought. Instead he faced me and bent a little, wrapping his arms around my legs, and before I realized his intent, he'd hefted me over his shoulder.

"Fletcher!" I squeaked, flailing my arms a little as I eyed the ground. I found purchase by propping my elbows against his back and turning my torso to try to catch his eye. Jack and Casey were chuckling and taking pictures.

Suddenly I felt I couple pats on my behind.

My eyebrows shot up. "Did you just…?"

He turned his head to smile smugly at me out of the corner of his eye. When I noticed out of the corner of mine that Chloe's mouth had dropped open, I couldn't help smirking back.

I decided to play along. I had promised to protect him after all.

"Two can play at this game, buddy," I mock-scolded him before lifting one of my hands to smack his attractively jean-clad butt. "Put me down or I'll spank you again."

He grinned. "You have no idea how long I've waited to hear you say that."

At Chloe's huff of frustration, I looked over to see her stalking away toward her brother and Jess.

"Okay, for real, put me down now. She's gone."

"These pictures are great," Casey grinned as Fletcher bent to set my feet on the ground. When he stood, his hands lingered on my waist before he let me go, making me think of when he'd lifted me onto the countertop during our moment in the kitchen.

"I imagine they are," I said, swallowing my sudden nervousness.

His eyes heated and his gaze sharpened on me, and I wondered if he was remembering the same thing I was.

As the four of us rejoined the others, I realized I'd called Darcy Fletcher for the first time without even thinking about it; when had he stopped being just Darcy?

Our group finished the maze and explored a few of the other activities before heading back in the same cars we'd come in. Chloe, who'd been grumpy and silent the rest of the afternoon, glared daggers at me on the drive back to the house.

Once back on her home territory, however, Catty Chloe returned with a vigor. She made sure she sat next to Fletcher at dinner, doing her best to monopolize his attention and conversation, alternately talking about the superiority of herself or his family, and not-so-subtly trying to belittle me.

Normally I would have shrugged it off, but Fletcher was tense. He looked like he was about to explode at Chloe, but I caught his eye as he opened his mouth, shook my head. Oblivious, Chloe chattered on; when she paused, looking expectantly to Fletcher and fluttering her lashes, Cameron used the opening to change the subject.

I'd missed what she'd said, but Fletcher visibly relaxed once conversation shifted to more pleasant things. Each time Chloe tried to derail things, someone else at the table picked up the conversation, so thankfully she was thwarted for the rest of the evening. And no matter what she said, she couldn't stop or interrupt the looks Fletcher sent me from across the table, or the ones I sent back to him.

What an interesting day it had turned out to be.

. . . . .

AFTER MY USUAL SWIM, I hopped in the shower. The last couple days had been better than I could have imagined—and certainly a lot more fun than I'd had in a long time. Not that I didn't usually have fun with Cam and Jack, or with my family, but Emerson's presence had a different effect on me. I'd truly enjoyed everyone's company as we picked apples, toured a local brewery, chose a place for dinner at random, and walked around town.

Emerson made me happy, and if the time we'd spent together since our talk was anything to go by, I was having an effect on her as well.

She'd started calling me Fletcher, instead of Darcy, and I loved hearing her say my name.

But she wasn't ready; that was fine. She was a woman worthy of being pleased, and I'd just have to keep proving that to her. We only had a few days of our vacation left, so hopefully whatever bond we were forming would keep growing once we got back.

I smiled as I stepped out of the shower, thinking of her delight as she'd expounded the deliciousness of Jess's apple cinnamon muffins while she'd carefully plucked an apple. And she'd been right, I thought as I grabbed my towel and began to dry off; I'd liked the muffins so much I'd asked Jess for the recipe for our housekeeper, Mrs. Reynolds.

As I rubbed the towel over my hair, I thought I heard the door to my room open and close. Frowning, I peered through the crack between the door and the wall, squinting at a movement. Then I blinked just to make sure.

It was Chloe, dressed in a thin silk robe.

What the…?

I could only blink again as she removed the robe, tossed it on a chair, leaving her wearing a very lacy bra and underwear set. I quickly looked around the bathroom, but the only clothes I had were my swim trunks.

Silently cursing, I wrapped the towel around my waist and looked into the bedroom again, double-checking the bathroom door was locked. Chloe was occupied positioning herself on my bed.

Torn between bafflement, frustration, and panic, I glanced at the door to Jack's room. It was my only method of escape, and I could borrow his clothes. *Perfect.*

I carefully opened the adjoining door and stepped into the room to see Jack holding a phone charger out to Emerson. I froze upon seeing them, my feet refusing to move any further; Jack's eyebrows raised in amusement while Emerson's eyes widened and began darting around the room.

"Um…" I cleared my throat. "Jack, could I borrow some clothes for a little bit?"

"What'd, you forget to do laundry?" Jack smirked.

"Chloe's in my room."

"What?"

As it was Emerson who had spoken, I risked a glance back at her. She looked as confused as I felt.

"I heard the door to my room open after I got out of the shower," I explained, "And when I looked through the door crack, she was climbing onto my bed in her underwear."

Jack and Em exchanged a look; then both of them burst out laughing. I gave them a bland stare.

"Yeah, it's hilarious. At least give me some pants."

Handing the charger to Emerson, Jack headed toward the bathroom. "I have a better idea."

Then he winked at us, walked through the bathroom to my door, and casually strolled into my room. Em and I could very clearly hear Chloe's yelp, angry *'what are* you *doing here?!,'* and Jack's responding, *'getting my cousin some pants,'* followed by some shuffling. I looked at Em again, and I could tell she was holding back laughter.

"I bet you're thinking how pathetic this situation is."

"That's not even close to what I'm thinking," she said, running her gaze over me before finally meeting my eyes. She quirked an infuriatingly sexy brow that had me grinning back at her. This was a good sign.

I was trying to think of something charming to say when Jack came back with a pair of my jeans.

"Here you go, hotshot. Room's clear."

"And that's my cue to leave," Em said, waving the charger as she headed to the door. "Thanks for letting me borrow this, Jack."

When she was gone, Jack turned to me and gave me a significant look. "Now if Em had wanted to sneak into your room to surprise you in her underwear, something tells me you'd be having a very good time right now."

I said nothing, only deigning to return the look, then headed back to my own room to dress.

. . .

AT LUNCH THAT AFTERNOON, we were all gathered outside on the deck—all except Chloe, who'd claimed not to be feeling well. I smiled to myself as I remembered the look on Fletcher's face when he'd walked into Jack's room.

Jack, of course, was telling the story to the others, who had mixed reactions. As I could clearly picture Fletcher in nothing but his towel, his hair damp and dripping beads of water onto his lean shoulders, I could only hope I wasn't blushing. Casey burst out laughing, Cam looked chagrined but chuckled, and Jess looked downright shocked, only allowing a smile and shake of her head when she saw that Cam wasn't upset.

"I'm sorry, Fletcher." Cam ruffled his hair, making it stick up a little in a way Jess had told me she found endearing. "I never thought she'd do something like that."

Fletcher shrugged casually, though the stiffness of the gesture told me he was embarrassed. "Neither did I, and I'm more aware of her antics than you are."

Casey leaned across the table conspiratorially. "What would you have done, I wonder, if you had walked out of the bathroom to see her there?"

Now Fletcher pursed his lips. "Probably turned right around and walked back in."

Jack let out a guffaw and Casey dissolved into laughter again. The rest of us snickered a little, but seeing how uncomfortable Fletcher was, Jess kindly changed the subject.

After a while Cam asked her what she planned to do after graduation. As she spoke and the others continued the conversation, Fletcher leaned toward me a little and said quietly, "Did you ever get out to see the waterfall?"

"No," I said. "We've been so busy the past couple days I haven't had the chance."

"Would you like to go tomorrow?" He paused. "With me?"

My heartbeat did a double-dutch jump. "What time?"

"Say mid-morning? We could bring a picnic for lunch."

It sounded so delightful and romantic I couldn't stop a smile from spreading over my face. Though I felt I didn't deserve his attention after the things I'd said to him, if he was braving the wilderness by asking me out again, this time I would give him all the encouragement he needed.

"I'd like that."

FIVE

I WAITED for Emerson at the start of the waterfall trail carrying a light pack and a basket made up for us by Mrs. Nicholls—with some additions of mine. The others knew of our plans, except Chloe, and I hid myself in the trees a little just in case she was looking for me.

Ridiculous as ever, I knew; I was starting to think she was delusional. But that was a problem for another time.

I peeked around some branches at the sound of footsteps approaching, relieved when Emerson started down the trail. Her smile was warm as she noticed me, gestured to what I carried.

"Is that an actual picnic basket?"

"It is indeed."

"Need help with it?"

The thought of the two of us carrying a picnic basket between us made my heartbeat pick up a notch. "Sure," I swallowed.

I held out the basket and she took one of the handles.

"Geez, what did you put in this thing?" She laughed as she adjusted her grip. "Bottles of wine?"

I only shrugged.

"You did, didn't you?" She shook her head but smiled. "So it's a fancy picnic."

"If you say so."

"I do say so, if indeed there is wine in this basket."

"Then fancy it is."

We chatted amiably for a while about school and our families. I told her about my teenaged sister and my plans to join my father's company after grad school, she talked about her plans for her senior year and her three younger sisters.

I mentioned how loving my parents' relationship was, and my hope that I could someday find a love like theirs. I couldn't help glancing at her, and she surprised me by meeting my eyes. Her skin flushed a little, and she looked down at the basket we carried, her voice quiet among the rustle of leaves.

"That's really nice," she said softly, turning her gaze back to the trail. "I'm unsure about my own parents' relationship, but I am sure I don't want to emulate it. They're complete opposites and they hardly spend any time together. Still, they do seem to love each other, so I suppose there is that."

I nodded. "Love is different for everyone. What works for them won't work for you; that's not a bad thing. In fact, I think knowing what does and doesn't work for you in a relationship is important."

She gave a small smile. "Then I suppose I should thank them for their example."

Then she stopped, her face brightening as she motioned to put the basket down.

"What is it?" I asked.

She tilted her head toward the trees as she pulled her camera from her pack. "There's a bird's nest. The birds are perched so prettily it's like they're posing for me."

She readied her camera quickly, took a few shots from where we stood. Then she crept closer, stood on a boulder and got a few more. She was smiling when she returned and put her camera away.

"I would've climbed the tree but I didn't want to scare them away."

"We can climb trees later," I grinned.

She returned my grin with her own. "Promise?"

We picked up the basket and continued on; it wasn't long until we reached the falls. The end of the trail opened up on one side while the other gave way to the stream that flowed from the waterfall's shallow pool. The falls couldn't be more than ten feet high, but the water flowed clear and foamed white as it met the pool's surface, which was at least as wide around as the waterfall's height, if not more.

I watched her face as we approached it, catching the way her breath caught, and her calm, dreamy smile. We set the basket down and she immediately moved to take as many pictures as her heart desired, while I pulled a blanket from my pack and laid it out on the ground near the pool's bank.

I laid out some of our picnic while she climbed the rocks for different angles; when I was satisfied I climbed up to join her.

"I take it you like it?"

"Like it?" She shook her head. "This trip was worth it just for this."

I quirked a brow in imitation of her. "Just this?"

Her answering smile was coy. "Among other things." Then she lifted her camera and snapped a shot of me just as I smiled. Shocked, I could only gape at her.

"What?" She tilted her head. "You took one of me, can't I take one of you?"

I recalled the urge I'd had to take her picture as she stood on the bridge and wondered if she'd had the same impulse. Before I could ask to see the picture, she anticipated me, turning the camera around to show me. The falls made a picturesque backdrop; I was angled toward her, with the waterfall behind my shoulder, and my grin one that was surprisingly flirtatious.

"I hardly recognize myself," I finally said. "It's perfect."

"I thought so, too," she said quietly.

"Can you take one of us?" I asked.

"Sure." She smiled.

She fiddled with the camera settings, then walked over to a taller rock and spent some time framing a shot; I was about to ask what she was doing when she pressed a button and scampered back over to me.

"I set the timer," she explained as she put an arm around my waist.

I put my arm around her shoulders and smiled when she told me to smile.

"Looks good," she smiled when she checked the photo and showed me. "Good idea."

"I have them sometimes," I said, thinking we looked good together.

Carefully, she began stepping down from the rocks.

I followed her to the picnic I'd set up and opened the basket again while she put her camera away; when I pulled out two tin camping mugs and the bottle I'd packed, she let out a laugh.

"Only you," she said, shaking her head.

"What?"

"Champagne? On a hike?"

I shrugged. "Fancy picnic, remember?"

Still smiling, she shook her head again as I popped the cork and poured out the champagne. When I handed her one of the mugs, her smile faded a little into something like sadness.

"What's wrong?" I asked.

She looked down into her mug. "I feel like I don't deserve this."

"Everyone deserves champagne," I said lightly.

She laughed a little, but it came out as more of a sigh. "No, I mean…

after the way I treated you, I don't feel like I deserve another chance…
with you."

Now it was my turn to shake my head. "I'm still kicking myself for
giving you such a bad impression."

"I think we've established it wasn't completely your fault. I didn't
want to be impressed."

"That may be, but I made a complete blunder of things." I took a sip of
champagne to clear my dry throat. "I was taught to respect women; when
you turned me down, I should have just accepted your answer. You didn't
owe me an explanation."

"No, but I did push your buttons," she pointed out. "And you didn't
deserve the terrible things I said."

"It doesn't matter," I asserted. "It's me who doesn't deserve another
chance, but I'd hoped to at least make things better between us. When you
agreed to this picnic, it gave me hope."

I paused to look at her, her green eyes bright as she listened, the sun
catching hints of the red in her hair. "I was really hoping to think of this as
our first date, but if you tell me that it's not, I'll let it go, and I won't ever
bring the subject up again, no explanation required."

She looked away, toward the waterfall, and took a sip of her own
champagne. Then a small smile crept back onto her face.

"As far as first dates go, I think you've outdone yourself." She
gestured to our surroundings, finally turning the smile on me. "How are
you going to beat this?"

Relief, joy, excitement all burst through me at once. "You'd be
surprised," I managed to say.

Then, to my delight, her eyes softened, and she reached up a hand to
run her fingers over my cheek and into my hair. "I'm so glad I was wrong
about you," she murmured, leaning into me.

I sat still and let my eyes close as she brushed her lips gently over
mine. I could taste the tang of the champagne on her, even as she pulled
back.

I laid my hand over the one she'd leaned back on. "We should eat."

Suddenly her smirk grew flirtatious. "You can if you want. I think I'm
going to cool off first."

She set down her mug, stood, and pulled her t-shirt over her head,
revealing a simple black bikini top. Tossing the shirt on the blanket, she
kicked off her shoes; my eyes widened and I watched slack-jawed as she
tugged off her socks and shorts, revealing the matching bottoms.

I set down my mug absentmindedly, entranced as she carefully walked
over to the rocks. She paused at the edge of the water and sent a come-
hither look over her shoulder.

"Are you going to join me?"

I scrambled up, nearly upending my champagne as I yanked off my own shoes, socks, and shirt. I had also worn my swim trunks in anticipation of a dip under the waterfall, but I hadn't imagined anything like this.

As I joined her on the rocks, she slowly stepped into the water.

"Ooh, it's cold!" she remarked.

"Yeah, but you'll get used to it after a few minutes," I told her.

She braced herself and walked to the center of the pool, where the water came up to just under her breasts; it hit me about mid-abdomen. As I made my way over to her, she moved toward the falls, trailing her fingertips along the water. When she reached the falls, she lifted a hand and ran her palm under it. Then she turned and backed into it, tilting her head back to let the water run over her hair. When I reached her I did the same, letting the force of the water gently pummel my shoulders.

She sank down a little, so the water nearly covered her shoulders, her hair moving sinuously over the surface. She looked like a sea goddess as she rose back up, water rolling over her skin, and at the smile she gave me, I glided toward her.

Putting my arms around her waist, I pulled her flush against me, delighting at how she ran her hands up my chest and linked her arms around my neck.

This time her mouth met mine fiercely, almost demanding. I felt rather than heard the hum in her throat through the crashing of the waterfall.

I dug my hands into her hair and deepened the kiss, her tongue sweeping to meet mine. She moaned as her hands roamed down, up my back. After several moments, she let a hand wander under the water, sliding it playfully over my ass and causing me to groan.

Her smirk died on a gasp of pleasure as I nipped my way down her neck, my hands moving to cup her breasts. They fit so perfectly, and I could feel how her heartbeat kicked up under my palm.

"Fletcher," she sighed as her eyes flitted shut. Since her mouth was near my ear I heard her soft moan as I rubbed my thumbs in circular motions across her nipples.

I slowed the motions, letting my head rest in the crook of her shoulder.

"Oh, God, Em. I want…"

"I know."

I straightened, glancing around just in case someone else happened to be on the trail, then sank a little in the water until I was nearly eye-level with her breasts. Softly, I moved aside the wet fabric covering one breast, then the other, my hands resuming their motions as I looked up to meet her eyes.

"You're so beautiful," I said before taking a breast into my mouth. Her hands came to grip my shoulders, and the sounds she made nearly undid me as I moved from one breast to the other. I could feel her quivering, and hoped it was from pleasure rather than cold.

On a sudden groan, she dipped down to crush her mouth to mine, her lips moving slow and sensuous, her bare breasts pushing against my chest as water lapped around us. We were breathing heavily when we finally pulled apart.

She swallowed. "Maybe we should eat now."

"Definitely," I agreed.

She nodded and adjusted her top before rising, and we walked hand-in-hand back to the blanket. Though the air was warm, it was chilly getting out of the water—though thankfully it helped me…calm down.

We each pulled a towel from our packs, and she wrung water out of her hair before wrapping the towel tight across her shoulders.

I stared at her as she reached for a little tomato, mozzarella, and pesto sandwich.

"What?" she said, blushing.

I repeated my words from earlier. "You're so beautiful."

"Oh." She smiled shyly. "So are you."

Pleased, I grinned before taking a sandwich of my own. She bit into hers thoughtfully.

"So should I expect you to stare at me a lot?" she asked as she chewed.

I swallowed a bite and nodded sagely. "Yes."

Her laughter warmed me. "I suppose I should get used to it then."

I nodded again, truly unable to take my eyes off her.

"Yes, you should."

SIX

OUR WALK back to the house was pleasant, if not a little distracted; we held hands, and if the way his eyes still followed me was any indication, Fletcher was thinking about our interlude in the waterfall's pool as much as I was.

What was it about the man that made me lose my senses in the most inappropriate places?

One of these days, I thought, we'd make it to a bed, and then there wouldn't be anything holding us back. I looked at him as the thought went through my mind, and the way he waggled his eyebrows at me made me wonder if he knew what I was thinking.

I laughed and shook my head.

The others gave us knowing glances when we returned, and we each went to our rooms to shower—alone. There were thankfully no surprises, though if I were Fletcher, I would have locked my door.

Not long after I'd dressed, there was a knock at my door.

"Come in."

Jess came in, followed by a grinning Casey.

"I told you," Casey said. "I told you he liked you."

I responded with a dry look, taking a seat on the bed. "Yes, oh Wise One, you were right."

Casey just smirked.

"So…" Jess bit her lip. "How was your picnic?"

"Delicious," I answered honestly, thinking of more than the food.

Casey rolled her eyes.

"I'm serious," Jess insisted.

"So am I."

"We don't want to know about the food, you dork," Casey said as she sat next to me.

I raised a brow. "Even if there was champagne?"

"Champagne?" Jess perked up. "Okay, now we really need details."

"Yes, but first," Casey nudged me with her shoulder, "What I meant was, how was Darcy?"

"Delicious," I repeated.

Casey snorted and clapped her hands together. "Okay. Yes. Details now."

So I told them—about how lovely our hike was, how beautiful the waterfall was, the pictures I took of him and us, which I showed them while I explained our swim; I didn't tell them how carried away we got, just that we spent a lot of time kissing before going back to the picnic.

I left out our little heart-to-heart before the swim; neither Fletcher or I had told anyone about our argument, or the subsequent apologies, and we agreed to keep it between us. It was too personal and intimate an experience to explain, even to those closest to us. And it was more meaningful to us as something only we shared.

I wasn't sure what our relationship looked like to the others, especially Jess and Casey, who knew I hadn't liked him before. They'd noticed us growing closer throughout the week, so I'd merely told them he and I had talked, and I'd gradually changed my mind about him. It may have been vague, but it was the truth.

At dinner, it seemed Fletcher and I couldn't help ourselves, constantly glancing at one another across the deck table. I caught myself staring at him more than once, absorbed in the lines of his face and the intensity of his blue eyes. He was so damn handsome—if this was why he stared at me, then I could say I understood the feeling.

Chloe would have been blind not to notice our exchanges, and, though I never looked at her to confirm, was undoubtedly glaring at me again. But I hardly cared. I was too happy to let her dampen the day for me.

After dinner, we all sat around the fire pit chatting and drinking beer as the sun went down. The evening was cozy, and though I wasn't sitting next to Fletcher, I could feel the heat of his gaze over the warmth of the fire.

Inspired, I sat up straighter.

"Who wants s'mores?" I asked.

Cries of assent sounded around the circle, so I stood and said I'd get the supplies when Cam assured me they were stocked. I'd just made it to the kitchen and was rummaging around in the pantry when Fletcher came in.

"Thought I could help," he said, and, spotting the box of graham crackers, took the opportunity to slide his hand over my bottom as he reached for the box.

"I suppose it's helpful to have a tall person around," I said.

When I found the marshmallows, I moved to place them on the counter. He came up behind me and set the box of graham crackers down, but didn't move back.

Instead he laid his hands on my hips, and bent to trail kisses down my neck. I shivered at the sensation.

Smiling, I reached back to cup my hand around the back of his neck and tilted my head to give him more access.

"Are you trying to re-create our first kiss?" I asked him.

"No," he said, turning me to face him. "But we can if you want."

I shook my head. "No, but we could definitely create a new, happier memory."

He smiled just before he molded his mouth to mine in a hard kiss, tugging me against him until I stretched my arms around his neck and stood on my tip-toes to lessen the distance. After a few moments, his hands rested on the small of my back, and he slowed the kiss.

I set my feet flat on the floor again, pulling him with me and bumping into the counter behind me. A muffled laugh escaped him, and one of his hands dug into my hair at the back of my neck, keeping the kiss slow and deep. I moved my hands to his chest and sighed in pleasure as he changed the angle, his nose brushing mine, his tongue seeking a dance partner.

He straightened at the sound of a gasp followed by glass breaking.

We both turned our heads, arms still around each other, to see an angry Chloe, an amused Cam, and the remnants of an empty beer bottle on the floor.

"What are you doing?" Chloe screeched.

Since it was rather obvious what we'd been doing, my eyebrow rose on instinct.

"What does it look like we're doing? Playing croquet?"

Fletcher gave a quiet snort; Cam chuckled and laid a hand on his sister's shoulder but she jerked out of his reach. She sent me a fulminating stare, but since she didn't actually seem hurt by the situation I only tilted my head at her.

I could tell there were a lot of things she wanted to say, but wasn't sure she'd say them with Fletcher and her brother present. Fletcher seemed to sense this, too.

"Why are you so angry, Chloe?" he asked her calmly. "Em and I are unattached adults. We have the right to kiss each other if we want to."

Shocked, she opened her mouth, but Cam stopped her from stepping forward.

"Don't step on the glass," he told her.

Fletcher moved to the pantry, took out a broom and dustpan, held it out to Chloe. She stared at it as though it were covered in spiders.

Cam nudged her. "Your mess, Chloe. It's only fair you clean it up."

Sighing, she snatched the broom from Fletcher and yanked off the dustpan. When she bent to sweep at the glass, Fletcher glanced at the couple other empties in Cam's hand.

"It took two of you to carry three empty bottles?"

On a half-laugh, Cam shrugged. "No. Chloe said she was going to toss hers; I followed when I remembered the chocolate isn't in the pantry. I figured I'd save you the trouble of searching for it and clean up a little while I was at it."

I managed to hide my smirk—mostly. We all knew what Chloe had really wanted was to make sure I wasn't alone with Fletcher. In that, I supposed, she had succeeded, though her ultimate goal of gaining his attention for herself was destined to fail, even without me. I would have felt sorry for her if I thought she actually had any romantic feelings for him.

Cam glanced at the graham cracker and marshmallow packages on the counter and grinned. "Evidently, you either gave up trying to find the chocolate, or got too distracted."

Though Fletcher blushed a little, he did smile at me and admitted, "Definitely distracted."

Still grinning, Cam nodded, gave his friend a light punch on the arm as he made his way to the giant refrigerator. He opened the bottom drawer that was the freezer and dug around for a few seconds before he pulled out a handful of chocolate bars.

Chloe finished sweeping up the glass, dumping it unceremoniously in the trash under the sink and walking stiffly to the pantry to return the broom and dustpan. Since I was still at the counter, I grabbed up the other s'mores supplies.

"Shall we?" I asked.

"Here." Cam handed the chocolate to Fletcher and turned back to the refrigerator. "I'm going to grab another six-pack."

Fletcher and I went back to the fire pit, followed a few moments later by Cameron, who explained to the group that Chloe had decided to turn in for the night. Though Fletcher and I exchanged a look, we decided to be nice and not comment on the reason for her absence.

The six of us enjoyed our s'mores, chatting and laughing idly; at some point Fletcher pulled me into his lap, hugging his arms around my middle, and I rested an arm around his shoulders. It wasn't long before the others followed our example and cuddled up as well.

I looked around in contentment and sighed, absently playing with the hair at the back of his neck.

"What are you thinking?" he asked.

"Just how nice this is," I answered, gesturing around the circle. "We should make it a tradition to come here every year."

Jess, though she had been snuggling with Cameron, heard me and piped up. "Oh, yes that's a great idea."

Cam laughed. "It already is a tradition for me, Jack, and Fletcher. But I think I speak for all the guys when I say we can update the tradition to include you."

"I'm for it," Jack agreed, as did Casey, and I made a note to myself for later to grill her as mercilessly about Jack as she'd grilled me about Fletcher.

And so we made a plan to return at the same time the next year. Fletcher tugged me a little closer and tilted his head to murmur quietly in my ear.

"So you think we'll still be together a year from now?"

Startled, I looked at him. His eyes were teasing and his smile was full of possibilities.

"Did I say that?" I mused.

"You suggested the six of us come back here next year—together." He twined his fingers through mine. "That tells me you're confident we'll still be together. And that's a thought that makes me very happy."

"I hadn't really thought about it," I admitted, my heart warming. "But now that you point it out, I find it makes me happy, too."

I kissed him lightly, there in the glow of the cozy autumn fire, and leaned my forehead against his, eyes closed in contentment.

"We'll go back to the waterfall," he whispered. "It'll be our place."

I opened my eyes and smiled.

"I like the sound of that."

EPILOGUE

One Year Later

THE FAMILIAR SOUND of water crashing against water made us both smile, and a few moments later, we reached our waterfall.

"I can't believe it's been a whole year since we were here," Em said, opening our picnic basket as I laid down a blanket, then pulling out containers of food.

I draped a light blanket over her shoulders before I pulled out the champagne and opened it; though the weather was still nice and reasonably warm, we had decided it was too cold for a swim this year. Though I had very much wished for a repeat of our last waterfall swim, she looked just as good in flannel as in a bikini, so I couldn't fault the view.

"It went by pretty fast, didn't it?" I agreed, pouring out the champagne in the tin mugs, just as before.

"And so much has changed," she continued, taking a mug. "I remember when we first got here last time—I was struck by the contrast of you and Jack. Him smiling and explaining your family naming tradition, you frowning at me when I said it was cool."

My brows furrowed at the memory. "Was I frowning?"

"Yes." She smiled knowingly. "But it was that particular frown I now know means you were thinking about something."

"I was." I nodded in remembrance. "Do you want to know what I was thinking?"

The teasing brow I loved made its appearance. "I don't know, do I?"

"I had the sudden thought that Bennet Darcy sounded like a cool name."

Her lips parted in surprise, and I smiled as I sipped my champagne. "Then I scolded myself for thinking it because we weren't even together, and I didn't even know if you wanted to have kids."

Her hand covered mine, squeezed. Not long into our relationship we'd gotten talking about relationship and life goals out of the way, agreeing that marriage was in the cards—though she made it clear she didn't want to consider it until after graduating college—and that we would like to have kids someday, but not for several years at least.

Knowing we were on the same page early on helped us grow closer, as it made it easier to discuss more serious things, and also meant neither of us ever wondered where we stood with the other.

We ate and talked companionably, taking our time and enjoying our surroundings. Eventually, Em pulled out her camera, and we climbed over the rocks. We'd decided to add to the tradition by taking a photo in front of the waterfall each time we made it out there.

She set up the camera and I pulled her into my arms when she joined me. She looked like she was about to say something, but I stopped her with a quick kiss. As I pulled away and looked down at her, her eyes fluttering open and a small smile playing on her lips, I heard the familiar click and shutter of the camera.

My own smile widened. "Perfect."

"How do you know?" She chuckled. "We haven't looked at it yet."

"Just a feeling."

She ran her thumb over my cheek. "I believe you."

I caught her hand in mine. "I love you, Emerson Bennet."

"I love you, Fletcher Darcy."

She kissed me softly before going to retrieve her camera. I watched a luminous smile spread across her face as she pulled up the photo.

"You're right," she said. "It's perfect."

I smiled back, already planning exactly how perfect I would make next year's photo.

VITRIOL AND VINEYARDS

ONE

TALL, trimmed trees lined the dirt road that would take Elliot Burke closer to a place he never thought he'd see. He'd been traveling with his aunt and uncle, and they'd spent the past few days touring California's wine country; so far the trip had been just what he needed—hiking around Sugarloaf Ridge State Park, wandering the Napa Valley Museum, and of course, visiting vineyards. But there was one vineyard he hadn't considered, despite its popularity.

Pemberley.

He'd tried to convince Aunt Maddie and Uncle Ed he wasn't interested in seeing it, but they weren't fooled; fortunately his uncle had learned when he made a tasting reservation that the owners were visiting the Pemberley offices in San Francisco that week.

He tapped his fingers nervously against his knee and focused on watching the trees go by.

She's not here, she's not here, he repeated to himself.

"Elliot, look!"

He snapped his gaze away from the line of trees to look where his aunt Maddie was pointing. And his heart gave a not-so-subtle lurch.

The house that came into view was, much like its owner, stunning and surreal. It nestled perfectly into the land, the villa-style stonework blending into its surroundings, the creeping ivy giving a three-story tower with a balcony a fairytale effect.

He barely heard his aunt and uncle's exclamations as they passed the house, continued down the drive to the vineyard, and parked. He couldn't tear his eyes from the endless rows of sweeping vines, the picturesque silhouettes of rolling hills and peaks in the distance.

He should have known her home, her livelihood, would be idyllic.

A host met them at the entrance to the winery, and Elliot did his best not to gawk.

"We have a reservation under Gallagher," his uncle Ed told her.

"Perfect, right this way."

They were shown to a table on the winery's rustic but elegant patio, where they enjoyed a tasting along with some other tour-goers, and Elliot couldn't help but be impressed, with the wine and the vibe. Everywhere he looked he noted little touches, like the fairy lights strung among the woven ivy canopy that provided shade to the terrace, the beams carved to look like tree branches, the tables with bases made from wine barrels, and the copper lanterns filled with string lights in the center of each table. Though it was midday now, he imagined it was magical lit up at night.

He'd expected the wine to be good but pretentious, but it wasn't—it was just really good wine. Every note of flavor his tongue detected solidi- fied just how much everyone at Pemberley cared about what they did.

And the staff were so nice; they all spoke so well of Pemberley's owners he had to resist the urge to cringe. Their host even commented on how well the owners took care of their staff.

More evidence of how wrong he'd been.

Next, the tour showed them through a little of the wine-making process, and through the edges of the vineyard from behind a fence. But Elliot hardly paid attention.

He loved everything he saw, and it only made him feel more guilty and uncomfortable. He had no right to be here, in her place. The haven she and her family had created. He had no doubt he would disturb that peace if she discovered him here. He could imagine the way her deep blue eyes would widen, and then not be able to meet his own.

She's not here, he reminded himself. *She's in San Francisco for the week.*

"We're going to browse the store." Aunt Maddie laid a hand on his arm. "Coming?"

"Nah," he told her, putting on what he hoped was a convincing smile. "I think I'm going to wander and take in the view. Pick out a cabernet for me, though?"

She didn't look like she believed he was that cheery, but she was aware of his moods and didn't question it. "Alright."

He only wandered a little before he found a quiet spot on a wooden bench overlooking the vineyard, its back carved to look like twining branches. It was so inviting he decided it would be the perfect place to be alone with his thoughts, so he sat and automatically pulled up his email on his phone. By now, he knew her letter by heart, but it was easier to hear her voice as he read the words than to go over them in his head.

Dear Elliot,

Don't worry, this isn't a love letter. It's just that I find it hard to say what I feel out loud sometimes; writing is easier. So if you have the decency (and I believe you do) to let me explain my side of the story, I would like to defend myself—and there are some things you should know.

There are a couple (very different) things you accused me of yesterday, but it was the second accusation—that I deliberately and callously dumped Gabriel Windham, fired him, and blacklisted his name in the wine business—that hurt the most, because it is completely and utterly false.

I should probably explain some of our history. Gabe's father was the marketing manager for Pemberley, and a good friend of my father's; Gabe and I spent a lot of time together growing up. Eventually, our senior year of college, we started seeing each other. I thought I was in love with him, and that he loved me, but it turns out he was just using me.

The summer after we graduated, a couple months after we'd started dating, he began training with his father to one day take over the MM position, and I began working closely with my father. It was at this point that Gabe started wanting more in our relationship; he kept pressuring me to sleep with him, but I wasn't ready. I remember once while we were kissing, he asked if I wanted to have sex, I said no, and then he asked again five minutes later, as if that was a substantial enough amount of time for me to change my mind.

Then one day, I walked in to my father's office to find him tangled up with one of the interns, both of them already half undressed. I broke up with him then and there, but I'm ashamed to admit I had too much pride to report him or the intern, though their behavior certainly warranted it. Even more ashamed because not long after that, I found him in my father's office again—but this time he was alone, and had broken into the safe where my father keeps our wine recipes.

This time I called security, and when he finally admitted he had planned on selling the recipes to our competitors, my father fired him. Though our fathers remain friends, Gabe's father decided it would be best if he took a position somewhere else. That's when my cousin Seth became the MM.

Unfortunately, that wasn't the end of it.

My brother Aspen, who is six years younger than me, started college last year. Aspen has always been shy, and sometimes he has trouble making friends; I know he's struggled some with bullies and social anxiety. He was nervous about college, but excited too.

This next part is the hardest to write, and I trust I can count on your discretion.

Aspen had been away at a music program the summer all that stuff with

Gabe happened, and other than telling him Gabe and I had a bad break up, we chose not to tell him about Gabe's actions. I hadn't wanted to disclose I'd been cheated on, and my father wanted to keep the attempted theft as quiet as possible. We heard nothing of Gabe for a little over a year, until I went to surprise Aspen with a visit on his 19th birthday this past fall.

I was horrified to find him with Gabe, who had apparently been spending a lot of time with Aspen the last few weeks. At first, Aspen defended Gabe, who had convinced my brother he had been the one to break up with me because he thought I was too controlling. Before I could tell Aspen what Gabe had done, Gabe started laughing. As he left, he confessed he'd only been talking to Aspen because he thought Aspen could be easily manipulated into revealing Pemberley recipes, though I suspect he also wanted revenge on me.

Aspen was devastated, and so was I. Aspen had always looked up to Gabe as a sort of older brother, so his betrayal was all the worse. I don't consider myself a violent person, but to this day I wish I'd kicked Gabe in his precious balls—I still hope one day I'll get the chance. Aspen's found a good therapist and is better, but still recovering.

I know it might be hard to believe someone as seemingly good-natured as Gabe could do something so shitty, so if you need verification, you can ask Seth. He was there for all of it, and in the case of my brother, managed to do what I couldn't—he blackened Gabe's eye that day.

Part of the reason I'm telling you this, even the hard things, is because I should have sooner. I learned the hard way that ignorance doesn't protect anyone, and yet I went and made the same mistake by letting my pride keep me from exposing Gabe. It's painful to realize you were right about that, at least; by keeping silent, I've allowed him to hurt others.

As for the other matter, breaking up Joy and Cal, I admit I may have had a role to play—to what extent, I don't know. To clarify, the idea that Cal and I are interested in each other romantically is absurd to both of us, but I suppose I understand others may not always see it that way. I can assure you I was never jealous of your sister; in fact, I like her quite a bit.

But I've never seen Cal be serious about a relationship. He's not a player, but I guess you could say he's more than a little commitment-phobic. Though when he was with your sister he could hardly leave her side, in private he kept waffling, asking me all the time what I thought of him and Joy.

At first I simply told him she seemed nice, then later that they seemed good together; but as the weeks wore on, and he still asked for my opinion, I finally told him that if he really needed my opinion to determine whether or not he wanted to be with someone, then the answer to that question was probably no—that if he loved Joy, he need only consult his own feelings, and that it would be unfair to raise her expectations if he wasn't sure.

When he and the others followed me back to San Francisco and he told me he'd broken things off with Joy, I assumed he'd come to the conclusion he didn't, or couldn't, love her. I didn't know she'd told him she loved him.

To put it bluntly, I think he freaked out; I do believe he cares about Joy very much, and to be honest, he hasn't been quite himself since leaving Medford. I'm sorry your sister was hurt. If she still loves him, and if Cal can get over his doubts—which really are about him, not her—then maybe they have a shot.

And that's it. The only thing left for me to say is I'm sorry I hurt you. I never intended to, but you know what they say about intentions.

As all of the things I've written here are deeply personal, the only thing I ask of you is to delete this email when you're done reading it.

Good luck in your future endeavors.

Sincerely,

Willow

HE SIGHED, tucking his phone back in his pocket. Here, at Pemberley, it hit him just as hard as it had the first time how wrong he'd been. It made him sick how easily Windham had befriended him, pouncing on his poor opinion of Willow and, through what he'd thought was commiseration, encouraging the disdain of a woman who'd rejected them both out of hand.

Except it turned out Willow was right to kick Windham to the curb.

"Fuck me," he muttered to himself.

"Elliot?"

At first he wasn't sure he'd actually heard the voice, but when he realized it was real, he lurched to his feet, whirling to face the person he both desperately wanted to see and avoid.

She's here.

Willow Davenport stood in front of him, eyes wide and blue as he'd imagined, casually dressed in denim shorts, a v-neck tee, and old scuffed boots for walking the vineyards, her wavy coffee-colored hair pulled back in a long braid and covered by a dirt-smudged cap.

"Hi...Willow."

＊

HE'S HERE.

Pemberley was the last place she'd expected to see the man who'd stomped on her heart. But there he was, flesh and bone, looking rugged and forlorn on her favorite bench, nut brown hair mussed from the breeze, the most fascinating gray eyes she'd ever seen penetrating her heart yet again. The last time she'd seen them, the flecks of gold and green among the gray were sparking in anger.

You're the last person in the world I'd want to be with.

The words still stung, precise as a bee sting, but the lost look on his face was a good reminder she'd hurt him, too. By closing herself off, over-protecting her heart, she'd inadvertently made the man she was falling for despise her; and when she'd finally accepted her feelings and told him, she'd done so in such an insulting way, rejection was the only reasonable response.

But now he was here, standing in a place she'd imagined him standing so many times. Here was an opportunity—to be different, to start over. To show him she was more than he thought, and that she'd listened to his criticisms and begun to work on them.

She began to say, "It's nice to see you," just as he began, "I thought you were—"

"You first," she said, smiling a little.

The smile seemed to put him more on edge. "I didn't...I wouldn't have..." He stopped, started again. "I don't mean to intrude. We were told the owners were in San Francisco. I never would have come if I'd known you were here."

"We were in town today, but we came back early. And it's alright, I'm glad you're here."

"You are?"

She looked away a moment before looking back at him and the eyes that haunted her.

"I've wanted to show you Pemberley for a while. Who's we?"

"Huh?"

"You said we."

"Oh." He paused, watching her closely. "I'm here with my aunt and uncle. They're checking out the store. We've been taking a tour of wine country."

Now she smiled more broadly. "Did you ride the wine train?"

"Yeah. And we went to see the museum, and Castello di Amorosa."

"Good choices."

He nodded, and just kept looking at her like he expected her to vanish at any moment. She imagined it was just as awkward for him as it was for her, especially if he'd read her email. She hoped he had, but she didn't dare ask. She also didn't dare ask the one thing she really wanted to know.

Do you still hate me?

"Well," she swallowed. "I was, um, on my way to get cleaned up..."

"I won't keep you."

She nodded and said, "Nice to see you, Elliot," as she turned. She could feel his eyes on her as she walked to the house.

Once inside, she bolted up the stairs to her room. She had planned on a shower, but there wasn't time for that now. She changed her shorts and exchanged her t-shirt for a black tank top with buttons in the front, shoved her feet into an old pair of converse. Hastily, she undid her braid and ran a light brush through her hair. Then she raced back down and over to the winery. She had just about reached the store side when she spotted Elliot with a couple who were loaded down with shopping bags.

He was ushering them out, but he stopped when he saw her, just as surprised as before.

She smiled at them. "Good, you're still here. Is this your aunt and uncle?"

"Uh..."

His aunt elbowed him with a raised brow, a gesture Willow found amusing and immensely charming.

"Yes," he blinked. "Um, Willow, this is Ed and Maddie Gallagher; Uncle Ed, Aunt Maddie, this is Willow Davenport, one of the owners."

Ed gave Willow a firm handshake, while Maddie clasped her hand in both of hers and beamed.

"This is the most beautiful place," Maddie told her. "I don't need to tell you how good the wine is, as you can see we've just come away from your shop with several bottles."

Willow laughed. "We like it here. And thank you. Did you come just for a tasting, or did you take the tour as well?"

"We did both," Maddie confirmed, then paused slightly. "I should confess this isn't my first visit, though I was never old enough to try the wine the other time I was here."

"Oh?" said Willow, curious about the tinge of sadness behind the woman's eyes.

"I spent my childhood in this area," Maddie explained. "Up through high school. Your mother and I did theater together."

Willow's own eyes went soft with understanding. "You knew my mom?"

"We weren't close, but we were friends. She was a dear woman."

"She was. She often told me how she met my dad building sets in theater."

Maddie chuckled. "Yes, I remember. He nearly spilled a bucket of paint on her, and he didn't apologize—"

"Until she wiped her paintbrush on his face, and he was hooked." Willow grinned, and couldn't resist flicking a glance at Elliot, who was gawking at her as if he'd never seen her before. Well, she supposed, maybe he hadn't exactly seen her like this. She turned back to Maddie and Ed. "Would you like a private tour of the vineyard?"

"Oh!" Maddie's eyes lit up, and she looked at her husband and nephew beseechingly. "You don't mind, do you?"

"Certainly not," Ed assured her. "Let me just go put these bags in the car."

As he shuffled off, Willow looked at Elliot expectantly. "You don't want to see the vineyard up close?"

"I'd really like that, actually." He paused. "Thank you."

She nodded. When Ed returned, she led them down an employee path that started next to the winery, sloped down toward the rows of rambling vines.

"So when was the last time you were here?" she asked Maddie.

"Oh," Maddie sighed in remembrance. "Your father threw a graduation party for all the theater kids on the terrace of the winery. It was a very lovely evening."

"I can imagine. My parents were married on that terrace."

"That doesn't surprise me."

Elliot had been watching the proceedings since Willow met them outside the winery with a mixture of fascination, curiosity, and wonder. A part of him wanted to turn heel and run away, and the other wanted to go back to the moment she'd come upon him at the bench.

Why hadn't he apologized? Why didn't he tell her he'd read her letter, and he was more sorry than he could truly express?

Willow was walking more slowly now, talking about the grapes, and both his aunt and uncle were in raptures, but he'd been so lost in thought he hadn't heard a word she said. He came up short when he realized they'd stopped; his aunt rested a hand on her uncle's arm, and she fanned herself with the other.

"It's spectacular out here, Willow dear, but I hope you don't mind if we turn back and find some shade."

"Of course." Willow smiled as she turned. "In fact, if you come up to the house, I can offer you some of Mrs. Reynolds' famous lemonade before you go."

"Mrs. Reynolds is still here?" Aunt Maddie perked up a little. "I wouldn't mind popping by to say hello."

Elliot followed Willow quietly, while Aunt Maddie walked with Uncle Ed; it wasn't long before he and Willow outstripped them, and they were essentially alone.

Willow must have noticed too, because she said, "Something on your mind?"

Elliot watched as she trailed her fingers along the vines, some of their leaves and wisps of her hair teased by the breeze.

"Yeah, actually." He shoved his hands in his pockets. "I've been trying to figure out how to apologize to you. I was so incredibly wrong about everything that I don't know where to begin."

"I appreciate that," she said softly, "but you don't have to apologize."

His gaze snapped to her; she was gazing ahead, watching the path they walked. "Of course I do. Willow, I was an asshole. You didn't deserve any of the things I said."

"You didn't deserve any of the things I said either." She finally looked at him. "And I don't just mean that day. There's something…I don't know for sure if you heard, but the night we met…"

"I heard."

She nodded as though she'd expected this. "You should know, I'm sorry about what I said that night. I only said what I did because I wasn't ready for any new male interaction. I admit I thought you might've been able to hear me, but at that point in time I didn't care because I just wanted to be left alone. I didn't want to encourage you, or any man."

"Well, you certainly succeeded," he said flatly, then winced when he realized he sounded harsher than he'd intended.

She gave him a wry smile when she caught his self-reprimand. "Yes. A little too well."

"I'm sorry," he said.

"I'm sorry, too," she said again.

They were silent for a few moments as they neared the path leading up past the bench and to the house, and Elliot couldn't help but pick up on the wry mood.

"So we're both sorry. What now, then? An argument over which of us is more sorry?"

She let out a small laugh as her lips curved. "That sounds like us, doesn't it?"

She said it so companionably, he couldn't resist the urge to smile back. He kept glancing at her as they made their way to the house, wondering if she was different, or if he was just looking at her differently. Perhaps it was both; if her behavior today was any indication, he had affected her as much as she'd affected him.

"So just how good is this famous lemonade?" he asked her.

But she shook her head, smiling slyly. "You'll find out."

He couldn't be sure, but he thought maybe there was something else behind that smile—something promising. He certainly hoped so.

And damned if he didn't want to find out.

TWO

WILLOW WENT INSIDE for the lemonade, leaving Elliot, Maddie, and Ed on her family's garden terrace. Mrs. R was already pouring out lemonade into glasses filled with ice when she entered the kitchen.

"How do you do that?"

The long-time housekeeper and family friend gave her a knowing smile. "I saw you lead them up. Who's the handsome young man?"

"A friend." Willow got down a tray for the glasses. "From Medford. I think you know his aunt; she said she grew up here and went to school with Mom. She wanted to say hello to you."

"To me? How sweet."

Mrs. R tittered as she set the pitcher on the tray, but Willow could tell she was pleased. And perhaps she didn't believe Elliot was just a friend, but she let it drop. When she finished arranging the lemonade tray to her liking, she waved her hands at it.

"Now you take this on out, and I'll bring out some snacks," she ordered Willow.

"Yes, ma'am." Willow carefully picked up the tray and made her way back out to the terrace, where Elliot and his family sat under the shade of the table's umbrella. She didn't miss how Elliot's eyes immediately tracked to her, watched her; it was all she could do not to tilt the tray and spill the lemonade.

"Mrs. R will be right out," Willow said to Maddie as she set the tray on the table, handed out glasses. She sat and watched as they all took a sip of the refreshing drink; what made Mrs. R's the best was that she freshly squeezed the lemons, then dropped the rest of the rind into the pitcher, along with her special ingredient, a few sprigs of lavender from the garden.

All of them sighed in bliss.

"Holy crap, that's good," said Elliot.

"I'd forgotten the taste itself, but not how good it tasted." Maddie took another sip. "She'll join us, you said?"

"She said she was going to bring snacks, but I know that means she's raiding her supply of fancy tea sandwiches and cookies. You're in for a treat."

"Did I hear someone say cookies? Because that's the magic word."

The voice brought an instant smile to Willow's face. "The magic word to what?" she asked as she turned.

"My stomach." Her cousin Seth beamed at her as he walked toward the table, held out a hand to Elliot. "Hello, Elliot, good to see you again."

"You as well." Elliot's return grin was warm and genuine, and Willow felt a little pang wishing he could be that easy with her. She knew Seth and Elliot had hit it off during that fateful spring break at her aunt's; it was another reminder of how wrong she'd been to think Elliot might return her feelings, when she and Elliot had never had that camaraderie.

"And who are your friends?" Seth asked.

Before Willow or Elliot could answer, they heard more footsteps and voices, followed by her father and brother climbing the terrace steps. They made a picture, Willow thought, with the sun picking up a little red in Aspen's short reddish-brown hair, and hints of gray in her father's near-black locks.

"See if Seth wants to—Oh. Hello." Sam Davenport stopped when he saw the small crowd on his terrace, but smiled lightly. His daughter hardly ever brought guests who weren't Callum and his siblings over to the house. "What's all this, Will?"

Willow smiled quietly. "Dad, Aspen, Seth, this is Elliot Burke, my friend from Medford, and his aunt and uncle, Ed and Maddie Gallagher. Elliot, Maddie, Ed, this is my dad, Sam, my brother Aspen, and the one who thinks with his stomach is my cousin Seth."

"Hey!" But Seth was grinning as he shook Ed and Maddie's hands.

"Maddie?" Her father looked almost...hopeful, Willow realized as he approached the table. "Is it...is it really Madeline Gibson? Gallagher now, you said?"

"Hello Sam," Maddie said warmly as she shook his hand. "Yes. It's so good to see you."

"I can't believe it," Sam said a little wistfully. "Aren't you a blast from the past. Anne would..."

When he trailed off, Maddie patted the hand she still held understandingly. "I know."

When her father only nodded, Willow tried to think of something to break the silence, and she was about to turn to Seth for help.

Thankfully, Mrs. R chose that moment to come out to the terrace, carrying a tray loaded with small finger sandwiches, homemade sugar cookies, a selection of fruits, and extra glasses for the lemonade. Willow didn't doubt she'd heard the tail-end of the conversation when she beamed at Elliot's aunt.

"Why, Maddie Gibson, you come give this old woman a hug."

Maddie had risen as Mrs. R set the tray down, and didn't hesitate to wrap her arms around her, squeezing tight. "Hello, Alice. You haven't changed a bit."

"How do you know each other?" Seth asked as he pulled up chairs for everyone else; as Maddie sat back down, Sam explained their theater history.

"Mrs. Gibson is a dear friend of mine; I haven't seen her much since they moved away, but we've kept in touch over the years," Mrs. R added. "How is your mother, dear?"

"She's good," Maddie told her. "She and my dad have been traveling a lot since dad retired, but they're thinking of moving back to this area, actually."

"Oh!" Mrs. R clapped her hands together. "Well, I hope they do."

Mrs. R stayed for a few more minutes, delighted to meet Ed and Elliot and catch up with Maddie. Though Sam assured her she should stay, Mrs. R waved him off and insisted she wanted to return to her kitchen. She and Maddie exchanged a warm farewell, and she left them to their own devices—but not before sending Willow a subtle wink on her way back to the house.

Willow pretended not to notice. She was trying to think of a way to talk to Elliot without making it obvious to everyone at the table that she really wanted to talk to him.

"Are you the Elliot whose family owns a brewery?"

Willow blinked, surprised the question came from Aspen. Elliot, too, was clearly surprised, but took it in stride.

"If you're referring to Isle of Burke Brewing, then yes."

Aspen's blue eyes lit up. "That's so cool! Willow told me how much she liked your stout, and Seth mentioned he tried your red ale when you were in Portland." Then he stopped, as though he thought he'd said too much, explaining, "I'm making a list of beers I want to try when I turn twenty-one."

"And you want to try ours?"

Aspen nodded.

Elliot's face turned up with his slow, heart-melting grin. "Then I'll save you one of each. Though the ones my sister Joy makes are the best of the bunch, including the two you mentioned."

By this time her father had recovered, and, Willow noted, was increasingly curious about the young man who was already bringing both his quiet children out of their shells. "Just how good is this beer?" he asked.

"One of the best I've had in a while," Seth answered companionably, just before draining his lemonade. "Same with you, Will?"

Willow nodded. "You know how picky I am. But that coffee stout hit all the marks for me."

"Really?" Elliot asked. "You never said."

"Sure I did." She tilted her head. "When Cal and I came to open mic night, I said it was good."

He shot her a teasing grin. "Yeah but, you could've just been saying that."

She laughed, but shook her head. "I promise I wasn't. I love cinnamon, and the hint of cinnamon with the coffee flavor really cinched it for me. I had two pints."

He hadn't believed her, Elliot remembered. She had said it was good, but he'd thought maybe she was just being polite, and that the look of surprise on her face when she first sipped it was one of distaste. Yet another example of ways he'd misread her.

"I believe you." He held up his hands in surrender, playful smile still in place, but Willow thought she saw his smile slip for a moment, and tried to think of a way to ease his mind.

She let her smile come slowly before she took a sip of her lemonade. "You were too busy performing at open mic to notice what all your patrons were drinking."

"Oh, you got to see him play?" Ed chuckled, winking at his nephew. "Did he break out any Oasis?"

"He did." Willow grinned. "Champagne Supernova."

Aspen, who had perked up in his chair, turned to Elliot with a new enthusiasm. "What do you play?"

"Just a little guitar," Elliot shrugged. "I should practice more than I do, but it's not usually a priority so I'm not that good."

"I disagree," Willow asserted. "I enjoyed your performance. And you sing very well. The duet you and Joy sang together was particularly good."

"You got Joy to sing with you?" Maddie blinked. "Now there's a surprise."

"Actually, Cal did." Elliot deliberately looked at his aunt instead of

Willow. "When he found out we sometimes sang together, he asked her to join me."

Willow remembered. Joy had come to their table to replace their empties, and Mrs. Burke had come over to see if they were enjoying themselves; when Cal said he was enjoying hearing Elliot play, Mrs. Burke had taken the opportunity to rave about how Joy had such a lovely singing voice, and how wonderful it would be if she and Elliot would do one of their duets. Cal had practically begged Joy to sing, and though she was obviously embarrassed by her mother's praises, she'd agreed.

"Cal likes hearing other people play music because he can't play worth jack," Seth grinned. "And he's tone deaf."

Eager to change the subject, Elliot turned to Aspen, who'd gone quiet again. "But you're not—I've heard you're a musical prodigy. What do you play?"

"Piano. And I'm starting to learn the violin." Aspen smiled quietly. "But I'm no prodigy."

"I disagree with that, too," Willow said. "You're talented, passionate, and you work hard—all things that make you a great musician."

Aspen looked at his sister with a cheeky grin. "I can't sing, though. Not like you."

"You sing?" Elliot raised his brows, pointed a finger at Willow. "You've been holding out on me, Davenport. Next open mic, you're up."

"I'd pay to see that," Seth smirked.

Willow looked down at her lemonade. "I don't…I don't sing in front of people."

Elliot only shrugged. "Neither does Joy."

"We should all play a song together," Aspen suggested. "Dad, we should invite Elliot and the Gallaghers over for dinner tonight."

Sam smiled warmly. "Excellent idea."

"I second the motion." Seth picked up Willow's glass of lemonade, raised it as if in a toast.

"I think that's technically third," Willow corrected him, grabbing her glass back before he could steal a sip.

"We'd love to," Maddie said apologetically, "but we have plans to have dinner with some old friends of mine tonight."

"Well, how about tomorrow, then?" Sam asked.

"We were planning on having a barbecue with Callum and his family, since we were supposed to come back tomorrow instead of today," Willow clarified, mostly for Elliot's benefit.

Though he quirked a brow, he nodded at his aunt and uncle. After sharing a silent exchange with her husband, Maddie nodded to the table. "Tomorrow would be lovely."

IF POSSIBLE, Elliot was even more nervous than the day before. Probably because this time he knew Willow *would* be there; and, damnit, now that there was peace between them, he had to admit he wanted to impress her.

He supposed he'd wanted to impress her all along; ironically, though he thought he'd failed, he'd actually succeeded without even trying.

Yesterday had gone well, despite the unexpected circumstance, and he and Willow had been civil to each other—more than civil.

He could only hope the others didn't pick up on the confusing emotions swirling around them. They both had their reserves down now, and he doubted either of them was sure what it meant.

If he were honest with himself, the whole thing made him nervous. He liked this warm, more open version of Willow—the version that could very well be the girl of his dreams. But dare he even think it?

Their history with reading each other wasn't exactly stellar, so he couldn't be sure how she felt about him now, or if she even knew herself.

He took time to shave and dressed more carefully than was his wont, in khaki shorts, a t-shirt, and a button down. He didn't usually go out of his way to put thought into what he wore, but sometimes the extra effort was worth it.

His aunt gave him a knowing look when he met her and Uncle Ed in the hall, though he did his best to seem nonchalant on the way to the car. But he couldn't relax, and he only became more agitated as they pulled up to the house.

Who was he kidding?, he thought as Uncle Ed knocked on the door. He was the same Elliot he'd always been, and Willow either accepted that or she didn't. So far it seemed she did, but if she didn't, he doubted there would be much he could do to change that.

Plus, could he really trust the Willow of yesterday wasn't an apparition?

Even as he thought it, the door opened, and she stood on the other side in high-waisted jean shorts and a short-sleeve blouse, her smile welcoming as she ushered them in. And if he wasn't mistaken, she brightened when he smiled back at her—though it was barely perceptible; he didn't think he would have noticed if he hadn't been looking at her.

By the time he finally managed to look away from her, she'd led them to the family room overlooking the patio they'd sat on yesterday, where everyone else was already gathered watching the ball game.

Elliot was relieved the room didn't feel stuffy. In fact, it was just a room like in anyone's home, as evidenced by the family photos arranged on the mantle and tabletops. The furniture looked luxurious but comfy, and though the grand piano in the corner near the fireplace certainly made a statement, it wasn't at all out of place—and the many disordered sheets of Aspen's music on the music stand added to the homey quality.

He relaxed as he shook hands with Sam, Seth, and Aspen, but tensed up again when he faced the other guests, the Barringtons.

Callum Barrington looked as easy-going and friendly as ever, though slightly less cheerful than Elliot remembered. *Good*, he thought as he recalled the sound of Joy crying herself to sleep at night in the weeks following Cal's departure.

"Elliot, it's great to see you!" Cal said, shaking his hand enthusiastically.

"Cal." Elliot only nodded, gripped Cal's hand a little harder than was necessary.

Cal had the decency to look sheepish as he asked, "How's your family?"

Elliot did his best to lighten his tone, but deliberately didn't mention Joy. "They're good. The brewery is doing well."

"Good! That's good."

For once, Cal didn't seem to know what else to say. *Good*, Elliot thought again. The guy could use a little awkward in his life.

"Hello, Elliot," the next voice purred.

Elliot resisted the urge to cringe. For some reason, Cal's twin, Clara Barrington had latched onto him, especially whenever he was in the same room with Willow, but he got the distinct impression she didn't actually like him. It was disconcerting, and since it was Clara's text to Joy that had suggested there was something more than friendship between Cal and Willow, he could only assume it had something to do with her wanting Willow to date her brother.

Why she thought pretending to hit on him would make Willow want to date Cal was beyond him.

Since she hadn't held out her hand to shake, he didn't bother offering his. "Clara," he said stiffly, then turned and gave a quick greeting to Lisa Barrington and her fiancé, Gerald Hastings, and Willow did a round of introductions between Elliot and his aunt and uncle, and Mr. and Mrs. Barrington, who seemed as friendly as their son.

"Well!" said Seth, rubbing his hands together. "What do we want to do first?"

Gerald held up his glass of wine and gestured to the television. "I'll be watching the game, but let me know if anyone wants to play cards."

"I thought Aspen and I could give Elliot and the Gallaghers a little tour, if they were interested," Willow said.

"Oh, yeah!" Aspen piped up. "You've got to see the music room."

Elliot smiled. "Music room, eh?"

"You go ahead, Elliot," Aunt Maddie told him. "I'm sure I'd love to see the house, but right now I'd rather catch up with an old friend."

Understanding, Elliot only nodded as Sam ushered his aunt and uncle to a loveseat.

"There's also a library," Willow mentioned as he followed her and Aspen from the room.

"Like, an *actual* library, not just a room with a bookcase?"

Both Willow and Aspen only smiled, exchanging the kind of conspiratorial glance that only siblings can share.

"Why don't you check that out first?" Aspen suggested. "I'll meet you in the music room."

At Elliot's confused frown, Aspen winked—a gesture Elliot found somewhat surprising for someone as shy as Aspen. As Aspen sauntered down the hall without them, Elliot turned a suspicious eye on Willow.

"Why do I get the feeling you're up to something?"

Willow shrugged and walked over to a set of thick wooden doors. "I enlisted his help since we didn't get much time to talk yesterday."

She pulled open the doors, gesturing Elliot through, and he walked into the most amazing room he'd ever seen.

It was the tower, he realized.

It felt almost ancient—round stone walls with arched windows stretched up three floors, a spiraling metal staircase on one side leading up to the other levels, which opened up to become a metal railing around the center of those floors. There was at least one cozy reading chair beside each window.

And each floor was lined with dark wood bookcases crammed with books.

"Holy shit," Elliot breathed.

Willow beamed. "I thought you'd like it."

He circled the room before nearing the staircase. "May I?"

"Go ahead."

He climbed the stairs and circled the next level, peeking out the window, which showed some of the property's trees and part of the vineyard, then did the same for the third level, where the ceiling formed a cone with dark wood beams.

"I bet you come up here a lot," he said when he heard Willow come up the stairs behind him.

"It's one of my favorite places." She smiled as she moved to sit in one of the chairs, drawing up her knees.

"Do you actually live here, or do you just come here a lot?" He took a seat in the other chair.

"I still live here, yes. I do have my own apartment in San Francisco where I stay when I'm there, and so does Seth, but Pemberley is home," she explained. "We both prefer it here, and the house is so big we don't all crowd each other."

"I can see why. So…you wanted to talk to me?"

"Yes. I wanted to make sure we're good."

"I'd say we are." He watched her carefully. "You apologized, and so did I. I admit I wasn't really sure where we stood, but it seems we've started over."

She nodded, but remained silent, staring out the window.

"Hey, Willow?"

She shifted her gaze to his.

"I'm sorry about what happened with Gabe. I'm especially sorry I let him play on my insecurities when it came to you."

"He's good at that," she said quietly. "Don't feel too bad. He's fooled us all at some point."

Now it was his turn to nod in silence. After a moment, she stood, deliberately putting on a smile. "Alright, enough melancholy. Shall we join Aspen in the music room?"

He followed her lead back down the stairs, to the hall, and to another room with double wooden doors. Elliot could faintly hear the sounds of a violin playing scales on the other side, and when Willow opened the doors, Aspen stood with his violin, eyes shut in concentration.

Without opening his eyes, he said, "That was quick."

"We didn't have much to discuss," Willow said.

"Hm," was all Aspen said as he finished his scale. After the last note, he set the violin and bow on a stand and gestured around the room.

"So, Elliot, what do you think?"

The music room had Elliot as much in awe as the library. There was another piano, though not a grand, and a keyboard, a small drum set, a few amps, and on the wall hung a bass guitar, a couple of electric guitars —he knew enough to recognize a Gibson SG and a Fender Player Telecaster—and an acoustic guitar.

"Is that a Taylor?" He pointed to the acoustic.

Aspen smiled. "It is. Wanna try it out?"

"No, that's not necessary."

Aspen shuffled his feet a little, cleared his throat. "I was hoping…we could all play a song together. The three of us."

Elliot recalled how excited Aspen had been at the idea the day before and glanced at Willow, who'd raised both her brows in surprise.

"What song did you have in mind?" he asked.

Willow's eyes widened as she looked at him.

"I told you, Davenport," Elliot grinned at her. "You're up. If Aspen and I play, you sing."

"I like that idea," said a voice from the doorway, and they all turned to see Mrs. Reynolds leaning against the door jam. "It's been too long since you've sang for company, Willow."

"Oh, I meant in here..." Aspen started to interject, but Mrs. Reynolds cut him off.

"You too, Aspen. Both of you stop hiding away in here and go entertain your guests."

"Yes, ma'am," brother and sister intoned quietly.

Mrs. Reynolds nodded in satisfaction, and to his surprise, she too sent Elliot a wink before she turned and left. Did everyone here suspect there was something between him and Willow?

"Well," Elliot said after a moment. "You heard the lady."

He carefully grabbed the acoustic from the wall and turned to the now wide-eyed siblings. "Any song suggestions?"

Willow looked at her brother beseechingly. "What have you been working on?"

"Oh!" Suddenly Aspen's eyes lit up. "Ever since we watched *Once* last week, the music has been stuck in my head. I've continually been playing 'Falling Slowly.'"

He went to the piano and pulled off a few sheets of music, smiling quietly as he scanned them—a smile similar to his sister's. The smile dimmed when he looked back at Elliot. "Oh. You might not even know the song."

"Are you kidding?" Elliot grinned. "I love that song."

At Willow's curious expression, Elliot shrugged. "Macy, my middle sister, loves musicals. A couple years ago she asked me if I'd learn it with her for an open mic night. She plays the piano, too," he explained to Aspen.

"Well, perfect!" Aspen turned to Willow. "Sounds like serendipity to me."

Resigned, Willow finally smiled. "Alright. Let's do this thing."

"Do you want to practice it?" Elliot offered.

"No, I'd rather get it over with," she said. "Aspen?"

"Same."

Elliot gestured toward the door. "Then lead the way."

THREE

WILLOW WAS silent as they walked back to the living room, and Elliot noticed she kept playing with one of the rings on her fingers, a sure sign of her nerves. Aspen didn't seem to fare much better, as his fingers lightly tapped the music he held.

The light sounds of conversation and laughter reached them just before they entered the room. Elliot noticed the older adults were all chatting happily, while Seth was left to fend for himself with Hastings, Lisa, Cal, and Clara, who was sidled up to him. Though Seth's expression was polite enough, Elliot knew from his own experience Seth was likely just trying not to grimace.

Sure enough, when they entered the room and Clara noticed Elliot, she completely ignored Seth, who looked relieved.

"Are you going to play for us, Elliot?" she asked saucily.

Elliot addressed the rest of the room. "How about a little concert? Willow and Aspen agreed to accompany me."

Though Sam seemed surprised, everyone else was enthusiastic and turned to face the piano. Elliot slung the guitar strap over his shoulder and waited for Aspen to take his place at the keys. Willow stood next to him and clasped her hands in front of her as though she were going to give a speech. Aspen, too, looked a little rigid.

"Relax guys," he whispered. "We're not doing this to be perfect, we're doing it to have fun."

When both siblings raised an eyebrow, he shrugged. "No one here is going to judge you—except maybe Clara, and she'll mostly be judging me."

Willow let out a quiet snort while Aspen was clearly trying to hold back a smile, and with that he lifted his fingers to the keys and began to play the tinkling melody to "Falling Slowly." After the opening, Elliot joined in with the guitar and began to sing the verse.

He noticed that Willow took a steadying breath, but he was pleasantly surprised when she added the gentle harmony to accompany his vocals, and her voice grew stronger, more confident as they went into the chorus.

Throughout the song, Elliot did his best to look around the room, and he often glanced at Aspen to make sure they were on the same page instrumentally, but he caught himself looking over at Willow just as often. She seemed to grow more confident as the song went on, and her soft soprano meshed well with the melody; Elliot had always thought he was a relatively decent singer, but with Willow as his duet partner, he thought he sounded even better.

The more they sang, the more he felt like the song was about them, somehow. And he could've sworn Willow felt it, too—they seemed to have kept their boat from sinking, and they still had time to get it back to shore.

As the song came to a close, his gaze shifted to Willow again, and her eyes met his as they sang the last several notes. It wasn't until the others in the room began to clap that he fully realized the song was over.

Seth let out an obnoxious whistle and a short 'Woo!,' while Aunt Maddie had a huge grin on her face, and Sam looked almost in awe; everyone else clapped with genuine enjoyment, except Clara, who only clapped politely, a plastic smile on her face.

"Thank you," Elliot said, giving an exaggerated bow. "That concludes today's performance by The Last Minute Band."

"You guys rock!" Cal enthused.

"Agreed," concurred Uncle Ed.

Willow and Aspen both murmured their quiet thanks while Elliot headed back toward the hall. "I'm just going to put this back," he said.

"I'll come with you." Aspen swiped up his sheet music and hurried after him. Elliot could sense the younger man's disquiet as they approached the music room, entered.

"Did you want to talk to me about something?" Elliot asked him as he crossed the room to the guitar wall to hang up the Taylor.

"How did you know?"

Elliot gestured to the music Aspen was putting away. "You could've just left the music at the piano and put it away later."

"Oh. Right." Aspen looked sheepish, then shrugged. "Well, anyway, I just wanted to thank you."

"Thank me?"

"Yeah. My sister doesn't make friends easily, and she can come off kind of prickly sometimes. She mentioned the two of you got off on the wrong foot, so…thank you for giving her another chance."

"Oh." Elliot didn't really know what to say to that. "You're welcome. Though I should point out, she's giving me another chance, too. In fact, I wasn't very nice to her; if she told you about that I doubt you'd be thanking me."

Aspen tilted his head as a smile formed. "She didn't give me specifics, she just said you'd had an argument rooted in misunderstandings on both sides. But now you're working it out."

"Yeah. I guess we are."

When they returned to the others, everyone was spread out, either sitting or standing with a glass of wine, watching the baseball game and conversing. Clara wore a look of triumph, as Willow stood off to one side with Cal, while she sat on the sofa next to Seth, who looked long-suffering.

"Oh, Elliot!" Cal waved Elliot over, motioning for him to come stand in the space on his other side. Admittedly, Elliot was relieved; as much as he liked Seth, he did not want to occupy the sofa with Clara. Instead, Aspen sat there, while Elliot joined Willow and Cal, and Clara glared at her brother.

"What's up?" Elliot asked Cal, though he had a feeling he knew. His suspicion was confirmed when Willow gave him a reassuring smile, and went to stand near the others.

"Uh, well…" Cal shuffled his feet. "I was wondering if you could tell me…how is Joy?"

Elliot shut down Cal's hopeful look with a bland stare. "You're seriously asking me that question?"

"Yes." Cal looked down. "I know I hurt her, and I have no right to ask. I just…I need to know."

"Cal. If you want to know how Joy is, you'll have to get the answer from her yourself—if she's willing to talk to you, that is."

Cal nodded solemnly. "Yeah. Yeah, okay. Thanks."

They made their way back over to the others, and Willow handed Elliot a glass of white wine. "Thank you," she said quietly.

There were a lot of thank-yous going around today, Elliot thought.

"For what?"

"For telling it to him straight."

He raised a brow. "You don't even know what I said to him."

She shook her head. "I don't have to."

The next half hour passed pleasantly, and to Elliot's delight, his aunt, at the urging of the others, decided it was her turn to entertain.

"Do you mind if I use your beautiful piano, Aspen?"

"Not at all," Aspen assured her.

Comfortable and confident, Aunt Maddie began to play a piece from memory. It was one Elliot had heard her play before, but he never tired of hearing it. His delight, however, was interrupted by the other Barrington twin.

Clara sidled over to him and gave him a simpering smile.

"Enjoying yourself, Elliot?"

"Yes, I am." He did his best to inch away from her without being obvious about it, and kept his eyes on the performance. "The company is good, and I always love when my aunt plays this song."

"Hm." He could feel her looking him up and down. "Would you like to dance, Elliot?"

He blinked, turned to look at her. "Uh…thanks for the offer, but I don't think this situation calls for dancing."

She put on her best pout. "I bet you'd dance with Willow."

You're right about that, he thought. Instead he said, "Willow hates dancing."

"Cal can get her to dance."

"Good for him." Elliot took a sip of his wine.

"They're so good together, Cal and Willow," Clara sniffed. "It would be a shame if someone were to try to come between them. They would inevitably fail, of course."

Elliot suppressed a smirk and pretended not to catch her meaning. "From what I can tell, they're very loyal friends. I highly doubt either of them would let someone come between that."

Before she could respond, he excused himself to go stand with Aspen and Seth.

"What do you think of my aunt's piano skills?" he asked Aspen.

"She's great!" Aspen responded enthusiastically. "Do you think she would mind doing a duet with me?"

"I think she would like that very much."

Aspen beamed and went to approach Maddie as her song ended; his aunt beamed back and scooted over to make room on the bench, and Elliot watched in satisfaction as the two animatedly discussed what song to play.

"I think your family has made his day," Seth commented.

"My aunt has that effect on people."

"Not just your aunt, and not just Aspen. My uncle is more cheerful than I've seen him in a while, and you managed to get both my cousins to perform for everyone. Neither of them has been very open since…"

When Seth trailed off, Elliot glanced at him and saw he appeared to be lost in thought, watching Aspen and Aunt Maddie as they began to play, aware he may have said too much.

"I know," Elliot reassured him.

Seth blinked. "You know?"

Elliot nodded. "Willow told me. A few months ago."

"Huh." Seth gave him a curious look. "Okay then. Speaking of, I think I'll do you and my cousin a favor, and head Clara off."

Confused, Elliot turned in the direction Seth was looking to see Willow walking toward them, followed by Clara. With a friendly slap to Elliot's back, Seth waltzed off and deliberately took Clara's arm, drawing her back toward Cal and Lisa; he had no desire for her company, Elliot knew, but he was very convincing.

Elliot raised his brows at Willow as she approached.

"Looks like Seth took one for the team."

"Yeah, he does that sometimes," she said affectionately. "He knows how to flatter her, which is a sure way to distract her."

"I don't think she'd like it if I flattered her."

Willow chuckled. "That's actually why I came over here. I wanted to say I'm sorry about Clara haranguing you."

His brows rose again. "You're not responsible for her. Besides, sometimes it's entertaining—she alternately insults me to my face or pretends she's into me, and I never know which one it's going to be. I could turn it into a game."

That got a smirk. "What kind of game?"

"I'm thinking a drinking game."

He could hear the laughter in her voice when she said, "What?"

"A shot of one thing for every insult, and a shot of something else for every flirtation," he explained.

Willow covered her mouth with her hand to hide how much she was shaking with laughter.

"You forgot one," she said companionably. "A shot for every time you take a dig back at her and it goes over her head."

Now a bark of laughter escaped him, and he shook his head. "We're terrible. I know I shouldn't make fun of her, but her actions really make no sense to me. I can tell she doesn't like me, yet she seeks me out. She just asked me to dance a few minutes ago, then started talking about how great you and Cal are together when I refused."

"So that's what that was about." Willow nodded to herself. "She's made it her mission in life to get me and Cal together, despite the fact we've both stated we have no interest in dating each other, more than once. I think she insults you because she perceives you as a threat to that, so she tries to point out your flaws to me, while simultaneously trying to make it appear to Cal that you're not a threat by hitting on you."

"That sounds...convoluted."

"It is," she agreed. "And Cal isn't any more fooled by it than me or you."

"And what about Seth? She hits on him, too," he pointed out.

"Yeah, I think it's just because he's wealthy. She would probably flirt with Aspen if he wasn't so much younger than us."

"Ah. Well then I'll be thankful for that, since it seems like he's enjoying himself much more without being subjected to her attention."

"Yes, he is," she said, glancing over at the piano. Aspen and his aunt were in the midst of playing, and though Uncle Ed had joined Sam at the grill to put burgers on, they'd left the patio doors open and were listening in delight. The others chatted among themselves—in particular, Seth was doing a brilliant job keeping Cal and Clara company; Clara was even turned away from he and Willow.

When Elliot looked down at Willow, he saw she was watching the scene unfold with a smile of contentment on her face, her expression almost dreamy, and he found he couldn't take his eyes off her. And all at once, all the things he hadn't let himself feel for her before blew threw him and left him stunned.

He loved her.

Oh, God. He *loved* her.

He couldn't even begin to process what that meant, especially not when she turned her face up to smile at him; he hoped to God his heart wasn't in his eyes.

She flicked a glance back at the group, and seeing they were distracted, turned back to him, setting down her wine and sliding her hand into his.

"Come with me," she said, her smile turning mischievous. He set down his own glass and she tugged him by the hand out the patio door and down the steps to the path that led toward the vineyard.

"You're not going to tell me where you're taking me, are you?"

She shook her head. "It's not that far."

As the trees cleared, he recognized the area. She slowed so they were walking side-by-side, finally coming to stop at the bench she'd found him at the day before.

"This is my favorite spot to look out at the vineyard," she told him as she dropped his hand and sat. He cautiously took a seat next to her. "And often my favorite spot to think."

He offered a small smile. "That's just what I was doing when you found me here. Thinking."

"May I ask what you were thinking about?"

He was silent for a moment, swallowing his guilt and bracing himself to face her. But he owed her this much, if not more. Turning his gaze to her hopeful face, he met her guarded eyes with his remorseful ones.

"You."

She straightened. "Me?"

"I was re-reading your email for about the millionth time," he confessed. "It seemed appropriate to sit here and absorb all over again just how wrong I was about you. About a lot of things." He gently laid a hand over hers, continued.

"I've been berating myself for months, and I don't know how you can be so welcoming to me after the horrible things I said to you."

She shook her head. "You put too much blame on yourself. I should have behaved better. I'm sorry I was such a jerk."

"I could just as easily say 'ditto.'" He smiled a little. "Neither of us have been our best, especially around each other."

"No we haven't," she sighed, looking down and turning her hand under his and interlacing their fingers. The gesture both comforted him and made him anxious. How was it possible she even wanted to be around him?

But she did. She was here, holding his hand, talking to him. Real and beautiful in ways he hadn't let himself acknowledge before.

He squeezed her hand. "Maybe we shouldn't think about the past too much right now, especially if it makes us unhappy."

"I'm not very good at that, but I'll certainly try," she said solemnly.

"Like anything, it takes practice, and isn't always easy. I've been dwelling on the past too much recently."

"Me too." She bit her lip. "I tend to dwell on things that hurt me, on my mistakes and failures. I have a hard time letting things go. I know none of that is helpful, and it gives me anxiety, but I can't seem to help it."

He thought of something similar she'd said once, back in Medford, and knew it was something else about her he'd misunderstood. He'd once thought she hardly felt anything, but now he knew better—she felt more deeply than most people he knew.

"Hey," he nudged her shoulder. "I'll help you."

"Will you?"

"As much as I can. But you have to let me." He paused to meet her eyes. "No more misunderstandings."

Her answering smile was one of both amusement and comprehension. "No more misunderstandings," she agreed.

Then she bit her lip again, seeming to mull something over. "Speaking of," she said quietly. "You said you'd been re-reading my email. Meaning you didn't delete it?"

"I couldn't delete it." He unconsciously stroked his thumb over the back of her hand. "It may sound clichéd, but it's all I had left of you. Besides," he said, a smirk forming on his lips, "You said to delete it when I was *done* reading it, and I'm not done. I can't tell you how many times I've re-read it over the past couple months."

Though she gave him a mock frown, her eyes softened, and after a moment the corners of her lips turned up. "Smart ass."

"Guilty."

"I suppose I understand why you kept it if it means that much to you." She tilted her head, studying him, almost in question.

Feeling her astute gaze, not ready to tell her that which was so new to him, he cleared his throat. "So, why'd you bring me out here?"

"I told you, it's my favorite spot to think. And you looked like you needed to think."

So she had noticed—but how well could she read him? Maybe he had just looked like he needed air. She looked out over the vineyard she loved, breathing a peaceful sigh in contrast to the way his heart seemed lodged in his throat.

"I can't tell you how often I've imagined us sitting here like this."

He hesitated. "Before we argued?"

"Before," she acknowledged. "And after."

"After?" In his chest, his heart squeezed with hope. "Are you saying you still…"

He trailed off—it seemed an impossible thing to ask.

Do you still love me?

When she turned her eyes on his, her expression was serious, but her eyes were soft. She spoke quietly, but he could hear the determination behind her words. "I still have feelings for you. If anything, I feel even more than I did."

He inhaled audibly, a combination of the emotion that swamped him and the need to slow his racing heart. He gripped her hand again and added a teasing note to his tone.

"So you imagined us here, like this?"

"Well…" To his delight, she blushed and bit her lip, looking down. "Not just like this."

"Oh, yeah?"

A slight smile played on her lips. "I always imagined kissing you in this spot. And when I saw you sitting here yesterday morning…" He waited when she paused; she gathered her courage, and looked back at him. "When you stood, for a moment I hoped you'd walk over and kiss me right then and there."

Her breath caught when he lifted his free hand to her cheek. Gently, he freed his other hand and brought it up to cup her face, and slowly tilted his head down until his lips met hers.

She wasn't fragile, he knew; she was actually incredibly strong. But his instinct was to keep the kiss slow and sensuous, and knew it was right when she sighed into him, her hands moving up his chest to settle on his shoulders.

He moved his tongue over hers, tilting her chin and angling his head to deepen the kiss. The hands on his shoulders gripped and tugged him a little closer, and his fingers dug into her hair.

He softened the kiss again, nibbling her bottom lip and massaging the back of her neck where her hair tangled around his fingers.

"Like that?" he asked, his voice husky.

She shook her head as her eyes fluttered open, a dreamy look on her face. "That was much better than anything I imagined."

"I certainly hope so."

She laughed, a musical sound he'd had the privilege of hearing more often in his few days in Napa than in the entire couple months she'd spent in Medford.

"Maybe you should do it again, just in case," she teased.

"Hm, good idea," he said before recapturing her lips.

A little more insistent now, he felt as though he was fused to her, their lips mating in complete accord with each other. He wrapped his arms around her and hugged her to him, stopping short of pulling her into his lap.

At the sound of a satisfied purr in her throat he thought, *the hell with it*, and was about pull her onto his lap anyway when the sound of someone very deliberately clearing their throat reached his ears.

They both whipped their heads around to see Aspen standing on the path, grinning at them.

"Thank God you came out here to release all that sexual tension," he said. "You might have set the house on fire otherwise."

Though she blushed, Willow's lips quirked in an attempt to suppress a smile.

"Are you here to tell us dinner is ready?"

"I am—and you should thank me for volunteering to find you before Seth could."

Willow gave in and let a wry smirk take over her face. "Then I do thank you, because he'd never let me live it down."

Still grinning, Aspen nodded, and turned back toward the house. Willow let out a sigh.

"I guess that's our cue to rejoin the others."

"I mean, we could stay here the rest of the day," Elliot teased.

"We could?" Willow asked doubtfully, but played along. "What happens when someone else comes looking for us?"

"We'll climb a tree where no one will think to look for us."

She shook her head in mock disappointment. "Unfortunately, my family would absolutely think to look for me up a tree. And what happens if it rains?"

"Then I will punch every raindrop in its dumb face."

Willow burst out laughing, clamping a hand over her mouth in surprise even as she continued to giggle. He imagined the grin on his face as he watched her was ridiculously wide.

When her laughter subsided, she cleared her throat. "And when it gets dark?"

"Sounds perfect for stargazing."

"Oh, it definitely is," she smiled. "Unfortunately, I am a mere mortal, so I have to eat at some point."

"Ah." Elliot feigned disappointment. "I knew there was a flaw in this plan."

Her smile pure joy, she cupped his cheek and gave him one more long, smacking kiss, then stood and pulled him to his feet. "Let's go before my stomach embarrasses me by growling at an absurdly loud volume."

They may have been able to sneak off without being noticed, but as they were the last ones to the table, no one missed they arrived together. Though Willow wasn't holding his hand anymore, Elliot doubted anyone who was paying attention wouldn't notice something had shifted between them.

He sat next to Aspen, and Willow took the remaining seat next to him so he was sandwiched between the siblings. They ended up shuffling the chairs a bit when Mrs. Reynolds brought out a plethora of side dishes— chips and dip, potato salad, fruit and cookies—and this time when asked she agreed to join them all. She sat next to Aunt Maddie, who was particularly delighted to chat with her friend.

The dinner passed in a blur of conversation and laughter, and Elliot found himself a little in awe of the situation. He'd never expected to be here—to even visit Pemberley, much less enjoy a companionable dinner hosted by Willow and her family.

To be with Willow this way.

They'd have to talk, eventually, about where to go from here. But they still had time, and the boat was no longer sinking.

At some point someone suggested they all get together for brunch the next day at one of the local brunch spots, and the party unanimously agreed. Though Elliot had hoped to spend time with Willow on her own, he figured they'd find a way soon enough.

Besides, who didn't like brunch?

FOUR

IN THE MORNING, Elliot woke up rested; he hadn't slept so well in months. He couldn't stop the grin as he thought of the events of the previous day; resolving things with Willow had certainly removed a lot of stress, but he could admit now that an emotional burden had been lifted as well.

And he loved her.

His grin faltered slightly at the thought—not that he didn't like the idea of loving her, it was just…well, scary.

A little terrifying, actually.

How could he tell her? She'd said as much the night before that she still loved him, though she hadn't actually said 'I love you.' It wouldn't surprise him if she was just as scared as he was. She had more reason to be afraid, considering what happened the last time she'd told him she loved him.

You're snobby, conceited, and unfeeling. You're the last person in the world I'd want to be with.

He winced at how harsh he'd been. He didn't deserve to be with her, he was sure of that, but there was no way in hell he'd toss a second chance back in the face of whatever universal power had thrown them together.

If God was giving them another shot, he'd take it and be grateful.

With that in mind he got up and hit the shower. They weren't meeting the others for brunch for a couple hours, but he was too antsy; he needed to *do* something.

When he got out of the shower, he studied the contents of his suitcase; he was in the middle of wondering if he should've asked if it was a fancy brunch or a casual brunch when there was a knock at the door.

"Coming," he called out, assuming it was his uncle. He wrapped the towel he'd tossed on a chair around his waist and went to the door; when he opened it to find Willow, fresh and pretty in a flowy blue sundress that deepened the blue of her eyes, dark hair framing her face and cascading over her shoulders, he froze.

Those luminous eyes widened in surprise when she saw him, and suddenly he remembered the state of undress in which he answered the door.

"Sorry," he said, glancing down, just in case. "I figured it was Uncle Ed."

She blinked before raising her eyes to his, her cheeks flushed.

"Do you need me to wait?"

"No." He opened the door a little wider, stepped aside. "Come on in."

She smiled now, a familiar smile he'd come to categorize as *quiet amusement*. "Alright."

"So what brings you by so early?"

"Well…" she tossed her bag on the chair where he'd tossed his towel earlier. "As much as I'm looking forward to brunch with everyone, I just really wanted some time alone with you."

He swallowed. "Oh?"

"I hope you don't mind that I just showed up here."

"N-no, not at all," he assured her. "I, uh…"

He looked down again at the towel around his waist.

"I'm just gonna…"

He snatched up a clean pair of boxer briefs and pair of jeans from his suitcase and headed to the bathroom.

"Take your time," she said, her amused smile still in place.

When he emerged, she was sitting cross-legged on the bed, waiting expectantly.

"Sorry about that."

She shrugged. "Nothing to apologize for. In fact, I rather appreciate the view."

When she stared unapologetically at his bare chest, he felt it was his turn to blush.

"Is that so?"

"It is. No need to put on a shirt if you don't want to."

God, she left him speechless. He felt like he was having an out of body experience, watching a beautiful woman flirt with him while is mindless body opened and closed its mouth like a fish.

"I'm sorry," Willow said, biting back a grin. "I seem to have discomposed you."

"Yes. I'm...not used to this openly flirtatious version of you," he admitted.

"Neither am I." The grin slowly appeared, and she shrugged. "You just make me feel flirty. Is that okay?"

Now he grinned back at her. "It's definitely okay. More than okay."

"Good," she said, rising. "Then you won't mind if I..."

She stepped to him, rested a hand on his chest over his heart, paused as she felt his heart beat. Then moved her hand down, up again. Just feeling. She lifted her other hand and ran both hands over his shoulders.

His skin was warm everywhere she touched. He didn't dare move for fear of breaking whatever spell had her so enchanted by him. He didn't realize he'd closed his eyes until she stopped, her hands cupping the back of his neck.

When he opened them, she was staring up at him quietly, but appreciatively—was that longing on her face? If so, he was sure his own expression mirrored hers.

Slowly, she pulled his head down to her, pressed her lips to his, whisper soft. Then she stood on her tip-toes, simultaneously deepening the kiss and pressing herself against him. Though the movement stirred him, he kept his hands lightly on her hips.

When she broke the kiss, she spoke against his mouth.

"I want you to touch me."

His hands clamped at her waist, loosened again. "I want to touch you."

But she sensed his hesitation, lowered, and he could see the vulnerability in her eyes. "Then why don't you?"

"Because if I touch you, here, like this," he gestured to his half-undressed body, the hotel room, the bed, "I won't want to stop there."

Her eyes heated as they met his. "What if I don't want you to stop there?"

"Willow."

"What?"

"I don't want to push you." Elliot couldn't help but think of the way she'd described how Gabe had tried to pressure her to sleep with him. "I want to be sure you're ready for this, with me."

Now her eyes softened, and her quietly amused smile made another appearance. "You force me to point out I'm the one who showed up here, and I initiated this."

When he said nothing, she sat on the edge of the bed again, but kept her eyes on his.

"Elliot, why do think I came here like this if I wasn't ready? You're *nothing* like Gabe," she said, as though she'd read his mind. "I trust you, and I want to be intimate with you."

He blew out a breath. "You make it really hard to say no."

"Do you want to say no?"

"No. I really want to say yes."

"Then come here," she said, crooking a finger and grinning.

He slowly grinned back, pulled to her like a magnet, not realizing his feet had moved him forward until she was once again running her hands up his chest. Using his shoulders to pull herself up, adjusting herself so she was on her knees on the edge of the bed, she was now slightly taller than him, looking down at him with the quiet intensity he'd come to expect from her.

Softly, he twined an arm around her waist and lifted the other to brush her hair from her shoulder.

"There's one more thing I need to clarify, so I know how to go about this," he murmured.

Curious, she tilted her head. "What's that?"

"In your letter, you made it seem like…" He swallowed, hoping he wasn't about to put her on edge. "Have you…had sex before? Or not?"

"Oh!" She leaned away from him a little to look at him more fully. "Yes, I have. Before Gabe, actually. A college fling. It just wasn't that pleasant an experience so I wasn't that eager to repeat it, and by that point that kind of intimacy had come to mean something more to me. I'm sorry I didn't make that clearer."

He sighed, relieved. "That's good. Takes some pressure off if I'm not your first—I'm nervous enough as it is."

She smiled. "Me too. Have you?"

"Hm?"

"Am I your first?" she clarified.

"Ah." He nodded. "No. But I don't have much more experience than you. Only a couple college flings myself."

"Anything else you need to know?"

He was about to say no when it hit him. Groaning, he ran a hand over his face.

"Shit. I'm sorry, Willow. I don't have a condom. I wasn't expecting…"

But she was smiling. "I know," she said, and got up to go to her bag.

"I have an IUD," she said as she opened one of the front pockets, pulled out the little square package. "But just to be extra safe, I brought this."

She stepped back over to the bed, held it out to him. He reached for it almost absentmindedly, mesmerized by the look in her eyes as she watched him, and the realization this was really happening rushed through him with a mix of relief, joy, and arousal.

The moment his fingers touched foil, he tossed the condom on the bed, yanked her to him, and took her mouth hard and deep.

Her response was immediate. He lit her up, she thought. When Elliot Burke touched her, kissed her, she simply wanted to burst—with passion, with happiness, with love.

The relief he hadn't turned her away, the euphoria of knowing he wanted her, made her giddy. It was a high she hadn't expected to feel, and she infused all she felt into every move she made, running her hands anywhere skin was exposed, into his soft, sexily unruly hair.

His own hands traveled over her, and his mouth broke from hers to brush kisses against her neck and collarbone as he cupped her breasts.

"Is this how you want me to touch you?" he asked as he nuzzled her neck and his thumbs rubbed lightly over her through the layers of fabric.

"God, yes."

She felt his lips curve into a grin before he brought them back to hers, softer this time, as some of his attention was occupied tugging the straps of her dress from her shoulders. He pulled the top of her dress lower, trailing his fingers down her arms, and her knees nearly buckled. When his hands reached her waist she stepped back a little, shimmied out of the dress.

She swore she could feel the heat of his eyes as they roamed over every inch of her, clad in a lacy, strapless sage green bra and matching underwear. When his gaze met hers, full of awe and arousal, she stepped out of the fabric pooled at her feet, hooked her fingers in the belt loops of his jeans.

She gave him a sultry look as she undid the button, trailed the zipper down.

"Aren't you going to keep touching me?"

He nodded as he watched her, entranced, and she grinned when his hands stayed at his sides—it was both gratifying and thrilling to have him so stunned by her he couldn't speak.

"Elliot."

She pulled his jeans down over his hips.

"Huh?" It came out almost as a grunt.

She only gave him an arch look as she gave a playful tug on his jeans. He blinked as though he'd just woken up.

On an intake of breath he yanked the jeans off, kicked them away from the bed. When he turned back to her she was laughing, and he gave her a sheepish grin.

"Sorry," he said. "You fried my circuits."

"You certainly know how to give a woman a confidence boost."

He shook his head. "Will, you've left me tongue-tied since I answered the door."

Confidence boost aside, he still made her blush. He took her hand, and this time it was he who sat on the edge of the bed, nudging her so she stood between his legs. Slowly, teasingly, he ran his hands up her body, traced a single finger across the top of the cups of her bra.

She'd wanted him to touch her, but oh, once again he'd outdone her imagination. She was tempted to close her eyes and enjoy the sensation, but she wanted to see his face as he felt her, absorbed her. His eyes met hers as his fingers danced up her back, flicked open the clasp of her bra. A gasp of pleasure escaped her lips as he palmed her, again using his thumbs to stroke and sending tendrils of pleasure across her skin.

"So perfect," he murmured, before taking a breast into his mouth. She quivered, gripping his shoulders when he turned his attention to the other one.

"E-Elliot…"

"Hm?" He mumbled, not moving his head from her breasts and simultaneously cupping her bottom.

"I want…"

She lost her train of thought when he hooked a finger in the waistband of her panties and tugged her closer.

"What was that?" he teased.

Since her hands were already on his shoulders, she simply shoved him back onto the bed as she straddled him. He grinned in acquiescence, reaching for her as she did for him and holding her close.

Now their kisses did the talking, pressing unspoken words to each other's lips, responding with sighs and moans and touches. His arms came around her and she resisted the urge to sigh again.

He ignited her, she thought. Body and soul.

Almost as an afterthought she noticed he was pulling off her underwear, so she moved off him to allow him to draw them down her legs, fling them to the floor. Delicately, he brushed his fingers along the curve of her hip, and the look of admiration on his face astonished her.

Mesmerized, she reached for him, drawing off his briefs and tossing them to the floor with the rest of their clothes. Now that they were both naked, the air seemed both intense and cautious; for a moment they stared, both startlingly aware of each other.

Then, inspired, she gripped him as gently as he had her; he hissed in pleasure as she teased him. After a few moments, he stilled her hand, panting a little.

"Willow, if you keep touching me like that I'm not going to last. Give me a second."

He sat up, scanned the bed for the condom, snatched it up the moment his eyes landed on it. As he put it on, she sat up too, and when he was ready, straddled him. When he twined his fingers in her hair, brought his lips to hers, she sank down onto him, bringing him into her.

They stayed like that for a moment, arms around each other, and he watched her eyes as she adjusted herself, the movement sending pleasure surging through him. Then on some silent cue, they moved together; she clung to his shoulders for balance as she rocked against him, and he held her close as he thrust into her.

She didn't know why, but she'd expected their lovemaking to be frantic. Instead it was slow and...*filling* was the word that came to mind. All of her felt full—her body, her heart, even her mind. No matter what happened she would remember this, the way he held her, caressed her. The way he looked and felt.

This was a moment worth preserving.

Even as she thought it, it built in her, the grasping, greedy rise of pleasure, and she let it take her. He felt her tighten around him, and the sensation spurred him toward his own release.

Spent, he rested his forehead on her shoulder, and she leaned her head against his. Though she wanted to savor this intimacy, she rose slowly off of him, and sat on her hip, leaning on her arm as she looked at him with a coy smile on her face.

He returned the smile, holding up a finger; he swung off the bed, and disappeared into the bathroom for a few moments. She took her turn in the bathroom after him, wondering if it would be awkward, or if he would immediately get dressed.

But her fears were for nothing, because when she returned he was back on the bed, still undressed, leaning casually against the pillows; his smile widened in an adoring, yet smug, way that she could only interpret as the smile of a satisfied lover. She imagined her expression mirrored his own.

When she climbed back onto the bed, he pulled her to him, drawing her against his side. She didn't resist, swinging a leg over one of his and laying an arm over his chest.

"Jesus, Will. I'd ask why we didn't do that sooner, but something tells me it was meant to happen this way."

This was what she'd craved most of all—just this. Lying snuggled up with him, talking about their life; or perhaps just enjoying the companionable silence.

"You think we had to misunderstand each other to get here?" she asked.

"Sort of." He paused. "We both had to do a little soul searching after that argument, right? We had to re-examine not just what we thought we knew, but ourselves. And we likely wouldn't have gotten here if we hadn't been willing to admit we were wrong, or if we were too stubborn to change.

"But we did; I think we're better because of it. Maybe we'd have gotten here if we'd never misunderstood each other, but our relationship might not be the same. Maybe we had to misunderstand each other to truly understand each other."

She craned her neck to look at him. "Our relationship is stronger because of everything that happened, you mean?"

"Yeah." He looked down, stroked a hand over her hair. "Willow. I…"

He only paused a moment, but it was enough to be interrupted by a rapping at the door. They heard his uncle call out, "You up, Elliot? We're going to leave for brunch in an hour."

"Yeah," Elliot called back. "I'm gonna hit the shower, then I'll meet you in the lobby."

"Sounds good," came the response, then all was silent.

Her heart pounded so hard she was sure he could feel it—was he about to say what she thought he was about to say?

But he was sitting up, forcing her to sit up as well.

"Sadly, we should probably get dressed," he said. "Society frowns upon naked brunch."

She sent him a sultry look as she stood. "Only in public."

His smile was automatic, his eyes tracking every movement of her body as she picked up her discarded clothes. "Now there's an idea."

Reluctantly, they began to dress, and Elliot determined on wearing a slightly nicer pair of shorts instead of the jeans. As he reached for a t-shirt, his phone rang.

He wanted to ignore it, but he saw it was Joy calling, and he could never ignore a call from her. Smiling, he yanked the shirt over his head.

"Hey, gorgeous," he said when he picked up.

Willow raised a brow at him, mouthed "Joy?" He nodded and winked at her. She shook her head in amusement; he was so distracted watching her finish putting her dress back on it took him a moment to process Joy's words, and he wasn't sure he'd heard her correctly.

"What was that?"

"Layla is gone." It was hard not to miss the distress in his sister's voice.

He frowned. "Gone. What do you mean gone?"

Willow gave him a questioning look, and the pause before Joy spoke instantly filled him with dread.

"She ran off with Gabe Windham. She left a note with Kate," she said of their next youngest sister.

Elliot's blood chilled. So many thoughts rushed through his head at once he wasn't sure he was thinking anything at all. In a daze, he closed his eyes and let out a shaky breath.

"*Fuck.*"

Concerned, Willow stepped to him, took his hand. He could only imagine how agonized he must look—how could he tell her the man she utterly despised had once more intruded in her life, her happiness? Whether he knew it or not, by involving Elliot's family, Gabriel Windham would be bringing himself to Willow's notice yet again. But Elliot couldn't keep this from her.

He swallowed, squeezed her hand as he put Joy on speaker.

"Gabe Windham? You're sure?"

Willow stiffened, and he kept his eyes on hers, searching for any sign of pain—but all he saw was that same concern, heightened by a sense of focus.

"Yes." Knowing his sister, Elliot could tell Joy was on the verge of tears. "In her note she said she was in love, and he was going to surprise her by whisking her away someplace special, just the two of them."

"So no one knows where they are."

"Dad was notified of a charge to his credit card—she used it to buy plane tickets to Las Vegas," Joy explained. "That was a couple hours ago. He's been working on getting another ticket to go there himself."

"I'll go," Elliot told her, finally taking his eyes off Willow. "I'm closer. Tell Dad to leave it to me. I'll ask Uncle Ed and Aunt Maddie for help if I need to. We'll leave right away."

When Willow laid a hand on his arm, squeezed the hand she held, he realized he was shaking—with rage for Windham, annoyance and fear for Layla, distress for his family, and with despair at the thought of losing the woman in front of him when he'd finally just found her.

"Alright." Joy sighed, clearly worried, but he could hear the relief in there as well. "I'm so sorry Elliot. I know you were having a good time on your vacation."

"It's not your fault, Joy. Just focus on taking care of Mom and Dad. I'll take care of the rest."

"Alright," she said again. "Be careful. I love you."

"I love you, too."

When he hung up, he clenched his jaw, stared at a random spot on the wall. Willow's hand in his kept him steady, and he wanted to hold on to it as long as possible, but he knew that might not be possible now.

His voice was hard and distant when he spoke. "I have to go."

"I know. I'm coming with you."

He whipped his gaze to hers. "What? No. You can't."

She straightened, and, lifting her chin, pulled her hand from his to cross her arms. "And why not? I know Gabe very well, remember? He's no stranger to the casinos of Vegas; there are several places he likes to frequent."

"So write them down for me." He dumped his suitcase on the bed, began tossing his belongings inside, not bothering to fold or organize. There was no time.

"Elliot, I can help you. My Dad can help, too—Gabe isn't just your problem, he's our problem, too."

"I can't ask you—either of you—to do that." He stalked to the bathroom, swiped up his toiletries and shoved them in their case. She only followed him.

"You're not asking. I'm offering—and need I remind you I'm just as stubborn as you are."

"That remains to be seen," he said as he stalked back out, threw the case in with the rest of his stuff.

She folded her arms again. "I'll just follow you, you know. I can go to Vegas with or without you, but I'd rather go with."

He slammed his suitcase shut, gritting his teeth. "I don't want your help."

He yanked at the zipper, putting weight on top to lessen the gap. He just wanted the damn thing to *close* so he could go and do whatever needed doing. He wanted to fix this damn mess but the zipper wouldn't *budge*.

He felt a hand over his, gentle and warm.

"Elliot."

Willow's voice was quiet, a contrast to his screaming thoughts, and somehow her touch settled everything again. He stilled and shifted his eyes to meet hers.

"You don't have to do this alone," she said.

"I know," he said wearily, all his anger draining. "But I can't let you get involved in this."

She kept her gaze calm. "Tell me why."

The true reason swelled up in him, the love for her newly blossomed, simultaneously a force of agony at the thought of hurting her. It was nearly crippling, this weight. God, and he'd once thought he hated her? No. Those feelings were sprouts of what was blooming in him now, and they paled in comparison to this overwhelming, gut-wrenching emotion. This time he was positive she could see all of it clearly written on his face.

"Because I love you too much to ever make you have to face that bastard again."

Though her heart ached for him, it constricted in utter joy at his words; the tension left her body, instead replaced by a strength she knew came only from love. His love for her, and hers for him. When she spoke, her voice was soft, but determined.

"And I love you, which is why I'm going to do exactly that."

He sighed, running a hand over his face in resignation—finally, he seemed to understand. Resigned, yes, but relieved, and she saw the love in his eyes when he cupped her cheeks in his fingers.

"You amaze me, Willow Davenport."

Touched by the sentiment—she didn't think she'd ever amazed anyone before—she leaned her forehead to his, let herself savor the moment. Then she squeezed his wrists.

"What do you want to do?"

He let out a breath. "I need to talk to my aunt and uncle; I want to leave as soon as possible, and they'll have to pack. Are you still planning on going to brunch?"

"No. I need to talk to my family, too. Why don't we meet you back here, pick you up on the way to the airport? We can all catch the next flight to Las Vegas."

"Alright. We'll wait here—and I'll find out what more I can from Joy."

"Good idea." She grabbed her bag and headed for the door. He followed, and she paused when she laid a hand on the handle. "I'll just tell Cal and the others you had a family emergency."

"Alright." He bent his head, gave her a soft peck on the lips. "I'll see you soon then."

She nodded, opening the door and stepping out; when she looked back at him, he was holding the door open, looking as lost as he had when she'd found him on the vineyard bench.

"I love you, Elliot."

His eyes seemed to clear a little bit; then he took her arm, pulling her back to him, and kissing her again. Harder, a little more desperately this time. When he broke his lips from hers, he just wrapped his arms around her and held on as she squeezed him back.

"I love you," he murmured. "Thank you."

"For what?"

"Grounding me."

He pulled back, let her go. She gave him an understanding smile.

"Any time," she said. "I'll be back soon."

He only nodded, watching her go as she rushed down the hall to the elevator. She gave him a slight wave before she disappeared around the corner, and he waited a moment before stepping back and letting the door close behind him, not entirely sure what he was feeling.

Grief? Happiness? Worry, loss, stress, hope? Perhaps all those things. The world had tilted a little without Willow there, even though he knew she was coming back. Even though this new understanding between them was in mint condition, and it didn't make sense to fall so hard so fast.

Was it fast though? He'd already acknowledged his feelings had likely been building since they'd met. They'd just been thwarted by misunderstandings and a particularly devious asshole.

An asshole who would be a pile of pulp by the time he was done with him.

With that in mind, he grabbed his phone and his keycard, and headed next door to his aunt and uncle's room. It was going to be a long morning.

FIVE

WILLOW CALLED out as she rushed into the house, clambering up the stairs to her father's office. "Dad? Seth? Aspen?"

She'd debated with herself on the drive home whether to bring Aspen into it, but they hadn't last time, and that had been a mistake. This time he would know.

"Willow?" Her father set down the book he was reading. "Are you all right?"

"Yes, but something's happened," she said, a little out of breath. "It involves Gabe."

"The slimy bastard again?" Seth said as he and Aspen entered the room. "What's he done now?"

"I was just with Elliot, when—"

"You were with Elliot? But we're about to see him at brunch." Seth interrupted.

Willow huffed. "Yes. Will you let me explain?"

"Are you blushing?" Seth started to smirk, then his eyes widened. "Wait, when you say you were with him, you don't mean..."

Though Willow pinked even more, sent her father an apologetic look, she stiffened her spine and sent her cousin a fulminating glare. "That wasn't what I meant, but yes, I went to see him at his hotel room. And since you're not a girlfriend, I'm assuming you don't want to hear about that, so shall I just skip to the part that's relevant?"

Seth only gaped at her. "But..."

"Oh, for Pete's sake." Willow threw up her hands.

"Um." Aspen laughed a little. "As much as I like Elliot, I really don't want to hear about my sister's sex life. If you need a minute, Seth, we can fill you in later."

That snapped Seth back to attention. "I don't need a minute. Well, what are you waiting for?"

Willow refrained from rolling her eyes. "Elliot's sister, Joy, called to tell him their younger sister Layla ran off to Vegas with Gabe. They don't know where in Vegas, but I have a few hunches where Gabe is most likely to go."

"You offered to help find them," her father finally spoke. "Do you have a plan?"

She sighed, relieved. She knew she could count on her father's support, but she was grateful he didn't question her instincts to help. "Right now, he's explaining the situation to his aunt and uncle. I came here to explain to you; then I and whoever wants to come with me are going to pick them up on our way to the airport."

"And you think you know where he might go?" Seth asked.

"I have a few ideas."

"So do I," said Aspen.

Willow gave her brother an understanding look. "I thought you might."

"I don't want to go with you, but I still want to help."

Seth nodded. "I'm definitely going."

"As will I," her father added, getting up from his desk and giving his nephew an authoritative stare. "Can you promise me you won't resort to violence this time?"

Though Seth frowned, he sighed. "Fine."

Willow deliberately kept silent. She would make no such promises.

"Alright," Sam nodded. "Let's all pack an overnight bag and meet downstairs in ten."

"I'll write you a list," Aspen told Willow as she headed to her room.

As she changed into jeans and a t-shirt, Willow shot off a quick text to Cal with an excuse; then she tossed a change of clothes and a few overnight things in her travel backpack, snatched up her purse, and headed back downstairs.

Seth was already waiting, and her father and Aspen came down just moments after her.

"I texted Cal," she informed them.

"Here," Aspen said, holding a piece of notebook paper out to her. "Those are all the casinos I remember him mentioning."

There were only a handful, Willow noted, and they were all ones on her own list as well, but for one.

"What's this one?" she asked him. "I've never heard of it."

"Oh, I think that one's newer." Aspen shrugged. "I just remember it because he talked about how he was friends with the hotel manager."

Now that was new. "Thank you, Aspen."

They all hugged Aspen goodbye, then clamored into Sam's SUV.

"Keep me updated," Aspen called out.

Willow nodded before she closed the back door. "Will do."

They discussed the list on the way to the Gallaghers' hotel, and the pros and cons of splitting up to search. She knew the others would want to weigh in, but it was a good distraction. Her anxiety grew as they neared the hotel—what if Elliot had changed his mind? What if he decided it was her fault after all, or that he didn't want her to help?

When Sam parked, she opened her door. "I'll go," she said, rushing up to the automatic doors.

When Willow spotted Elliott pacing in the hotel lobby, relief rushed through her. His own expression when he glanced toward the doors and saw her lost some of the tension it had been carrying, and he visibly relaxed as she approached. Any concern he might have decided to blame her for the situation vanished as he wrapped his arms around her.

"I know it's stupid, but I'd almost convinced myself I'd pushed you away earlier," he murmured into her hair. "Or that you would resent me for bringing him back into your life."

"I was worried you'd try to push me away again, or blame me for not warning you about him sooner," she admitted.

"You're not responsible for his actions."

"Neither are you."

Having wrapped up their checkout, his aunt and uncle approached with worried faces.

"Are we ready?" Ed asked.

Willow nodded. "My father and Seth are waiting in the car."

She turned to lead them out, and saw Seth standing near the doors, watching them with an expression she couldn't quite decipher. "Or just my father," she corrected.

The Gallaghers had a rental to return at the airport, so Ed would drive separately, but he stowed his bag in the SUV, where Maddie and Elliot would ride with the others.

On the way, Willow showed them Aspen's list and shared her theories, while Seth began checking flight times.

"Did you learn anything from Joy?" Willow asked Elliot.

His look was stony as he pulled up a picture on his phone. "She took a picture of the note Layla left and sent it to me."

Willow took the phone and began skimming the letter, a short missive full of the kind of selfishness, naivety, and innocence a teenage girl who believes herself violently in love would write.

Gabe could be charming and persuasive, she knew, and shuddered at the thought. Even so, and even though at nineteen Layla was legally an adult, Willow couldn't help but wonder at Layla's audacity—running off with some guy without really telling her family where she was going.

That didn't matter at the moment, Willow reminded herself. What mattered was finding her and dealing with Gabe.

"She mentions Gabe seems to have had a particular place in mind," she noted.

"You think one of his usual haunts?" Seth asked.

Willow pulled out the list Aspen had given her, scanned it again; again her eyes were drawn to the unfamiliar name. Everything in her gut told her to start there.

"No." She answered slowly, considering. "I think he has a new haunt, and I think he'd go there first."

. . . . .

ELLIOT'S KNEE bounced uncontrollably in the back of the cab he, Willow, and Seth had scrambled into.

Everyone had agreed on a basic plan—they'd all go to the casino Willow suggested based on Aspen's information, and if they didn't find out anything, then they'd split up and search the other ones on the list. Elliot and his aunt and uncle had exchanged their return tickets for tickets to Vegas while the others got their own tickets.

The flight was thankfully short, though worry and anxiety of course made it feel longer, and now that they were almost at their destination, he felt the cab couldn't go fast enough.

They'd been lucky to catch one, what with all the traffic; Uncle Ed, Aunt Maddie, and Sam had to wait a bit before they managed to wrangle one as well, but a text from Aunt Maddie had assured him they were on their way.

Willow laid a hand on his knee in an effort to calm his agitation. "Focus on what we'll do when we get there," she said in a soothing voice.

He let out a breath, dimly registering that Seth was staring at Willow's hand on his knee, lips pursed, but was too worked up to think anything of it. He automatically laid a hand over hers.

"I know worrying doesn't help, I just…"

"I know."

She did know, he thought, and it helped that she understood. They all did.

"Thanks, guys," he murmured. When Willow opened her mouth, he waved a hand to stall her protest. "No, really. You don't know Layla well, and Seth, you and Sam don't know her at all; but you've all put everything on hold to help her—help my family. I know you all feel some responsibility because of Windham, but you still didn't have to get involved. But you're here. That means a lot."

Seth had finally raised his eyes from their joined hands at the sound of his name, and now gave Elliot a nod of quiet respect.

"You're right about Windham," Seth acknowledged. "But you're welcome all the same."

Elliot nodded back.

When they finally made it to the casino, they rushed inside, pausing in the crowded lobby to take in the layout. Willow glanced in the direction of the casino floor.

"Chances are Gabe is hitting up the tables, but I doubt security would let Layla on the floor."

As much as Elliot wanted to find Windham and pummel him, he wanted to find his sister more, his eyes passing over faces in the lobby with a heightened sense of awareness. They roamed over the restaurant and bar area, the doors to an auditorium, the signs pointing toward the indoor waterpark, and the counter for the hotel check-in.

As his eyes began to sweep down the hall leading to the spa, he heard an elevator ding and glanced toward the sound.

And then he saw her.

She was across the lobby, but he could see her dark blonde hair was pulled back in a ponytail and she was hugging herself as though she were cold. She looked lost, he thought as he stepped in her direction.

"Layla!" he called out as she stepped onto the elevator.

But she didn't hear him. Cursing, he ran to catch it, but the doors closed several seconds before he reached it.

"Damn it!"

"It's alright," Willow said as she pressed the call button. "She was the only one on the elevator, we can watch to see what floor it stops at."

Even as she said it, the light on the scale showing the number of floors switched from one to two, and stayed there. As soon as the elevator came back down and opened, Elliot rushed in and immediately pressed the button for the second floor, repeatedly pressing the close-door button once Willow and Seth were inside.

Though it didn't have far to go, every second the elevator inched along was its own kind of torture—what if they couldn't figure out what room she'd gone to?

He could try calling her cell again, he thought. She'd looked kind of miserable, and she was alone; maybe now she would want to talk to her family.

The doors opened with a shrill *ding*, and he nearly leapt out into the hall, whipping his head in every direction to see if he could spot his sister.

And he did spot her, but at the sight before him, any relief he felt was immediately overshadowed by a kind of cold fury he didn't know existed. He heard Willow's gasp behind him as he took off at a sprint, barreling like thunder down the hall.

Neither Willow or Seth tried to stop him, following hot on his heels, and in a flash of black-tinted vision, he reached his sister and wrenched Gabe Windham away from her.

· · · · ·

LAYLA HUGGED her arms to her chest and rubbed as a shiver wracked through her body; being in the casino's air conditioning was like being inside a refrigerator. She was tired, and she couldn't find Gabe anywhere —some trip this was turning out to be.

She wasn't having any fun. She wasn't allowed past a certain point on the casino's floor since she wasn't twenty-one, their hotel room smelled like stale cigarettes, and so far Gabe had spent all his time gambling, so she was left to wander by herself. He'd hardly paid any attention to her.

She'd thought she was in love with him, but any warm feelings she had were now turning cold. Why had he brought her here if he only intended to ignore her and do whatever he wanted without her?

She sniffled as she pulled out her keycard. Everyone was going to be so mad at her.

"Hey, babe."

She jolted as Gabe appeared next to her, dark hair mussed and eyes bleary.

"Where have you been?" she asked sourly as she jammed the keycard in the slot. When the lock clicked, she shoved open the door.

She'd barely taken a step into the room when Gabe had her back against the door, pressing her into it as his mouth crushed hers, the keycard falling from her hand.

This kiss wasn't like the other ones they'd shared. This kiss was hard and bruising, and sloppy—she could taste the alcohol on him. As the muffled bell of the elevator sounded in the distance, she realized they were holding the door open, in full view of the doorway and anyone down the hall.

She pushed against him, but he wouldn't budge. She pushed harder and he freed her mouth to clamp it on her neck.

She winced. "Gabe, stop. You're drunk."

"I'm fine."

Instead of stepping back, his hands reached up to possess her breasts, squeezing none too gently.

"No, Gabe. Stop!" She struggled against him again, but he only tried to pull up her shirt.

The next thing she knew, his weight was whisked off of her.

Shaking and unsure, she froze when her brain seemed to register her brother dragging Gabe away from her, farther into the room, and she stared open-mouthed as Elliot drew back his arm and threw his fist into Gabe's face with a force she didn't know he had. Gabe cried out in pain and held his nose with both hands as he bent away from Elliot.

Layla flinched when she felt a hand on her shoulder, and shock turned to confusion when her gaze met that of Willow Davenport. All she could do was blink and glance between Willow and her brother, and another guy with wavy reddish-brown hair who had come up behind Willow. Willow gently led her over to the bed while the other guy closed the door to the room.

"Are you alright?" Willow asked softly.

Before Layla could answer, Gabe let out a rough groan.

"Touch my sister again, I'll break more than your nose," Elliot spat.

"I think I can take you even with a broken nose, Burke," Gabe said as he straightened.

Elliot only gave the bleeding man a pitying smirk. "I'm not the one you need to worry about," he said, turning to glance at Willow.

Layla watched the exchange with growing curiosity, but was still too stunned to speak. Willow gently squeezed her shoulder in comfort.

"Excuse me." Her voice was quiet, but steely, and something Layla supposed was disgust simmered underneath. "There's something I have to do."

She moved aside to let Elliot, who had approached them, take her place at his sister's side. Layla stiffened, assuming she was in for a lecture, but instead she was enfolded in her brother's arms and squeezed hard against his chest. She sagged against him as the sudden feeling of safety overcame her. He said nothing, and she let tears she didn't realize had been choking her quietly fall.

Elliot breathed deep as he held his sister, a little surprised when she not only let him, but clung to him. He flexed the hand he'd used to bash Windham's face, reminding himself to save his anger for later; right now, Layla needed him, and after what he'd just witnessed, he couldn't bear to be angry at her.

Now his anger was reserved for Gabe, who was eyeing Willow smugly as she swiped a box of tissues from the room's nightstand and thrust it at him.

"Here," she said dispassionately. "You're getting blood on the carpet."

"Pretty sure that's not my fault, babe." Gabe sent Elliot a glare as he yanked several tissues from the box and held them to his bleeding nose, then tilted his head back.

"How were you planning on paying for this room, Gabe?" Willow's voice was deceivingly calm.

"I won some money at the tables."

"Really?" Willow paused. "And how much money did you lose?"

Now Gabe straightened again, glaring at Willow with as much fervor as he'd glared at Elliot. "None of your business, Will. I get why *he's* here," he gestured to Elliot. "But why are you?"

Willow stepped toward Gabe slowly, deliberately. "Because my family has allowed you to cause problems for others long enough, and because it is my business if the money you lost belongs to the Burkes."

Gabe narrowed his eyes at her, flicked his gaze over Elliot, Layla, and Seth before finally landing back on Elliot, who had tensed up a little. A slow, malicious grin spread over his face as he dropped the hand holding the tissues to his side and let out a half laugh.

"Oh, don't tell me—you're with him now?" He laughed again. "Good luck with her, Elliot—this one's a prude *and* a handful."

Though Elliot could see Seth was itching to pummel the bastard, Willow's face remained stoic and impassive as Gabe laughed at her.

"Isn't that right, Will?" he asked her, reaching his free hand to run the backs of his fingers up her arm.

Seth and Elliot both tensed, automatically moving to pull Gabe away. At first, Willow was too surprised Gabe had the audacity to touch her to do anything but stare; but as his hand neared her breast, instinct kicked in. In a flash, she'd gripped his arm, shoving it away from her, and in the next moment, she was bringing her leg up to kick him where she knew it would hurt most.

Elliot and Seth both stopped in their tracks as Gabe sank to the ground and seemed to curl in on himself as he held his groin. Even so, he managed to gasp out a single word.

"Bitch," he rasped at Willow.

Willow only raised an eyebrow. "Oh, trust me. I'm not the bitch in this situation."

Seth chuckled as he pulled out his phone to call his uncle. "Yeah, we found them. Room two-oh-seven."

Willow and Seth kept watch over Gabe—not that he was in much condition to go anywhere at the moment—while Elliot iced his hand as he sat with Layla on the bed. She'd stopped crying, but she hadn't said a word, which was starting to concern him.

When finally a succinct knock came at the door, Willow went to open it. Aunt Maddie and Uncle Ed rushed in ahead of Sam, making a beeline for him and Layla, while Sam took in the scene. Seth had helped Gabe into a chair, and Gabe was once again holding tissues to his nose; he also had a bag of ice on his lap that Willow had graciously fetched from the hotel's nearest ice machine.

Sam sighed, though there was no admonishment in the tone. "Seth, I thought we agreed there would be no fighting."

"Don't look at me," Seth raised both his hands in defense. "But to be fair, they just beat me to it."

"I'm afraid the nose is my fault," Elliot explained. "I might have exercised restraint if we hadn't come across him trying to force himself on my sister."

Aunt Maddie gasped as she held Layla close and Uncle Ed turned a glare on Gabe.

"We were just having a little fun," Gabe asserted. "If she didn't want to have sex with me she wouldn't have come here with me."

"Then why was she trying to push you away, asshole?" Elliot rose to stand next to Willow. "Why didn't you stop when she said no?"

When Gabe opened his mouth to argue, Willow held up a hand to stall him. "Don't bother answering. There are three people here who all witnessed what happened, and one who experienced it."

Sam's voice was grim. "What about the ice?"

"Our girl here has good aim," Seth informed him.

Willow's smirk was slow and deliberate. "I never made any promises of non-violence."

Her father sighed, but said nothing more.

Elliot nudged her. "Hey, Will."

"Hm?"

"You finally got your wish."

When she lifted her head to give him a quizzical look, he clarified, "You told me you hoped you'd get the chance to kick Gabe in the balls someday, and you did."

She smiled at the realization. "I did, didn't I? I'll check it off my bucket list."

Seth laughed, and Gabe glared at all of them. Clearly resigned, her father turned to the Gallaghers. "Maddie, Ed, why don't you take Layla to another room. My family can handle Gabe."

Maddie looked like she wanted to protest, but her husband stopped her. "Now's not the time," he told her.

One glance at her niece had her nodding her head. Elliot gave Willow's hand a squeeze. "I'll come with," he said, and went to join his family.

He texted Willow the room number when they got another room with two beds, and Layla, who hadn't spoken at all the entire time, sat quietly on one of the beds with Aunt Maddie. She wouldn't look at any of them, and Elliot wasn't sure how to begin.

Then, softly, Layla finally spoke.

"Thank you for coming for me," she murmured.

"Of course, honey," Aunt Maddie said, slowly rubbing Layla's back. "We were worried about you."

It was the truth, but it made Layla's eyes fill with tears. "I'm so stupid," she said as she began to sob. "If Elliot hadn't…"

She swallowed, unable to finish the sentence.

"Hey." Elliot knelt in front of his sister, covered her hands with his. "You're not stupid. It was wrong to run off like you did, but it's not your fault he's an asshole."

"He said he loved me, and I believed him."

Elliot shook his head, thinking of Willow's words in the library. "He's fooled us all at some point. And he'll pay for what he's done, I promise."

He didn't know how, but he knew the bastard wasn't walking away unscathed—not this time.

Layla didn't say anything more, just stared blankly at the wall. He wished he knew what would help her, but though he could imagine her fear and her pain, since he wasn't a woman, he couldn't completely understand it.

Elliot stood, and after a few more moments of silence, there was a knock on the door. Uncle Ed opened it to Willow, who carried a duffel bag and a purse.

"I brought Layla's things," she said, stepping into the room. "And some news."

This at least caused Layla to look away from the wall, her attention now on someone she probably considered a near-stranger.

Willow considered Layla carefully, tilting her head, seeming to decide something. Then she pulled a credit card from her pocket, handed it to Uncle Ed.

"This is Thomas's credit card," he said, confused.

"Seth found it in Gabe's wallet," Willow explained, still watching Layla. Elliot had been looking at the card in his uncle's hands, but now he turned to observe Layla as well, and she seemed just as confused as the rest of them. Willow moved to sit on Layla's other side and made sure she met her eyes.

"Do you know if Gabe had access to your dad's wallet at any point recently?" she asked carefully.

Layla's eyes widened. "You think he…"

She trailed off, then her eyes lit again when a thought seemed to take hold. "He was at dinner last night. He excused himself to go to the bathroom, and he was gone for a few minutes."

"And he'd spent so much time with your family he probably knew where your dad kept his wallet."

Her eyes going sad, Layla nodded. "It's my fault, isn't it?"

"No," Willow said firmly. "Your family invited him into your home in good faith, and he broke that trust by stealing from you. That's on him."

Surprised, Layla could only blink at Willow. Then after a moment, she seemed to realize that everyone was looking at her and began to withdraw into herself, this time looking at the floor.

Looking at the rest of them, Willow said, "Do you guys mind if I talk to Layla alone?"

At a loss, Elliot could tell his aunt and uncle didn't know how to answer any more than he did, so he shrugged and nodded to indicate he didn't have any other ideas.

"Certainly," Aunt Maddie decided. "We'll just be out in the hall."

With that, she stood and ushered her husband and nephew out of the room. He just barely caught Willow's reassuring smile as Aunt Maddie closed the door.

Inside the room, Layla sniffled. Her eyes still on the floor she mumbled quietly, "Thank you for bringing my stuff."

"You're welcome." Willow deliberately kept her voice as calming as she could make it. "I thought you might want it."

Hugging herself, Layla finally glanced at Willow, watching her warily.

"You're probably wondering why I'm here," Willow said.

"Am I in trouble?" Layla asked quietly.

Willow only tilted her head. "That's not up to me. But I don't think you'll be in too much trouble. Your family is just glad you're safe."

Layla decided not to ask if Gabe would be in trouble. She wasn't sure what she hoped the answer would be, or how she would feel about it.

"Are you here to lecture me?"

"No." Willow turned to face Layla more directly. "I was hoping you'd let me tell you a story."

* * *

WAITING WAS AGONIZING. It had been more than ten minutes, and Willow was still talking to Layla. At least that gave Elliot hope she'd gotten her to talk about what happened.

Then finally, the door opened, and Willow stepped out.

"She's asking for you," she said to Aunt Maddie.

"Thank you, dear." Aunt Maddie hurried into the room, leaving Willow with Elliot and his uncle.

"Is she okay?" Elliot blurted out.

Willow smiled understandingly at his impatience. "She's shaken up, but she'll be alright eventually."

That wasn't what he'd hoped to hear, but logically he knew he couldn't expect everything to be fixed right away. Layla would need time to come to terms with her actions and heal from Gabe's.

"Okay. What did you talk about?"

Now Willow shook her head. "Sorry, big brother, that conversation is locked in my vault of confidentiality."

When he only blinked at her, she patted his arm in sympathy. "She'll talk to you when she's ready."

As he tried to think of a response, Seth and Sam exited from the elevator and headed down the hall toward them.

"Where's Windham?" Uncle Ed asked, his tone darker than Elliot had ever heard it.

"In custody," Sam told them. "He was arrested for theft and assault, and our lawyers will deal with him from here on out. We plan to bring to light some of the other things he's done, so hopefully he'll be put away for some time."

They all breathed a collective sigh of relief.

"Thank God," said Uncle Ed.

"How is your sister?" Seth asked Elliot.

Elliot could only shake his head. "I don't know. It may be a little while before she's really okay. But I think she's at least a little better at the moment," he said, shooting Willow a questioning glance.

She nodded. "I had a long conversation with her. She at least accepts Gabe's actions aren't her fault."

"That's good." Seth sighed. "It's not quite over yet, but this is the beginning of the end of our association with Gabriel Windham—and I don't know about you guys, but I could use a drink."

"Amen, brother." Elliot said, scrubbing a hand over his face.

"I'll buy a round," said Uncle Ed. "Maddie may be a while with Layla, but they can join us if they're up for it."

"Sounds like a plan." Seth clapped Uncle Ed on the back and headed back toward the elevator.

Before Willow could follow the others, Elliot took her hand. His eyes warmed with love when she looked at him expectantly.

"I don't know how to begin to thank you, or your family," he said.

"Elliot," she said, gently touching his face, "you are my family."

The squeeze of his heart was automatic, and he finally managed to smile. "And you're mine," he murmured.

He gave her a quick kiss, then tugged her down the hall to join their collective family.

SIX

THE SOUND of chatter and clanking dishes filled Elliot's ears as he sipped his beer. It was a good sound—that of a busy brewery and happy, satisfied patrons. He glanced at Willow and Aspen to see how they were doing.

Aspen had his eyes closed, and his fingers were twitching, a sign Elliot had learned meant he was running through the music in his head. Willow stood next to him, arms crossed and a frown on her face. It was a look that gave the appearance of boredom, the same appearance she'd achieved all those months ago, and one that Elliot himself had believed. But now he understood she was simply trying not to show how anxious she was, and in this case, she was nervous on top of it.

"You ready?" he asked her.

"As I ever will be, I suppose," she said quietly.

"Want any advice?"

Her brow rose. "Like what?"

"Like the classic 'imagine the audience in their underwear,'" he said, gesturing to the crowd.

That got her to crack a smile. "I've never understood that suggestion. It only makes everything more awkward, which is decidedly unhelpful."

"Never tried it myself." Elliot shrugged. "But I do know that this crowd is as laidback as they come."

"I know. Why did I agree to this again?"

Aspen opened his eyes. "Because it's fun," he reminded her.

"Exactly." Elliot put more cheer into his voice. "We've practiced the song, and we're in this together. And when we get to the end you'll wonder where the time went."

Willow tilted her head. "Is that what you tell Joy when you get her to sing with you?"

Elliot quirked a smile, spotting his older sister chatting with their aunt, uncle, dad, Seth, and Sam, as she set their drinks at their table. On a stool at the bar, Callum sat alone—Clara hadn't come with him—staring longingly at Joy. He'd come back to Medford to apologize to her, and they'd had a long conversation Joy wasn't ready to tell Elliot about; she'd seemed to have forgiven Cal, and though their mother still held out hope, whether Joy would be willing to give a relationship with Cal another chance remained to be seen.

At first, Elliot wanted to be glad Joy hadn't taken Cal back. But one look at Willow had reminded him of the power of second chances. If they had worked through all their misunderstandings, why couldn't Cal and his sister? And who was he to say what they should or shouldn't do?

"She knows how it goes by now," he said, looking back at Willow. "She gets nervous getting up on stage, but once she starts singing she gets more comfortable. But she leaves all the talking to me."

Willow nodded. "Sounds good to me."

She and Joy had gotten to know each other more over the past week; Willow was making an effort to spend more time with his family, but she'd found kindred spirits in Joy, and to Elliot's surprise, his father.

The even bigger surprise was Layla. She'd been much more subdued after their return from Vegas the past couple weeks, and the only ones she'd been willing to talk to intimately were Willow, Joy, and Aunt Maddie. Whatever they talked about, it was helping—even now, though not as boisterous, Layla was still her bright, bubbly self as she interacted with the people at the tables she waited.

The Davenports' lawyers had dealt with Gabe Windham; what with his previous attempt at stealing Pemberley recipes, and the theft of Thomas Burke's credit card, among others, it was enough that he would be doing some time—without Layla having to testify about what happened to her.

To everyone's surprise and delight, Aspen had hit it off with the Burkes on first meeting, and his confidence was growing as a result. Joy got along with everyone, he played music with Macy, discussed art with Kate, and had bonded with Layla over their shared Windham experiences. Even Mr. and Mrs. Burke were taken with him; Mrs. Burke showered the motherless young man with motherly love, and Mr. Burke was impressed by the literary knowledge of all the Davenports.

It was both a pleasure and a relief to find that his father got along with Willow and her family, and had made an effort to get to know Willow. His mother had been a little confused by his relationship with Willow at first, as she was still under the impression they disliked each other, but once she understood Willow was quiet and shy, much the same as Joy was, she had no problem extending her motherly love to include Willow.

Though Willow had been a little overwhelmed by all the attention, she was touched by the warm welcome, and in particular seemed to be closest with Aunt Maddie.

Even now, Elliot could tell Willow's eyes were on the table where her family and the Gallaghers sat with his father; and though her father smiled and Seth gave them a thumbs up, it was Aunt Maddie's encouraging nod that seemed to release some of the tension in Willow's shoulders.

It was a subtle change that only those close to Willow were likely to notice, and Elliot could now say with the satisfied certainty of one who loved her that he was very attune to her.

After glancing at his watch, Elliot signaled Willow and Aspen, and stepped up onto the little stage area, where a keyboard setup and his treasured acoustic waited to be played. There were also two microphones on stands set up in the front of the stage, and an extra in the back in case it was needed. He stepped up to one of the mics and gave the crowd his best audience smile.

"Hello out there, Medford—welcome to open mic night. I'm Elliot Burke, and I'll be your emcee tonight," he announced. Willow and Aspen quietly took their places on the stage as he spoke; Aspen readied himself at the keyboard, and Willow settled on a wooden stool in front of the other microphone.

Elliot gestured toward the side of the stage and continued, "We do open mic nights every Friday; if you're interested in performing tonight just add your name to the clipboard on the wall next to the stage, and I'll announce each person before they go on. Please stick to one song so we can get through everyone, and if there's time at the end or the list is short, we'll ask if anyone would like to perform again."

Now he took a pause to grab his guitar from its stand, then introduced his fellow performers.

"I usually kick these things off by myself, but tonight I have a couple of talented musicians joining me—please welcome Willow and Aspen Davenport."

Though he could see some of the regulars who remembered Willow were surprised, the crowd wasn't any less enthusiastic in their applause. After a nod from the siblings that they were ready, Elliot grinned.

"This is 'Make You Better' by The Decemberists," he said, then began to play the opening guitar chords. Part way through the verse, Aspen came in strong with the bright piano melody.

Since they'd practiced the song in anticipation of the event, Willow and Aspen were a little more sure of themselves, and Elliot was more prepared to look at the audience instead of Willow.

Even so, it captivated him how her voice blended with his in the duet. He still couldn't get over the feeling that they were singing only to each other; again the song they'd chosen seemed to parody their relationship so far, from love lost and found to realizing that they made each other better versions of themselves.

And he wasn't the only one mesmerized—every time his eyes roamed over the tables, nearly everyone was staring at them, enthralled.

Though they were playing the song acoustically, it seemed to swell with the three of them in sync. Willow's voice became stronger as the song progressed, and Elliot could even hear Aspen singing along behind them.

A smile took over Elliot's face, and when she caught it, Willow beamed back brightly; they spent the final refrain of the song looking only at each other. He didn't care if anyone made fun of him for it later, especially since what the crowd was witnessing was genuine connection.

Though he was sure there were still some trials ahead of them, he had no doubt they'd get through whatever came their way. This was the real deal.

He may not have always loved Willow as strongly as he did now—understatement—but he loved her now so very deeply he couldn't imagine life without her. And he'd have to remember to thank his aunt and uncle for dragging him to Pemberley, since their trip was the reason he and Willow were reunited.

With the song over and the next performer introduced, Elliot went to stand next to Willow at the side of the stage.

"That went well," she said as he took her hands in his.

"Yes it did," he agreed.

"You have the audience wrapped around your finger," she pointed out.

"Not as much as you." He grinned. "They're used to me. You put a spell on them and made them all fall in love with you."

She quirked a brow. "Oh, really? Is that how I made you fall in love with me?"

"No, you made me fall in love with your library first."

It made her laugh, and he kept his eyes on hers as he squeezed her hands. "I do love you, Willow. It took me a while to catch up, but now I know I've never loved anyone the way I love you."

Her eyes went soft and she stood on her tip-toes a little to kiss him, slow and sweet.

"I love you, too."

"When?" he asked, giving her a searching look. "When did you know you loved me?"

She bit her lip, her eyebrows furrowing in thought. "I don't know," she admitted. "It just sort of snuck up on me when I wasn't really thinking about it. I landed before I even knew I was falling."

He chuckled. "Me too, except I think I crash-landed."

When he went up to introduce the next person on the list, she went to join the table where her family sat. Even from across the room he could feel her gaze on him—he hoped that was something that would never change. And as he looked around at the place and people he loved, he couldn't help but think everything just felt *right*.

That was the feeling he'd been waiting for, he realized. To feel like everything just felt right.

And to think, it had all started right here in his family's brewery.

I'll drink to that, he thought, and raised his glass to his lips.

DISTRACTING DARCY

ELIZABETH BENNET ABSORBED the passing scenery with contentment, despite the silence and rigid posture of her traveling companion. They were the only two in the gondola, which was only big enough for a handful of people, and while normally she wouldn't mind the contraption's slow pace, every second it took to get to the top of the mountain was another spent with Will Darcy.

How could he not be amazed at the views? she wondered. Instead, his clear green eyes were engrossed in his phone. She rolled her eyes. His loss. It was a shame, though, that he was more absorbed in his business than the people and places around him.

Although, to be fair, she'd noticed he stared at her quite a bit. It was both unsettling and a little bit of a turn on—or maybe the fact that it stirred her was what was unsettling about it. Either way, she was grateful he'd barely looked at her since they boarded the gondola.

As she turned back to the window, the gondola gave a small shudder and stopped. After a few minutes without movement, she sighed.

"Great."

She glanced at Darcy again, and he was still looking at his phone, his hand now clenched around it like he was angry at the universe for the delay in his day. He really was handsome, rather unfairly so, but the disapproving expression he currently wore often marred his looks, in her opinion. Ignoring him, she stood pulled out her own phone to call Jane.

"Lizzy?"

"Hey Jane, our gondola stopped. Did yours?"

"Yeah. We're almost at the top, too."

She turned to face the forested landscape. "Well, at least it's not just us, I guess."

Oh, how she wished she were with her sister. Jane and her boyfriend, Charlie, had gotten onto a gondola with his sisters and brother-in-law, but there was no room for anyone else, which left Darcy and Elizabeth to get in the next one. The only plus was that the snobby Caroline Bingley had looked none too pleased she wasn't the one riding with Darcy.

Elizabeth would gladly have switched with her, but the attendant closed the door after Charlie and Jane, and it began its ascent soon after.

It was one of many moments during their vacation in which Elizabeth had wondered what she was doing there. Charlie had invited Jane to join his family on their annual stay at their vacation home in Park City; when Jane had said she didn't want to leave her sister alone in their apartment for a week, he'd gladly included Elizabeth in the invitation as well.

Elizabeth had assured Jane she would be fine spending a week by herself, but had eventually decided to go to please her sister.

So far it had been…interesting.

"It'll be fine," Jane said. "I'm sure we'll be moving again in no time."

"That's good, because I'm hungry." Elizabeth thought of the restaurant they were going to at the top of the mountain with longing.

Jane laughed, then paused, and Elizabeth heard the muffled tones of other voices. "Oh, hold on, Lizzy."

As she waited, Elizabeth noticed a movement out of the corner of her eye. She looked at Darcy, who was now pacing back and forth, his movements stiff and his eyes downcast; his steps were limited though, considering there wasn't much space to pace. Elizabeth nearly rolled her eyes at his impatience when Jane spoke again.

"Lizzy, Charlie says Darcy is afraid of heights."

"What?" Elizabeth watched Darcy more carefully. "Really?"

"Yes, so be nice to him."

Elizabeth had a retort on the tip of her tongue, but another look at how tense Darcy was stopped her from voicing it. "I…I will. I promise."

"Good. See you at the top."

"You too."

She slipped her phone back in her coat pocket, considered Darcy. He was obviously uncomfortable; before, she had assumed it was because of her, but now she realized he just didn't want to be on the gondola at all. When his pacing didn't let up, compassion moved her to him, and she calmly placed a hand on his arm. He stiffened, but raised his eyes from the floor.

"Pacing won't make the gondola start moving again, you know," she teased gently. "Why don't you come sit."

He slowly raised his gaze to hers. "I…need a distraction."

She nodded. "You could always talk to me."

He studied her carefully as she studied him. Then he frowned even more, if that was possible. "Charlie told you."

She angled her head. "If you're referring to your fear of heights, Charlie told Jane, who relayed it to me. We are stuck together, after all."

He looked down at the floor again, seeming to deflate as his shoulders slumped. The sudden vulnerability had her taking his hand, pulling him back to the bench along the windows.

"Sit," she ordered.

He obeyed without comment or resistance, resting his elbows on his thighs and dropping his head in his hands. She sat next to him.

"Hey." She nudged him with her elbow. "It'll be fine."

He sighed. "Logically, I know that. I just…"

"Fear isn't always exactly logical."

"Yes, but I meant..." He paused, then slowly sat up straighter. "I don't like to show weakness."

She let out a half-laugh. "Does anyone? So you have a completely normal and not uncommon fear; as far as I'm concerned that makes you human, in which case I would say you should be grateful."

When he looked at her incredulously, she knew her way of distracting him was working.

"Grateful for my fear?"

"Yeah. It makes you approachable. Until now you were so stoic I had a hard time imagining you being friendly, much less afraid of anything." She softened her tone when she saw how surprised he was by her statement. "Now I know you're just as human as the rest of us."

"Have I really been that bad?" he asked quietly.

She shrugged. "You don't have a problem being rude, but again, until now I just kind of assumed you had a stick up your ass, like Caroline."

He snorted. "And now?"

She shrugged again. "Jury's still out."

He smiled a little, and they sat quietly for a few moments; she could tell he was deep in thought and didn't want to interrupt him.

"So you think my fear is a good thing because it's a vulnerability that reminds me I'm human?" he finally said.

"Yeah. Basically."

"Even if it means others may look down on me for it?"

She turned to face him more directly. "Look, Darcy, everyone has vulnerabilities—no one's perfect, which is a phrase I'm sure you've heard before. If you look down on yourself for yours, then of course others will; whereas, if you embrace them as part of who you are, then maybe they'll look down on you, maybe they won't. But, in my opinion, if someone thinks less of you when they don't really understand you, then fuck them."

He raised a brow as he faced her. "Even you?"

"Even me," she said with an acknowledging smile.

He glanced out the window for a second, an odd smile on his face. "You're doing a very good job of distracting me."

"Evidently not good enough, if you noticed that's what I was doing."

"No really," he shook his head. "If I had to be stuck in a gondola with anyone, I'm glad it was you."

"Really?"

He brought his gaze back to hers. "Your presence...calms me. No one else has that effect on me. Sort of like how your sister tempers Charlie's exuberance."

She blinked. "That sounded like a compliment."

"It was."

And here she'd thought he resented her presence and disapproved of Charlie dating Jane.

"I don't know what to say."

He reached out to place a hand over hers, squeezed. "You're not required to say anything. I just wanted to say thank you for helping me."

"You're welcome." She looked down at his warm hand covering hers, and curse it all, she couldn't deny the little flutter in her stomach. "So what now? Any other distraction ideas?"

"Just one."

When he said nothing else, she looked up to find him staring at her intently.

"Are you going to tell me what it is?"

"No." He shook his head, that odd smile appearing again.

"Why not?"

"Because I'm not sure you would approve."

Her eyes narrowed in utter confusion. "What does that even mean?"

"I…" He withdrew his hand to run it over his face. Finally he let out a breath and leveled his gaze on her again. "Can I kiss you?"

She only stared back, but the flutter moved up to her throat. "What?"

Suddenly he could only look anywhere but at her. "I've been thinking about kissing you since you first opened your mouth to me, to the point where it sometimes distracts me from everything else." He looked back at her, his expression unsure.

Heat flooded her, but she couldn't move. "Is this a joke?"

"No." He scrunched up his face. "Why would I joke about this?"

"Because you've never acted like you like me."

"I do like you, Elizabeth. Quite a bit, actually." He reached for her hand again, but she pulled hers back.

"But…you told Charlie I wasn't anything special."

He started. "What? When did I say that?"

"You don't remember? It was at the bar when we met."

He winced and shut his eyes in remembrance. "I do remember now. I'm so sorry. I was hardly paying attention to anything that night, much less who I was looking at when Charlie was trying to get me talk to strangers. I just wanted to be invisible."

Her brow quirked. "So you didn't know it was me you were talking about?"

"No. I know that's no excuse for saying something so rude in the first place, so I can only apologize and assure you it's completely untrue. You have the most spectacular blue eyes I've ever seen, and you are wonderful, Elizabeth Bennet. And if anyone says otherwise, fuck them," he said in reiteration of her words to him.

Fighting the smile that wanted to take over her face, she decided to go easy on him and say the words she was sure he was hoping she'd say.

"Including you?"

"Including me."

She let the smile spread slowly. "I suppose I can forgive you, then."

His eyes darkened and zeroed in on her lips. He swallowed. "You never answered my question."

She knew what question he was referring to. She opened her mouth but no sound came out. Eventually she found her voice, despite the fact he hadn't taken his eyes off her.

"Darcy, I—"

"Will."

"What?"

"Please don't call me Darcy. I want to hear you call me Will."

She couldn't help the upward curve of her lips. "You know, you should ride gondolas more often. I like this side of you." She paused. "Will."

Before she realized she'd subconsciously begun to lean toward him, he dipped his head and pressed his lips to hers. He lifted both his hands to cup her face, his fingers moving through her hair. Though surprised, her eyes fluttered closed at the sensation. She moaned when his tongue swept over hers, and she gripped his shoulders.

On a groan, he pulled back just slightly. "You have no idea how often I've wanted to kiss that sexy smirk off your face."

"You don't know how often I've wanted to slap the smug one off yours."

He frowned, but when he saw that she was smiling, he tugged her closer. She reciprocated by sliding her arms around his neck.

"So, you really like me?" She said, her brow arched again.

"I must have hidden my feelings too well if you have to ask," he said, moving his lips to within a breath of hers. "To clarify: I more than simply like you."

"You wouldn't ask Caroline to kiss you if she was here instead of me?"

He jerked back to look at her amused face. "*Fuck* no."

A laugh bubbled out of her, and she leaned her forehead against his chest. After a moment, she felt his body shake as he joined her laughter. When their laughter subsided, she lifted her head, grinning.

"You know I'm teasing you?"

"I do," he grinned back. "I love it when you tease me."

"You do?"

"Yes." He cupped her cheek. "I have feelings for you, Elizabeth. And at this point I think it's fairly obvious I'm insanely attracted to you."

"Lizzy."

"Hm?"

"Call me Lizzy."

"Lizzy," he murmured, and her heart warmed at how breathless he sounded.

Who knew? she thought. Lizzy Bennet could make Will Darcy breathless. She couldn't deny it was empowering, especially since he'd succeeded in stealing her breath more than once. She couldn't deny that anymore either—which was a relief.

Evidently there was no longer any need to suppress her attraction.

Her fingers feathered into his hair as his lips met hers again, his hands roaming down and grasping her back. It was like a battle of wills; her heart pounded as her mouth clashed against his, fighting for more of him.

A sexy growl escaped his lips as he moved them over her cheek, her jaw, her neck.

"God, Lizzy. Is this real?"

"Yes." She managed to get the word out before her mouth was occupied again. He pulled at her legs until they were strewn across his lap and her torso was flush with his. Fumbling with the zipper on her jacket, he pulled it down far enough for his hand to reach inside and palm her breast. Even through her sweater, the feel of him touching her drove her crazy. She hummed to show her approval and grazed her teeth along his earlobe.

His eyes opened on a gasp. "Jesus."

She grinned in satisfaction at the hot look in his eyes; to her surprise, his next kiss was tender, and he sighed as his lips gentled over hers.

And then, on a lurch, the gondola moved.

Eyes wide, Will smiled in relief as they finally moved toward their destination. Elizabeth set her feet back on the car's floor, but twined her fingers through his.

When they finally reached the top and exited the confined space, Elizabeth scanned the crowd for the rest of their party.

Will squeezed her hand. "I'm so glad to be off that thing I could kiss the ground."

She deliberately stepped closer to him. "The ground, huh?"

"Or I could do this."

In one sweeping movement, he gripped her waist and laid a smacking kiss on her lips. Since she'd been expecting it, she stood on her tiptoes and gripped his shoulders, kissed him back.

"We should find the others," she said after lingering a moment.

"Do we have to?"

Her stomach loudly proclaimed its emptiness, and she gave him a pointed look. "Yes."

His laugh came easily, and he took her hand. "Alright, then. But you have to promise to sit by me at dinner."

She smiled, thinking how strange it was how much things had changed in only half an hour. Before, she'd dreaded riding the gondola with him. Now, she relished the idea of sitting next to him at dinner, and it was a promise readily made.

"Done."

SEAGLASS AND SIMPLICITY

ONE

BREATHING DEEP, Evie inhaled fresh summer air tinged with the spray of sea salt, a subtle fishiness, and that inexplicable beach scent often simply described as "sun."

Waves rolled and lapped at her toes as she meandered along the stretch of beach she and her friends would be calling home for the next week. The mint green she'd painted her toenails was still visible even through the sand that was starting to cake around them, and it made her smile.

She was the first to arrive at the pretty powder-blue beachside bungalow—aptly named Seaglass Cottage—they'd booked for the five of them. They'd had a couple girl-time getaways in the few years since their college graduation, but this would be the first time in over a year. Even though they all lived in Chicago, or a suburb thereof, conflicting schedules were a common deterrent. Life too often got in the way, Evie thought, but now they'd have this time to reconnect.

She'd been hoping they could all fly to the little coastal Maine town together, but those conflicting schedules meant Josie and Lucile would have to take a later flight; and Cassie and Grace had been suspiciously secretive when they'd decided to come separately, with the excuse they were bringing "a surprise."

At least they all had the same flight back.

Since she had time, she took the opportunity to stroll farther down the shoreline, relishing whenever the tail end of a wave swept over her feet. The cottages spotting the stretch of beach were pretty and cozy, adding to that idyllic-beach setting she'd anticipated for the past few months, and the tall wood pier in the distance made the charming picture complete.

As she rambled, she kept her eye out for bigger shells and pieces of sea glass, swirling sand and water with her toes while her sandals swung from her hand, a calm smile on her face. It was this image of her—a free-spirited young woman simply enjoying her surroundings, her wide-brimmed sun hat perfectly accenting her long, dark blonde waves—that captured the attention of someone walking down the pier, and made him smile.

Absorbed in watching a crane trudge through the water, it was a moment before Evie got the sense someone was watching her. She turned to face the pier, tilting her head at the man who'd stopped on the boardwalk.

It was too far away to really see his face, but he was tall, his hair dark, his skin lightly tanned. He stood with his hands in his pockets, gazing out over the beach and at her. She pulled off her sunglasses and sent him a small smile and wave.

He seemed surprised, but smiled and waved back; then, to her delight, he gave a slight bow. Amused, she laughed and gave him a curtsy.

She wondered if he would come down, debated climbing the pier's steps, when her phone buzzed. She pulled it from her back pocket, unsurprised at the text from Josie informing her she and Lucile had arrived. When she glanced at the guy on the pier, she saw he was still watching her, and as she looked up, he tilted his head. With a shrug, she held up her phone in indication she had to go, then put it back in her pocket.

Was it her, or did his shoulders slump a little?

Well, she could understand his disappointment, as she felt a twinge of it herself. But perhaps they would meet again.

To cheer him a little she gave him another wave, and in a bold move—even for her—blew him a kiss. She saw him straighten—probably in surprise—but a moment later, he held his hand over his heart as though he'd caught the kiss.

Smirking in amusement, she turned and went back the way she came. It was a pleasant walk, but she found her solitude wasn't as appealing as it was before, and she wondered if she should have invited her pier Romeo to walk her back.

As she approached the back French doors of the cottage, one of them opened, and Josie and Lucile burst out, kicking up sand as they ran to enfold Evie in a group hug.

"If I'm not alone, then girls' beach week has officially started," Evie said as she squeezed them back.

"Well, actually." Luce gave them a conspiratorial grin. "It might not be just a girls' week."

"What do you mean?" Josie asked.

"I may have wrangled the surprise out of Grace."

Evie smirked. "Sneaky. And are you going to tell us, or are you going to lord it over us?"

"Oh, it's too good not to share." Lucile paused, leaned in, and in a stage whisper said, "They're bringing their brothers."

Evie choked out a laugh. "They're bringing their brothers on a girls' trip?"

"No," Lucile clarified as she rolled her eyes. "The guys are staying at a separate rental, having a guys' trip. But we'll finally get to really meet them!"

The elusive brothers in question were Grace's brother, Daniel, and Cassie's brother, Brandon. They'd seen pictures over the years, and had been told countless stories about the pair, as well as Grace and Daniel's cousins, Matt and Richard. But they'd only very briefly met the two after their college graduation ceremony before being whisked away for pictures and time with their families.

"I'll believe it when I see it."

"This is great!" Josie said. "We'll have to plan some activities with all of us."

"I fully agree," Lucile nodded. "Anyway, Grace said they're getting the guys settled, having lunch with them, then the guys will drop them off."

Josie looked at her watch. "What should we do while we wait?"

"Well, I don't know about you guys," Evie cocked a thumb toward the wide open water, "but that ocean is calling my name."

"Perfect," Josie grinned. "Let's start the week as we mean to go on."

And so it was that after donning their suits, the three of them found themselves lounging in some of the inflatables Josie had picked up, chatting and soaking up the sun.

Evie watched as Josie, on her giant unicorn, lazily trailed her fingers through the water, eyes closed while her sunglasses sat on top of her perfectly coiled coppery-red hair. Though Evie could never begrudge her friend her beauty, with her crystal blue eyes and titian locks that fell in soft waves, Josie looked like the real life version of Ariel from *The Little Mermaid*.

Evie's own hair was a naturally streaked dirty blonde, with shades ranging from a light sandy brown, to a golden honey; though Cassie had once insisted on teaching her how to make them into the effortless look known as "beach waves," it often hung in untamed limp waves down her back since she couldn't be bothered most of the time. She had a smattering of freckles over her nose and cheeks—something her mother despaired of, but she herself adored—and bright hazel eyes accented with green, gray, and brown.

And Lucile, Evie thought, was classically pretty, with sharp features and high cheekbones, bright green eyes, and thick, straight hair the color of brown sugar, which she often kept up in a ponytail.

Stretching herself out of her reverie, Evie submerged her lower half into the water, her arms dangling over the side of her pineapple, and kicked herself closer to where Lucile floated on her shark. As she moved she thought she felt something brush up her thigh, and she squealed, kicking out her legs.

"What?" Luce asked her.

Evie peered into the water. "Seaweed, I think. Felt weird on my leg."

"Oh," Lucile laughed. "Yeah, there's a lot of that around."

"I noticed."

It was true. They'd had to wade through clusters of seaweed to get out far enough to float. Even so, Evie would rather avoid the slithery feeling on her legs. She shook off a shiver, and decided she'd lazed about enough.

She let go of her pineapple and let herself sink under the surface, closing her eyes as warm seawater rushed over her. She re-emerged feeling pleasantly refreshed, as the water really was that perfect bathwater temperature, then dived down again to swim farther out. When she felt she'd gone far enough, she let the momentum of the waves speed her return.

And she was rewarded with the sight of Cassie and Grace walking toward the water dressed to swim, clutching the remaining inflatables—a penguin and a dolphin. The three in the ocean moved to shallow water so they could stand and hug their friends.

"Boy, do we have news for you!" Grace bounced up and down, her curling dark hair floating around her in the water, soft blue eyes wide with anticipation. With her glowing olive skin she seemed to have a perpetual tan; and with her sun hat and sunglasses, Evie thought with amusement that her friend was currently the epitome of the 'coastal' vibe.

Cassie, with her mahogany hair picking up hints of red in the sun, grinned widely but kept silent. There was something secretive about her smile, a different kind of anticipation behind her bright green eyes.

"You already told us about your brothers," Lucile smirked.

Cassie's mouth dropped open. "Grace!"

But Grace only smiled. "But I didn't tell you everything. I didn't tell you our cousins are also here."

Evie laughed, nudging Lucile playfully. "And you thought you were so clever."

Lucile shook her head, but couldn't hold back a smile. "You got me, G. So we're meeting the whole gang?"

"Yep! And..." Grace's gaze slid over to Cassie, who had gotten comfortable on her dolphin. "Cassie has a development to share."

Climbing back onto her unicorn, Josie perked up. "Ooh, that sounds promising."

"Alright." Cassie bit her lip, and the others got comfortable on their floaties as she spoke with deliberate calm—Evie wasn't fooled though. Cass was supremely giddy about something. "I didn't say anything because it's only been a couple weeks and I wasn't sure what would happen...but I'm officially dating Richard."

Josie clapped her hands together. "For real?"

And suddenly, Cassie's face broke out in a huge grin—there it was, Evie thought, grinning back.

"Well, finally," Lucile teased.

"I know, right?" Grace flicked some water at Cassie. "They've only had a crush on each other *forever*."

"Shut up." Cassie put on her best haughty face, flicking some water back at Grace, but it wasn't long before she was smiling again.

"So when will we meet them?" Evie asked.

Grace stretched out on her penguin. "Well, when we were at lunch, there was this poster for a party on the beach. Hosted by locals, but encouraging vacationers to come, too."

"Beach party?" Lucile sat up straighter, the plastic of the shark squeaking with the movement. "Heck yeah, let's do it."

"Good, because the guys want to go," Cassie said. "So, what else have you guys been up to today?"

"I took a walk on the beach," Evie started.

"Nice, but uneventful," Lucile interrupted. "If only you'd met a handsome stranger."

Evie shot her friend a wry grin. "As a matter of fact, I did—at least I assume he was handsome."

"Oh, well in that case, please continue."

She told them about the brief flirtation she'd engaged in with the guy she'd seen on the pier. Lucile was disappointed she hadn't introduced herself, but suggested she might run into him at the party; they all agreed it was a possibility, but since Evie hadn't been able to see his face, she might not even realize if she did meet him.

They stayed out on the water a little longer, talking about work, TV shows, and random bits of daily life—Josie in particular had some entertaining stories about her cat—before heading back in to shower and dress for the party.

Feeling the beachy mood, Evie chose a flirty green sundress with a very twirly skirt she was now very glad she'd packed. Cassie wore a billowy off-white shirt with jean shorts and colorful sandals, while Grace slipped on a black sundress, and Josie donned a light blue romper. And Lucile surprised them all when instead of her usual shorts and t-shirt, she wore a flowy black skirt with a summery red blouse, and left her hair down.

Grace motioned for them all to gather on the back deck, pulling out her phone. "We look pretty hot, if I do say so myself. This calls for a group photo."

In agreement, they all leaned in close as Grace stretched out her arm, beaming as she took the picture, and preserved the memory.

· · · · ·

THE FIVE OF them sat comfortably on several of the beach blankets laid out along the beach. People milled around them, chatting, grabbing drinks, and playing beach volleyball.

"There's some pretty hot guys here," Lucile said, scoping out the crowd.

"Yeah," Evie said, her tone deadpan. "Because we came here for hot guys."

"Well, I did." Lucile shrugged. "I want to get laid, so if he's hot enough he'll suit me."

They all blinked at her.

"Even if you have no connection?" Josie asked.

"Just because a guy is good-looking doesn't necessarily mean he's good in bed," Cass pointed out.

Luce only shrugged again. "I'm willing to take my chances."

Evie could only shake her head. "How—"

"There they are!" Grace jumped to her knees, waving an arm to capture the attention of a group of four guys coming down the beach steps.

Seeing her, they all smiled—well, all but one—and headed toward them. The blonde one Evie assumed was Richard bent to kiss Cassie before sitting down next to her. The others remained standing as Grace introduced them.

"You remember my brother, Daniel." She gestured to the unsmiling one, a tall, almost lanky guy with a sweep of curling ink-dark hair and nearly golden olive skin, identical to that of his sister, which Evie knew came from their mother's Greek heritage. With a spurt of attraction, Evie recalled his eyes were also the same soft blue. He nodded at the group in acknowledgement, barely looking at them while Grace continued.

"You probably guessed that's Richard," she said, pointing to the blonde-and-blue-eyed guy next to Cassie, then one of the others who could have been his twin, "and this is his older brother, Matt."

Matt and Richard both grinned, while the fourth member of their party—a guy with a curly mass of mahogany hair—began to shake hands with them all while Grace introduced him. "And you've also met Brandon, Cass's brother."

Brandon's bottle-brown gaze lingered on Josie as he clasped hands with her. "It's nice to finally meet you all for real this time," he said.

Evie didn't miss how Cassie rolled her eyes at her brother, but she cheerfully picked up the introductions for Matt and Richard. "And these are our friends, Josie, Evie, and Luce."

"It sounds corny to say, but we really have heard a lot about you guys," Richard said, draping an arm around Cass.

"It's true," Matt seconded. "It's hard to believe it took us all this long to meet."

Josie smiled. "We've also heard a lot about you."

"That's an understatement," Evie teased. "Grace and Cass haven't shut up about you guys for four years."

"Aw." Richard put his hand over his heart and sniffled as though he were particularly moved. "I never knew you guys cared so much."

"Wise-ass." Cassie elbowed him, smiling as the group chuckled—all except Daniel, of course. He stood slightly behind everyone else, looking out at the ocean more than at anyone, a blank expression lining his face.

Brandon gestured to the row of coolers lining the sand near the stairs. "Anyone want a drink?"

"Ooh, yes! What do you want?" Grace looped an arm through her brother's, trying to draw him into the group. "Daniel, come help us get drinks for everyone."

"Sorry, G," he said, frowning. "I was going to find a bathroom. Excuse me."

He pulled away and headed toward the set of outhouses the host had set up near the stairs without another word. Grace let out a huff.

"Someone's grumpy today."

"He was fine earlier." Matt frowned as he watched his cousin make his escape. "Must have been that phone call."

Now Grace frowned. "What phone call?"

The guys only shrugged.

"He wouldn't say," said Richard.

A moment of awkward silence followed, and picking up on it, Josie rose to her feet. "I'll help you guys with the drinks. What does everyone want?"

Most of them settled on a beer or a seltzer, and since there were nine of them (Grace figured her brother would want a beer), Matt also volunteered to help carry. As they headed off, Richard turned to Cass and whispered something in her ear, causing her to smile and bite her lip.

"We're going to take a quick walk on the beach," she said. "We'll be back in a few minutes."

Lucile wiggled her eyebrows suggestively. "Don't do anything I wouldn't do."

Richard chuckled, and though Cassie blushed, she returned her friend's teasing by sticking her tongue out at her.

When they were out of earshot, Luce leaned back on her arms and sent Evie a look. "What do you want to bet 'walk' is code for k-i-s-s-i-n-g?"

Smiling, Evie only shook her head. "You're so romantic today, Luce."

"Hey, sometimes you've got to live a little vicariously. Besides, I'm not really romantic. You know that."

Evie opened her mouth to respond, but the others returned with the drinks.

"Where'd they go?" Matt gestured to the empty space where Richard and Cassie had been sitting.

"A walk on the beach," Evie informed them.

"Which undoubtedly means alone time," Lucile added.

"Ah." Matt nodded. "Can't say I blame them."

It wasn't long before the others, including Daniel, returned, and as they sat around chatting, the low hum of music began playing.

"Ooh, dance with me!" Cassie jumped up and tugged on Richard's hands. He made a show of reluctance, but was ultimately dragged to the section of beach where a dance crowd was forming with a grin on his face.

"Would you like to dance, Josie?" Brandon asked with a near-puppy expression.

With a small smile, Josie took his outstretched hand. "Sure."

Now it was Grace who rolled her eyes, and Evie didn't miss the look of disappointment on Matt's face. *Poor guy,* she thought. Josie just had that effect on people. But he recovered quickly and turned to her.

"How about you, Evie, would you like to dance?"

"Absolutely," she said as she rose. "But I have to warn you, I am an excellent dancer, so if you can't keep up I'll ditch you."

He laughed, tugging her hand to give her a quick twirl. "Oh, I can keep up."

And he did. It seemed all the Flemming-Locke cousins knew what they were doing on the dance floor—she caught Richard effortlessly leading Cassie, and even Daniel smiled a little as he danced with his sister. Brandon didn't have the same finesse, but he made up for it with enthusiasm.

She found that out herself when he asked her to dance next.

They were all asked to dance by each guy, except Daniel, who only danced with Grace and Cassie, then went to go sulk near the food tables. Grace assured them that wasn't unusual behavior for him, but Evie noticed she looked a little concerned regardless. Throughout the dances, Evie could have sworn she saw Daniel watching her, but it was hard to tell.

At some point they all broke off to grab their drinks and get food; Evie and Lucile each made up a couple of hot dogs for themselves, sitting on a flat wooden log acting as a bench near the ring of large rocks where the bonfire would be when the sun went down. They'd lost sight of the others for the time being, but it was nice to have a moment to just sit and people-watch.

When they'd finished their hot dogs, Lucile began gathering up their trash. "I'm gonna hit the bathroom."

"I'll hold down the fort."

Finishing off her beer from earlier—it had long since lost its chill, but she found she didn't mind—Evie stretched out her legs, digging her toes into the sand and looking out at the ocean, grateful for the momentary respite.

Her pleasant solitude was interrupted when someone sat down next to her—rather closely. She turned her head to find a pleasant-looking guy with trim, light brown hair covered by a fedora, a straight nose, and an overconfident look about him peering at her.

"I couldn't help but notice how lonely you look, and thought I'd offer to keep you company," he said suggestively.

"Oh, actually—"

"I'm Hunter," he continued, and thrust out his hand.

She shook it reluctantly. "Evie."

"Nice to meet you, Evie," he said, slinking an arm over her shoulders. "How about we head back to my hotel room—or your place if you prefer?"

"No, thank you," she said politely as she used her free hand to lift his arm off her, then let go so that it fell listlessly back at his side.

Leaning a little closer, he wiggled his eyebrows. "I assure you I can make it worth your while."

"Still no."

"I've been told I'm very good with my hands."

"Good for you," she said blithely. "I'm still not going to sleep with you."

He frowned. "Are you a lesbian?"

Was this guy for real?

"Not that that's any of your business, but no."

"Then you have no reason not to accept my generous offer."

"Actually, I have lot of reasons." Evie deliberately scooted farther away. *Where was Luce?* "I don't owe you any explanation, but since you don't seem to know how to take no for an answer, I'll inform you my main reason is because I don't even know you."

"Ah, but I'm offering to let you get to know me *very* well."

When he tried to put his arm around her again, she rose to her feet. Though she nearly told him to fuck off, she restrained herself, as she wasn't sure even that would get through his clearly over-amplified ego. Walking away was the better choice.

"I'm going to the bathroom. Goodbye."

She stalked away before he could respond, and thankfully she hadn't made it far when Lucile appeared, looking past Evie's shoulder at Hunter.

"Who's that?" she asked. "He's cute."

"He's an ass." Evie gripped Luce's arm and pulled her into the crowd, back toward the drinks. She tossed her empty can in the giant recycling bin and yanked another beer from a cooler at random, cracked open the top, and took a few long swills.

Lucile raised a brow as she grabbed one for herself. "That bad, huh?"

"He asked if I was a lesbian because I said I wouldn't sleep with him."

"What the fuck?"

Evie replayed the conversation for her, feeling better once she'd ranted about it a little. But her mood soured again when Lucile seemed to shrug the whole thing off.

"I'm sorry he was a dick about it, but I think maybe you expect too much of the casual vacation crowd. Lots of people here are just looking for a fling—he just went about it really badly."

Evie narrowed her eyes. "So that means some guy can insist I don't mean it when I say I don't want that?"

She sighed, knowing this was something she and Luce had always disagreed on—Lucile had never been the romantic type. Now that she'd gotten her insult and frustration off her chest, she was able to regain some equanimity. She wasn't one for melancholy, and she wasn't going to start now—looking around, she let the vibrancy of the seaside and the party soothe her.

The sand was soft and welcoming, there was a breeze just strong enough to be annoying, but not enough to be unpleasant, and the last dregs of light were fading, leaving behind streaks of Dreamsicle orange, coral pink, and the early gray of nightfall, making the clouds look like cotton candy.

The sound of rolling waves was constant—not loud, but noticeable enough to drown out any whispered conversations, as was the cheery music playing from a set of speakers on the host's deck.

It was perfect, Evie couldn't help thinking. Then recalling her earlier swim with her friends, thought the only real thing to complain about was the ridiculous amount of seaweed.

She shuddered at the thought of it slinking around her legs.

It was just a plant, but dang, it freaked her out a little to have unknown bits of ocean life brushing against her unexpectedly.

But though the moon was a great source of light, no one would be going for a dip in the dark. Everyone was gathered for the bonfire—which was in the process of being lit—and booze; and maybe, like Lucile, some were looking for some particular company for the night. She wasn't naive enough to think otherwise.

"All I'm saying is," Lucile continued as she scoped the crowd, "realistically, if you want a hot vacation hookup, you shouldn't expect him to be perfect. If you're attracted to him, why not?"

"I don't want a vacation hookup," Evie reminded her. "And even if I did, I don't think having standards is a bad thing. Mutual respect, mutual trust, and mutual affection or attraction is all I ask for. Because if you don't respect, trust, or like each other, what's the point?"

"Um, possibly great sex?"

Evie heroically restrained from rolling her eyes—she understood her friend, but just couldn't agree with her.

"Sorry, Luce. Sex isn't just physical for me. It's an intimate experience, and I don't know how to be casual about it. I sure as hell could never sleep with someone who doesn't respect me. I'm attracted to more than just looks."

Lucile sighed. "I get that. I do," she insisted when Evie raised a brow. "I just…according to society, I'm not fashionably beautiful, and so I have to set my expectations a little lower than someone like you or Josie."

"Society is stupid," Evie glowered. "And you're just as attractive as Josie or me."

"It is, and that may be." Lucile only shrugged. "But I don't feel like I have any right to be picky, so for now at least, I'm going to base whether or not I would sleep with anyone here on how attracted I am to them."

Unsure what else she could say to her friend, Evie contemplated her response. Before she could form one, she noticed Brandon break off from the dance crowd and approach Daniel off by the end of the coolers, facing away from the crowd.

She hadn't realized he was standing so close by—she was surprised he was still here, to be honest—but she and Lucile were close enough to hear their conversation in the crowd.

"Dude, you're bumming everyone out standing over here by yourself. Come on and dance with us."

"I'm really not in the mood."

"Doesn't mean you can't end up having a good time," Brandon insisted.

"Doubtful."

"How do you know if you don't try?" Spotting Evie and Lucile, Brandon perked up. "Look, a couple of Grace's friends are right over there. I know you saw how good a dancer Evie is—why don't you ask her?"

"Which one was that?" Daniel stopped brooding long enough to turn his head in their direction. Though it was almost full dark now, she knew the moment his eyes met hers. She didn't know what she was expecting, but it certainly wasn't his next words.

"She seems nice enough, but I'm not interested in some shameless flirt, even if she is Grace's friend."

TWO

EVIE BLINKED in utter shock as the words left his mouth. Eyes narrowing, she lifted her chin in defiance, and her brow automatically raised in a challenging arch. To let him know what she thought of his insult, she folded her arms and stuck out her tongue with as much defiance as she could portray.

She knew she'd hit the mark when his eyes widened. To her amusement, his mouth dropped open.

"Yeah, I heard you, asshole," she muttered to herself, turning away and taking a sip of her beer.

"Well, you got his attention," Lucile said, nudging her. "He's coming over here."

"Ugh. Why?"

"Guess you'll just have to ask him."

And a moment later, she felt his presence next to her and turned her head to directly meet his eyes. He was stiff, clearly uncomfortable, as it took him a moment to meet her gaze.

He finally said, "Hi."

Evie raised her brows. "Hi," she said slowly, and took another pull of her beer.

Lucile cleared her throat. "Umm, I'm just gonna get another beer."

When she was gone, Evie looked at Daniel expectantly.

"I, uh..." He started, stopped, started again. "I'm sorry about what I just said. I don't usually go around being so rude for no reason; I should never have said something so shitty."

"Then why did you?"

"Pardon?"

"If you don't think you should have said it, then why did you?" Evie said slowly.

He shuffled and cast his eyes over the growing crowd. "I guess I'm just not very comfortable in crowds. Brandon was pressuring me to be more sociable."

Something Evie understood, but she wasn't about to let him off so easily. She nodded, bringing a slightly teasing tone to her voice. "I find that people tend to tell the truth more openly when they're either drunk, or when they feel cornered. With the latter, they may lash out with words they know will hurt, and there's usually some truth to those words."

"Exactly." He seemed relieved for a moment, but then frowned. "Wait, no."

He turned to face her more directly, and took a moment to pull himself together before looking her in the eye. "Are you saying you think I meant what I said, that I'm just apologizing because I feel like I should?"

Evie shrugged as though she didn't care. "It's a possibility. It's more that while I understand your excuses, it doesn't really make me feel any better about you using me as an excuse not to interact with people."

When he opened his mouth, she held up a hand to stall him. "Look, I get where you're coming from. We all say stupid or hurtful shit from time to time. But if you're going to apologize, I don't want you to beat around the bush. No prevarication, just own your mistake and be honest."

"I have been honest."

"Yes, but you've also been reluctant," she pointed out. "I can partially chalk that up to your social awkwardness, but I imagine part of you is a little too proud to properly humble yourself."

She watched as he took a slow, deep breath—in and out.

"You're Evie, right?" he asked quietly.

"Evie Bishop," she nodded. "And you're Grace's brother."

He winced, but nodded and held out his hand, and she cautiously took it. "Yes, and I sincerely apologize for degrading you. It was uncalled for, and untrue. In fact, I think I reacted so strongly to Brandon pushing me because you're one of the most beautiful women I've ever seen, and quite honestly I had no idea what to do. I just said the opposite of what I felt to get him to leave me alone."

Her brows showed her skepticism as she shook his hand. "Not to be nit-picky, because I appreciate the more forward apology, but don't you think you're laying on the flattery a little thick?"

"Oh, no. I never flatter," he said earnestly.

"Never?" she smirked, letting go of his hand.

He shook his head. "You can ask my friends, or Grace, if you don't believe me. I tend to be rather blunt, even if I'm saying something positive."

Evie shook her head back, but revealed her growing amusement with a small smile. "You shameless flirt, you."

He let out a short laugh, then shoved his hands in the pockets of his shorts. "Yeah, you may have guessed I'm pretty terrible at flirting."

"Mm." Evie neither agreed nor disagreed, and took another pull on her beer. "Can't say I'm very fluent in flirtation myself, but I am pretty sure that such an art takes practice."

He nodded, but for the first time the corner of his lips began to twitch upward. "What are you fluent in?" he asked.

"Sarcasm."

"Figures." His smile grew, as something in her air and manners—not to mention her looks—was familiar. He decided to take a chance. "I got the impression you're a bit of a free spirit, and I have to say I think my assessment was accurate."

Her brow raised of its own accord. "And what, may I ask, gave you that impression?"

Daniel shrugged, but kept his smile in place. "It's not every day a guy is blown a kiss from an enchanting stranger, then mocked by that same woman later that same day."

The amused smile dropped from her face, her demeanor softening into something resembling surprise, confusion, and interest.

"You...you're the guy from the pier?"

He nodded sheepishly. "And you're the girl from the beach."

"But..." She blinked at him. "This morning, you were so...*charming*. And then you came to this party all grumpy?"

"Yes, and I really am sorry about that." He sighed. "It's a long story. But the last thing I wanted was to insult the woman I was hoping to impress, if I found her."

Despite herself, Evie felt heat warming her cheeks, and her lips tugged in a small smile. "You wanted to impress me? But you didn't know I was Grace's friend."

In answer, he held out his hand again.

Intrigued, she took it, felt the gentle pressure when he squeezed—was it her, or did it feel more like a caress? "Evie, my encounter with you this morning was the first thing in the past couple weeks to make me smile. You have no idea how much I had to resist the urge to run after you. I've been remiss avoiding spending time with Grace's friends, and I'm the biggest fool in the world not to realize it was you I saw this morning the moment I saw you dancing."

Her smile was slow and teasing. "Are you sure you don't know how to flirt?"

He let out a half laugh as he let go of her hand. "You are literally the first person to call me charming."

"Well, you were," she shrugged. "Bowing at a stranger, catching her impromptu kisses."

"It was the boldest I'd been in a while," he confessed. "Perhaps because there was distance between us—it felt safer."

"Ah, so it's up close human interaction you don't like."

He shook his head. "I'm not sure how to respond to that."

"I'm just teasing you." She nudged him with her elbow.

"Yeah, Grace told me you do that. She said it helped bring her out of melancholy whenever she thought about Wickham."

Evie nodded solemnly. "I tried to get her to see it wasn't her fault he cheated on her, but I never knew if anything I did really helped."

"You helped her. You all did," he confirmed. "I've been meaning to thank you guys, but we never had opportunity to meet properly."

She tilted her head. "Yeah, why is that? We all live in the same city."

He shrugged. "Brandon and I were always busy, and I guess I, admittedly, was reluctant for the longest time. Grace and Cassie were always talking about how awesome their roommates were, and I got the sense they wanted to set at least one of us up."

She gave a nod of understanding. "And you didn't want to be set up. That's fair; I think I would also be reluctant under those circumstances. What changed your mind?"

"A few things, I guess." He paused for a moment, thinking about his response, and she took the opportunity to study his face. He was frowning slightly, and she determined it was just his 'thinking face'—her own thinking face sometimes made her look sad, she knew, as people sometimes asked her what was wrong and she had to assure them she was fine.

Up close, she realized he didn't necessarily look displeased, just a little uncomfortable.

"Grace started wearing me down when she mentioned this trip," he continued. "She pointed out it had been a while since I went on vacation. Then at some point Cassie showed Brandon a more recent picture of all of you together, and he started insisting we come and finally meet you."

Evie laughed knowingly. "If a pretty face was all it took, I'm surprised we didn't meet a few years ago."

The corner of his eyes crinkled as he smiled back at her. "Anyway, then

Grace had the idea to invite our cousins, too, so the four of us could have a guys' trip, and Rich and Matt were excited about it."

"The final nail in the coffin."

Now he laughed. "Basically. I didn't have much choice other than to concede. But I'm glad I did," he said, his eyes roaming back over to her.

Smiling, Evie polished off the last of her beer to keep herself from blushing again.

"Do you want another one?" he asked as she tossed it in the nearest receptacle.

"Sure."

He went over to one of the coolers, and when he returned with two beers, handed her one, she turned to him.

"So I know you said it's a long story, but do you want to talk about what had you in such a bad mood earlier?"

He cracked open his beer, the sound a pleasant soundtrack to the background chatter and the roll of waves. He took a sip, thinking again, his frown deepening.

Then he glanced at her, seeming to decide something. "Will you take a walk with me?"

Smiling, she looked out at the sky over the sea; some of the shoreline was dotted with the light of the long tiki lamps stuck in the sand, and with the addition of heightened flames from the bonfire, the beach was aglow with flickers of warmth. "You want to take a nighttime beach walk with me? How romantic," she teased, fluttering her lashes in an overzealous manner.

It worked.

He laughed, a deep chuckle that had him grinning at her. "Yes, I do. If I'm going to talk about this, I need to move."

"Alright. Lead the way, Casanova."

As she turned with him toward the water, she spotted Lucile, who caught her eye, and grinned, mouthed *told you.* Evie only rolled her eyes.

There were a handful of other people slowly walking along the shoreline, taking in the views, and they walked in silence for a few minutes. She didn't want to press him; if anything, his silence made her wonder if the question she'd asked him was too weighty a subject for two people who hardly knew each other.

"You don't have to tell me," she said softly. "I'm just now realizing it might be super personal, so I understand if you don't want to talk about it with someone you hardly know. I'm sorry for being so invasive."

He turned his head, regarding her with a quiet expression. "You're not invasive," he assured her. "And if I may say so, because of Grace I don't feel like I hardly know you. It's just, the situation is an odd one, and I don't really know how to talk about it."

She stopped to kick off her flip flops, picked them up. "Why is it odd?"

"It...involves a person who doesn't seem to understand how ridiculous she is." At Evie's inquiring brow, he chuckled. "My dad's business partner, Catherine. She's very...overbearing. And she thinks she knows what's best in any situation, even if it's a subject in which she has no experience."

"O-kay..."

He sighed. "She wants me to date her daughter."

Ignoring the unexpected flare of disappointment, she asked, "Do you want to date her?"

"No, and Anne doesn't want to date me, which we have both told her multiple times, but she keeps insisting."

Evie scrunched up her face in confusion. "Insisting how?"

"Well, almost every time she sees me she asks when I'm going to ask Anne out, trying to sell me some crap about how when Anne and I were kids, she and my mom had the idea we should get married someday." He kicked at the sand as he walked. "But I know it's crap because my mom said so herself.

"*And*—" he paused for dramatic effect; she didn't know if it was intentional or not, but either way it was endearing. "She's constantly saying things like, 'when you and Anne are married,' and sometimes even telling other people we'll be married someday."

"So basically, she's harassing you." Evie pointed out.

"I guess that would be accurate, yes."

"And your dad still works with her?"

He shrugged. "Despite her personality, she's good at what she does. He usually has someone else interact with her if he can avoid it. Plus, he's training me to take over in a few years; he assumes she'll retire when he does."

With a huff, Evie kicked at the water. "Something tells me if she weren't a partner, she wouldn't get away with it."

Daniel caught the look of exasperation on her face. "What do you mean?"

Rolling her eyes, Evie stopped to face him. "What do you mean what do I mean? It's pretty obvious the only reason she's still around is because her position is a powerful one—and she knows it. The way you've described it, she seems to think it's her prerogative to force her will on others, and apparently even people as powerful as she is let her get away with it. Sounds like a sorry excuse to avoid drama if you ask me. But is all that avoidance truly worth the harassment? What if she doesn't retire and it only gets worse? Just because she's a higher up doesn't make her behavior acceptable."

She held up a hand before he could respond. "So she's good at her job —so what? Someone else might be just as good, or better. No one is irreplaceable."

"I...never thought about it that way."

"Well, then," she shrugged, "Hopefully I'm helping you challenge your perspective."

"You are," he said as they started walking back toward the party. "Especially since—well, I never actually said why I was a grouch earlier. But it was because Catherine called me not long before we were going to head out to this party, and I don't recall ever giving her my personal number."

"What?"

"Yeah. I don't know how she got it, or who told her about this trip, but she seemed to think it would be a great opportunity for me to take Anne on a getaway. I told her I was already here and in no uncertain terms that it's a guys' trip, but she just kept going." He punctuated the last three words with such frustration, Evie couldn't help placing a hand on his arm.

"Please tell me you hung up on her."

"I did. She started calling back immediately, so I just turned my phone off."

"Definitely block her. And talk to your dad," Evie insisted, "or to HR. If it's causing you this much stress, it needs to be dealt with."

He looked at her then, his eyes tired but taking in every inch of her concerned face. "You're right," he acknowledged. "Enough is enough."

Satisfied, Evie nodded. And to her surprise, he gripped her hand in his, squeezed lightly before letting it go.

"Thank you," he said.

She cleared her throat as her belly fluttered. "No problem."

They'd walked farther than intended, so they turned back. It was full dark without the torchlight, the sky lit with pinpricks of stars, shining brighter with the new moon. Approaching the glow of the bonfire and torches in the distance somehow made everything feel more magical, Evie thought. They walked in companionable silence the rest of the way; she imagined he was mulling over her words and thinking about what he should do.

"You want another drink?" she asked him as they reached the bonfire, slipping a teasing tone into her words. "My treat."

He chuckled. "Yeah, sure."

As he took their empties, Evie wandered over to the row of coolers.

She grabbed him a beer, and was debating picking something else for herself when Lucile found her.

"You two seem to be getting on swimmingly."

Evie raised a brow at her smug friend. "We've been having a lovely chat, yes."

"Oh, come on." Lucile rolled her eyes. "I could see the sparks flying between you from halfway down the beach."

Laughing quietly, Evie pulled a hard cider from a cooler, grinned at her friend. "Turns out he's the guy from the pier."

"No shit?"

"None whatsoever."

"Well, damn." Lucile grinned back as she picked out a hard lemonade. "Maybe you should bring me with you next time, so I can find my own Romeo."

As if on cue, the guy from earlier popped up in front of them.

"Hello, ladies," he said slowly, in a low tone Evie assumed was supposed to sound seductive, but sounded more like he was talking to a pair of puppies.

Here we go, she thought as she stifled a mix of laughter and annoyance. She quickly settled on annoyance when he looked at her with a smug smile she couldn't like.

"Hello, Hunter."

Though she kept her tone as disinterested as possible, he didn't catch on. "Babe, won't you introduce me to your friend?"

Though it grated, she ignored the unwarranted nickname. "Hunter, this is Lucile; Luce, this is Hunter."

"Pleased to meet you," Hunter held out his hand.

Lucile tilted her head, assessing him as she shook it. "The pleasure is mine."

He winked. "Don't I know it."

With the formalities out of the way, he dropped her hand and turned to Evie as though Lucile wasn't there.

"The party's almost over, so I expect you're ready to take me up on my offer. Want me to take you to the dance floor first, or do you just want me to take you?"

Evie nearly shuddered—that was definitely the most cringe-worthy line she'd ever heard—but instead managed to stare him down.

"As I already told you, I'm not going to sleep with you. Ever."

"Babe—"

"*Stop* calling me that," she bit off. "We don't even know each other."

A little miffed, he raked his eyes over her body. "I mean, you're hot and all, but I doubt anyone else here would make you an offer like mine."

"I sincerely hope so."

Hunter opened his mouth, but Evie was spared whatever nonsense he was about to say when Daniel appeared at her side and casually slid his arm around her waist. He nodded to Lucile as he rested his hand lightly on Evie's hip, his face a questioning mask of calm when he looked down at her.

"I see you got held up." His eyes only briefly flicked to Hunter, but she understood.

"Indeed I did." She met his gaze and smiled as she spoke to let him know his presence was appreciated, then held out the beer she'd grabbed for him. "This is for you."

"Thanks, *babe*." He took a sip to hide the smirk twisting his mouth.

So he'd heard that. Well, two could play at that game. "You're welcome, *hon*."

"Who's this?" Hunter exclaimed.

Evie leaned into Daniel a little as she pursed her lips at Hunter. "That's really not any of your business."

Hunter folded his arms. "Actually, it is my business since I asked you out first."

"*Actually*, no, definitely still not your business. At all."

She was pretty close to junk-punching him, and she was positive Daniel and Lucile could sense it—Daniel because he could likely feel how tense she was, and Lucile because she knew her well. Daniel narrowed his eyes and seemed like he was about to say something, but Lucile beat him to it.

Stepping forward, she laid a hand on Hunter's arm. "If you'd still like to dance, Hunter, I'll dance with you."

For a moment, Hunter blinked in confusion, but as he registered what Lucile was saying, his eyes roamed over her much as they had over Evie. If she noticed, Lucile didn't so much as bat an eye.

"Of course—I'd never deny a lady anything." He cut Evie a look as he took Lucile's hand as though to tell her she was missing out. "Lucy, was it?"

"Eh, close enough." Lucile shrugged, sharing a look with Evie, who mouthed "thank you" to her friend as she let Hunter pull her into the dance crowd.

"Do I want to know what offer he was talking about?"

Though his grip loosened, Daniel kept his arm around her. When Evie looked up at him, he was glaring after Hunter, and a frown was forming on his face again.

Evie sighed. "I'll only tell you if you promise not to be grumpy about it after."

His gaze shifted to her, and softened. "Alright."

So they found a blanket to sit on, and she regaled him with the tale of Hunter the Ass, deliberately pumping amusement into her tone and imitating said ass in an exaggerated way. Though a crease often formed between his brows, she did get Daniel to laugh—since he seemed pensive afterward instead of reserved, she considered that a victory.

The party was starting to clear up by then, and they both had messages from the others letting them know they were about to head out, asking where they were.

"Can I walk you back?" Daniel asked her.

"Sure." She didn't know why, but for some reason she suddenly felt a little shy, and bit her lip to hide her smile. She texted her friends that Daniel was walking her back and to go ahead, and he did the same.

It was a relatively short distance down the beach, and he was quiet for most of the way, much as he had been after their walk on the beach.

It wasn't uncomfortable, but she decided to break the silence. "I feel like something's on your mind."

He nodded. "I was thinking about what that guy said to you. I'm sorry you had to endure that, and then the crap I said."

"Thanks." She nudged him with her elbow, tossing a half smile his way. "At least you got your act together."

Shoving his hands in his pockets, he said, "I'm glad you think so."

"You don't?"

"Maybe." He shrugged. "There's too much going through my mind to be sure."

They'd reached the back porch, aglow with outdoor string lights hung on poles, and climbed the few steps up to the deck. When they stopped in front of the French doors, he ran a hand through his hair.

"I really appreciated our talk earlier," he finally said. "Thank you for listening, and understanding. Not everyone does."

She met his eyes, which she noticed were a shadowed blue under the soft glow of the stringed bulbs breaking up the darkness. Her heartbeat kicked up a notch when she realized how close he was.

"Not everyone wants to."

He only nodded, staring back at her before his lips lifted in a small smile. His fingers gently gripped her hand, and he tilted his head down to press a soft kiss to her cheek.

Surprised, she could only blink at him before managing to give him a shy smile.

"Goodnight, Evie."

She couldn't quite read the expression on his face—longing? Curiosity?

Appreciation? And she wondered if perhaps she was imagining feeling those things in the way his fingers brushed hers as he let go of her hand.

"Goodnight."

She keyed in the code, opened the door quietly as he headed back down the steps; she couldn't help pausing, turning back to look over her shoulder to watch him walk down the beach toward his own rental.

He didn't look back, but despite herself, she could have sworn her cheek still felt a little warm where his lips had been.

THREE

AS WAS HER HABIT, Evie rose early the next morning, surprised to find Lucile already up.

"Coffee?" she asked as Evie came into the kitchen.

Eyeing her friend, Evie took the mug she held out, took a contemplative sip. "Thanks."

Lucile rolled her eyes. "I can hear the suspicion in your voice from Mount Everest."

"You're never up this early." Evie tilted her head, wondering if she should be concerned. "Did you get any sleep last night?"

"A little." Lucile bit her lip, suddenly quiet as she traced a finger over the rim of her own mug.

"Luce, what's wrong?"

Lucile sighed, not looking at her. "Nothing's wrong, I just know you won't be happy with me."

"I..." Evie trailed off, not sure what to say to that. "What does that mean, Luce?"

Before Lucile could answer, there was a shuffle from the hall, and in walked Hunter, wearing the same clothes he'd worn at the party. Eyes widening, Evie opened her mouth, then closed it. Swallowed.

Hunter waltzed around the island to Lucile, wrapping his arms around her waist and giving her a smacking kiss.

"Good morning, my lovely Lucile," he said.

Evie could only stare. She was grateful for the coffee, as holding it gave her hands something to do and it provided her with a bit of defense against the shock.

Though he surely saw her when he entered the room, Hunter turned to her as though he'd just noticed her. "Oh, hello, Evie. Good morning."

"Morning," Evie said absently, her gaze flitting back and forth between him and her friend warily. She decided it was good moment to drink some of her coffee.

Hunter kept one arm around Lucile, taking her coffee mug from her and taking a sip. "I don't know about you, but I just had the *best* night last night."

Evie noticed how Lucile grimaced, but sent her a pleading look that unmistakably asked, *please be nice.* Swallowing and doing her best to genuinely smile, she responded. "I'm glad. And I had a great time last night, thank you."

Though he seemed a little confused, Hunter nodded and began heading out to sit on the porch.

"Hunter," Lucile stopped him, nodding toward the mug in his hand.

"Oh, sorry." He seemed sincerely apologetic as he handed Lucile's mug back to her. "I'll just be outside."

When he was gone, Evie was pretty sure she could hear a drop of water hit the ocean with how silent it was. Lucile spoke first.

"Go ahead. Say it."

Evie shook her head. "I don't understand."

Lucile finally looked at her. "I don't expect you to."

"I just...why *him?*"

Lucile shrugged, but the gesture was half-hearted. "I told you if a guy was attractive enough he would suit me, and it turns out he wasn't just talk. He wasn't the only one who had a good time last night."

It stung, Evie thought—the knowledge one of her closest friends was selfish enough to sleep with a guy who'd blatantly demeaned her. But the last thing Evie wanted was to make her friend feel ashamed, and she felt a flare of shame herself for judging Lucile for making a different choice than she would—even though she couldn't stand Hunter. But the same was obviously not true for Lucile.

Deflated, she said, "I'm happy for you, Luce. I'm just having a hard time getting past the fact he expected me to sleep with him just because he paid me attention."

"I know, and trust me," Lucile held up her hands as she explained, "We had a pretty long talk about why his behavior was insulting. I don't think he fully understands, but I think he gathers that he offended you."

Evie had stared into her coffee as Lucile spoke, and now shifted her gaze out the kitchen window to the spot of sea.

"I need to process this. I'm going to go for a walk, but I'll be back for breakfast."

"Okay." Lucile bit her lip. "You're not mad?"

"No." Evie set down her coffee and pulled her friend into a hug. "I'm not mad."

Disappointed maybe, but she could never truly be mad at Lucile.

Lucile went out with her and sat with Hunter on the deck; Evie waved to them as she put on her sunglasses and made her way down to the water.

Putting her hair up in a messy bun to keep it from whipping around in the wind, she continued down the beach much as she had the day before, but with less pleasant thoughts. Was her friend so desperate for male affection that she'd give herself to a man who seemed to have little respect for women? Or was she being too judgmental?

Luce's choices were her own, Evie reminded herself. And she knew her friend wasn't as romantic as she was; if anyone could bring some sensibility to Hunter, it would be her. The show of sheepishness when he'd almost walked out with Lucile's coffee was a hopeful sign.

She sighed. Logically, she could follow Luce's line of thought—Hunter would give her the vacation fling she was looking for—but emotionally… the reasoning eluded her. Physical attraction was all well and good, but for her, without a real connection, there was no true attraction.

She just couldn't fathom making the same choice herself.

She was so lost in her tumult of emotions she didn't realize she'd stopped, and was staring out over the water. When she was fully present again, she turned to keep walking, but halted when she saw Daniel walking toward her.

He must have spotted her from the pier—and this time he did join her. She resisted the urge to touch her cheek where he'd kissed her and sent him a smile.

"Hey," he said, smiling back. "I thought it was you."

"I'm that predictable, huh?"

He shook his head. "Nah, I never would have pegged you for an early riser. Can't say I'm surprised, though."

"I'm not surprised in the slightest." She settled into her customary stance—raising a brow. "I bet you were up at sunrise."

He chuckled. "I was, but not for the reason you think."

When she said nothing, only waited, he continued. "I couldn't sleep."

"Ah." She frowned, looking out at the sea again, her voice distant when she said, "You're not the only one who didn't get a lot of sleep last night."

"Is something wrong?" He asked, shifting toward her. "I'm sorry if I—"

"No, I'm not referring to myself." Rubbing her arms, she looked at him warily. "You know that guy from last night, Hunter? Lucile spent the night with him. He was in our kitchen this morning."

"Wait, what? After he insulted you?"

She shrugged. "Her standards are different than mine. I've been standing here trying very hard not to criticize her for it."

"Yeah, but…" He shook his head. "Standards are one thing, but she's your friend, and he was so rude to you."

"I'm as baffled as you are. And a little hurt, and just…sad, I guess. I feel like maybe she thinks she's not good enough, like she has to settle for guys like him. I don't want her to feel that way."

"It seems I'm more pissed off about it than you are," he frowned.

"Thank you." With a half-smile, Evie laid a hand on his arm, then let it fall at her side. "But don't be mad at her. I just want her to be happy, and though logically I've always known this, I'm beginning to realize what makes me happy isn't necessarily what would make her happy."

He nodded. "Standards."

"Standards," Evie agreed, then took a big breath. "Now, enough philosophizing. Shall we walk?"

"Sure." He followed when she started walking in the direction he had come from, watching her with interest as she scanned the ground, pausing every so often to trail a toe lightly in the sand under the water.

"What are you looking for?" he finally asked.

"Seashells," she told him, "or sea glass if I can find it."

"Sea glass?"

"Pieces of glass that have been tumbled by the ocean. It's a process that takes years, and the glass ends up with this frosted look because the soda and lime in the glass dissolves over time," she explained, and listed the different colors one might find. "There are some beaches where you can find a lot—though you usually aren't allowed to take any."

"I had no idea," he mused. "I thought people just bought stuff like that in stores, like you can with shells."

"I'm sure some do. I've always wanted to find my own piece, though."

"Are you allowed to keep any from this beach?" he asked.

She bit her lip and nodded as she concentrated on the waves rolling over her feet. "I looked on the website for this area, and it turns out beach-combing is pretty popular around here."

"Well, then, I'll help you look."

They meandered a little more, talking, enjoying the water, and discovering a handful of pretty shells. She took a picture of them in her hand, but decided to leave them.

"I'm sorry you didn't find any sea glass," he said.

She shrugged. "I didn't expect to. It's just fun to look. Though I'd probably have better luck at low tide."

When they reached the pier, she climbed the steps without hesitation. He followed quietly as she walked a little ways down the boardwalk, then stopped to lean forward against the railing, her elbows propped on the flat wood surface.

The ocean breeze teased strands of her waves, and she closed her eyes to breathe it in. Noticing her relaxed smile, he said, "You look how I felt yesterday morning when I saw you on the beach."

"Oh?" She kept her eyes closed, but arched a brow. "And how do I look?"

"Content."

Now she did open her eyes. "Seeing me walk on the beach made you feel content?"

His brows scrunched together, and he took a few moments to think about the question, gazing out over the water.

"I think it was more that your contentment was infectious. You were just enjoying the simplicity of the beach, and there's a certain sense of peace that comes with that," he finally said. "It made me realize why I'd walked out on the boardwalk in the first place. To find some of that peace."

When he looked back at her, her smile was small and secretive; it wasn't until later she would realize what she'd been feeling was affection. "That was very poetic. I suppose I was feeling rather content yesterday. Nature in general tends to bring me that sense of peace you mentioned."

"And did it help you feel better this morning?"

She took a deep breath before answering, letting the atmosphere roll through her emotionally tired heart. "It did," she decided.

Then she sighed, turned to him. "I should head back now, or I might be late for breakfast."

"We can't have that." His smile was crooked and teasing, and it warmed her—an unexpected feeling, considering how little she knew him.

He offered to walk her back, and she accepted, but with the warning that he would probably be invited to stay for breakfast.

They entered the kitchen to the alluring scent of cinnamon rolls, and found Lucile and Josie squeezing out the icing from their packets onto the swirled rolls. Evie brightened considerably.

"Oh, you know me so well," she sighed as she breathed in the sweet fragrance, and Josie looked up from her task and smiled. At Daniel's questioning look, Evie clarified, "Cinnamon rolls are a favorite of mine."

Amused, he let out a quiet laugh. "Good to know."

"I hope you'll stay, Daniel," Josie said, using a butter knife to spread the icing a little more. "We made like three packages of these."

Lucile finished the icing on her half of the rolls, looking at Evie warily, as if asking if the gesture was accepted. In answer, Evie reached for a roll, pleased it was still warm, and took a bite. As the deliciously gooey combination of cinnamon and sugary icing met her taste buds, she smiled. Though Lucile's responding smile was small, she breathed in relief.

It turned out Hunter had already left, but since Daniel had been invited for breakfast, Josie suggested inviting the others. Daniel happily agreed, and shot Brandon and his cousins a group text. Josie had met Hunter briefly, but didn't know about his role in Evie's party experience, and Evie graciously decided not to enlighten her, or the others.

Breakfast was a pleasant affair, where they enjoyed the cinnamon rolls and some fresh fruit, chatting amicably about the day-to-day routines they were taking a break from.

Josie talked cheerfully about the event she'd had to cover last minute for the event-planning company she worked at when the original planner called in sick; though it was surely a lot of work to do on such short notice, Evie noted she didn't have a single complaint. She wasn't the only one who noticed.

"You sound like you love your job," said Brandon, who was seated next to her.

"I do." Josie smiled at him. "It's really satisfying when I can give clients exactly what they want."

Beside Brandon, Grace laughed. "Especially when they're demanding. Like that one marketing firm that changed their flower order half a dozen times, and you wrangled it all together like the boss you are."

"You do corporate events?" Matt asked Josie. "Richard and I are actually looking to hire someone to plan a work anniversary celebration for our dad at our law practice."

"That's exciting." Since he sat at her other side, Josie turned more fully to face him. "What kind of anniversary?"

"Thirty years as partner at Locke and Sons," Richard supplied from across the table.

"You're a family firm?" Josie's eyes softened. "That's lovely."

As Matt began to talk potential party details, and Richard and Cassie—who sat at the end of the table—joined in, Daniel asked Evie about her work.

"I'm the social media coordinator at the Newberry Library," she told him.

"Really?" He grinned. "I love the Newberry. What made you want to work there?"

"I love libraries and I've always wanted to work in a museum." She lifted a shoulder in contemplation. "I double majored in communications and history, and after a few years temping for the Field Museum, the opening at the Newberry came up. While not technically a museum, it's so full of history it was still a great fit."

"I bet. And the Field Museum, huh? Was your favorite exhibit the room with all the gem stones?"

Chuckling, she nodded. "Yes, actually. Nailed it in one."

"Oh, I love that room." Across from Evie, Grace sighed. "There's so much to look at."

Brandon grinned at her. "You could say that about museums in general. I love looking at everything, but I don't have the patience to take my time with it."

Daniel rolled his eyes. "Ain't that the truth."

Lucile, who sat between Richard and Daniel, pointed out, "Taking your time in a museum usually means you don't get to see everything."

"Exactly," Grace grinned back at Brandon affectionately. "He wants to get through everything, so he rushes through each exhibit like he's on a mission."

"What about you?" Evie asked Daniel. "Would you rather see it all or take your time?"

"I definitely take my time," he said. "I either plan out what I'd like to see most, or make sure I have enough time to get to everything."

"Which is solid," Brandon concurred. "But like I said, I don't have that kind of patience."

By this point, the others had finished their conversation, and since most had finished eating, Josie started clearing the table. Matt waved her off, telling her those who'd cooked didn't clean up, and all the guys followed his lead.

Inspired by their conversation, they made plans to check out a small local natural history museum in the afternoon, then go out for dinner. To Evie's delight, the museum boasted a detailed and beautifully displayed sea glass exhibit, and Daniel spent at least twenty minutes wandering it with her.

True to form, Brandon finished going through each section before anyone else. He doubled back for some of the things he found more interesting, but when it was obvious he was getting antsy, Grace took pity on him, and offered to go get ice-cream with him while they waited for the others to finish their exploring.

The group spent their dinner stuffing themselves full of seafood at a restaurant by the dock, and their evening swapping stories over drinks at a tiki-themed bar.

Though she always had a good time with her friends, Evie couldn't help but notice how much more they all laughed with the guys around— herself included. And the dour version of Daniel from the day before hadn't made another appearance; he laughed just as much as everyone else.

She ignored the hitch in her breath when she caught him staring at her over the bar table, her eyes meeting his as they both laughed at something Richard had said. When his gaze lingered a little too long, she brought her straw to her lips, and looked away, blushing.

He really was unbearably handsome when he smiled.

FOUR

THE NEXT FEW days were full of leisurely activity, and time, as it is wont to do when one is enjoying themselves, seemed to fly by.

They'd had a beach day, full of swimming, spreading out on the sand with a beach read, and frisbee; they'd popped into shops around town and bought kitschy souvenirs; they'd even driven to the nearest waterpark and spent the day there. They often ate out, sampling local fare and ending the day relaxing at a local bar—Evie's favorite was a little seaside dive bar with a pirate theme, where she'd had a drink called Captain's Beard: A rum and coke (with Captain, of course), and a splash or two of Guinness on top.

The group camaraderie was light and easy, and Evie found herself increasingly wanting to spend time with Daniel. They often walked together on the beach in the morning, sometimes getting to know each other, sometimes simply appreciating each other's company.

She couldn't ignore the hum of attraction she felt for him (good Lord, did he look good in his swim trunks), nor did she want to, but she wasn't sure what to do about it. She had a feeling he might be feeling the same (she'd noticed him checking her out in her swim suit, too), but she hesitated to initiate anything more than friendship while they were on vacation.

For all she knew, he might not enjoy her company the same way once they were back home; vacation was very different from regular life. So, she decided, she would enjoy this time with him while she could.

The only damper on their pleasant party was the presence of Hunter. Feeling like the odd one out in a group of four men and five women,

Lucile had asked if she could invite him along to some of their outings. She'd checked with Evie first, and Evie didn't have the heart to admit to her friend it was uncomfortable for her to be around Hunter, so she agreed. No one else had any objections, and when Evie agreed, so did Daniel.

Hunter had accompanied them around town and to the waterpark, often interjecting completely obnoxious thoughts into conversation, and tending to talk over everyone else. But the more time he spent with them, and especially with Luce, the less he did so.

Evie didn't know how she'd done it, but Lucile had made Hunter somewhat palatable—and even, dare she think it, less of an asshat. He actually apologized to Evie—at Luce's behest, no doubt—for his initial rudeness.

It wasn't a great apology, but she could tell he was trying, so she gave him the benefit of the doubt. And even now, as they sat around playing Jackbox games in the guys' cottage (which had turned out to be right across from the pier), he was listening carefully to something Lucile was telling him.

Later that evening as the women walked back to Seaglass Cottage, Lucile hung back with Evie. Though Hunter had come back with Lucile the past couple nights, she'd told him she wanted some time with her friends tonight, and Evie was relieved to see he didn't seem annoyed about it.

It was Luce who broke the silence first.

"How was the apology?" she asked.

"Could have been better," Evie admitted. "But I appreciated the thought. I'm surprised he apologized at all."

Hearing the question behind the statement, Lucile smirked. "Let's just say I convinced him it would be in his best interest to make nice with my friends."

"You're a little devious sometimes, you know that?"

Lucile laughed. "I do. Growing up with brothers will do that."

Hesitating, Evie asked slowly, "And what about you? How's... everything?"

Quirking a brow, Lucile snorted. "Well, the sex is fantastic, if that's what you're asking."

Evie felt heat rise to her cheeks, but she was saved a response when Lucile continued.

"But in all seriousness, things are good. He takes a little getting used to, but I've gotten him to talk more openly, and I've come to understand he hasn't had the best male role model in his dad. And despite that, he has these moments of...sweetness." She shrugged, and Evie wondered at her normally confident friend, as she was clearly a little shy about the subject. She was quiet for a few moments, but then took a breath.

"I…I like him," she confessed. "I know what I've said about romance, but I'm finding that a little romance isn't so bad after all."

Evie found herself slowly grinning at her friend. "Are you telling me you've been drawn away from the Dark Side?"

"Well, I wouldn't go that far."

Laughing, Evie slung an arm over Luce's shoulder, side-hugging her as they walked. Luce returned the gesture, asking, "How's Daniel?"

"Daniel is good, too." Evie couldn't stop her smile at the thought of him. "I'm not afraid to admit I like him, and I think he likes me, but we haven't talked about it."

"Why not?"

"Well, I don't know about him, but if we're going to start something, I want it to start off right, you know. Not rushed, or because we happened to spend a lot of time together on vacation."

"Evie," Lucile used the arm still around Evie's shoulders to shake her a little. "If you like each other, there's no reason not to go for it. Being on vacation doesn't change that, so if I were you I wouldn't waste time on the details and just tell him how I felt."

Evie considered Luce's words, mulled over what she meant a few times before responding.

"You know, you're right. If things are meant to work out, they will."

Lucile grinned. "Damn straight, I'm right."

. . . . . .

"So, I talked to my dad about Catherine."

Evie and Daniel were taking their daily beachcombing walk the next morning, and though Daniel had been happy to see her, he'd also been relatively quiet. Evie sensed he was just lost in thought, but thinking of Luce's words from the night before, she had begun to feel a little discouraged. Now, though, she understood his contemplative state.

"You did?"

"Yeah, and I didn't pull any punches," he said. "I told him about how she'd called me, how it affected me. I even told him about my conversation with you that first night, and the advice you'd given me."

Her eyebrows shot up. "Really? And what did he say?"

"About Catherine? He was appalled, and sorry he hadn't taken my complaints more seriously. About you?" He turned his head to grin at her. "He was impressed, and he had bunch of questions."

"Really?" She asked again. "But he knows me a little. We all met your dad after the Wickham fiasco, and as you recall, at graduation briefly."

He winced. "Yeah, on a side note, I'm sorry I didn't try harder to get to know you after either of those events. I have no excuse."

"That's alright. You can't change the past, and dwelling too much on things you can't change doesn't do anyone any good; you should only think of the past if doing so makes you happy, or if it actually serves a purpose."

"I suppose I could try that. Especially since I know you now, and I'd rather not waste time regretting lost time."

His words echoed what Lucile had said, ricocheting around in Evie's mind. She didn't want to waste time, either, and she agreed there was no point regretting lost time. But still she hesitated, unsure what to say.

"Anyway," Daniel continued, "He said he's not surprised you were the one to call me out on my shit, or to listen and give me solid advice."

Evie chuckled at that summary of her. "Is that a good thing?"

"Very. But he kept asking about all the time I've been spending with you."

"And that's not good?"

"No, it's just…" He cleared his throat. "I haven't spent quality time with a woman in a while. I think he's just curious."

"I see." Evie bit lightly on the inside of her cheek to hide her smile, and her nerves. "So what happens now? With Catherine, I mean," she clarified at his wide-eyed look.

He rubbed at the back of his neck. "Ah. He said he'd talk to her."

"Then let's hope that conversation goes well, and the demoness will be slayed."

He sputtered on a laugh. "Demoness. I like that."

Later that evening, after a dinner of grilled kabobs and corn, and Josie's peaches and cream pie for dessert, the group (including Hunter) moved from the deck to the beach, where Seaglass Cottage had a small fire pit several feet from the steps. They opened a couple bottles of wine as they tossed around ideas for their last day.

Matt had grabbed some firewood from the supply on the deck, and now got a small fire going as the sky began to turn baby pink. Evie couldn't say how long they all sat around just talking and drinking wine —it was easy to lose track of time—but it didn't matter. She just felt present in the moment, and was grateful for her friends.

There was a little bit of a breeze, so she was glad she'd worn a light flannel shirt—her favorite dark navy blue one—over her tank. But she scooted closer to the fire to keep her legs warm. Daniel must have noticed because he got up, and when he came back he held a beach blanket out to her.

Surprised, but touched, she took it. "Thank you."

Cassie had been curled up against Richard's side, but after a while they rose, expressing their desire for a moonlit walk on the beach.

"Oh, that sounds nice," Grace sighed as they headed off.

"It does," Josie agreed. "I'll go with you."

They both got up, and it only took a moment for both Brandon and Matt to offer to accompany them as well. Evie shook her head as the four of them scampered off; she felt a little sorry for Josie, having two perfectly nice guys competing for her attention. Her tender-hearted friend wouldn't want to disappoint either of them, and Evie just hoped Josie was up to the task of letting one of them down.

Glancing after them a moment longer, she shook off her sudden melancholy by finishing her glass of wine, then turning to the rest of her companions.

With the others all split off, it left her and Daniel remaining in awkward silence by the dying fire with Hunter and Lucile.

"More wine, anyone?" Daniel asked, likely to cut the tension.

"Sure," Evie said quickly. She wanted something to do with her hands, and holding a glass of wine would suffice—plus the buzz from more liquid sustenance would dull some of the awkwardness.

"We're good," Lucile said, laying a hand on Hunter's knee when he opened his mouth. Evie suspected he'd been about to say yes, but Lucile had learned over the past several days when he should be cut off. Though Hunter pouted, he didn't contradict her, and Evie hid her mirth by turning to hand Daniel her glass.

It only took a few moments for her to realize Hunter and Lucile wanted to be alone, and joining Daniel was as good an excuse as any. They seemed not to notice when she slipped away and through the back door of the cottage.

She found Daniel staring out the kitchen window, leaning on his hands as they gripped the edge of the sink. He came out of his reverie when she stepped in, and for a moment she was a little undone by the way his eyes roamed over her face, her body. His expression showed such transparent desire she had to suppress a shiver.

But in the next moment he'd hidden the expression and picked up the bottle of wine he'd already opened. He had yet to pour it out, but did so now with such decided calm Evie tilted her head at him.

"What has you so lost in thought?" she asked carefully, folding her blanket over a kitchen chair.

He took a sip of wine before answering. "I was just thinking how nice this vacation has been. It's too bad it'll be over soon."

"Yeah." She sighed. "I love home, but it's always hard to jump back into things after time off."

"Yeah, there's that...But I also meant I've enjoyed this time with everyone." He paused before looking at her. "Especially you."

She hoped she wasn't blushing too profusely, and ignored her racing heart. "I've enjoyed spending time with you, too. But we'll see each other back home, right? Now that we're all friends, I'm sure we'll get together more often."

His eyes crinkled as he smiled. "I hope so."

She didn't know what else to say, unsettled by his gaze, so she cleared her throat.

"I'm a little afraid to go back outside," she joked. "I really don't want to walk out to see Luce and Hunter making out or something."

"Me either. Let's stay inside, then," he suggested.

"And do what?"

He shrugged. "We could play a game or something."

"You know," she grinned. "That sounds cozy."

She settled on the couch while he rummaged under the coffee table for a two-person board game. Maybe it was the wine, or maybe it wasn't, but she couldn't help ogling his butt a little while he was bent over on the floor—it was a very nice ass, after all.

She took a sip of her wine to keep herself from staring.

"How about Connect Four?" He sat up, held up the cardboard box, and she quickly re-adjusted her thoughts.

"Classic. You're going down, Flemming."

"We'll see about that, Bishop." He hopped up and plopped down on the couch, whipping off the lid to the game. "I'll have you know I was the Camp Eastlake Connect Four Champion two years running."

Her eyes slitted at him over her glass. "You're making that up."

He grinned. "Nope."

When he won the first two games, she realized he really wasn't kidding; but her competitive streak kicked in, and she used what she'd learned of his moves to beat him in the third game.

They were a few moves into a fourth game when there was a thud at the kitchen door. They both turned to glance over the back of the couch; the light was still on in the kitchen, and she could make out a person-like shape on the other side of one of the French doors through the shade covering the glass, accompanied by a peculiar grunt.

The door handle rattled, turned, and the door burst open as Hunter and Lucile stumbled into the kitchen, Hunter kicking the door closed without removing his mouth from hers.

Evie ducked so that her head was hidden by the back of the couch, and Daniel did the same. She was grateful they'd only turned on an end table lamp, so the lighting in the living room was dim, and she covered her mouth with her hand to stifle her laughter. She definitely did not want to interrupt them.

Daniel lifted a fist to his own grinning mouth as the sounds of their moans and kissing grew closer, and Evie held her breath, avoiding Daniel's eyes. The noise stopped for a moment, then picked up again closer to the stairs; Evie risked a peek over the couch to see that Hunter had lifted Lucile, who had wrapped her legs around his waist, and he was now carrying her up the stairs, their mouths still fused together.

She raised her eyebrows, finally letting out her breath in a quiet chuckle as the two lovers disappeared upstairs.

"Jesus, that was close." Daniel whispered, shaking with his own laughter.

"Tell me about it." It was only when she looked back at him that she realized just how close his face was to hers. Even in the dim lighting, she could see flecks of gray in the blue of his eyes, and her heart shot up into her throat when she noticed their noses were practically touching. Her breath caught when he blinked at her, his eyes unmistakably drifting to her mouth.

He swallowed, his gaze meeting hers again, and before she could wonder if he would kiss her, she felt his nose brushing hers, and she instinctively tilted her head just slightly, her eyes closing. She wasn't sure which of them moved first, or whether they'd both been drawn toward the other at the same time, but just when she'd realized it was really going to happen, she was kissing him.

It started soft, testing. A teasing press of lips.

Then she let out an involuntary sigh, which spurred him to lift his hand to the back of her neck, his fingers gently gripping her hair, and deepen the kiss. Far from displeased, she scooted a little closer, causing them to straighten a little more. She ran her hands up his chest to cling to his shoulders, and his other hand rested on the other side of her head, his thumb moving over her jaw.

She moaned when he dipped his tongue into her mouth, his kisses slow and sensual and tasting of sweet red wine, and her tongue met his with equal fervor. His arm came around her waist, tugged her closer.

When her breasts pushed against his chest, he groaned, and it made her quiver. She nearly cried out when his lips left hers, but instead they began to trail over her jaw, her earlobe, her neck, and his other hand began to trail up her side. He nipped at her collarbone before lifting his head, bringing his lips back to hers, his thumb brushing just under the swell of her breast in question.

She brought her hands to the sides of his neck, slowly broke the kiss. His thumb continued to stroke her; it was driving her crazy with need, and she could only imagine how turned on she would be if he really touched her.

"I've been wanting to do that all week," he said, his voice a low rumble.

"You have?"

He nodded, leaning his forehead against hers. "But I wasn't sure what you wanted."

I want to climb into your lap, she thought.

He let out an amused chuckle. "I would not be against that at all."

"Oh my God, did I say that out loud?"

Mortified, she pulled back and covered her face with her hands. She felt his hands close gently over her wrists, tug her hands down.

"Don't be embarrassed." He intertwined their fingers. "Wanting me isn't anything to be ashamed of. I'm not ashamed to admit I want you. A lot."

"I know, I—" She looked at their unfinished game of Connect Four. "I'm not ashamed, I'm just hesitant to rush into something."

She forced herself to look back at him, relaxing a little when he didn't look annoyed or disappointed, just expectant. She bit her lip, then thought again of Luce's advice and decided she should be honest with him.

"I really like you. And I'm guessing you like me. But I'm not looking for a vacation romance." She swallowed. "I'm sorry if it's too much to ask, but I don't want you to kiss me again if you don't see this being more than a casual thing."

He surprised her by tucking her hair behind her ear and giving it an affectionate tug. "Are you asking me out, Evie?"

"I..." Caught off guard, she wasn't sure how to respond. Was she asking him out? She'd never asked a man out in her life.

"Because if so, my answer is yes." He bent his head and pressed his lips to her collarbone again. "I was going to ask you if I could take you out when we get back to Chicago, but it seems you've beat me to it."

He punctuated every few words with kisses up her neck, and finally his lips brushed over her cheek, stopping just a breath from her lips, which were already tingling in anticipation.

"You were?" she breathed out.

"Mm-hm." He nuzzled his nose against her cheek. "I really like you, too. I should warn you though, it's been a while since I've been on a date.

I've kind of avoided meeting women in general, since none of them seemed interested in me as a person."

"Why me, then?" she asked softly, her hands beginning to glide up his torso. "What changed your mind?"

"Just you." He brought his hands back up to cup her face. "Everything about you is different, and honestly, as corny as it sounds, I can't seem to resist you."

She was tired of resisting, too, and decided they'd talked enough.

"Then don't."

And his mouth was on hers again, sweet, but just rough enough to send flutters through her belly. He wrapped both his arms around her, straightening a little, and she used the momentum to do just as she'd said she wanted.

She leaned forward, and understanding her intent, he adjusted himself so he was sitting up, his back against the couch, just as she swung a leg over him so that she straddled his lap. *Oh, God,* she thought with a moan as she settled against him, his hands roaming from her hips to grip her bottom.

The movement caused her to grind against him, and he pulled her mouth back down to his with a groan. She ran her tongue across the seam of his lips, and his mouth opened to her with a wicked grin.

This time there was no hesitation when his hands explored, finally coming to rest just under her breasts; his thumbs stroked back and forth over peaks that had gone taut. She hadn't bothered with a bra under her tank, and he pulled back to look at her a moment, fully cupping her as his eyes met hers.

"Fuck, Evie." His voice was rough with desire, and he moved his hands to her shoulders, slowly pushing the light flannel shirt she wore down her arms. She shrugged the rest of the way out of the shirt, a strap of her tank sliding down her shoulder in the process.

He trailed a finger along the strap, nipping lightly at her shoulder, and down, down until he bit gently on her nipple through the cotton. Her gasp had him providing the same attention to her other breast.

"We should stop," he rasped out. "They could come back down."

"Right. Anyone could walk in," she agreed.

But neither of them moved.

He cleared his throat. "Um, you first."

She bit her lip, listening for any noise coming from upstairs or outside. When she heard nothing, she leaned further into him, wiggled her hips slightly.

"I'm comfortable where I am," she said in mock innocence.

He moaned, but shook his head. "Evie, our first time together isn't going to be on the couch of your vacation rental, hurrying in the dark like a couple horny teenagers. I want to take you on a real date first."

Smiling, she shook her head right back. "I agree, and I'm not saying we should have sex right now. I'm just saying I want to be close to you a little longer."

He sighed, hugging her close, and to her surprise, turning and leaning them back until her back met the cushions of the couch. "You sure?" he asked.

She nodded, grinning playfully. "Let's make out like horny teenagers instead."

And his lips met hers on a laugh. It was dangerously arousing to have him positioned between her legs, but with their intention set, the urgency of the moment was gone. Though he lavished attention on her breasts, they removed no more clothing, and their kisses were long and languid.

Eventually they sat up, and Evie put her flannel back on. But now he lay back on the couch and opened his arms in invitation, and she positioned herself so she could lay curled against him. She began to yawn as they discussed date ideas, and it wasn't long before she drifted off, the steady rhythm of his heartbeat under her head a lullaby she could get used to.

· ⸳ ⸳ ·

EVIE WOKE to someone poking her shoulder, and opened her eyes to find Grace grinning at her. She felt Daniel take a deep breath and mutter, "Hm?"

"You two are too cute," Grace beamed, but kept her voice at a near-whisper. "But I thought you might be more comfortable in a bed."

Blinking, Evie pushed up to a sitting position, her eyes adjusting to the darkness of the room. Beneath her, Daniel stretched and sat up as well.

"Where is everyone?" she asked Grace.

"Upstairs," Grace said cheerfully. "None of the guys wanted to leave, so Richard is staying with Cass, and I'm going to sleep with Josie tonight so Brandon and Matt can have my room. I'll let you two discuss your sleeping arrangements."

Winking at them, she practically skipped up the stairs, leaving them alone to stare at each other awkwardly.

"I can stay down here," Daniel offered. "I don't want you to feel obligated to invite me to your bed."

It was the safer choice, she knew. Having him sleep next to her would be very tempting; but the thought of him alone on the couch while everyone else had a bed didn't sit right with her.

"I don't feel obligated," she said softly. "I…I want you to share my bed. Besides, it's not fair you should have to sleep on the couch because the beds are already taken."

"If you're sure, I won't argue with you."

"I'm sure."

They made their way quietly up the stairs to her room in the middle of the hall, and he was still silent as she closed the door and turned on the nightstand light.

"Do you, um, need to change?" he whispered.

Oh. She hadn't thought about that. She supposed she could go change in the bathroom.

"I can turn around," he continued. "Or…"

"That should be fine," she said quickly, grabbing her sleep shorts and t-shirt off the end of the full-size bed. He nodded and turned around to face the wall, and she could have sworn a blush was creeping up the back of his neck, but it was too dim in the room to be sure.

She hurriedly pulled off her tank and yanked on the t-shirt, then changed into her cozy sleep shorts. Clearing her throat to indicate it was okay for him to turn around, she shoved her clothes in her suitcase.

"Do you need something to sleep in?" she asked him.

"I can sleep in this shirt and my boxers if that's okay."

"Okay."

She glanced away when he reached for the button on his shorts, and focused on pulling the bed sheet aside. What was wrong with her? She'd shared a bed with a man before. This wasn't any different, was it?

Except they'd agreed not to rush things. And being on the couch was one thing, but being in a bed together was a different scenario entirely.

Biting her lip, she climbed into the bed, pulled the sheet up over her legs. When she managed to look at him, he was looking at her intently, his expression hard to read.

"Are you going to join me?" She tried to sound casual, but she just felt awkward.

Wordlessly, he slid in next to her, pulling the sheet over his dark gray boxers as he lay on his back, then spent more time than necessary getting settled against the pillow. She did the same, folding her hands over her stomach as she stared at the outline of her feet under the sheet.

She swayed her head to look at him, and he, too had his hands folded on his stomach; he had his eyes closed, but he seemed too tense to be relaxed. Picturing what they both must look like, politely doing their best not to make contact with the other, she wondered why they were both suddenly feeling so shy. Before she knew it, a laughed rolled up and bubbled out of her.

He opened his eyes to watch her, confusion clear on his face.

Giggling, she rolled onto her side to face him and took a breath to slow her laughter. "I'm sorry, I was just thinking how ridiculous we must look."

He blinked at her, looked down at himself, and finally his lips pursed in a wry smile as he let out a quiet snort. "I guess we are being overly cautious," he said, laughing as he ran a hand over his face.

Then he turned on his side to face her so they faced each other.

"Do you snore?" he asked her.

"No. I also don't talk or kick in my sleep. You?"

"Me either."

She sighed, relieved the tension was gone, and leaned over to give him a quick peck. "Goodnight," she said, and rolled to turn off the light.

"Goodnight," he murmured.

She tended to sleep on her stomach, so she got comfortable, snuggling into the feather-soft pillow, her head still facing him; she could feel him re-adjusting before he settled, and when her eyes adjusted she could make out he was still facing her as well.

Smiling to herself, she let the sound of ocean waves and the unexpected comfort of his presence lull her to sleep.

FIVE

THE MORNING of their last day of vacation came before she knew it, bright sun spotlighting into the room through the picture window. Her room didn't have a view of the beach, instead facing the neighboring cottage, but it didn't lessen the pleasantness one bit.

She'd woken slightly spooned against Daniel, his arm loosely draped over her middle, and wondered how that happened. She didn't usually move much in her sleep.

Now she rolled slowly onto her back, stretching the sleep out of her limbs with a yawn. When she looked back at Daniel, his eyes were open and on her, his lips curved in a sleepy smile.

"Morning," he said through a half-yawn.

"Morning," she said, reaching out to run her fingers over the light morning stubble covering his jawline.

He chuckled at her touch. "You like?"

She nodded. "It's sexy."

Grinning, his arm came around her waist, and he tugged her closer for a long morning kiss.

"How'd you sleep?" he asked.

"I must have conked out," she said, laughing. "The last thing I remember is laughing with you before turning out the light."

"Same."

She sighed in contentment. "So should we get up?"

"In a minute."

He brushed his lips over hers again, sliding his other arm underneath her to pull her body flush with his. Intoxicated by the feel of him, she slid her hands over his shoulders, around his neck, and found herself pressed back into the mattress as she drew him down to her.

She didn't know how long they kissed, but it was more than a minute.

When she said as much to him as they finally got out of bed, he barked out a laugh.

"Okay, smart ass," he said as he yanked on his shorts. "I'm going to go see about coffee."

She got dressed in shorts and a t-shirt when he went down, then brushed her teeth, unable to stop smiling the whole time. Waking up with Daniel might just be her new favorite way to wake up.

It was a little bit of a scary thought, but she didn't mind so much anymore. Especially since there were probably many other ways she could wake up with him that were just as delightful.

With that thought in mind, she crept down the stairs, surprised when she found the kitchen empty. The coffee maker was going, the carafe slowly filling with the dark liquid that was her life force, and two mugs sat beside it, waiting patiently to be filled.

Assuming maybe Daniel had gone to the bathroom, she went to stand by the coffee machine, idling as she waited for it to finish brewing.

She was surprised again when she heard Daniel's voice radiating through the kitchen window.

"What's up?"

"Well, first I want you to promise you won't get upset with me."

"Okay."

The other voice was Brandon's, Evie realized. They must be on the deck, and they probably assumed their conversation was private. She shouldn't hear it, she thought, and moved to the sink, pushing up on her tip-toes and reaching out to close the window.

"I uh...I kissed your sister."

Evie froze. *What?!*

"You kissed Grace?" she heard Daniel ask.

"Yeah, well I mean she kissed me first, and I kissed her back."

She shouldn't be listening to this, Evie thought, even if Grace would undoubtedly tell them all at some point.

But wait—when did this happen? And what about Josie?

Daniel voiced the same thought. "When did this happen?"

"Last night, when we went for a walk on the beach," Brandon answered. "Look, I know she's your sister, but I've sort of had feelings for her coming on for a few years now, ever since that shit with Wickham, I think. It took me a while to figure it out, to realize she was more than just your kid sister, but I got to spend some quality time with her on this trip and it just kind of…hit me.

"I decided to just let her know what I was feeling so she could decide how she felt about it, and her response was to kiss me."

Evie couldn't see Brandon, but based on the tone of his voice she thought it safe to assume he was grinning like an idiot.

"After," Brandon continued. "She told me she'd had a crush on me forever. We had a lot to talk about."

After a few moments of silence, Daniel spoke. "I'm not surprised."

He wasn't?

"You're not?"

"Not really. I know my sister, so I could tell she had some feelings for you, I just wasn't sure what you felt."

"You never said anything," Brandon pointed out.

"You're both adults," Daniel said. "I trusted you'd figure out your own feelings when the time was right. And if I'd said something, the timing might not have been right."

"I guess that makes sense. So you're not mad?"

"No. Why would I be mad?"

"I don't know, I guess because I'm your best friend and she's your baby sister?" Brandon suggested.

"Dude." Evie heard Daniel laugh a little. "Like I said, you're adults. And I want both of you to be happy with someone special, so if you find that with each other, that's even better. If there's any man I would trust with my sister, it's my best friend."

At the sentimentality in Daniel's voice, Evie felt the pricking of tears behind her eyes. Thinking she'd heard enough, and that their conversation was probably ending, she turned from the window and headed back toward the stairs. She heard Brandon say, *"Thanks, man,"* and hurried her steps, rushing back upstairs.

The back door opened as she hopped the last few steps. She took a breath and waited a few moments before turning around and going back down the stairs. This time, when she entered the kitchen, Daniel was pouring coffee into the mugs he'd set out, with the addition of a mug for Brandon.

With her focus on the conversation, Evie hadn't even realized the coffee was done. She felt guilty for listening, especially since Brandon was undeniably happy, and so was Grace if her bubbly demeanor the night before was any indication.

But that still left the question of Josie. Was there something she was missing?

Daniel smiled brightly at her as he handed her a mug. She thanked him and inhaled a few gulps for fortification.

"Anyone else up?" she asked.

At that moment, Grace came into the kitchen, her smile radiant as she glanced at Brandon. "Morning. I think Josie went for a morning walk on the beach," she said in answer to Evie's question.

Perfect, Evie thought, smiling genuinely at Grace's joy. "Ooh, I think I'll join her."

She finished off her coffee and slipped on her flip flops, heading out the back door to find Josie—and hopefully, give Brandon, Grace, and Daniel some actual privacy in case they wanted to clear the air.

As she got closer to the water, she could see some fresh foot prints along the shore, heading in the direction of a set of rocks. As she approached she heard splashing, followed by giggling.

Confused, she edged closer, calling out. "Josie?"

"Evie?"

If Evie had been unprepared for the surprise she'd already had that morning, she was doubly so for the sight that greeted her when she turned the corner around the rocks.

Josie, in her pink bikini bottoms, hair in a wet braid over her shoulder, held the unicorn inflatable over her topless chest as she made her way to shore. Behind her, Matt followed, clearly a little embarrassed.

Evie could only blink as Josie made it out of the water and walked over to where she'd left her bikini top on a rock. She glanced back and forth between the flushed faces of Josie and Matt as Josie picked up her top, shook out the sand.

"I thought..." Evie trailed off. She'd seen Matt's interest in Josie, but had thought Josie liked Brandon—maybe that was what she'd been missing this whole time. The benefit of hindsight had her recalling how Josie had often initially talked to Brandon, but spent most of her time talking to Matt; similarly, Grace had been the one to accompany Brandon when he was done with the museum, not Josie. Had she really been that oblivious?

"...you were taking a walk," she finished instead.

Blushing, Josie hugged the unicorn tighter around her.

"Actually, Matt and I planned to go for a morning swim." Then shrugging, she let the unicorn drop, hastily pulling the still-tied top strings of her bikini top over her head, tugging the fabric over her breasts.

Laughing at Matt's simultaneously mesmerized and frozen expression, Evie gestured for Josie to turn around.

"Here, I'll tie that for you."

Josie adjusted the fabric some more as Evie re-tied the back of her top, then turned to give her a sheepish smile.

"Sorry about the show."

Evie shrugged. "Nothing I haven't seen before."

"True," Josie laughed while Matt, blushing and avoiding Evie's eyes, picked up the unicorn. "Oh, but guess what, Evie? Grace kissed Brandon last night!"

And yet another shock, Evie thought. Apparently she really was that oblivious. When she only blinked at Josie in surprise, Josie continued, "We talked about it last night. She told me she's had a crush on him since high school. Isn't that sweet?"

Well, Evie thought, this was certainly their most memorable vacation yet. Deciding to follow the ocean's example and go with the flow, she embraced Josie's enthusiasm.

"Yeah," she responded. "I hope it works out for them."

⁘ ⁙ ⁚

FOR THEIR LAST EVENING TOGETHER, the group decided to have a cookout at the guys' rental. Richard suggested burgers, and Matt and Daniel volunteered to run to the store for ingredients and beer.

While the others waited for their return, they sat around in the living room playing Apples to Apples, which they'd found in the rental's coffee table board game stash. They'd been playing for a good fifteen minutes when a sudden, succinct knock came at the front door.

"What the?" Richard glanced at the door. It was too soon for Matt and Daniel to have returned, and even if they had, they had no reason to knock.

"I'll get it," Grace offered when the knock came again. She stood and went to the door, opening it part way. But her movements halted and her mouth dropped open.

"Ms. DeVry, what a surprise."

They all looked up as Grace abruptly moved out of the way for a tall, slender woman, who stepped into the cottage without waiting for an invitation, and with an expression of clear distaste. Evie noticed Grace very deliberately pronounced her moniker *miz*.

She wore a dark red blazer and matching pencil skirt with a crisp white shirt underneath. Her slick silvery-blonde hair was half up, perfectly coifed, and diamonds—real or fake, Evie couldn't tell, but they looked real enough—glinted at her throat and ears. She wore the minimum of makeup, with the exception of a rust-colored lipstick.

She ignored Grace, standing tall and staring down her nose at the rest of them from towering red heels. She neither introduced herself nor asked for an introduction, and her voice was harsh amid the hush that had fallen over the room.

"Where is Daniel?" she demanded.

Brandon straightened up. "He and his cousin went to the store, ma'am."

"Then I'm here to speak to whichever of you is Evelyn Bishop."

Evie couldn't help the smirk that played on her lips as she met the woman's gaze. "I'm Evie. You must be Catherine."

Since Catherine was already basically glaring, it was hard to tell if the informality irritated her. If it did, she didn't let it show, instead looking Evie up and down with a distinct frown. Based on what she'd heard of the woman, Evie supposed anyone would be found lacking under Catherine's discerning eye, so she didn't take it personally.

Her assessment complete, Catherine turned her head to look past the dining area to the back screen door.

"I see there's a boardwalk out back. We can speak there."

Without waiting for a reply, she glided past the living room, through the kitchen to the back door. Then she stopped and turned, clearly impatient for Evie to follow.

While the others looked absolutely confused, Grace gave Evie a wary look; but Richard gave Evie a nudge as she stood, and when she looked at him, he gave her an encouraging nod.

"She's all hot air," he said. "You can take her."

Evie gave him a grateful smile. "I'll keep that in mind."

When Catherine didn't move upon Evie's approach, Evie slowed, paused. Catherine pursed her lips impatiently.

"Well, what are you waiting for?" She asked sharply.

"You asked me to follow you," Evie pointed out. "What are *you* waiting for?"

"For you to open the door," Catherine said, as though it were obvious.

Evie glanced at the sliding door, then back at Catherine with a deliberately unaffected expression, though she wondered at the woman's audacity.

"Oh, my bad," she said flippantly, flipping the lock, "My mind reading powers only work from eight to noon."

She thought about stepping out ahead of Catherine, but feeling more amused than irritated, she opened the door and turned swiftly, arching her free arm and bowing as though she were a butler, then affecting a suave tone.

"After you, my liege."

Whether Catherine took the impression seriously or not she couldn't say, but the snickers coming from the living room told her those watching were vastly entertained. Evie looked back at them before stepping out onto the deck; Richard sent her a thumbs up, and though Grace was now chuckling, she had gotten out her phone.

Likely to inform Daniel the demoness had arrived.

Catherine nimbly went down the deck steps and crossed the sidewalk, and kept going to the pier entrance without a backward glance.

She looked so out of place in her power suit on the laidback beach boardwalk Evie found herself smirking at the sound of Catherine's pumps on the wood; she wouldn't be surprised if the stilt-like heel got caught between the boards. She followed as Catherine marched about a third of the way down the pier, stopped abruptly, and turned just as sharply on her heel to face Evie.

"I'm sure you understand why I'm here."

Evie, arms already folded and brows preemptively raised, merely tilted her head.

"Actually, no," she said honestly, "I can't think of a single reason you would come here, much less demand to speak to a complete stranger."

Catherine's glare, if possible, deepened even further. "I had a disturbing discussion with Robert Flemming yesterday, and he informed me that his son is involved with some woman—with you. I came to confirm that this is just a rumor."

Though Evie highly doubted that was the true subject of their conversation, she deduced it was the only part the woman chose to hear. When Evie only quirked a brow, Catherine stomped her foot in exasperation, reminding Evie of a petulant child.

"Well?" Catherine snapped. "Are you involved with Daniel Flemming or not?"

Now Evie gave her bland stare. "I shouldn't have to point this out to you, Ms. DeVry, but that's absolutely none of your business."

"Of course it's my business. Daniel Flemming is my—"

"Coworker," Evie interrupted. "Daniel is your coworker, and even if for some reason that made you entitled to know his personal business— which it doesn't—it certainly doesn't give you the right to know mine."

Catherine straightened, peering down her nose much as she had when she'd entered the cottage.

"And if I told you he is my future son-in-law?"

Evie couldn't help it—she laughed. "Nice try, but Daniel told me about that little delusion of yours himself, as well as the fact that neither he nor your daughter have any intention of humoring you."

Evie had heard the phrase "red-faced" before, but until now, as Catherine's pale skin seemed to darken with pink, she'd thought it was just a fanciful description.

"Let me be frank." Catherine was nearly shouting now, her tone clipped. "Daniel Flemming is one of the most eligible bachelors in Chicago. But he will be the laughingstock of the city if he involves himself with a nobody like you. His friends and family will think he's lost his mind."

"Actually, his sister is one of my best friends, and his friends are fast becoming my friends, too."

"Tell me now, are you involved with him?"

Putting a hand on her hip and bringing a finger under her chin, Evie pretended to think about it, then said, "I thought we established that's not your business."

Catherine huffed. "Fine. Then at least promise me you will not enter a relationship with him."

"Um, no," Evie scoffed. "I'm not going to base my life decisions on someone else's whims. You don't get to dictate my life or my happiness any more than you do Daniel's."

"I will not leave until you promise me."

Taking her time, Evie exaggerated the movement of glancing behind Catherine for other people. "I'm sorry, did I miss the army you brought to keep me here? If you want to stay out here, that's fine by me, but I think this conversation is over, and I'm going back inside."

Catherine stamped her foot again. "I will not tolerate such rudeness."

Evie shrugged. "I'm only rude to people who are rude to me—and you're officially the rudest person I've ever met."

Which is saying something, Evie thought, thinking of Hunter.

Catherine stood ramrod straight, clearly gearing up to say something else completely unreasonable, but when she opened her angry lips, it wasn't her voice that came out.

"That's enough, Catherine."

She blinked, her anger draining in satisfaction as her eyes shifted behind Evie; Evie turned around to find Daniel, hands in his pockets, standing with his stern gaze focused on Catherine.

The poor woman didn't realize he was irritated, Evie noted. She still assumed Daniel would listen to her.

"Daniel, darling," Catherine purred. "You've come at just the right time."

"I'll say," Daniel muttered, so only Evie could hear.

Catherine continued, "Tell this shameful girl your little holiday romance is nothing but a fling."

Daniel only blinked, moving to stand by Evie's side. "Why would I do that?" he asked.

"Because anything more between you would be a disgrace," she insisted.

"To who?" Daniel frowned. "No one outside my inner circle cares about my personal life, and if they do, that's too damn bad, because their opinions have nothing to do with me."

Catherine squared her shoulders. "I highly doubt your father would approve."

"Funny you should say that." Now Daniel's lips curved into a devastatingly smug smile, and he folded his arms over his chest as though he were a parent who'd caught a naughty child. "After my initial conversation with him about your harassment of me, he told me to let him know if your behavior continues. Since my sister took the liberty of informing me you were here, I did just that. I just got off the phone with him."

For the first time since she'd arrived at the cottage, Catherine's demeanor showed a crack in her unflappable confidence—her eyes widened slightly, and her demanding frown became one of nervousness.

"He's positive he didn't give you any information about where I was staying, and yet, here you are," Daniel continued.

Though still wary, some of Catherine's hauteur returned. "I had to come. I had to make sure you weren't throwing your life away for some silly infatuation."

"That's not for you to decide." Daniel dropped his arms, walked slowly toward Catherine with a look of such quiet fury that Catherine took a step back.

"You stalked me to my place of vacation," he continued, "Barged in to our rental uninvited, and demanded to speak to someone you don't even know, and for what? Because you can't stand not having your own way?"

Catherine's face contorted, and Evie could see her calculating her response; when she spoke she'd molded her voice into one that almost sounded well-meaning.

"I only want what's best for you, Daniel."

"No, you don't." Now Daniel stepped back, shaking his head in disappointment. "You only care about yourself. And this time you've crossed a line."

Catherine scoffed and Daniel turned his back on Catherine, held a hand out to Evie. Smiling, she took it, and turned with him as he began to lead her back toward the cottage. They'd barely taken a step when Catherine called out.

"Just where are you going?"

"To have dinner with our friends," Daniel answered. Then with a squeeze of Evie's hand, he stopped, and the same smug grin he'd worn earlier made another appearance. Turning slightly, he glanced back over his shoulder as if in afterthought.

"Oh, by the way, my father asked me to pass along a message for you," he said to Catherine. "You're fired."

Catherine blanched. "You can't fire me!"

"I'm not firing you." Daniel tilted his head, all innocence. "My father is."

Then he tugged on Evie's hand, and they walked back toward the cottage, leaving *Miz* Catherine DeVry gaping after them.

"Is he really firing her?" Evie asked him.

"Oh, yeah," he confirmed. "He's done with her shit."

"How did she find out where you were staying?"

He shrugged. "No idea, but he's going to look into it. HR will do an official investigation."

"Good." Evie nodded. "I'd be willing to replay our conversation if necessary."

"I appreciate that." He lifted the hand he held, kissed it.

The others were already in the process of starting dinner by the time they made it back up to the deck. Matt and Josie were manning the grill, from which the the aroma of burgers wafted and made Evie's mouth water. Through the screen door she could see Cassie and Lucile cutting up fruit for a fruit salad.

Grace rose as they climbed the last step, wringing her hands, and Richard was ready with a couple freshly opened beers.

"If you tell me you don't need one of these after dealing with the demoness, I'll call you a liar," he said as he handed one to each of them.

Evie grinned—Daniel must have told his friends her off-the-cuff nickname for Catherine. "We made it unscathed."

"Dare I say we're the victors?" Daniel grinned back, tipping his beer toward her, and she tapped it with hers in a toast.

"What happened?" Grace asked, worrying her lip. Her hands were still clasped together, but she'd stopped fidgeting when Brandon rose to stand next to her, rubbing a hand back and forth between her shoulder blades in comfort.

"Catherine is caput," Daniel told her. "Dad told me to tell her she's fired."

Grace exhaled in relief, finally unclasping her hands. "Good riddance."

Evie replayed her conversation with Catherine for the group as they prepared the rest of their meal, and while they ate, much of the discussion revolved around stories of Catherine's past antics. And now that the demoness had been conquered, those stories had a happy ending.

When they'd cleaned up from dinner, they began to break off into couples. Since they would leave late the next morning, Evie figured they each wanted to savor the remaining free time with their special someone.

She and Daniel had wandered back down to the boardwalk, stopping at an ice-cream stand for a treat as the sun began to set. She sampled some of his Mexican hot chocolate cone, while he tried some of her gin and lavender cone, and neither could decide which flavor was best. Smiling to herself, she took it all in one last time when they made it to the end of the pier, watching as the sky filled with an explosion of misty tangerine and pearly violet, and sky merged with sea.

When they'd polished off their cones, Daniel cleared his throat.

"So…" he started. "I have something for you."

Since he seemed nervous, she poked him playfully. "What kind of something?"

"Well…"

In answer, he reached into his pocket; when he pulled it out, opened his fingers, he held up a smooth-looking stone. It took her a moment, but when she realized what it was, she inhaled softly.

"You found one," she breathed out, looking up at him in awe.

There in his palm sat a small piece of lightly frosted sea glass. Even in the fading light she could still make out its color, a translucent turquoise.

"Yeah," he said sheepishly as she picked it up, holding it between her fingers and feeling its smooth, rounded surface. "I just happened to see it partially poking out of the sand when I was walking back yesterday. It would have been perfect if you'd been there with me. I know you wanted to find a piece yourself."

She shook her head, clasping the pretty little treasure in her hands against her chest. "This is just as perfect. I know it's a simple thing, just a whimsical quest, but it means a lot to me that you found this for me. Thank you."

Smiling softly, he gave her a look of such affection her heart skipped a beat. "You're welcome. But maybe I'm the one who should be thanking you."

"Why?"

"You've changed my life in some pretty significant ways, and I've only formally known you for a week." He reached to cup the back of her head in his hands. "You're a wonder, Evie."

"So are you," she said, and wrapped her arms around his waist as he kissed her, soft but deep. He still tasted like rich dark chocolate, a hint of spice on the tongue that tangled with hers. They lingered for a few moments, savoring the newness of discovering each other before pulling apart.

"I can't wait to take you on a date," he murmured.

Laughing, she pulled away far enough to pocket the sea glass, then laced her fingers through his. "And I can't wait to take *you* on a date."

He swung their hands between them as they headed back to the cottage. "Oh, yeah? What'd you have in mind?"

Heart full, she shifted her gaze away from him with a secret smile.

"Guess you'll just have to wait and see."

EPILOGUE

One Year Later

"WE'RE GOING TO BE LATE."

Daniel popped his head into the bathroom, where Evie was putting the finishing touches on her makeup.

"No, we're not. You worry too much." She slicked on her favorite lipstick—a soft, rusty pink color inspired by Catherine DeVry (what could she say, the demoness knew how to color coordinate)—before turning to her anxious boyfriend.

"All done. I just have to grab my shoes." Glancing down, she smirked at his shoeless feet. "And so do you."

He looked down. "Crap. I knew I was forgetting something."

When they'd donned their shoes, Evie picked up her purse, and Daniel patted his pockets to make sure he had everything.

"Got everything?" he asked her.

She shook her head. "There's one more thing."

A crease formed between his brows, and his face deflated into a worried expression she'd become very familiar with over the past year. "What?"

Smiling as only a patient lover can, she stepped to him, laid a hand on his chest. "This," she said, giving him a soft kiss.

She could feel the tension leave his body, and when she pulled away, he breathed out a sigh.

"I know, I know. I need to loosen up."

"It's an engagement party," she reminded him. "We're going to have fun with our friends, and I doubt Cassie or Richard would care if we're a little late."

"But we won't be late," he reiterated.

"We won't," she agreed. "So there's no need to stress."

He blew out a breath. "Okay. Let's go."

He took her hand, pulling her out the door of their apartment; she smiled when he ran his eyes over her body as he locked the door.

"Have I told you how sexy you look tonight?" He put an arm around her as they exited the charming brownstone they called home, whispering in her ear as he pulled her close.

He had. She'd twisted up her hair, and the short sleeve black dress with a wildflower pattern and low-v neckline was a favorite of hers, and apparently of his—he'd commented on it when she put it on. She'd chosen it specifically, hoping he would be inclined to peel her out of it after the party. She'd paired it with her favorite necklace, one he'd had custom made for her for her birthday—a thin silver chain that held the turquoise sea glass he'd found, inlaid in silver like a pearl. She lifted a hand, stroked it affectionately.

"Mm-hm. Why do you think I wore it?" she teased.

"Oh, so you are trying to torture me?" He smiled, letting go of her so they could get in his car.

"No, I thought I'd save that for later."

Chuckling to himself and shaking his head, he started the car and pulled away from the curb. She looked out the passenger window, watching the city they loved go by as he drove to the bar Richard and Cass had rented out for their party.

No one was surprised when Richard had popped the question and Cassie said yes; the two had been inseparable for the past year.

The same could be said of their other friends, Evie mused, as well as of herself and Daniel. Grace and Brandon were still thick as thieves, and Matt and Josie were still going strong. Lucile had stayed in touch with Hunter for a few weeks after returning home from their fateful trip, but long distance hadn't worked for either of them; however, a few weeks after that, she'd met a nice guy named Carter, and had yet to change her mind about romance.

As for Ms. DeVry, she had long been out of the picture; once it came to light she'd hired a private detective to keep tabs on Daniel, Robert Flemming had no problem convincing the board to back up her termination. The PI, once he'd learned Catherine's true motives, gladly handed over her file.

Daniel and his father had yet to replace her; instead, they were training her daughter Anne—who, free from her mother's overbearing shadow, had blossomed and become a real friend—to take her place.

"You look happy."

At his wistful tone, Evie glanced back at Daniel with a contented smile. "I am. Two of my friends are getting married, I'm deeply in love with my boyfriend, and life is good."

His eyes crinkled with his wide smile, and he took one of his hands off the wheel, held it out to her. When she placed her hand in his, he kissed her fingers before twining them with his, then resting their hands between them.

"Good," he said softly. "Because you make me blissfully happy."

"Good," she echoed him. "Now save all that sappy sentimentality for your cousin and his bride-to-be."

His laugh was bright and endearing, and she reveled in the feel of his hand as it loosely held hers over the console. It was a small gesture of affection, but one that connected them, and reminded Evie that joy could be found even in the simplest of places.

Clasping her necklace again, she thought of that first week with Daniel, when he'd told her her contentment had brought him a measure of peace. But it was these moments, for her, that truly brought on that peaceful contentment.

And not too much later, as they watched their closest friends mingle and celebrate a new stage of life, she knew she wouldn't trade those moments for anything.

MY RELUCTANT ROOMMATE

ONE

"NO WAY. ABSOLUTELY NOT."

I cannot believe what my sister is asking me to do. The very idea is unthinkable. Ridiculous. Laughable, even.

Utterly, sincerely impossible.

I fold my arms over my chest and stare Julia down with a glare I hope manages to be both baffled and stern. "Ask someone else."

"But you're the best option," Julia says gently, shrinking a little under my gaze, her moss green eyes shifting down to where she's been picking at a thread on her shirt.

I sigh, feeling guilty—I know Julia hates asking me to do something that might make me uncomfortable, so the fact she's doing it anyway must mean it's important.

"Am I, though?" I argue. "Darcy and I can hardly stand each other; living together would be its own circle of hell."

"I know, but it's only for a few months," Julia insists. "You have a spare room, and—"

"Cole has a spare room, too."

Julia sighs. "Yes, but his commute would be farther from Cole's. It would be the same from here. Plus, he would be paying half the rent—you could save the money you would normally put toward that."

I pause. It's the first thing Jules has said that appeals to me—I'm responsible with my money, so I have a decent cushion, but even so, saving on half my rent for a few months would be nice. I could put the money toward my student loans instead; I was fortunate enough to have scholarships in both undergrad and grad school, but it would be a big help since I've only been out of school a few years and have only made a small dent in the loans on my small town librarian's salary.

Julia catches the wheels turning in my mind. "At least think about it? You don't have to decide right now."

Pursing my lips, I glance down the hall toward my spare room, briefly trying to imagine the somber, disapproving Felix Darcy in my space, and failing.

"I'll think about it."

* * *

I STARE, unblinking, at my closest friend, several contradicting thoughts running through my mind. But first and foremost is confusion.

"You think I should what?"

I'm at Cole's house to watch the game, as my house is currently out of commission; a violent thunderstorm a few nights before caused damage all over town, and my home was one of the hardest hit—literally.

The oak tree in my front yard had practically been ripped out of the ground, crushing part of my roof, while detached branches smashed the front windows. The tree had only just today gotten fully cleared, and, just my luck, an inspector had noticed some rot in the old Victorian's rafters—the whole roof has to be replaced. It'll be months before it's livable again.

Now, Cole, who sits on the couch next to me, jiggles his leg nervously, clears his throat. "Ask Elise if you can stay with her."

I finally blink. "Why can't I stay here? You have an extra room."

"Wouldn't staying with me add a half hour to your commute?"

"True. I could just stay at the hotel I'm at now," I point out.

Halfway to lifting a beer to his lips, Cole pauses and turns to me. "You want to live in a hotel for the next few months?"

"Not particularly," I shrug. "But it's not a big deal."

"I know money isn't an issue for you, but it would be cheaper to pay half the rent at Lissa's than the cost of three months at the hotel."

"True…" I trail off, my mind whirling as I run a frustrated hand through my coal-colored hair. It's not that I don't think I could get along with Elise, but my unexpected attraction to her is frustrating enough—consistently sharing the same space as her might be…problematic. Even now it's hard not to think of how silky her chestnut curls might be, or in particular the look of her soft brown eyes, the color of root beer flecked with golden amber, whenever she arches that teasing brow of hers at me.

"Look," Cole continues, "I know you don't like her much—"

"What?" I interrupt. "Why do you think that?"

Cole looks as baffled as I feel. "Because you're always frowning at her, and arguing with her, and you called her frumpy when you first met her."

Running a hand over my face, I contemplate my friend's words. I don't even recall that comment about her appearance, but apparently it stuck in Cole's mind. I'm not sure if Elise heard it, but if she did, maybe Cole isn't the only one who remembers.

If she was hurt by my comment, it would explain a lot.

I nearly brush off the thought—Elise Bennet is an unflappable, confident spitfire. But, I remind myself, that didn't mean her feelings couldn't be hurt. Warily, I watch Cole for a reaction.

"Is that what Elise thinks? That I don't like her?"

He looks away, which isn't a good sign.

"Cole." I wait until Cole looks back at me, hold his gaze. "What do you know?"

Cole blows out a breath, running a hand through his hair. "Jules told me Lissa thinks you're an ass. I've tried to play up your good qualities, but you haven't made the best impression on her."

"Great," I mutter dryly, "Then I bet she'll jump at the chance to have me as a roommate."

"Julia said she got her to think about it."

"Then Julia must be a miracle worker." Maybe it's for the best, I think, if Elise doesn't like me. I might have some feelings for her, but that doesn't mean I should pursue them.

And yet.

Maybe this is the perfect opportunity. To really get to know her, to discover the depth of my feelings, and hopefully to change Elise's opinion of me. If nothing else, we could become friends.

"Julia seemed pretty optimistic," Cole assures me. "Elise is stubborn, but she has years of practice wearing her down. Plus, at the core of it, Lissa is just as kind as Jules—I bet she'll find it in her heart to help the ass who insulted her."

"So she did hear that?" I know that will likely set me back—it's probably the root of the problem—and I'm not sure how to fix it. I couldn't just bring it up, could I? Would she hear me if I apologized, or would she think I'm just saving face?

With Elise, I have a feeling words won't be enough. I'll have to show her in other ways how wrong I know I've been.

"Yep." Cole emphasizes the "p" with a pop.

Narrowing my eyes, I sip my beer. "Just how much has Julia told you?"

"Not that much, I swear." Cole holds up his hands. "But she did say she had a feeling…never mind, it's probably nothing."

"A sibling's intuition isn't nothing," I push.

"Well…" Cole rubs the back of his neck. "Julia thinks Elise is at least… attracted to you, because if she wasn't, then your 'frumpy librarian' comment wouldn't have made her so antagonistic toward you. But that's just speculation."

I have to laugh, but it comes out as a partial groan as I drop my head in my hands. "Well that's ironic."

"What is?"

I look up, decide this is an area in which I could use Cole's advice— after all, he's the one in a relationship with a beautiful brunette. And my friend is light in all the ways I'm dark—physically, yes, with his honey-blonde hair and grey eyes, but his cheery, open personality is a stark contrast to my own brooding reserve.

"Promise you won't laugh."

Cole nods, setting down his beer and giving me his full attention. "I'm listening."

"I don't think Elise is frumpy at all. In fact, I'm very attracted to her," I explain.

"O-kay…" Cole says slowly.

"And now you're telling me the woman I might be infatuated with would have been attracted to me, too, if it weren't for a stupid comment I made about her."

Cole opens his mouth, then closes it as a grin spreads over his face. "I'm not laughing, but…," he shakes his head. "Only you, Darce."

"Which is why I'm telling you," I inform him. "I want to fix things with Elise, and if she'll let me stay with her, it'll be the perfect opportunity."

"Are you asking me for help?" Now Cole does laugh. "You never ask me for help with anything, unless it's help getting rid of Celeste."

I snort. "Yeah, well, it's been a long time since I've actually wanted to earn a woman's good opinion."

"Don't worry." Cole slaps a hand on my shoulder. "I'll be your inside man."

· · ˙ ‧ · · ·

I CARRY a box of perishables from Darcy's refrigerator up to my second-floor apartment—our apartment—wondering what on earth I'm doing.

Why had I agreed to this again?

At the moment, I'm not sure. Behind me, Darcy drags a large rolling suitcase and duffel bag, saying nothing, just following me down the hall. When we enter the apartment, I go straight to the kitchen—which I ruthlessly cleaned this morning, along with the rest of the apartment—and set the box on the counter.

His dark blue eyes survey the living room and dining nook before he stops next to the kitchen and watches me take things out of the box, his tall frame taking up much of the doorway.

"What?" I grind out.

"Which room is mine?"

"Oh." Right. He probably needs to know that. "The one across from the bathroom. Bathroom's on the left, my room is the one at the end of the hall."

He nods. "Okay. Thanks."

I store a carton of almond milk and a package of cheese in the fridge, taking a deep breath. It hadn't occurred to me before to be nervous, but I realize now that I am. It's a good room; not as big as the master, but cozy with a thrifted queen-size bed, rummage sale chest of drawers, and other second-hand finds, like nightstands, lamps, and wall art.

But my place, and thus his new room, are smaller than what he's used to, I'm sure, and despite my surly feelings toward him, I don't want him to be uncomfortable.

Stupid Darcy.

He comes back out, pauses on his way out the door. "I'm just going to grab the rest of my stuff."

"Okay."

I focus on my task and try not to think about the situation too much. When he comes back, he has a messenger bag slung over his shoulder, and carries a guitar case. Since I've seen him with the bag, I know it holds his laptop, and usually a book or two, but I've never seen the guitar.

He stows his things in his room and comes back out again.

"Not gonna unpack?" I ask, wondering if he's already regretting this and plans on reneging tomorrow.

"No rush." He shrugs. "I was thinking, if you don't have plans for dinner I could order a pizza, and we could go over roommate stuff."

I quirk a brow. "Roommate stuff?"

"Yeah, you know. Chore rotation, how to split groceries, stuff like that."

Ugh. I've been so busy preparing for his arrival I haven't really thought about what we'd do once he actually moved in. Hoping this isn't the start of him trying to take control of everything, I force back a retort; if he's being nice, then I can play along. "Okay. Pizza sounds good."

"Great." To my astonishment, he actually smiles.

When he pulls out his phone, I have to remind myself to stop staring— why does he have to have such a nice smile? He actually seems nice and approachable when he smiles, and it…does things to me. Despite myself, I can't look away.

Stupid Darcy.

"Avanti's okay?" he asks.

I blink rapidly, grateful he hasn't looked up because I'm pretty sure I'm blushing.

"Avanti's is always okay," I say as I come back to myself. "I would give a kidney for Avanti's."

"I know." He smiles even more. "That's why I suggested it."

He knows my favorite restaurant? Maybe Jules told him as a suggestion to smooth the way for our new situation.

But no, I recall talking about the little family-owned Italian café—and my undying love for their meatball sub—in his presence. I just hadn't thought he'd been paying attention. This more considerate version of Darcy doesn't really vibe with my impression of him, but I have to admit either explanation is plausible.

He goes to do some unpacking while we wait for the pizza, and I curl up on the couch to read. I'm so absorbed in my book, I don't even realize the delivery has come until Darcy sets the pizza box down on the coffee table, and the scent of garlic and basil hits me full force.

I suddenly remember I'm hungry when my stomach grumbles—loudly —and I slap a hand to my stomach, as if that would shut it up.

Way to embarrass me, belly tiger.

Darcy's lips twitch as he sits down next to me, flips the lid. "After you."

Grinning, I reach for a slice, use my other hand to gather up the cheese that continues to stretch and pile it on top. I hum with pleasure when the combination of gooey mozzarella, tomato, fresh basil and garlic seduces my taste buds.

I swallow and say, "Their margherita pizza is the best."

"I won't argue with you," he replies, taking a bite of his own slice.

"First time for everything, I guess," I quip.

"Hey, look who's talking." He arches a brow as he chews.

"Touché," I assent. "So, what roommate rules did you have in mind?"

He shrugs. "Nothing too crazy. I was thinking we could each be responsible for washing up any dishes we use, or cleaning up the kitchen after using it. And if we both want to cook, we can both clean."

"Sounds reasonable." I don't know why I'm surprised; I've been to his place a few times, and it was always tidy. "What about the bathroom? I usually give it a scrub about once a week."

"Then we can rotate weeks. Same with vacuuming."

"With the caveat that we clean up our own messes," I add, eyeing him as I eat.

He chuckles. "What am I, an animal?"

I jerk a shoulder. "I know your bachelor pad was all spick and span, so I don't doubt your abilities; but you're still a bachelor after all, and I don't want you to think I'll clean up after you."

He smirks as he polishes off his slice. "Not all bachelors are a walking cliché, Elise. Besides, for all I know you're the one who likes to leave your socks everywhere."

"Darn." I roll my eyes, reaching for another slice. "Guess I won't be able to leave my bra on the bathroom door handle anymore."

Am I seeing things, or is that a blush creeping up his neck?

He clears his throat. "Preferably not."

We agree we'll each buy our own groceries, but switch off on communal things, like milk, eggs, and bread.

"What about TV usage?" Darcy asks.

"What about it?"

"Well, what happens if we want to watch something at the same time?"

"First come, first serve, I guess."

He narrows his eyes. "And you'll make sure you're always there first?"

My lips twitch in one corner. "Something like that."

He grins again, and again it bewilders me. Blinking, I grab another slice of pizza.

"Any other ideas?" he asks.

"Yeah, I was thinking about guests," I chew thoughtfully.

"Guests?"

"Yeah. Like, if we want to have friends over, or a date or something. Let me know if you want me to make myself scarce."

"Oh." He stares at his pizza as though it contains his response. "I mean, I guess I might have Cole over to watch baseball sometimes, but that's about it."

"I can't object to baseball. But that's it?" I eye him skeptically.

"Yeah. What, do you think I bring home a new woman every week?"

I take a bite of pizza, shrug again. "I don't know your life."

"No, you don't," he agrees, sighing. "But just so you know, I haven't even been on a date since I moved here."

"What, the women of Meryton not good enough for you?" I quip, even as I realize how contradictory I sound.

"That's not it." Frowning, he pauses. "I don't think you'd believe me if I told you why I haven't been with anyone in a while."

"What's that supposed to mean?"

He gives me a discerning look. "I think we've both noticed I tend to bring out the argumentative side of you."

"Yeah, well maybe—" Bristling, I start to get defensive, but he holds up a hand.

"Lissa, I'm just saying. I don't think you would like my answer right now."

Right now? I wonder. And what did *that* mean? He's cagey; I don't like it, nor do I like how my heartbeat picked up when he so casually used my nickname all of a sudden. But, I remind myself, he'll be here for a few months, and I agreed to it. We don't have to actually spend any time together, and I doubt we will, but we'll constantly be in each other's vicinity. I could at least do my best not to be hostile.

He keeps his eyes on me as he waits for a response, but he doesn't seem impatient, just assessing.

"Well, since you're stuck here," I say, meeting his eyes in challenge, "I think we should at least try to be civil."

"I agree." He tilts his head, expression thoughtful. "It occurred to me that while there are things we know about each other, we hardly actually know each other. I think if we're going to get along, we should get to know each other better."

What? Disinterested Darcy wants to get to know me? Where is this coming from?

"Are you saying you want to bond with me?"

"I supposed that's one way to put it. Though I also suppose some bonding is kind of inevitable." At my baffled look, he explains, "It's just usually what happens when you live with someone."

"That's not why I'm confused," I say. "I kind of thought you'd want to spend as little time together as possible."

He smiles a little, one corner of his mouth twitching up, but it's almost a little sad. "Believe it or not, Elise, I enjoy your company. Even when you completely misunderstand everything I say."

Torn between confused stupefaction and insult, I eventually decide on the easier emotion—insult. "Oh? And when have I misunderstood you?"

"Let me count the ways."

"So when you were mocking me for my extensive reading habits, that was a misunderstanding?"

"Actually, yes." He frowns even more deeply than before. "I didn't know you thought that. I assure you I wasn't mocking you. I was trying to point out to Celeste that reading is a more worthwhile pursuit than what she was listing—and also just good for you."

Watching him, he seems sincere; but then again, I thought he'd been sincere in his dislike. Is this a trick?

I would hate to admit I've just been misreading him the whole time, so I won't. Not yet anyway. I also hate to admit he's right—there's a lot we don't know about each other.

And whether we like it or not, living together will likely enable us to learn things about each other without even realizing it. If I'm lucky, maybe I could learn subtle ways to torture him.

"So you weren't making fun of me?" I ask for clarification.

"Of course not—partially because it's your job, which is important, but also because I would never do that, at least not intentionally," he says earnestly. "Especially not for something I enjoy doing myself."

I shake my head. "You know, I can't figure you out, Darcy."

He smiles again, eyes crinkling. "Well now you'll have plenty of opportunity to try."

TWO

AND TRY SHE DOES, at least at first. Since I constantly find myself staring at her, I almost always catch her when she's looking at me—and the moment when she catches herself watching me. Sometimes I'll be in the kitchen, or working on my laptop at the dining table; other times I'll be playing my guitar, sprawled on the couch on the rare occasion I play outside my room.

She doesn't realize how mesmerized she looks when she listens to me play, but I do. It's that look that pushes me to practice in the living room more often.

I'm learning little endearing things about her—the way she hums when she's cooking something, how she sets the alarm clock in her bedroom ten minutes ahead so she feels like she has more time in the morning, how cranky she is without coffee when she wakes up.

I love especially to watch her read.

She likes to curl up on the window seat—flanked by two filled book-shelves—with a book or e-reader and be lost to the world. I enjoy watching various expressions and emotions play over her face, but my favorite is when she laughs, often having to put the book down and clap a hand over her heart or mouth.

And she gets so into whatever she's reading she doesn't notice when I leave or enter a room; sometimes I have to call her name to get her attention, and she blinks at me as though just remembering where she is.

She often misses texts or forgets to eat while reading, but otherwise it's endearing.

It's only been a couple weeks, but I'm already finding it hard to keep my distance. If she notices how often I'm home, she doesn't say anything.

I suspect she does notice, though, and often deals with it by finding something else to do to avoid me. I know it'll take time for her to adjust and warm to me, but I'm not quite sure how to go about gaining her friendship—and maybe something more. It didn't take me long to realize I'm probably falling for her; but that won't end well if she never develops feelings for me.

I can only hope. I'm not sure I can be confident where Lissa is concerned.

But I do thoroughly appreciate the opportunity to get to know her better, and to have an excuse to be in close proximity with her.

Even though she keeps me at arms length.

Neither of us are used to sharing our space with someone else after so long living alone, so we both tend to be irritable from time to time, but I'm starting to wonder if she feels crowded. Despite our short time together, I can tell her patience is already wearing thin.

I do my best not to set her off—sometimes it's like walking on eggshells—but a lot of the time she's just politely distant.

I'll ask how her day was when we're both home from work, and she'll give me one-word answers like, "good" or "fine," without returning the question. A couple times I could tell she was tired and did all the dishes so she wouldn't have to, but she accused me of being so controlling as to be unable to deal with a slightly cluttered kitchen. And she stomped off in a huff when she'd wanted to do her laundry on a Saturday morning, but saw mine was already in the washer.

I also know better now than to try and have a conversation with her while she's reading.

I'm a patient man, but I'm starting to feel a little discouraged. I have to admit I thought things would have gotten better at this point. Instead, her walls are still thoroughly up. I'm at a loss how to get her to stop being abrasive and *talk* to me.

Now, we're out at Phillip's, the town's favorited local dive bar, and while Lissa agreed to carpool with me, she darts toward the bar—away from me—as soon as we enter.

I find Cole and Julia at a u-shaped booth with his sister Celeste, who looks like she wants to be literally anywhere else. Knowing World War III might erupt if Celeste and Elise sit next to each other, I sacrifice myself and slide in next to Celeste, leaving the end next to Julia for Elise, and order a drink from the server that stops by the table.

Celeste flips her sandy hair over her shoulder, a move she does often around me, but I don't pay much attention.

"How's the house coming, Darce?" Cole asks me.

"Good," I tell him honestly. "I've been stopping by to check in on the process every few days, and so far everything is satisfactory."

I don't really have anything else to say, so after that I only half-listen to the conversation at the table as I wait for Lissa, sip at my beer when it comes.

The bar is crowded, but it's taking her longer than I thought it would to get a drink; glancing over, it doesn't take me long to spot Lissa's curling dark hair, which she'd tied up in a ponytail.

She's leaning an elbow on the bar, a beer in her other hand, as she chats with the bartender. And when my eyes alight on the man across from her, I stiffen.

My brain registers the corresponding shock on the man's face, as well as his smirk when Lissa glances back over shoulder, then back to the bar. I clench my fists under the table; it takes every ounce of my self control not to storm over there and drag the smug bastard over the bar.

But that wouldn't do any good. If anything, it would make matters worse, and my former friend would probably slink away again, like he always does. Frowning, I brood into my beer.

. . .

AT THE BAR, I take in the furious look on Darcy's face, and the stunned one on that of the hot new bartender's. They clearly know each other, and not in a pleasant way.

I'd been having a nice, slightly flirtatious conversation with Garrett, as he'd introduced himself; he didn't hesitate to start charming me, and I couldn't help be a little charmed, even though his ease and confidence with me, and other women at the bar, informed me he's either a womanizer, aiming for more tips, or both.

Then he'd noticed something behind me, and I turned a little to see Darcy staring at us with barely concealed contempt. Garrett shakes off the encounter and smiles at me.

"I didn't realize you were Darcy's girl."

My eyebrows shoot up. "Me and Darcy? No, no. We're just... acquaintances."

Amused, Garrett starts drying a glass. "Acquaintances? Ouch."

"Well, we only know each other because his best friend is dating my sister," I explain, feeling a little off as I realize I don't have the heart to badmouth Darcy as I once did. "And now he's also my roommate for a few months while his house is being repaired."

He laughs. "Well, I don't envy you that. We were roomies once in college, so I speak from experience when I say he's a pretty stuffy room-mate. And he was constantly telling me what to do, especially when it came to chores—he was pretty anal about it."

"Is that so?" I narrow my eyes. Stuffy was what I had expected from Darcy myself, but as much as I hate to admit it, so far he's actually been a pretty decent roommate. He's super organized, and can't seem to help patronizing me sometimes—he'd even been impatient enough to do all the dishes a couple times—but he's never complained or tried telling me what to do. Maybe he is a tad anal, but he's stuck to the rules we agreed on and is pretty quiet most of the time.

Maybe Garrett was just a lazy roommate.

Plus, I was secretly grateful for the dishes thing, because both times I had been asleep on my feet; it had actually occurred to me he may have noticed and done it to spare me, but I'd snapped at him because I'd felt guilty I hadn't done it yet. If he did, he was more thoughtful than I gave him credit for.

And as much as it annoys me to realize, I love it when he plays his guitar; he seems like an entirely different person when he's relaxed, and that, reluctantly, pulls at me. "I can't say I've found him to be quite *that* bad."

Garrett's smile falters, but only for a moment. "Lucky you. Maybe he likes you better."

I snort. "Doubtful."

Grin widening flirtatiously, he leans in closer to me. "His loss."

Only half the table is happy to see me when I get there; Julia scoots a little so I can sit next to her. Across the table, Darcy scowls at me. I ignore him and do my best to make pleasant conversation; he, of course, doesn't say a word. Every once in a while he glances toward the bar, his scowl intensifying; every time I follow his gaze, it's on Garrett, who's always chatting up a different woman, to the detriment of some of the men waiting at the bar.

After a while, Darcy and I both have to stand to let the others out; Celeste reluctantly leaves Darcy's side to go to the bathroom, and as she heads off, Cole pulls Julia over to the dance floor.

He shoots Darcy a look as Darcy and I sit back down, and Darcy returns it, but I can't figure out what the exchange means. Just as I've resigned myself to spending the next few minutes in silence, Darcy speaks.

"Wanna play twenty questions?"

I turn from watching Cole and Julia, brow lifting. "With you?"

"No, with Mr. Bones over there." He tilts his head toward the life-size skeleton with a bow tie sitting on a bench by the entrance; even though it's the middle of September, Phillip's already has their Halloween decorations up, and I, for one, am here for it.

"I bet Mr. Bones is a better conversationalist than you."

The side of his mouth quirks in a lopsided smile. "Probably."

"Why the sudden interest in talking to me? You've hardly said anything all night," I point out, taking a sip of my beer.

He winces. "I know. I guess I've just been…thinking."

I give him an unimpressed stare. "Thinking."

"…Yes."

"Well, don't think too hard, there, Einstein."

"What's your favorite color?" he asks.

"Really?" I deadpan.

"C'mon." He runs a hand through his raven hair, mussing it up sexily, and leans over the table. His gaze on me is insistent; it's impossible not to look at him, so I don't try to look away, my courage rising under the intensity of his attention. "It's been a couple weeks since I moved in, and we hardly talk to each other. That's not just on me."

I wilt a little at the assertion, because I know he's right. He watches me carefully as I ponder this, causing me to sigh in acquiescence. "Turquoise. You?"

He perks up at this, and a little fissure of pleasure spreads through my chest with the knowledge I'm capable of pleasing Felix Darcy. It shouldn't delight me this much, but it does.

"Purple," he says. "Your turn."

"Favorite food?"

"Burgers. You?"

"Ice-cream."

This gets a smile out of him. "Good choice. I feel like it's a loaded question to ask your favorite book, so…favorite genre?"

"Ooh…" I press my lips together. "I'll read any genre, but I do read a lot of fantasy and romance. You?"

"Probably mystery."

We shoot a few more trivial questions at each other, and I figure that's the purpose of this game, so I'm surprised when he asks, "Is there anything you find challenging about your job?"

"Hm." I take a moment to really consider the question. "There are typical challenges with any public service occupation, and specifically within libraries. But for me, the hardest is dealing with book ban challenges."

"Ah." He nods, twirling his beer bottle around with his fingers. "I imagine that's frustrating."

"Very." Since the mood has shifted to more serious subjects, I contemplate something deeper to ask him. "Why'd you move here? Why Meryton?"

"Well," he sighs thoughtfully. "I like working in the city, but I also like peace and quiet. I'd gotten tired of living there, especially after Cole moved out here. I have other friends there, but I missed him, and he kept raving about this place. So I took a chance.

"What about you? You could've gotten a job at a different library."

"I could've, but this is my home." I shrug. "I wanted to come back."

He nods like he expected this answer, and I ask, "Why marketing?"

"I've just always liked graphic design. And in school I discovered I liked helping businesses discover how they could use branding to send messages about themselves. Whether we like it or not, people really do judge a book by its cover, and so I wanted to help spruce the cover up, you know?"

"I do," I smirk. "Thank you for the analogy."

It occurs to me the others have been away longer than expected, and I search the dance crowd for Cole and my sister, only to find them at the bar with Celeste. She does not look happy to be held up, and her frown only deepens when she glances back at us.

"You're welcome," Darcy says as the others start heading back. When he sees what I'm looking at, he gives me a knowing smile. "Guess we'll have to finish our game later."

I tilt my head, wondering if there's some subtext to the statement. "Guess so."

. . . . . .

DARCY IS his usual quiet self on the drive back to the apartment, but almost eerily so. Celeste had doubled her efforts when she'd gotten back to the table, but he wasn't very cooperative, much to her dismay.

Eventually he'd excused himself to go to the bathroom—whether he actually had to go, or just wanted to get away from Celeste, I couldn't tell —and when he came back, his expression was stony.

I'd also gone to the bar for another drink at one point, and ended up chatting with Garrett some more, flirting subtly. He not-so-subtly flirted right back, eventually leaning toward me with a seductive smile.

"Wanna grab drinks sometime?"

I grinned back, giving myself a moment to appreciate his silky-looking blonde hair, bright blue eyes, and full lips. But I had a feeling he wasn't looking for anything serious, and for reasons I couldn't comprehend, another pair of blue eyes—darker and more serious—flashed through my mind. Unnerved, I'd decided not to shoot Garrett down entirely.

"We'll see," I said.

When I'd returned to the table, Darcy's face was stormier than ever, and he scowled into his beer for the rest of the evening.

I know Darcy's sour mood must have something to do with Garrett, but I don't dare ask. In fact, I'm a little broody myself; he was starting to be companionable earlier, and now he's closed off again.

When we make it inside and he's closed the door behind us, he finally speaks.

"Did you have a good time tonight?" he hedges. I can tell he's trying to sound casual, but I suspect he really just wants to know about my conversation with Garrett. Well, I can oblige him if it gets under his prickly skin.

"Yeah," I tell him. "I even had a pleasant conversation with the new bartender."

"I'm sure you did," he says evenly.

"What exactly is that supposed to mean?"

Ugh, a phrase I seem to be repeating all too often. I move to the kitchen. If he's gearing up for a fight, I need some tea.

He follows me. "It means Garrett is good at making himself agreeable to people, so I'm not surprised your conversation was pleasant."

"Then why do I get the feeling you disapprove?"

"Because everything is a game to him." He leans against the counter, folds his arms. "He always has an angle, with everything he does. Especially with women."

I pick out a tea bag as the electric kettle boils water, send him a searching look. "And if he asked me out for drinks, would that be an angle, too?"

"Yes. Are you going out with him?" His eyes zero in on my face with such intensity I nearly take a step back. Why should he care who I go out with? I debate asking him just that, but I can't bring myself to go down that road.

"No," I admit. "I told him 'we'll see.'"

His shoulders relax, and he nods, more to himself than to me.

"Alright," he says. "Just don't get too close to him."

My head snaps up, eyes blazing with indignation. "You don't get to tell me who to date, or how to feel."

His face falls, arms collapsing listlessly to his sides, and for a moment I think he looks like he's going to be sick, but whatever he's feeling, he tamps it down.

"That's not what I meant," he says gently, almost like he's talking to a spooked horse, looking me in the eyes as though willing me to understand his sincerity. "I…I just don't want you to get hurt. And if you get too close to Garrett, then I guarantee you will. Get hurt, I mean."

Though the fire in me quiets, I remain skeptical. Darcy could just be jealous of Garrett, but that would mean...no. It can't have anything to do with me. He keeps his eyes on mine as I search his face; the furrow in his brow is unrelenting, as is the worried look in his eyes. Slowly, I soften into uncertainty, swallowing visibly.

"You mean that, don't you?" I say softly. "You're actually trying to protect me?"

He takes a step forward, hesitates as he watches me. When he steps back again, I feel bad—I've done such a good job of needling him, he's not even sure if he can approach me.

"Of course. You might not believe me, but I consider you a friend, Elise. And I do what I can to protect my friends."

My eyebrows scrunch together. "How did you know?"

"Know what?"

"That I might not believe you."

His lips twitch. "You haven't exactly kept your dislike of me a secret. If you don't like me, why would you trust me?"

"I..."

Well, shit. He's right—and maybe I'm the one who's not a great room-mate, I think as I deflate. I'm definitely the one who's been prickly. "I suppose I haven't. And after we agreed to be civil, too."

"It's alright."

I tilt my head. "No, it's not. You've been trying, and I haven't, and that's not fair to you. I'm sorry."

His answering smile is quiet, and not a little teasing. "Lissa Bennet is apologizing? Apology accepted if I can get that in writing."

"Shut up." I roll my eyes, but pause, unsure of myself. "If it makes you feel better, I didn't say yes to him because I could see he was playing the crowd. He was charming, but a little too charming for my liking."

Suddenly, but slowly, he pushes off the counter, picks up the electric kettle, and pours the hot water into my waiting mug. I haven't moved, so he's close enough for his arm to brush against mine as he replaces the kettle.

"Thank you," I croak out, my heart rate kicking up a notch.

"You're welcome," he says, his eyes flitting over my face. "And thank you."

"For what?"

"For trusting me. I think we're making progress."

I stay in the kitchen when he goes to his room, staring at my tea, pulling the tea bag string up and down to facilitate the steeping. My emotions are all over the place, jumping from confusion to anticipation—anticipation of what, I don't want to think about.

He said he considers me a friend. I called him merely an acquaintance earlier, just my temporary roommate. But deep down I realize we've built a certain level of trust over the past couple weeks, despite Snarky Lissa's active dislike. I have to give Felix the credit for that; he's been patient with me, and I've been short with him. But he's taken a step toward friendship, so maybe it's time I do the same.

Friends with Felix Darcy. Who'd have thought?

THREE

OVER THE NEXT COUPLE WEEKS, I take those steps toward friendship carefully, and as September edges into the first days of October, I feel lighter. I'd been so self-satisfied by my dislike of Darcy, I hadn't stopped to consider how much easier it would be to be friends with him.

Or how draining an intense dislike could be.

But I have to admit as we sit around the dining table at Cole's house, the more I actually get to know Darcy, the more I like him.

He was right about Garrett, of course. We've been to Phillip's a few times since that night, and when I twice had to take a trip to the ladies' room, I'd seen the handsome bartender making out with someone in the hall by the bathrooms both times.

He never noticed me during those moments and remains suave as ever behind the bar, but my responses are no longer even slightly flirtatious.

Instead, if I'm not mistaken, it's Felix who's been flirting a little. At the very least, he teases me as much as I tease him.

I don't know what to make of it. At first I wondered if he was seeing if I would be open to taking advantage of our living situation sexually, but he hasn't said anything suggestive or come close to making a move. Once I discard that thought, I'm relieved; I can now admit I'm attracted to him, but I don't want to sleep with him out of convenience, and I don't want to trod all over our newfound common ground.

And that's if he even wanted to sleep with me, which he doesn't, because as far as I know he still thinks I'm a frumpy librarian.

Or does he?

My Spidey-senses have detected something akin to desire in the way he looks at me sometimes, but I must be imagining it, right?

Really?, Snarky Lissa asks me. *What about this morning?*

Snarky Lissa has a point. This morning I realized I only had a dribble of shower gel left, and used Felix's as a last minute resort. It's labeled Bourbon and Amber, and I knew it smelled heavenly because I'd caught a whiff of the scent on him many times and had to hold myself back from sniffing him.

He, of course, noticed as soon as I stood next to him at the coffee machine.

"Did you use my body wash?" he'd asked. Though he'd stiffened, he hadn't sounded annoyed, only curious.

"Um, yes," I'd admitted tentatively. "Sorry. I ran out."

"It's alright." There was an awkward pause as he watched me pour my coffee, his eyes seemingly raking in every detail of my newly Bourbon and Amber-scented skin. "It smells good on you."

I'd blinked and looked up from my coffee at that, but he was already on his way out of the kitchen. And once again, I'd wondered, *what does that mean?*

So, maybe it's possible he's a little attracted to me. A tiny bit. We're talking miniscule.

But my resolution remains the same.

I have, however, slowly started to call him by his first name instead of his last. I confounded myself with how much I like calling him Felix, and with the thrill that'd shot down my spine the first time I did so, when he'd snapped his head around to look at me, lips slowly curving into a pleased smile.

Our relationship is precarious at best; we've gotten used to each other and have developed a routine of sorts, but still tip-toe around anything that resembles an emotional connection.

My heart sags a little when I realize that's mostly my doing. He hasn't had much of a problem being more open with me; I'm the one holding back. When I look at him across the table, discover his disconcertingly handsome gaze is already on me, it doesn't take a genius to reason why.

He's the kind of man I could fall in love with.

But it would be humiliating to fall for a guy who claimed me to be 'frumpy' upon meeting me (even if he may not mean it anymore), especially after proclaiming my own dislike so vehemently.

Oh, Pride you fickle creature. In only a month, I've gone from reluctantly letting him stay to possibly crushing on him. I do my best to keep a straight face, lest Celeste Bingley notice me developing feelings.

The last thing I need is a merciless interrogation.

Thankfully, Jules pulls me from my reverie.

"Lissa, how did last week's events go?"

"Really well," I tell her. The previous week we'd done a Freedom to Read campaign at the library, with informational programs, games, and displays about banned books all week long. "We had a lot of patrons thank us, and all our handouts were gone within the first few days."

"Oh, yeah," Cole perks up. "It was Freedom to Read Week, right?"

Celeste snorts. "Freedom to Read Week? Is that some kind of convention for bookworms?"

"No," I say seriously. "Freedom to Read is about exposing censorship and promoting intellectual rights and freedom. It's a constant campaign, but one week of the year, libraries highlight it just to let people know about all the attempts to ban books all over the country."

"Ban books?" Celeste blinks. "Why would someone do that? They're just books."

I resist the urge to roll my eyes since I sense her genuine bafflement. "Because some people think they have the right to decide for others what they should or shouldn't read. Without consideration for personal preference or values, they challenge books they think are inappropriate in public and school libraries—sometimes without even having read the book themselves, or even if they don't have kids in school. And sometimes they unfortunately succeed in getting books banned. Which, of course, then means those materials may not be available for someone who wants them."

To my surprise, Celeste stiffens in anger. "But that's...that's awful."

"It is," I agree.

"What one person considers inappropriate, another might consider perfectly acceptable. It's completely subjective," Celeste points out.

"Exactly." I nod to her, and I can feel Felix watching me. "And it's happening now more than ever. And the worst part is, most of the books that get challenged are books written by authors of color, or young adult and children's books that have LGBTQ characters, or tackle subjects like sexual education, race, or mental health. I'm not sure they realize how diminishing banning books is to the human experience. Or maybe they don't care who they hurt."

When I look at Julia, a tenderhearted elementary school teacher who often deals with opinionated parents, she's frowning.

"I understand some parents may not want their kids to read about certain things, but why they think they can choose for other people's kids I'll never understand," she shakes her head, though mostly to herself. "And at some point, even a kid is old enough to decide for themselves what they want to read."

"Actually the parents aren't the biggest problem," I elaborate. "Recently there's been an influx of groups who claim to represent liberty, but publish lists of books to challenge and make it their mission to convince people libraries are trying to 'groom' their children—which is bullshit, because if anyone has an 'agenda,' it's them. And they've succeeded in a lot of places because the community doesn't really understand what's happening. That's why we've been encouraging our patrons to publicly state how much they love the library and support the collection. It's proof that these groups don't speak for the community, and are actually in the minority."

Pursing her lips, Celeste eyes me. "For a librarian, you seem pretty calm about it."

Felix chuckles. "I assure you she's not. I've been subjected to a number of rants about banned books for the past week."

Though I smile, I shake my head. "I'm definitely not calm about it. In fact, I'm downright angry and disgusted. As corny as it sounds, books are powerful because they contain knowledge—even fictional ones, because we tend to see ourselves in stories, and also come to understand the situations of others, which is why representation is important. Reading helps us develop empathy for ourselves and others."

I stop, clear my throat. "Sorry, I'll shut up now, otherwise I'll go on forever."

Celeste glances between me and Felix, her expression thoughtful. "I never thought of books that way. I just thought they were either for learning or for escapism."

"You're not the only one," I shrug. "But one of the reasons I love my job is helping people discover the pleasure of reading. Finding that one book that gets them hooked."

"Has Meryton's library banned any books?" Cole asks.

I shake my head. "Thankfully, no. We've had a few complaints about books, and we listen to the complaints; we even thank them for sharing their opinion because we don't want anyone to feel like their feelings aren't valid—because they are valid, even if we disagree with them. But we have no intention of removing materials from our shelves just because someone makes a complaint. It's our policy to have something for everyone."

Julia changes the subject not long after that, and we speak of more pleasant things for the rest of dinner. Interestingly enough, Felix does more talking than usual, while Celeste is abnormally quiet.

I wonder at the role reversal, and am on my guard when I go to put my plate in the kitchen, and Celeste does the same. But unlike usual, she doesn't have some snarky comment to make.

She sets her plate on the counter as I rinse mine. If I'm not mistaken, she seems hesitant. Just when I think she isn't going to say anything, she asks, "Does the library have any books with bisexual characters in them?"

She asks so quietly, I'm not sure I heard her. I turn off the water and set my plate in the sink.

"We do," I say slowly. "Are you asking for a recommendation?"

"Perhaps," she says primly.

I smirk and lean against the counter. "Well, *An Absolutely Remarkable Thing* is a popular one, and one of my personal favorites is called *Payback's a Witch*, which has a lot of bi or pansexual characters. Both are series if you're interested in that."

Her eyes flit around the kitchen. "What are they about?"

I can't help wondering at her reasons for asking, but I know it's not my business; and regardless of her attitude toward me, the librarian in me is happy to see her taking an interest in something she's openly scorned in the past. So I deliberately relax and do what I do best: Talk about books.

It isn't long before she visibly relaxes, too, and even gives me a tiny smile of acknowledgement. "Thank you, Elise," she says, sounding a little surprised at the words coming out of her mouth.

"Thank you," I say, returning the gesture. When she tilts her head in question, I clarify, "For genuinely asking my opinion on something you know I enjoy, and setting aside whatever about me irritates you to listen."

I think perhaps the statement might make her dislike me again, but instead she looks confused. "You don't know why you irritate me?"

Wow. I wasn't sure she'd admit it. I guess we're both being blunt today.

"Should I? I mean, I think you have a thing for Felix, but I don't know what that has to do with me, other than that he's currently my roommate."

She narrows her eyes, watching me shrewdly, then appears to decide something. "I have been interested in him for a little while, but I've never had his attention the way you do."

I decide not tell her it's likely because I haven't been trying to get his attention.

"We're just friends," I shrug. "And we weren't even that only a few weeks ago."

"Hm."

There's that shrewd look again. She doesn't look like she believes me. But she lets it go, instead thanking me again for the book recommendations as she heads back to the dining room.

"You're welcome."

She pauses in the doorway, glances back at me with an arch look. "You know, you're not nearly as terrible as I thought you were."

I laugh. "Neither are you."

As I say it, I realize it's true. Celeste and I may never be real friends, but now I'm not nearly as worried as I was about her as Julia's potential sister-in-law.

If I was curious as to whether or not she was considering giving up her pursuit of Felix, returning to the dining room to see her cornered with him while Cole and Julia whisper to each other at the other end of the table certainly assuages that curiosity.

Felix gives me a look that begs me to be a buffer, but I head to my sister and Cole instead.

He can handle himself. Besides, I think Celeste and I have struck up some kind of truce. I'll let her have this one.

. . . . . .

I'M in a good mood today, sitting on the couch with my guitar, futzing around with melodies. It's the middle of October, my house repairs are coming along, and Lissa has gone all out for what she refers to as "Spooky Season." Our apartment is decorated, among other things, with figures of skeletons, black cats, and jack-o-lanterns, floating ghosts and bats, and a witchy display of apothecary bottles labeled things like "wolfsbane" and "hemlock tonic." A fake book of spells sits on the coffee table under a black cauldron that has carved frogs for feet and is decorated with brushed golden moons; the cauldron holds overpriced Halloween candy that has been steadily disappearing.

I find the whole ensemble whimsical, just like Lissa.

Our pantry contains a few boxes of Count Chocula, since Lissa stocked up once it hit the shelves. Her reaction when I mentioned never having tried it was one of horrified shock.

"You poor man," she'd said, thrusting the bowl she'd just poured at me.

I have to admit it's growing on me.

So far it's been a quiet Saturday afternoon. Lissa reads in her usual spot, drinking coffee out of a jack-o-lantern mug, and nibbling on candy corn from a bowl printed with ravens and skulls.

How she can eat the stuff I don't understand, but thankfully she'd only shrugged when I insinuated candy corn is the devil's idea of candy.

I can't help thinking how homey it all is. I miss my house, sure, but Lissa's place feels like home, too.

I don't doubt it's because she's here. I'm a little worried about what will happen when I can move back into my house, how big and empty it might feel.

And with that thought, I stop playing, the last chord I strummed ringing softly as I glance over at the window seat, surprised to find Lissa is no longer there. I set my guitar down, leaning it against the couch cushions, and stand to look around. I realize it's nearly dinner time and neither of us has mentioned cooking or ordering anything, so I go the kitchen and open the fridge to skim the contents.

I'm wondering if I should just throw in a frozen pizza when I hear Lissa come out of her room.

"Hey, I'm feeling lazy. Wanna throw in a pizza?" I ask, shutting the fridge.

But when I look out to the living room, she's on the couch lacing up a pair of black boots.

"Actually," she says, not meeting my eyes, "I'm going out."

"Oh. Okay."

My mind blanks. Does she mean she has plans with Julia, or does she have a date? When she stands, I struggle to keep a straight face.

She's wearing black tights under a plaid skirt, a slightly oversized sweater tucked into the front. She took the time to put on some makeup and put some colorful dangles in her earlobes. She looks tempting and sweet, and so utterly Lissa I just want to scoop her up and carry her to bed.

I swallow. "You look great. Got a date?"

"Thanks." She tugs at the sleeve of her sweater, fidgets her feet. "Yeah, kind of."

A lump forms in my throat at her hesitation, wondering if it's with Garrett, even though she'd assured me she wouldn't go out with him. The thought makes me sick to my stomach.

"Kind of a date?"

"Well," she sighs, "My mom set it up. She met the new associate at the De Bourgh law firm, and when he mentioned wanting to meet someone, she told him I would be happy to go on a date with him, then called me and insisted I go."

"Wait, what?" I'm relieved it's not Garrett, but balk at her words. "She set you up on a blind date without asking you first?"

"Yep."

I try to wrap my head around this. I knew Mrs. Bennet was eager for her daughters to meet successful men, but I can't think of a single reason she wouldn't at least ask Lissa if she was interested in being set up. "Why would she force you to go on a date? And why you? What about one of your other single sisters?"

She shrugs, but I can tell she's as bothered by the situation as I am. "My mother is frustrated by my lack of ambition when it comes to men. She wants us all married off so she can brag about it to her friends, but she doesn't think I can 'get' a man by myself because, and I'm quoting verbatim here, 'No man wants a woman who always has her nose in a book.'"

"That's bullshit," I bite out, my tone more forceful than I intended, and her eyes finally meet mine. "You're a smart, funny, passionate person. You don't need help getting a date."

As much as I don't want her to be going on a date with another man, it pleases me beyond reason to see a blush rise to her cheeks, her eyes widening at my words.

She smiles hesitantly. "I agree, thank you."

"You don't have to go if you don't want to," I point out.

"Technically," she says flatly. "But if I don't go my mom will call and berate me for my bad manners and tell me how ungrateful I am."

My mouth drops open, but she holds up a hand before I can so much as think of a response.

"It's alright. I'm used to it."

"It's not alright, but I'll let it go for now."

"Thank you," she says, clearly relieved. "Sorry to leave you alone so last minute."

I jerk a shoulder. "It's fine. Maybe I'll see if Cole is free and go to Phillip's for a bit."

She nods. "You should do that. I should go, or I'll be late."

I watch her pull on her coat and grab her purse, not looking back at me as she heads toward the door. When she opens it I call after her, doing my best to sound upbeat.

"Have fun!"

She rolls her eyes, but gives me a sardonic smile. "I'll try," she assures me before closing the door.

When she's gone, I blow out a breath, a mixture of confusion and jealousy swirling around in my stomach like oil and water. I don't want her to have a bad date, but I also don't want her to end up liking this guy.

But I'm not her protector, and as long as there's nothing more than friendship between us, I can't stop her from seeing other people.

Maybe I will go to Phillip's, if only so I won't be alone with my thoughts. But first, I should definitely eat something.

Frozen pizza it is.

FOUR

I FIGHT off the burn of angry tears as I stomp my way down Main, adrenaline still pumping, not giving much thought to where my feet are taking me. They kick up a few curled yellow leaves lingering on the sidewalk as I pass by street lights decorated with cornstalks and twinkling orange lights around the poles, smiling plastic pumpkins hanging from the top.

My date with Wilbur Collins was the absolute worst, but I'm more mad at myself than anything. Cursing myself would be more accurate.

I knew, I just *knew* it would be terrible. Not just because my mother had set it up and demanded I go, but because I'd mostly agreed out of cowardice.

I was afraid of how strong my feelings for Felix were growing, and I guess some small part of me was hoping the date would go well and I could put an end to the confusing situation with my roommate.

Well, mission failed.

Universe: One. Lissa: Zero.

Absently, my pace slows as I get to the door of my usual haunt; I can't decide if I'm hoping Felix will be here as he said he might, or if he's the last person I want to see right now.

The crowd at Phillip's is at its typical Friday night peak, and I pull my jacket tighter around me at the gust of wind that blows past when the door opens behind me. God, I just want a drink.

What goes good with indignation? Bourbon? Vodka?

As I head toward the bar, I catch sight of a familiar tall, dark frame facing away from me, and I feel myself relax a little. If he's at the bar, it means Garrett isn't, which is good—I have no more patience for sleazy men tonight. As I near Felix, I notice he's standing sort of stiffly, despite Garrett's absence, and through a break in the crowd finally determine why.

He's surrounded—I nearly laugh out loud. Three women form a half-circle around him, one standing just in front of the others, simultaneously leaning on the bar, and leaning toward him, pawing at his arm. The closer she gets, the more rigid his stance, and the more his shoulders hunch.

Can't she see he's uncomfortable?

Of course she can't. All she sees is a handsome face, like how I only saw his scowl once upon a time.

Well, I know better now, I remind myself. And since I owe him for warning me about Garrett, I can help him out. I continue my steps toward him, and, taking a breath, approach from the side so he'll catch sight of me. I deliberately smile brightly when he notices me, and though he's clearly surprised to see me, he relaxes a little and smiles back.

The leading woman trying to get his attention glares when she sees it was taken by me.

"Hey." I smile apologetically as though he'd been expecting me when I reach his side, then casually lay a hand on his arm, stand on my tiptoes to press a kiss to his cheek. "Sorry I'm late."

"It's alright."

He takes my improvisation with surprising ease, loosely sliding an arm around my waist as though he does it all the time and looking down at me with no small amount of intensity. "I haven't been waiting long."

I suppress a shiver. Why does such a small interaction between us feel so natural?

Felix turns back to the bar, absently saying, "Nice to meet you," to the group of women, and orders an Old Fashioned for me and another Scotch for himself. Nose in the air, the woman at the bar glides away, shooting daggers at me.

I valiantly pretend not to notice.

"No Cole?" I ask Felix.

"He had plans with Julia."

I'm surprised he willing came to a crowded bar by himself, but I nod. "Ah. Observe my shocked face."

He chuckles and tugs me a little closer.

When we have our drinks, Felix takes my hand and pulls me to a newly emptied table. Leaning over the table top toward me, he asks. "So what happened to the date?"

"It ended early." I take a long sip of my drink. "Ooh, that's good."

"You sound like you need that drink."

"I do. And it just answered my question." I take another sip.

He gives me a baffled look. "What question?"

I inch forward on my stool, lean in so our faces are only inches apart. "What liquor pairs best with indignation? Turns out the answer is bourbon."

A quiet chuckle passes his lips, as though he nearly snorted in laughter, but held back.

"That bad, huh?"

"You have no idea. Boy, my mom sure knows how to pick 'em."

"I can't tell if I'm going to be amused by this story, or annoyed."

I take another fortifying sip of my drink before getting into it, somehow not astounded that I *want* to tell him about my terrible evening.

I tell him Wilbur had scolded me for being late when I arrived, even though it was only a couple minutes past seven, and that he expected me not to keep him waiting next time—*next time,* assuming we'd have another date when we hadn't even started the first one.

He'd already ordered us each a glass of wine, which I'd been okay with, but when the server came to take our food order, and I gave her mine, he'd protested, telling me it was too much food for me. He tried to tell the server, "the lady will have a salad," winking at her as he said it, but thankfully she'd met my gaze and I'd given her a subtle shake of my head.

He nearly threw a fit when our food was brought out, calling the poor woman incompetent, which had forced me to point out she'd brought me exactly what *I* asked for, and therefore had done nothing wrong. This had seemed to mollify him, but when the waitress left, he'd smugly assured me she would not be getting a tip.

He hardly paid any attention to me as we ate because all he did was talk about himself, which was fine by me, because I'd rather he not know anything about me. The only time we talked about me was when he mentioned my mother had told him I worked at the library; he insinuated I must find my job boring and therefore wouldn't mind giving it up once I was married, and didn't seem to understand when I assured him I loved my job and fully intended to keep it whether I was married or not.

Felix watches me as I speak, clearly enthralled with my storytelling if the look of disgust in his expression is anything to go by. Then I tell him how stunned Wilbur was that'd I'd been able to finish my meal, and how he'd raked his eyes over my body, informing me I would never keep my figure if I continued to eat like that. I was already uncomfortable, but way he leered at me had put me on edge. Apparently this puts Felix on edge too, because the knuckles gripping his glass are turning a little white.

"Why didn't you just leave?" he asks me.

I shrug. "I was hungry, and the food was good. Plus it's just ingrained; lots of women are inadvertently trained to be polite to man, even if he's a jerk, either as a safety precaution, or just to make him feel more comfortable—never mind her own comfort. I guess I'm no exception, at least to a point."

This pulls a sad smirk out of him. "I recall being a target of your snark more than once. Please tell me you unleashed it on this guy."

"Something like that..."

When he raises a brow, I smile wryly and continue. "When the check came and I saw he had indeed not added a tip, I excused myself to go to the bathroom, but actually went to find our waitress and give her a generous one in cash for her trouble. I was just going to leave the restaurant without a farewell, but he was waiting for me when I stepped outside."

"Uh-oh."

I nod. "He proceeded to ask me if I would rather go back to my place, or his."

Felix sputters out a cough as his drink goes down the wrong pipe. "I beg your pardon?" he chokes out.

"That's what I said. He thought I was being coy."

"I have a bad feeling about this."

"As you should," I say grimly. "So, Wilbur decided we'd go this place and, apparently not considering birth control, informed me he refuses to wear a condom as he dislikes the feel. Never mind my feelings on any of those matters."

"What the fuck?" Felix tenses. "I can't even...what the fuck?"

"My thoughts exactly. I informed him in no uncertain terms I would not ever be sleeping with him, and he took that to mean he would have to wait until the second date for sex. I said if he thought I would go on another date with him after his behavior, he was delusional."

I bring my glass to my lips to steady my shaking hands, tilting my head back to swallow the last of my drink, steadying myself for the climax of the story.

I'd started to walk away, but he'd caught my wrist, insisting that since he'd paid for an extravagant dinner, I owed him, explaining it as though I were a child who didn't understand.

I'd pushed down the automatic fear and yanked my arm away, pointing out he didn't have to do any of those things, nor had I asked him to, and that no woman was ever obligated to repay a man with her body, for any reason.

He'd smiled—*smiled*, like he thought I was flirting—called me a tease, and leaned in to kiss me, but I pushed him away, and straight up ran in the other direction.

I don't realize a tear has escaped down my cheek until Felix reaches out to sweep it away with his thumb.

Stunned, I can only stare at him.

"I'm sorry that happened, that he upset you."

"I know I shouldn't care what a creep like him thinks," I say, my eyes downcast.

"Bullshit," he says darkly, and my head whips back up. "What he thinks matters on some level because it hurt you, and your feelings are valid. Don't put yourself down for having perfectly natural feelings in an upsetting situation."

"O-okay," I stutter. Without my even asking, Felix has given me something I didn't realize I needed: Vindication. I needed a man to understand what another man made me feel, and have him tell me the guy was a jerk and I acted appropriately. Jules would have assured me of the same thing, but for some reason it feels better coming from Felix.

When a server stops by our table to take our glasses, Felix orders another round and a basket of fried pickles. We're silent until the order comes, and needing to lighten things up, I prop my elbows on the table.

"So what's the verdict?"

"Hm?" He says, munching on a pickle.

"Amused or annoyed?"

"Oh." He swallows, frowning. "Definitely annoyed."

"Good. Me too—even I couldn't be amused by that schmuck."

"Pretty sure no one's said schmuck since 1926."

"We should bring it back, it's fun word." I pop a pickle into my mouth. "Schmuck...schmuck."

"I think you're a little tipsy."

"I think so, too. But in a good way, where I feel better instead of objectified by a garbage person who says garbage things."

He just smiles at me, his eyes glinting with amusement, and shakes his head. We finish off the pickles in no time at all, and he watches me thoughtfully over the table, seeming to consider something.

"What?" I ask.

"Nothing. Just curious about something, but it's a very personal question for two people who aren't dating."

I quirk a brow. "Is it a question a friend would ask another friend?"

His brows scrunch together in thought. "I think so, if both those friends were female."

"Okay, now I'm curious. Just ask, Felix."

"Okay, but feel free not to answer."

I just give him a look. He sighs and clears his throat.

"Are you…" He lowers his voice, "On birth control?"

Both my eyebrows shoot up to my hairline, but I'm even more intrigued now, unable to help the zing of attraction in my center when I wonder if he has a personal reason for asking. But I want him to know this, too. "Yes, I have an IUD. Why do you ask?"

"I just…when you mentioned that Collins guy didn't even consider it, I realized I haven't seen any pills in the apartment, and I wondered. I know as your roommate, I don't have a reason to know that, but as your friend I'm glad to know you have that protection."

Touched, I smile at him. "I'm glad, too, even if I've had no use for said protection of late."

I can't tell if it's the buzz I've got going on, wishful thinking, or what, but I swear his gaze turns heated. But he only says, "Me either."

"How long for you?" I pry.

He blows out a breath. "Several months."

I nod understandingly. "A little over a year for me."

Conversation tapers off after that; we both appear to be thinking deep thoughts as we finish our drinks. At least, I am, and as I head to the restroom, I try to puzzle out what exactly I'm feeling. When I return to the table, Felix has taken care of the bill and I'm no closer to an answer—aside from being attracted to him, that is.

I'd walked to my date, and he'd walked to the bar, so we head back to our apartment together, idling and enjoying the view of the street lit up at night, the plastic pumpkins looking whimsically eerie under the harsh glow of street lights.

I loop my arm through his companionably, and his face lights up. We don't say anything, just enjoying the quiet evening, and again it strikes me that this feels pleasantly natural. I let go once we reach our building, follow him up the stairs.

He opens the door, gestures me in; I turn on the hall light and shrug off my coat as he closes the door, and when I turn to hang it on the coat rack, I bump into him.

His hands land on my shoulders, steadying me, and I look up at him to see his gaze is on me, intense and searching. His fingers squeeze a little as his eyes unmistakably flick down to my lips, and I instinctively tilt my chin up.

Just when I think he's going to lean in, my phone buzzes in my pocket.

I jolt, his hands falling away as I shuffle my coat to one arm and pull it out. I groan when I see "Mother Dearest" lighting up the screen, and ignore the call. When I look back at Felix, he lifts a brow.

"She probably wants to ask about my date."

"Ah. I imagine she won't be happy about what happened."

"No, she won't, but probably not the way you think." When his brows furrow in confusion, I pocket my phone and move around him to hang my coat, and explain, "She'll probably blame me for chasing him off, or even accuse me of being rude to him."

"But he's a dickhead."

A laugh sputters out of me. "He is a dickhead. But she'll tell me he's the only kind of man who would put up with me and I have too many expectations."

"But…" He trails off, clearly baffled but probably not wanting to offend me.

"But she's my mother?" I finish sadly, and shrug. "That's just how she's always been."

"I'm sorry. What about your dad?"

"I'm the favorite when it comes to my dad," I say, perking up a little. "He was a librarian, too."

"That explains it." His voice is teasing, but his eyes watch me carefully. I still want to kiss him, but the moment is lost; there are still too many questions looming between us.

"Well, I think I'm a little emotionally exhausted, now," I say honestly. "So I'm going to go to bed."

"Good idea. Goodnight, Lissa."

"Goodnight."

I get ready for bed, but when I finally fall into it I lay awake for a while, unable to stop thinking about my eventful evening, and lingering on what might have happened if my mother's call hadn't interrupted us.

Despite the date-that-shall-not-be-mentioned, I had a pretty pleasant evening. And with the memory of Felix's heated gaze on my lips, I have even more pleasant dreams.

FIVE

I BREATHE a sigh of relief as I step through the front door; it's been a long day, and I want a bath with a glass of wine. I stow my coat and bag, head to the kitchen and pull a bottle of red out of the fridge, pull out the cat-shaped stopper.

It wasn't really a *bad* day, I think as I pour the liquid into a tumbler with ghosts painted on it. It was just a little emotionally draining.

We had someone call in to complain about a display—one highlighting LGBTQ young adult novels. The patron had told our teen librarian, Charlene, that no one in the community wanted the display up, but we knew that wasn't true—we've gotten a lot of positive response from the community about it overall.

But it was still upsetting.

I've always thought of our community as a pleasant, inclusive one; it's jarring to realize there are some who would spoil that. Although it's possible the caller was from another town, it still boils my blood.

I've just taken a long, contented sip of my wine when there's a banging on the door.

"Elise! You open this door right now!"

This time when I sigh, it's with annoyance and resignation. I've been putting my mom off all day, ignoring her calls and finally responding to her "CALL ME NOW!!!!" text with "I'm at work." I should have known she wouldn't give up; Francine Bennet is no half-assed meddler, and I know she'll demand to hear how my date last night went.

I go to the door, bracing myself over the sound of her still banging on it, and turn the handle. She doesn't wait for the door to open all the way before storming in in a flurry of lace and hairspray. I close the door quietly, walk wordlessly back to the kitchen to pick up my wine.

She follows, lips pursed in displeasure.

"Now you listen to me Elise Bennet," she starts. "You are going to call Wilbur and apologize to that poor man right this instant."

I sputter. "I beg your pardon? I have nothing to apologize for."

"I knew something was wrong when you didn't answer my calls, so I called him to ask how your date went. He assured me he'd be willing to give you another chance if you apologized."

"Excuse me?" I blurt, gripping my glass. "That's not your business! And I don't want to go out with him again, which I already informed him of."

She places her fisted hands on her hips—her signature stance with me. "Elise, I went through a lot of trouble to get that date for you—"

"Without asking if I would even be interested."

"And you," she continues as though I hadn't spoken, "Just had to go and be rude to the poor man. What am I going to do with you?"

I glare at her. "Actually, it was *him* who was rude to *me*, not to mention the poor waitress; I think I was pretty dang polite under the circumstances."

"He says you attacked him!"

I scoff. "That's a full out lie, mom. He tried to kiss me even though I made it very clear that would not be welcome, and I pushed him away from me. But I'm glad to know you believe some guy you hardly know over your own daughter."

She shakes her head, disappointment clear on her features. "You could have at least given him a chance. Maybe if you'd kissed him you'd feel a spark."

"I did give him a chance—I went on the date, despite my better judgment. And why on earth would I feel a spark with a man who spent the evening insulting and talking over me?"

"Oh, is that all?" She rolls her eyes. "You ungrateful girl. I set you up with a nice man and you throw it all away because—"

"Because he's not a nice man!" It bursts from me, and tears begin welling in my eyes. I think of Felix, how angry he was on my behalf, and wonder how my own mother could overlook Wilbur's behavior. How can she possibly thing I'm in the wrong here?

"Have you heard anything I've said?" I continue. "All he did was demean me; he even assumed I would sleep with him after one date and didn't understand when I told him 'no.' I literally ran away—that's how disgusted I was by him. I was even afraid of him for a second."

"Well, what am I supposed to do with you, then?" She asks again, eyes shifting uncomfortably, and I almost think I've gotten through to her. "You haven't liked any of the men I've sent your way."

Fuck it. Just fuck it.

I down the rest of my wine in one long gulp and set the glass on the counter, blow out a breath to hold back the tears, and turn to stare her down.

"That in and of itself should tell you the kind of man you think might be good for me isn't the kind of man I want. I don't need you to 'send men my way,' nor have I ever asked you to. I'm perfectly capable of getting my own dates, should I desire to."

She sniffs, tilting her chin up so she can look down her nose at me. "Fine. I can see my help isn't wanted here."

It never has been, I think. Then she continues, "Good luck getting a man without me. You may be pretty enough for some men, but you ruin it by constantly sticking your nose in a book and being sarcastic. When I mentioned you were a librarian to Wilbur, I had to talk you up like you were a quiet sort of girl who wanted to get married so you could quit."

I feel my cheeks heat and my face contort, and I hope my expression conveys the absolute disgust I feel. My stomach rolls.

"No. You didn't *have* to do any of that. And now I'm wondering how much of what you said influenced the way he treated me."

"Well, what do you expect, Elise? You chase men away with your attitude; I wanted him to have a good impression of you before he met you."

I don't bother holding the tears back now, letting them roll hot and miserable over my face. "And instead you gave him the impression I would let him walk all over me. Has it ever occurred to you that I don't want anything to do with a man who doesn't want me for exactly who I am?"

It's like a slice to my heart when she scoffs. "And just what man would want a mouthy, opinionated woman who spends all her time reading? It's like you're purposefully remaining single just to spite me. You've even had a man living with you for weeks and can't make him fall in love with you."

"I don't want to *make* anyone love me; that wouldn't be real love." I straighten my spine. "I would never degrade myself by building a relationship based on lies. That's not healthy or fair to anyone. And don't worry, you're not a failure as a mother if you don't get all your children married off."

She huffs. "And this is what I get for trying to help you. I wash my hands of you, you selfish child."

"Hypocritical much?"

Her face flushes. "What was that, young lady?"

All energy gone, my voice is quiet, but forceful, and I brush at some the tears that have slid down to my jaw. "The only selfish one here is you. For years you've tried to interfere in my life without any consideration for my feelings. I've never done anything wrong, yet you continue to berate me instead of support me—even now, when I've told you there was a moment I didn't feel safe with Wilbur. Hell, I'm not even sure if you love me."

I don't realize how true it is until I say it. And it's utterly crushing. I can't look at her face, creased in an angry frown, any longer, and move past her to the front door.

"I think you should leave now."

She does the chin-raising thing again, like I've done something to offend her—which, I suppose I have, if telling the truth is offensive. Nothing I've said appears to have any affect on her.

"Well, I never," she crows, marching stiffly out the door.

I slam the door behind her, the tears of hurt and anger welling in my eyes again. Feeling a crying jag coming on, I rush to my room, closing the door behind me and sinking to the floor at the side of my bed.

Why I'm always the butt of my mother's cruel streak I don't understand. And the worst part is, she doesn't seem to care if she hurts my feelings—maybe she thinks I don't have any feelings.

Whatever the case, it may be time to face the facts. Unless my mother can change, I might have to cut ties with her.

I think I hear a soft knock on the door, but only belatedly look up after hearing it open. My heart sinks when I see Felix approaching me, concern etching his face; I just want to be alone with my misery, and I don't want him to see me like this.

I start to wipe at my tears, but he sits down next to me, wordlessly sliding his arms around me. I try to push him away, but he only pulls tighter until he holds me against his chest.

Since it's obvious he isn't leaving, I give up struggling, at first trying to slow my tears. But when he begins to stroke my back in soothing motions, the idea that Felix of all people is more of a comfort to me than my own mother—that he seems to care about me more than my mother does—brings them back to the fore, fresh and hot.

I curl into him, allowing myself the comfort of his strong arms around me, breathing him in. He smells like his shower gel—it's definitely my favorite now, and I may have to get some for myself when he leaves.

Even if Felix and I go our separate ways after he moves out, I doubt I'll forget his kindness in this moment.

· . ˙ ˙. . ·

I CLOSE my eyes as I hold Lissa close. I don't know what exactly made her cry, but I have an idea—I saw Mrs. Bennet storming out of the building as I came in. I was grateful she didn't notice me, but when I entered the apartment, I could feel that something was off.

It was too silent.

Since I didn't see Elise, I wandered down the hall, finding the bathroom door open, but her door firmly closed. I hesitated, but when I heard the soft, muffled sounds of her crying, I went with instinct.

I used a knuckle to tap lightly on the door, opened it to find her on the floor by her bed, arms hugged around drawn up knees, head against her arms.

She looked up and, unsurprisingly, wasn't happy to see me, but I went to her anyway; and when she shoved at me, I refused to let go until she sagged against me, her breath shuddering in and out, over and over.

Now, as I recall how my mother used to rub my back when I was upset, I decide to see if it will help.

I'm both relieved and touched when she curls toward me, leaning her head on my chest. I savor the feeling of holding her until her breathing becomes more even, and she sniffles. I loosen my hold when she sits up a little.

"Do you want some tea?" I ask her.

"Can there be whiskey in it?" she mumbles.

I chuckle. "Absolutely."

I pull her up and hold her close as we walk down the hall, only letting go when she breaks away to go curl up on the couch. I get the water boiling and pull out my phone to send a text.

Once I've doctored Lissa's tea and poured a regular cup for myself, I bring the mugs out to the living room. I hand hers to her, sitting next to her and draping one arm over her shoulders, hugging her to my side. Her lip wobbles at the action, but she sips her tea slowly.

"I saw your mother leave. Do you want to tell me what happened?"

"She talked to Wilbur and came to get me to apologize to him," she says absently, her voice devoid of emotion.

I stiffen. "What?"

She runs through the gist of their conversation robotically, and by the end I can feel myself reaching my boiling point. Thankfully, I'm saved from a possible outburst by a gentle knock at the door.

Lissa frowns in confusion. "Who could that be?"

"Julia," I tell her. "I asked her to come."

"You did?" She looks at me with wide, bleary eyes, tired from crying. I smile softly as I get up to answer the door.

"I figured you'd need her."

She nods, her unguarded expression one of wonder and gratitude. "You sweet man. Thank you for thinking of that."

"Of course." It warms my heart that I was able to comfort her some, but I know what she really needs right now is her sister.

"Hey, Felix," Julia says as she shuffles in. Her eyes immediately go to her sister, who stares back, clutching her mug like a lifeline.

"Jules," Lissa whimpers.

Julia doesn't hesitate, not even bothering to remove her coat, and rushes to the couch, throwing her arms around Lissa, who begins to sob again. I move quietly toward my room to give them some privacy; over the back of the couch, Julia meets my eyes, gives me a thankful and encouraging nod. I nod back and go hole up in my room.

I try to read a book, one I checked out from the library after Lissa recommended it to me, but I just end up pacing my floor. Eventually I hear movement in the hall, and the sound of Lissa's bedroom door closing. After a few minutes it opens again, and I go to my own door, opening it to find Julia, fist poised to knock.

"How is she?" I ask as I step into the hall.

Julia looks sad, an expression I don't think I've ever seen on her face, and she rubs her hands over her arms as though she were cold.

"Upset, but asleep," she says. "I got some of the story out of her, but she's exhausted, so she didn't really get to tell me what happened last night. But she did mention she talked to you after. Can you tell me about it?"

"Sure."

I take her through Lissa's retelling of her date as we sat in the bar, my own responses. Julia's eyes fill as I talk, and though she lets the tears quietly trail down her cheeks, she doesn't interrupt. When I finish, she sighs, pulling a pack of tissues from the purse she'd left on the coffeetable and dabbing at her eyes.

"I didn't want to believe Mom could stoop so low. But I think it's time I had a long, hard talk with her. And I'll tell Dad what she said to Lissa; he won't stand for it either. Maybe she'll finally listen to us."

"And if she doesn't?" I ask.

Julia's face hardens. "Then our relationship will be very different. I've never understood why she places me on a pedestal and knocks Lissa down. Lissa never let it bother her before, so I never said anything, but I regret that now. I should have stood up for her."

"You're standing up for her now," I point out.

She sniffles, tilts her head at me, searching with discerning green eyes. I don't doubt she can see right into my heart. "So are you," she says, her lips forming a tiny smile.

"I do what I can," I shrug awkwardly, trying to come off nonchalant.

"You're a good friend, Felix."

Julia smiles knowingly and pats my knee before rising. She shrugs on her coat, slips on her shoes, and gathers up her purse.

Then she turns to me, pausing with her hand on the door. "When are you going to tell her you have feelings for her?"

I don't bother denying it.

"When she's ready."

⁎ ⁎ ⁎

OVER THE NEXT week and half, I have to admit it's a struggle not to tell her, to just take her in my arms and kiss her. With each day, I become more and more aware I'll be moving out soon, and though I know I'll still see her, I won't be in her presence nearly as much.

In the week leading up to Halloween, we watch a bunch of classic horror films and other Halloween movies, cozied up on the couch together —there were a couple times when Lissa propped her feet in my lap, and it almost felt like we were a real couple.

Though if we were a real couple, I wouldn't be able to resist giving her a foot massage.

We also spend the week helping Cole and Julia prepare for the Halloween party he's throwing at his house, and coming up with costume ideas. I admit I'm not the biggest fan of dressing up, but Cole won't hear of me coming to his Halloween party without a costume. He and Julia want to do a couples costume, and Cole *innocently* suggested Lissa and I do, too. Lissa had lifted her eyebrows at this, but made no protest.

I let her take the lead with the costumes, and she decides I should be the Phantom from *Phantom of the Opera*—one of the movies we'd just watched—and she'll be Christine. I point out I should be Raoul if we're doing a couples costume, to which she replies that as friends, it makes more sense; plus, the Phantom is more mysterious.

Though the emphasis on friends is discouraging, I can't fault her logic.

The four of us hit up thrift stores and a local costume shop in a neighboring town for pieces, and miraculously find what we need.

On the night of Halloween, I wait for Lissa by our front door, pacing in my costume. I actually feel pretty damn good in it. I wear a billowing white linen shirt that makes me feel like a pirate tucked into pair of slim black trousers, and a pair of shin-high black boots; a long, black cape is pinned around my shoulders over an even longer black coat. The only thing I'm not wearing is the Phantom's half-mask—I'll put that on when we arrive. I stop pacing when I hear her enter, look up from the floor.

And my heart stops.

She looks like an ethereal queen in a flimsy, lacy white gown that slicks down her body to the floor. A white corset cinches it around her torso, and she wears a long, white woolen robe with frilly sleeves she found in a vintage shop to act as Christine's dressing gown but still keep her warm. Her hair is half pinned up in a mass of curls, falling down her back and over the curve of her breast, and on her feet are a pair of white lace-up boots.

She hardly ever wears makeup, but she did something to her eyes that makes them pop like golden brown moons against thick, dark lashes. There's a little bit of color on her cheeks, and her lips are painted a dark pink that makes me want to nibble them. She's a goddess.

But it's not just that; it's the look in her eyes. Her appraising gaze roams up from my feet, lingering on my chest where the shirt billows open before finally reaching my face.

"Don't you look dashing," she says, her smile flirtatious.

It strikes me then how appropriate our costumes really are—the Phantom wants Christine, and I want Lissa. But unlike the Phantom, maybe I'll succeed in making her mine.

I don't hesitate to run my eyes over her again. "Back at you."

She puts on her coat while I grab my mask, and we head down to my car in silence. I don't know if it's the costumes, but something feels different between us. The air is somehow more charged.

Maybe it's just me, and the blood I'm trying to force back into my brain. The last thing I want to do is make things awkward by adjusting my crotch.

We make it to Cole's in one piece, arriving just before the party is supposed to start. The place is decked out with decorations and string lights inside, and the dining table is stuffed with food. Cole set up his stereo in the living room to play Halloween music.

He and Julia are dressed as Gomez and Morticia Addams, and I have to say, they pull it off really well, wigs and all.

Cole stows Lissa's coat with Julia's things, and we head to the kitchen, where the drink station is set up, to help ourselves. Once people start trickling in, I put on my mask. To my surprise, Lissa pulls out a mask from her robe pocket, a simple white one edged with black trim and lined with black lace. She shrugs when I raise the brow not covered by my mask.

"Seemed appropriate," she says.

Most of the party whirs by in a sequence of average events that mostly involves making small talk and hiding by the food when I don't want to. It's a relief to find I don't have to expend energy avoiding Celeste, who's dressed as Tinkerbell; when she spots me she acknowledges me with a friendly smile and nod, but doesn't approach, and goes back to talking to someone else.

So instead, I utilize my time trying to stay near Lissa, and talking with Cole and Julia, who is back to her serene self after having it out with Mrs. Bennet and talking to Mr. Bennet.

I haven't asked how those conversations went; I suspect Julia thinks Lissa will tell me, and Lissa will tell me if she wants to.

Lissa drags me to the living room, which has been cleared for dancing, a couple times, though she makes sure she does it with upbeat songs. I don't mind because I'm content to watch her dance around me.

Normally I'd be feeling the press of the crowd by now, but sticking close to Lissa has made my party-tolerance more resilient. Plus, I don't have to say much; she does most of the talking and it makes me seem more approachable.

After watching Cole and Julia try to dance a tango, Lissa laughs her way to the kitchen to get another drink. It's getting late, so she opts for water; I stopped drinking over an hour ago since I have to drive, so I pull out a Coke, take a swig.

She chugs about half her water bottle, blows out a breath.

"Are you having a good time?" she asks me.

"Actually, I am. Parties will never be my favorite, but I'm enjoying this one."

She nods understandingly. "I'm about ready to go. Want to go home and watch *Hocus Pocus?*"

A smile tugs at the side of my mouth; I love the way she said that, like she considers her apartment *our* home. "Sounds good to me."

We give it a few minutes, finishing our drinks while we chat with a few other people who go through the kitchen. Then, somehow, there's a moment when we're alone. We both tacitly decide now is the time to make our escape, and she turns to toss her bottle in the recycling. I reach around her to toss my empty can just as she turns back around.

She bumps into me, her hands slapping at the lapels of my coat to keep herself steady just as mine grip the sides of her shoulders to steady her.

We both freeze.

Her lips, still pleasantly pink, part on a short intake of breath when my gaze shifts down to her mouth. When I glance back up, her eyes are smoky under her mask, accentuated by the black trim, and I can't look away.

I find myself leaning in, tilting my head; she must lean in, too, because our lips meet sooner than I expect. My chest burns with joy and desire, and unable to resist, I scoop her against me, my hands roaming up her back, plunging into her hair.

She's soft and pliant, and her hands skirt up my shirt to where my chest is exposed, fingers trailing over bare skin. I struggle to contain a groan. Instead, I tease her lips open with my tongue, and she lets me in.

I know we should stop before we get carried away, so I give her one last deep kiss and lift my head, breathing her name against her mouth as I open my eyes.

Her eyes blink open as she comes out of the haze of my kisses, and I'm ecstatic about the response I got from her until she straightens, dropping her hands as though she were caught poking in the cookie jar.

She looks like she wants to say something, but when her mouth opens all that comes out is a shaky breath. I give her a patient smile and brush a long ringlet of her hair from her shoulder.

"Ready to go home?" I ask gently.

She swallows and nods. I figure she might need a minute, so I tell her I'll meet her at the car. I say my goodbyes to Cole and Julia, then go start up my car, turning up the heat. Lissa comes out a few minutes later bundled in her coat.

She unties her mask, quirks a small smile as she buckles up.

"You gonna drive with your mask on?" she asks wryly.

"Right." I pull off my mask, sending her an affectionate look. She squirms a little under my gaze, but I take it as a sign she's not unaffected by me. I think she's finally ready to hear me; I can only hope she doesn't push me away.

SIX

WE DON'T TALK on the way back to the apartment, but the atmosphere in the car is charged with stifled emotions—or at least, I'm trying to stifle mine. This whole night I've felt like I'm in a trance, like Christine mesmerized by her Phantom. And my Phantom looks especially dark and handsome, his thick dark hair grown unruly over the past few weeks and nearly falling into his deep blue eyes, his shirt still open at the top of his chest.

I keep my head turned toward the passenger window, not seeing anything that goes by, but in my peripheral I can see Felix stealing glances at me every now and then.

Every time he does, my skin breaks out in goosebumps.

I can't get the kiss out of my head, and I'm guessing he can't either. And who could blame him? That was the most sensual kiss I've ever experienced.

I want it to happen again, and yet I'm afraid of it happening again— what would it mean? If we wanted to, we could brush off that one kiss as being caught up in an intoxicated moment.

But do I want to? Does he?

At the thought that he might, my heart sinks, and I have my answer.

It's still silent as we walk up to the apartment, the only sounds our shuffling feet and the jiggling of the key in the lock. Felix opens the door and gestures for me to go in ahead of him; I do, removing my boots and only turning around once I hear the door close behind me.

We stand there looking at each other but not quite meeting the other's eyes.

"Are you going to say something?" he finally asks.

I bite my lip. "Are you?"

"I asked you first."

I scoff, and he smirks, and the swarm in my stomach intensifies.

"Do you..." I hesitate, rubbing a hand down my arm and looking away from him. My heart tries to escape from my chest, kicking wildly against the confines of its chamber. "Do you want to forget it happened? Or do you want to talk about it?"

I hear him step closer. "Lissa, look at me."

Sucking in a breath, I finally look him in the eyes. I stare him down, trying to find Defiant Lissa, daring him to say he doesn't want me.

But he doesn't say that. Instead his voice lowers and he says, "Right now, what I want more than anything is to kiss you again, but I'll settle for talking about it if that's what you want. But we're definitely not pretending it didn't happen."

Goosebumps erupt over my arms again at the demand of his last words, despite the rush of heat under my skin. All I can do is breathe out, "Okay."

He tucks a finger under my chin, tilts my head back and leans down, stopping when his lips are hovering just above mine.

"Are you agreeing we're not ignoring this, or are you saying I can kiss you?" He asks, his voice still low and rough.

"All of the above." Reaching for his hand, I slowly move it from my chin to my chest as I say, "but I have a better idea."

His eyes darken, and his fingers tenderly skim the tops of my breasts over the edge of my corset, sending tingles through me, but his brow furrows.

"I don't want to take advantage of this situation."

Dumbfounded, I step back abruptly. "How is it taking advantage when I'm giving you permission? Hell, I just offered myself up on a platter."

"Because a kiss is one thing, but there's no going back from being intimate." His eyes soften. "I want to be with you, but I don't want you to regret being with me. I want you to be sure."

The heat leaves my body, and I feel like someone filled my insides with icy water. I realize it's disappointment I feel and, stiffening my spine, I let that disappointment show. "You don't give me enough credit if you think I don't know my own mind. If I wasn't sure, I wouldn't have suggested it."

And with that, I swivel around and head straight for the bathroom. I want out of my costume, and I want a hot shower to warm me up again.

"Lissa—"

I cut Felix off by closing the bathroom door behind me—quietly. I turn on the water, then hang my robe on the hook on the back of the door and yank at the ties of my corset; once they're loosened, I strip off the rest of my costume. Leaving the hairpins on the counter and everything else in a heap on the floor, I pull up the pin for the shower and step under the spray. The hot water helps calm me a little as I tilt my head to wet my hair. Then, pumping my facial cleanser into my palm, I scrub all the makeup off my face.

As I reach for my shampoo, I hear the bathroom door open, and freeze. Heart pounding, I ask, "Felix?"

"Expecting someone else?" he asks, and I dare say he sounds amused.

"Expecting no one. Has it escaped your notice I'm in the shower?"

"Not at all. In fact, I thought I'd join you."

"Wh—"

I don't even have time to think as he pulls the shower curtain back and steps in, sans costume—he must have undressed before he came into the bathroom. My eyes automatically roam over his form, taking in all of him, and in my distraction he lifts his hands to tug at my arms, which had reflexively moved to cover my breasts.

I swallow as he sweeps his hands up my arms to cup my face, and I shudder out a breath when his thumb traces over my lips. My hand raises to rest on his chest, solid and smooth, and I can feel his heart thudding under my palm. I close my eyes to steady my own thundering heartbeat.

"I thought you didn't…" I croak.

"I've wanted you for a while," he murmurs. "I needed a moment to accept you want me back. That it's real."

God I hope it's real. "How…how long is a while?"

My eyes meet his as they open; the deep blue of his darkens even more with desire. "Since before I moved in."

I blink, lips parting in confusion. "But—"

He stops me with a gentle kiss, abrupt but sweet, and once again igniting prickles along my skin.

"Are you sure you want to have this conversation in the shower?" His voice is teasing, but he steps just a little closer, under the spray with me, and I can feel how hard his body is against me. Any thoughts I might have had about teasing him back leap off the foreplay tightrope; I'm too revved for the final act.

"No," I say, and grip the back of his neck, pulling him down as I stand on my toes to kiss him. He hums in pleasure, wrapping his arms around my back and hugging me tight against him. Warm water beats down on us as relentlessly as our kisses, and after a few moments, Felix turns us so his back is to the spray, then reaches for his body wash.

As he pours some into his palm, he says, "That time you used my shower gel, it drove me crazy. I had to restrain myself from kissing you."

He starts to lather me, starting with my shoulders.

"So..." I say softly, melting into his touch, "When you said it smelled good on me..."

"I wanted to do this."

He leans down, breathing me in as he nuzzles his nose just under my ear and his hands move, his fingers beginning to make circular motions over my breasts. I gasp when his tongue flicks out as he presses kisses down my neck.

Taking his time, he continues to rub his soap over my body, his hands gently massaging and leaving me aching, and I can't recall ever feeling more desirable or attended to. When one of his hands leaves my backside to slide between my legs, he covers my moan with his mouth, tongue searching for mine.

I run my hands up his chest, his back, wanting to touch all of him. Needy, I press against him, my sudsy breasts slicking over him, and he groans as the hand between my legs drops. Eager, I reach down to grip him, slowly pumping, running my thumb over the head of his length. I smirk with pride and delighted lust when his legs begin to shake and he grips my hair, kissing me hard.

Too soon, he pulls away, once again turning us so we're back under the spray, and swiveling me so my back is pressed against him.

His voice is husky in my ear. "You need to rinse off," he says, reaching around to rub my breasts with his thumbs.

When he's satisfied we've washed all the soap away, I let him move me again; this time he maneuvers us and carefully walks me backward until my back is against the cold tile of the shower wall. I don't have much time to react, however, as he bends to take a breast into his mouth. I arch into him, ripples of pleasure causing me to clench my legs together.

I quiver when he moves on to the other breast, flicking his tongue over me—now it's his turn to smirk.

"God, you're perfect," he whispers as he cups me, his lips roaming lower, lower, until he's kneeling in front of me, and his hands slide over my thighs.

There's no way the tub floor is comfortable on his knees, but he doesn't seem to notice.

"Felix—"

Whatever I was thinking is cut off with a gasp when his thumb rubs circles over my center, right where I ache, followed by his mouth. I'm so worked up, my hips begin to writhe as the pressure builds; gripping my hips, Felix lifts one of my legs over his shoulder, and I cry out as his tongue strokes relentlessly.

Flutters start in my core, my body tingling and reaching for the peak of pleasure it knows is within reach.

"Felix, I'm…going to—"

I can't seem to finish a sentence when his mouth is on me, but that's alright because I break in the most glorious way, crying out again as indescribable tingles of sensation rush through my body, starting inside my center and spreading up to my scalp. My hips buck and my head falls back against the tile when the burst begins to fade, and I can tell how sensitive I still am when he stands to kiss me and my legs quake.

I'm practically melting, and I smile, anticipating my turn to pleasure him. I reach to stroke him again, and his breath shudders out, his fingers tightening on my hips. I wet my lips, start to bend my knees, but instead he gently pulls my hand away.

"Not this time," he says, maneuvering me into the corner. "I want to be inside you."

My eyes widen a little. "Here? But I'm too short, and what if we slip?"

"I've got you. Do you trust me without a condom?"

I recall our discussion after my shitty date, and nod. "I'm clean. You?"

"As a whistle."

He takes my hand and places it on the bar; my fingers automatically wrap around it.

"Hold on," he grins, and lifts one of my legs over his hip, bending a little as his other hand moves over the back of my other thigh. "Ready?"

I set my free hand on his shoulder. "Yes."

I grip the bar tightly, pushing off of it and his shoulder as he lifts me with little effort. He braces me against the wall, and my legs wrap around his waist as he holds on to my hips. I hold myself up a little as he reaches down to line himself up with my entrance.

And then he's sliding into me, slowly so my body can adjust to take him in. When he's all the way in I squeeze my legs a little tighter, and he begins to move. My still-sensitive nerves have me quivering again as he strokes in and out, smooth as silk. I can't help looking down to where our bodies are joined, fascinated.

"You feel so good," he groans, and begins to pump faster.

I rock against him, concentrating on holding myself in place so he can lose himself, thrilled with the pleasured grunts escaping him. I myself can't help the sounds ripping from my throat, and it only seems to spur him on more.

He watches my face, and I watch him back, our eyes meeting with a combination of wonderment, affection, and unadulterated desire.

Finally he lets out one last groan, and his movements still with a few long strokes. He leans his head on my shoulder, breathing heavily, and I manage to run my free hand through his wet hair.

It isn't until now I realize the water is getting lukewarm, and I shiver. He lifts his head, his grin lopsided as he carefully lowers me.

I can feel myself blushing, trying to wrap my head around what we just did as we quickly rinse off, and he turns off the water. He gets out first, hands me my towel before grabbing his own.

We smile at each other as we dry off, and he grins when I twist my hair up in my towel.

"What?" I ask, suddenly shy.

He shakes his head. "You're just cute."

I wrinkle my nose. "Just what every grown-ass woman wants to hear from the man she wants to have sex with."

"You already had sex with me," he says, smirking and reaching over to give me a light smack on the butt. "I don't think it's a secret I think you're sexy and beautiful, but I'll tell you anyway: You're beautiful and sexy, Lissa. And right now, with that towel on your head, I also find you adorable."

"Well." I blink, feeling my cheeks warm, and try to keep my cool. "I suppose I can't be annoyed about that."

"Good," he grins. "You still want to watch *Hocus Pocus?*"

I tilt my head in surprise. "Absolutely, if you're up for staying up late."

"I'm up for it. Especially if it means I can take you to my bed afterward."

"Ah, the true motive is revealed."

He winks and opens the door, heading across to his room.

Smiling to myself, I go through the motions of blowdrying my hair—I'll have to shower again tomorrow since I didn't actually get it washed tonight—and brushing it out, a bit dazed by everything that's happened. My body is still warm and relaxed, my mind half disbelieving I didn't imagine the whole thing. I hang my towel, not bothering with a robe, and head to my room to toss my costume on the bed and put on my favorite sweats and a t-shirt.

I smell popcorn before I've finished dressing, and when I join Felix in the living room, I see he's already on the couch, pulling up the movie. He looks ridiculously sexy in his pajama bottoms and tee—or maybe it's just me. The popcorn is in a ceramic bowl patterned with cobwebs, and he's also taken the liberty of setting out two pumpkin ales for us, and lit my Witch's Brew candle.

Don't ask what Witch's Brew smells like, because I still can't figure it out, but I can tell you it smells musky, autumn-spiced, and cozy.

At the sight of his home-movie date setup, my heart catches in my throat, then plummets and explodes into a whirl of butterflies.

"Well this is cozy," I say, sliding onto the cushion next to him and crossing my legs.

"It is; it's only missing one thing."

"What?"

When he angles himself more toward me, opens his arms, I grin and lean into him. I rest my head on his shoulder as he presses play and wrap an arm over his stomach.

It's a good thing I've seen this movie a million times, otherwise I might not know what's happening—I'm too distracted by him slowly running his hand up and down my arm. Not to mention I have no idea how to feel.

I mean, don't get me wrong—I'm nearly giddy with happiness. But I'm also wary, because I have no idea what comes next. Will we date? Does this count as a date? Will it be easier or harder when he moves out?

Am I overthinking this?

I'm overthinking this.

To clear my head, I reach for the popcorn and my beer.

We spend probably half the movie kissing instead of watching it, the other half trying to keep our hands off each other by finishing the popcorn —though I nearly give in when I put my feet in his lap and he starts rubbing his thumb over the arches, squeezing them in a gentle massage that makes my scalp tingle. The beer is gone too soon, but we both decide one is enough.

As soon as the credits begin to roll, Felix turns off the TV. Taking my hand, he pulls me down the hall to his room, and I make no protest. He lets go of my hand to turn on the bedside light, and I notice the remnants of his costume strewn at the foot of the bed, except the mask, which is on the dresser.

When he turns to me, running his hands over my hips and toying with the waistband of my sweats, I give him a seductive smile.

·　·˙·.· ·

THE PAST FEW hours have been a literal dream come true. I lost count of the number of times I'd imagined Lissa wrapped around me, and now here she is, letting me touch her—again—and smiling at me under hooded brown eyes that darken like well-oiled leather at my touch. The scent of my soap on her skin is alluring as hell; last time it was all I could do not to pin her against the counter, but now I won't have to restrain myself from pinning her to my bed.

I recall the jolt of shock at her earlier boldness, inviting me to touch her, and the hurt of her disappointment at my hesitation; I knew I would have to repay her boldness with my own, and tell her the truth of my feelings.

But I'm not done yet.

"You," I whisper throatily, pressing my lips under her ear, "Are too tempting for your own good."

She whimpers and clamps her hands on my shoulders to steady herself. "You didn't…always think so."

"I did," I tell her, nipping down her neck. "Once I really looked at you. Talked to you."

In one swift motion, I push her pants down her legs, and when she steps out of them, I wrap my arms around her waist and lift her, turn to the bed.

We flop onto the mattress, and she giggles as I cover her, her hands roaming up my back and taking my t-shirt with them. I let her tug it off, then take her hands and pin them over her head so I can kiss her unhindered.

She arches under me, hitching a leg over my hip and parting my lips with her tongue. Her foot slides over my lower back, toes wiggling their way under the waistband of my pajama pants.

The sneaky little temptress.

Her lips smile against mine when I groan, and I release her hands to run a hand up her leg and torso, and finally to her breast, where her nipples are taut under the cotton of her shirt; I'm still dazed by how perfectly it fits in my palm.

Once freed, her hands explore the dips and muscles of my back, and she uses both her feet to begin pushing my pants off my hips.

Laughing, I roll off her to strip the rest of my clothes off, and she pulls off her tee, leaving only her underwear.

"Impatient much?" I smirk.

"Yes."

And she pushes me back against the pillows, straddling me before I can roll back on top of her. I run my hands over her curves as she leans down to take my mouth, slow and deep. Then she slides her body down mine, trailing her fingers in her wake, before cupping me, squeezing lightly.

She raises her eyes to mine, questioning as she flicks her tongue over me the way I did to her, and when I nod, she gives me a sultry grin and takes me into her mouth. I immediately groan, surrendering to her ministrations; but as much as I want to prolong the delightful torture of her tongue stroking me, it isn't long before I want to be inside her more.

My stomach muscles clench when she spreads her hands over my abdomen, and I crave all of her, reaching down to tug at her wandering hands.

"I want you to ride me," I say, pulling her up.

She hums in pleasure at the idea, releasing me to crawl back on top of me, and I tug at her underwear. She shifts to pull them off; I don't have much time to miss the loss of contact before she grips me, guiding me into her wet heat, sliding up and down again until I'm seated fully.

Smiling, she leans down to kiss me, hands on either side of my head, and begins to move. We meet each other, rhythm for rhythm, murmuring how good the other feels, exploring each other with hands and lips, and eliciting gasps and moans.

"Liss, I need you to come," I groan when I feel myself getting close, and reach down to clamp my hands on her ass. The words seem to have an effect on her, because it isn't long before I feel her clench around me, sighing my name as she shudders.

I watch her ride it out, heart swelling with affection, and pride that I can push her over the edge. Then I flip us so she's writhing under me; she hooks her ankles together around my back and makes the same demand of me. I pump faster as my own pleasure builds and bury my face in her neck, finally giving in to release.

We stay there for a moment, just breathing, then I nuzzle my way to her mouth, kiss her long and deep. When I pull back, pull out of her, we both grunt, then grin at each other like idiots.

She sits up, sliding off the bed. "I want to cuddle, but we should clean up first."

"Does that mean you'll stay with me tonight?"

She meets my gaze as she picks up her underwear and shirt, her smile shy but teasing. "I thought you'd never ask."

And later, when we've gotten cozy under my covers, I hold her tight as she snuggles against me. Her sigh is tired and contented, and I long to tell her I want her here every night.

But is she ready to hear that?

"You're so warm," she whispers. "Like a space heater."

I chuckle. "Glad to be of service."

"Mm."

"...Lissa?"

"Yeah?" She responds, fighting a yawn.

I take a breath. "I...I hope you know tonight wasn't just sex for me."

It's silent for a moment, and I worry I've said too much, or that she's fallen asleep, but then she stretches, rolls over to face me.

"It wasn't for me either."

I sigh in relief, leaning my forehead against hers.

"Am I..." She pauses. "Am I why you haven't dated anyone since you moved here?"

Ah. Now I remember our conversation on the day I moved in, and her skepticism about my dating life. "Yes."

She snorts softly, drifting her fingers over my cheek. "Well, you were right. I wouldn't have believed you. But I believe you now."

I turn my head to kiss her fingers. "Good."

. . .

IN THE MORNING I wake well-rested, relishing in the feel of Felix's arm around my waist. I can feel him breathing softly, his breath tickling my hair; for a moment I consider giving him a proper wake up call, but the gurgle in my stomach has other ideas, and when a glance at the clock tells me it's after ten, I carefully ease my way out of his bed.

In the kitchen I start the coffee, and am in the middle of mixing together some pancake batter when I hear Felix shuffle in. My heart melts a little when he comes up behind me, gives my butt an affectionate pat; I smile and tilt my head to look at him, hair still tousled from sleep, and he presses a long kiss to my lips.

"Morning," he says.

"Morning."

The scene is so natural and homey, and I feel delightfully warm all over at the thought. It's a little scary, these feelings, but it feels so good I hardly notice.

"Pancakes?" He grins. "Well that makes this day even more perfect."

"How so?"

"I got some very good news this morning."

I still, turning from the bowl of batter to take in his ecstatic expression. My stomach lurches. "Your house?"

He nods, grin widening. "It's done early. I can move back in."

It's good news. It's *great* news. And yet...

"Oh," I say, cringing at how forced the cheer sounds. I'm not surprised I don't fool him, and he steps to me, takes my face in his hands, and smiles.

"You're disappointed."

I slit my eyes at him. "You're happy about that."

"Of course. It means you don't want me to leave."

"Arrogant much?"

I don't want him to leave. And what felt so good only a few moments ago is now a little paralyzing.

He ignores my comment. "It means you want to be with me as much as I want to be with you," he murmurs.

I fight a smile. "Do I?"

"I hope so." His expression turns serious. "I think you're ready to hear me tell you I'm falling in love with you."

All the air whooshes out of my lungs, and right back in again. I release the tension with a small huff of laughter at the irony. "I am ready. And just when I figure out I'm falling for *you*, you're about to leave."

His lopsided grin sends my heart rolling. "Perfect timing if you ask me."

The only appropriate response is to raise a brow. He tugs affectionately at a curl of my hair, twines it around his finger.

"I want to ask you to come with me, but I don't want to scare you away."

My eyes lock onto his, and I can't help teasing him, if only so he knows I'm not scared anymore. "Do women have a habit of running away from you?"

His eyes crinkle with his smirk, and he tugs on my hair again. "Only one very stubborn woman."

I don't dignify that with a response.

"Your lease is up in a few months," he continues. "We can wait until then, or you can sublet it, or you can tell me right now that I'm moving too fast."

I shake my head, watching his eyes light up when I say, "It doesn't feel fast; our situation is just an unusual one. It feels right."

"So you'll do it? You'll move in with me?"

In answer, I pull his mouth down to mine. "Yeah."

"When?"

"We'll figure it out."

EPILOGUE

A Few Weeks Later

THE BENNET HOUSEHOLD is in an uproar when Felix and I arrive with his sister Giselle. My dad answers the door, greeting us with his usual sardonic smirk.

"You knew about this, didn't you?" he asks.

As we step inside the house, we can hear my sisters squealing, and my mom screeching, "A daughter married!"

Neither Felix or I deny it, as Cole and Julia had informed us of their engagement the week before; Julia wanted to savor that happiness before telling the rest of the family and suffering our mother's attention. Poor Giselle's eyes widen with anxiety; she's such a quiet young woman, but I doubt my sisters will let her remain so for long.

I, for one, am grateful for all the distractions. The relationship between my mother and I is still tentative; though she's apologized and her behavior has improved, I'm still not totally comfortable around her. I owe what improvement she's made mostly to Julia—it took her sweetest, most obliging daughter scolding her to make Mom understand she was truly in the wrong.

Julia convinced Mom and Dad to go to couples counseling, and so far it's had a positive impact on both their marriage and our family.

The rest I owe to Felix, who stood by me, and through the simple act of loving me, proved to my mother that some men do like bookish, opinionated women.

I'm not fully moved in to his place yet, though I am practically living there, leaving more and more things there each time I stay. I decided to keep my apartment for the last few months of my lease to give us time to adjust to the change in our relationship, and my family is aware I'll be moving in with him at the end of it.

I don't regret that decision, but I'm fast becoming impatient for my lease to be up.

After hanging our coats, we follow my dad into the kitchen, where Cole is drinking a beer and my mom is clutching at Julia's hand, admiring the ring; when my eyes meet my sister's, I roll my eyes with a knowing smile, and she gives me a long-suffering look in response. I can hear both my dad and Felix chuckle lightly at our silent communication, and the sounds of chatter from the living room tell me my sisters have moved to the living room.

The turkey and stuffing is already made, and I see the pumpkin pie Jules and Cole brought settled on the counter; when my mom finally looks up from Julia's ring and notices us, I hand her the cranberry espresso cheesecake Felix and I spent half the day yesterday making before we picked up Giselle from the airport.

She takes it gingerly, not quite meeting my eyes, but perking up at the decadent-looking dish.

"Oh, my," she says as she sets it next to the pie. "This looks sinful."

"It was my mother's recipe," Felix tells her.

"And this must be Giselle?" Mom asks when she turns back around and spots her standing slightly behind Felix.

"Yes." Felix makes the introductions, and Mom goes into full hostess mode.

"Would you like a drink, dear? The girls are in the living room, they'll be just delighted to meet you."

Giselle's eyes widen again, but Julia gives her a reassuring smile, and she and Cole lead her to meet the rest of the Bennet sisters. When they're gone, Mom finally turns to me and wraps me in a hug.

It takes me a second to hug her back; I can't remember the last time she did so. But my arms come around her, and I breathe her in. She smells like hairspray and jasmine perfume.

"I'm glad you came, Lissa," she says quietly, and if I'm not mistaken, she sounds a little choked up. She hasn't used my nickname in a while. "It's not the same when the whole family isn't together."

I don't really know what to say to that other than, "Thank you."

When she lets go, she seems like she wants to say something else, but giggles erupt from the next room and break the moment. Dad turns to Felix and gives him a cheeky smile.

"Well, young man, you may want to go and rescue your sister. My girls are probably peppering her with questions."

"Yes, sir."

Dinner is a rather interesting affair. It's different having Felix, Giselle, and Cole at the Bennet Family Thanksgiving, the newness of Cole and Julia's engagement lifting everyone's spirits. Mom is mostly distracted with visions of wedding bells dancing in her head, and since I'm no longer single, she can't harp on me about that.

Felix, Cole, and Dad ignore the wedding ravings by commandeering a corner of the dinner table and chatting amongst themselves.

Giselle sits next to her brother and is still relatively quiet, but her shyness is no match for Mallory's shared love of the piano, and Kit and Lila's boisterousness and genuine spirits. As the youngest and most spoiled, I sometimes worry about Lila; she'll graduate college next year, and she's more focused on dating than anything else.

My worry increases when she mentions having gone to Phillip's last night and flirting with one of the bartenders.

"Garrett is the hottest man I've ever seen," Lila says. "*Excellent* boyfriend material."

My eyes snap to Felix, whose own eyes are on his sister. Giselle is gripping her fork.

"He asked me if I wanted to go out when his shift was over, but Harriet Long dragged me away. She said he's a jerk, but she was probably just jealous," Lila is saying. "We should go tonight and see if he's there."

"Garrett Wickham?" Giselle asks.

Lila shrugs, so it's Felix who answers, his tone dark. "Yes."

"Oh." Giselle frowns, then straightens and turns to Lila. "You shouldn't go out with him. All he cares about is getting laid. Sometimes he'll lead multiple women on at the same time; you should listen to your friend."

Lila scrunches her face up. "You know him?"

"He was Felix's roommate in college one year," Giselle explains, her cheeks pinking a little. "I'd come to visit him, and Garrett hit on me at a party, not knowing I was his sister, and I agreed to go back to his apartment with him. Luckily for me, Felix was home. He wasn't happy to see me with Garrett, and Garrett..."

She pauses, and I have a sinking feeling. "He told me I was a nice piece, but that if I was as uptight as my brother I'd probably be boring in bed, and no wonder it was so easy to get me to go back to his place."

The whole table is silent. Even Mom is shocked, and though Felix looks surprised Giselle just shared that experience, he also looks proud. He gives me an apologetic look when his eyes shift to mine, but I shake my head with an understanding smile—it hits me now why Felix never elaborated about Garrett beyond the fact he had a propensity for breaking hearts. It wasn't his place to tell me his sister's story.

"I'm sorry he said that to you. Thank you for warning us," I tell Giselle, then do my best to move the conversation away from her to make her more comfortable. "Can't say I'm surprised he's such an ass; I've seen him kissing different women at the bar more than once, and on the same night, too."

"He probably has an STD," Mallory points out. "Would you want to get herpes, Lila?"

"Ew." Kit, who was about to take a bite of mashed potatoes, grimaces and sets her fork back down.

"Definitely ew," Lila agrees, pouting. "That's too bad. He's so handsome."

"I'm sure you'll meet someone else just as handsome," Jules assures her.

Lila perks up again at this suggestion, shrugging and changing the topic to something else. Giselle gives me a grateful look, and Felix sends me a wink that tells me we will be having a very not-boring time in bed later.

Shows what Garrett knows about his erstwhile roommate.

After dinner, I volunteer to make the coffee as Mom divvies up the pie and cheesecake at the table. I need to do something mundane while I process the last couple hours.

Felix joins me, pulling out mugs for everyone who requested one.

"That went surprisingly well," he comments.

"We probably have Julia and Cole to thank for that," I muse.

"Probably. But it got me thinking."

"About?"

He shifts his feet, eyeing me carefully. "What if we hosted Christmas?"

I choke on a half laugh. "What?"

"You'll be all moved in by then, and your family will want to see the place anyway," he clarifies, rubbing his hands over my shoulders. "Plus, I want to have my extended family over. Our house is big enough to accommodate both our families."

Our house.

I soften. "You know, that actually sounds really lovely."

"Good." He beams, leaning down to give me a soft kiss. "I'll bring it up with your mother."

"Have fun with that," I call after him.

"I will," he teases.

I don't doubt it. He knows Mom will do pretty much anything he asks if she thinks it'll get him to propose to me that much sooner. I'm sure she thinks she's being subtle, and I let her; she can't entirely change who she is, and I'm okay with that. Things are better.

And even if they weren't, I'd still have Felix.

Mom commandeers me into talking about Julia's wedding with her and Julia after I bring out the coffee, and I pretend to be interested since I can see Julia is getting tired of it. I find it isn't too hard when I have pie and cheesecake to cheer me, and when I take a sip of my coffee, my eyes search out Felix, who's across the room with his sister and Cole. My gaze meets his over the rim.

I lower my mug, mouth "love you" to him.

His responding smile is one of those from-the-heart ones that reaches his eyes, and he mouths back, "love you, too."

I don't care if anyone notices how sappy we are. It's these little stolen moments that remind me how grateful I am to have him in my life. I didn't know what I was missing until he came along and showed me how happy we could be.

And to think, I'd once been reluctant to have him as a roommate.

A TALE OF MISTLETOE SHENANIGANS

shenanigan (n.)

"nonsense; deceit, humbug," 1855, American English slang, of uncertain origin. Earliest records of it are in California (San Francisco and Sacramento). Suggestions include Spanish chanada, a shortened form of charranada "trick, deceit;" or, less likely, German Schenigelei, peddler's argot for "work, craft," or the related German slang verb schinäglen. Another guess centers on Irish sionnach "fox," and the form is perhaps conformed to an Irish surname.

-ONLINE ETYMOLOGY DICTIONARY

THE BIG HOUSE at the end of Netherfield Lane gleamed with such enthusiastic Christmas cheer, it left one in no doubt as to who lived there. In the front yard, a giant, grinning inflatable snowman lit up from the inside and waved to passersby, while an actual sleigh, big and red with painted gold trim, sat boldly in the snow. The light of a spotlight revealed creepily realistic dummies of Santa Claus and a few elves sitting on the plush purple cushions in front of a ridiculously large burlap sack threaded at the top with red ribbon; and to complete the elaborate display, eight wooden reindeer with painted detailing were harnessed to the sleigh.

As he opened the little white gate at the property's front fence and trudged up the walk, Elijah Bennet smiled with a shake of his head.

Brit Bingley's love of Christmas was both boisterous and genuine, and he couldn't fault her for that—especially since her affection for his best friend seemed genuine as well.

To match her exuberance, bright, twinkling lights covered the bushes that lined the walk, the edges of the porch and garage roofs, and wrapped around every porch railing. They flickered between yellowy-white and a rainbow assortment every every half second or so.

Almost like the turn signal of a car, but with more Christmas, Eli thought.

In one of the front windows, a Christmas tree filled the frame, and even from outside he could see there were an abundance of ornaments. And at the bottom of the steps, a tall metallic pole striped in red and white stuck up out of the snow, the silver ball at the top gleaming in the lights. He shook his head again as he passed it, walked up to the porch where an enormous wreath with a red velvet ribbon twined in its branches and tied in a perfect bow hung on the door. He stomped off some of the snow from his boots before stepping onto the doormat depicting a scene of the animated Grinch and his dog Max driving the sleigh full of stolen Christmas goodies.

It was a rather pointed contribution to the decor, he thought. Brit was friendly and cheerful, but her best friend was antisocial and hardly smiled —the Grinch to Brit's Cindy Lou Who.

The thought of Dani Fitzwilliam put a damper on Eli's Christmas spirit.

There was no doubt she was one of the most gorgeous women he'd ever seen, with long, silky dark hair and mesmerizing green eyes framed by thick lashes and stylish bangs. It was only her disposition he found unattractive, and he would be faced with plenty of it tonight.

Taking a fortifying breath, he rang the doorbell, glancing down at himself as he waited. Brit had said casual, so he wore jeans, and under his coat was his favorite wool sweater, knitted by his aunt in a soft and dark blue, chosen, as she'd told him, to bring out his blue eyes; even so, he hoped he hadn't underdressed.

Not that anyone would care. Probably not even Dani.

As soon as he thought her name, the door opened wide with a rush, and the Grinch herself was on the other side.

"Hey, Eli, come in."

Her eyes crinkled with the small smile that pulled at her scarlet-tinted lips as she stepped back, gesturing him inside.

He was surprised at her pleasant greeting, much less that she'd answered the door. "Hey," he replied, cursing himself when he couldn't help roaming his eyes over her. She wore a pair of dark skinny jeans and a deep forest green sweater that made her eyes an almost ethereal green; on her feet were a pair of socks depicting cats in Santa hats.

He didn't realize one corner of his mouth had lifted.

"Can I take your coat?" Dani asked.

"Oh, sure."

He pulled off his coat and scarf, handed them to her, and she found a hanger in the front hall closet for them while he pulled off his boots, set them by the door with the other shoes.

"Everyone's in the living room," she told him when she'd stowed his things. "Jason and Luke are already here."

For a moment he assumed she was politely scolding him for being late, and it irritated him; but her tone was pleasant, and a glance at the hall clock told him he was a few minutes early. He mentally kicked himself for jumping to a conclusion.

The sound of laughter and chatter reached his ears, and he recognized his best friends' voices among the others. Stuffing his hands in his pockets, he followed Dani past the stairs strung with holly and around the corner, where the hall opened up into a wide room.

He paused in the doorway, hesitant to enter the lion's den. Brit, her blonde hair pulled up in a messy bun, sat in the middle of a plush couch with her twin brother, Bradley, on one side of her and Jason on the other. Their older sister Becca sat on a loveseat with her husband, Harrison. His other friend Luke sat in a big wingback chair, his girlfriend Willa sitting on his lap. None of them had noticed Eli yet.

As he switched his attention, taking in the spectacular tree dripping with whimsical, colorful ornaments and figurines, sparkling with more twinkling lights, and stocked with shiny wrapped presents at the base, Dani stopped beside him.

She looked at him curiously, tilting her head in question, and seemed about to ask him why he'd stopped when Brit called out.

"Ooh, the first kiss!"

Both Eli and Dani whipped their heads around to stare at her. Everyone was looking at them.

"Did I miss something?" Eli asked.

"Mistletoe!" Brit beamed, pointing above their heads. "You guys are the first to get caught under it."

For a moment all the air left his lungs, and he reminded himself to breathe as he slowly turned his gaze back to Dani's.

Her eyes were wide, her lips parted in a small "O."

They both glanced up, inadvertently turning toward each other, and sure enough, a cluster of the fingered leaves and small red berries hung between them. When Eli swallowed, looked back down at Dani, his eyes automatically drifted to her lips. He blinked when she bit her lower lip, and saw the pinkish tint rising to her cheeks.

Great, he thought. She was cursing her luck.

Well, she'd have to make the excuses. It was no skin off him if Bradley —who was currently glaring holes into him—had another thing to sneer at him about. Or if Luke had another reason to suggest Dani liked him and tease him about it. But the last thing he needed was for kindhearted Jason to gently accuse him of being rude and embarrassing Dani.

But Dani didn't make any excuses.

She relaxed her shoulders, straightening a little as she brought her eyes to his. He raised his brows when she stepped closer, so they were only inches apart, tilted her head expectantly. She must have interpreted his astonishment as shyness, because she stood on her tiptoes, reaching up to pluck a berry from the offending plant, and held it between her fingers.

"I promise I won't bite," she said softly, with a small, teasing smile. "Not during Christmas, anyway."

She surprised a laugh out of him, and it came out in a huff as he finally withdrew his hands from his pockets. What the hell, he thought. As much as it went against the grain of insult, he could admit to himself the idea of kissing her sent his heart racing.

"Oh, this is childish," Bradley declared when he realized they were going to go through with it. "You're not really going to kiss him, are you, Dani?"

"Lay off, *Brad*." Brit scolded him. "It's tradition. And it's romantic."

Though Eli was sure she'd heard them, Dani didn't so much as spare them a glance. Instead she kept her gaze level with Eli's, closing the berry in her fist and laying her free hand on his chest as he gingerly cupped her face. As he leaned in, he caught her scent—sweet and slightly floral—

above the holiday candles scented with pine, cinnamon and clove, and cranberries. It was intoxicating, and a tickling thought in the back of his mind told him to be prepared, but the moment had already arrived.

She must be impatient to get it over with, because the fingers on his chest curled into his sweater. And that thought had his reluctance turning on its head to determination. He was a good kisser, damnit; he'd show her.

He'd kiss her senseless.

To tease her, he skimmed his nose gently against hers, causing her eyes to flutter and close, before brushing his lips overs hers with the barest touch. And on her intake of breath he finally captured her lips fully, his own eyes shutting as he sank into her.

And he was completely unprepared.

Her lips were slightly chapped, as were his, but they were so soft and giving the entire sensation was heady enough to fog his brain. And when her lips parted under his without losing contact, pressed more firmly to deepen the kiss, he had to fight back a groan. It was probably a longer kiss than it should have been, and yet a handful of seconds didn't feel like near enough.

To his chagrin, it was she who pulled back, a dazzling smile lighting her face as her grip on his sweater loosened. Her eyes were dark and sultry, cheeks pleasantly pink, and he was tempted to lean in again, but the whoops and cheers from the small crowd in the room—especially Luke and Brit—reminded him where he was.

Well, shit. He'd wanted to mesmerize her, to prove something to her, but instead she seemed to have mesmerized him and got under his skin.

Wasn't that poetic justice?

He was more alert now as he and Dani finally entered the room, no longer particularly dreading the company, but certainly not comfortable. What the hell was happening?

Dani glanced at the berry still in her hand, then to Brit, amusement softening her features. "What am I supposed to do with this?" she asked.

Brit shrugged. "I don't know, toss it I guess."

Dani sighed, but smirked when she shook her head at her friend. "Anyone want more mulled wine?" she addressed the group. "Eli, you want something to drink?"

"Uh, sure," he replied. Why did it feel like everyone was watching him? "Mulled wine is good."

Bradley asked for more wine, as did Harrison, and Dani nodded and headed off toward the kitchen. Eli didn't realize his gaze followed her until Brit spoke his name.

"Well, damn, Eli." She smirked into her wine. "That was one hot kiss."

He hoped he wasn't blushing. "Oh, yeah?" he asked, raising a brow at Jason, who was watching him carefully, then Luke, who of course was also smirking.

"Yeah." She grinned. "I'm almost jealous of Dani."

"Almost?"

"Well..." Her grin turned sly as she slid her eyes toward Jason. "I'm hoping to get caught under the mistletoe with someone else."

Now it was Jason's turn to blush and Eli's turn to grin—and Bradley's turn to roll his eyes. Willa giggled and whispered something in Luke's ear, causing a blush to creep up Luke's neck.

"Well, now that everyone knows about it, I'm sure they'll do their best to avoid it," Eli pointed out, secretly thinking Willa would do the opposite, and drag Luke underneath it. Though he could imagine Bradley hovering in the doorway, waiting for Dani to walk under it again, and for some reason the thought made his stomach churn. "It's a little awkward to be put in the spotlight."

"Oh, not to worry," Brit chirped. "I put some everywhere."

Everyone, including Dani, who had returned with her hands full of wine glasses, stopped and blinked at Brit.

"Everywhere?" Jason practically gulped.

Brit nodded. "Mm-hm. All over the house."

Resigned, Dani raised a brow. "Only you, B."

Then she turned to Eli, held out a steaming wine glass with a Christmas tree shaped charm around its stem to him. He took it gingerly, thanked her, and forced a smile he hoped didn't show his agitation or apprehension. She smiled in acknowledgement and turned to hand Bradley and Harrison their glasses. He noticed Dani's stem charm was shaped like a penguin when she sat on the other couch, directly across from Jason.

Eli sipped the wine, calmed by its warmth and spiced flavor. Feeling a little like he was in an alternate universe, he sat at the other end of the couch and focused his attention on the others as the conversation shifted. Most were dressed pretty casually—across from him, Bradley was wearing a crisp white button down, which he supposed counted—but it helped steady his unsettled emotions to see Brit, Luke, and Willa wearing ugly or fun Christmas sweaters.

In fact, Willa was basically dressed as an elf, complete with a long-sleeve green dress, red and white striped tights, and a floppy green hat with elf ears that covered her own. Luke wore a green sweater featuring the heads of golden retrievers wearing glasses and Santa hats that rather nicely accented his own ash blonde hair, glasses, and Santa hat, while Brit sported a bright red oversize vintage sweatshirt with a giant satin gingerbread man sewn on the front.

Meanwhile, Jason looked cozy in some checkered flannel, his hair—a shade or two lighter than Eli's own oak brown—freshly trimmed; Eli finger-combed his windswept locks, suddenly feeling a little self-conscious.

He was so caught up in distracting himself, he nearly jolted when the doorbell rang. Wordlessly, Dani set down her glass and slid off the couch; when she returned, she didn't so much as glance up at the mistletoe, merely stepping into the room just ahead of the new arrivals. As a small crowd had just arrived, those sitting decided to get up to greet them. Though he stood, Eli found himself lingering behind, staying near the couch to watch everyone mingle.

The Long sisters, Amy and Pen, were trailed by Steven Goulding—who had a long-time crush on Amy—Ryan Forster and his brother Denny, and lastly, Eli's cousin Leah and her girlfriend Gia.

Leah and Gia were already laughing about something; Eli watched Dani carefully for her reaction, as when he'd met Gia, she'd told him she used to be friends with Dani. Gia had implied they'd drifted apart after she'd come out to Dani.

But Dani only wore her usual distant expression as she turned to offer them all some mulled wine, and pointed out the dining room with a cooler of other drinks and a table crammed with Christmas party food.

Eli hadn't even noticed the food; he'd been too caught up in the emotions the past few minutes had stirred in him. Now his stomach grumbled.

"Ooh, Christmas cookies!" Leah exclaimed, gripping Gia's arm to pull her toward the table.

"Wait!" Willa called out. "You're under the mistletoe!"

"Mistletoe?"

Leah's eyes lit up when she spotted it, and she grinned at Gia, who blushed but grinned back. Bouncing on her toes, Leah grasped Gia's face, gave her a long, hard kiss, then gave the auburn braid slung over Gia's shoulder an affectionate tug.

"Now it's a party!" Leah declared, then turned to Dani. "I'll have the wine. It sounds good!"

A small smile graced Dani's lips as she nodded, then turned her gaze to Gia expectantly. Gia, who had reached up to pull a berry from the mistletoe, fidgeted and looked away, rolling the little red fruit between her fingers.

"No, thanks, I'm not really a wine person," she said flatly.

The smile faded from Dani's face, the set of her shoulders falling just enough that when she nodded again and headed toward the kitchen, Eli was almost positive she'd looked dejected. For her part, Gia had finally entered the room, watching Dani leave with something like regret.

Eli took another sip of his drink as his mind raced.

It was none of his business. He'd only known Dani since their first semester of grad school had started that fall, and the Bingleys had rented the Netherfield Lane house near campus—much to the notice of the locals in their quaint college town, including his parents. Even though they'd been in company plenty, he couldn't claim he and Dani were friends, especially since Dani had made her disinterest in him known before even meeting him.

Gia he knew even less; she'd just transferred to Meryton University the month before.

"Well that was an interesting exchange."

Eli shifted his gaze to Luke, who now stood next to him, watching him with a smug expression as if to say, *"You're still in denial, aren't you?"*

Eli shrugged, fiddled with the charm on his glass. "I guess so."

Not buying it in the slightest, Luke gave his friend a hard stare. "Dude, I can practically see all the questions dancing in your head."

"Like sugar plums?"

"Yes."

"Well, 'tis the season."

Luke grinned. "You can't seriously tell me you still think she doesn't like you."

Eli stared back flatly. "You can't seriously be reading into a tradition that practically forces you to kiss someone."

"You think she couldn't have found some way out of it if she wanted to? She could have offered her cheek, or made sure it was just a peck—but no, she offered her lips, and she didn't pull away right away." Luke shot him a discerning look. "And neither did you."

As he couldn't deny it, Eli made no excuse. And as his friend was too observant not to notice him squirming, the expression that now graced Luke's face could only be described as triumphant. It didn't help the turbulence roiling around in Eli's mind—or was it his heart?

"I don't know what to think right now, man," he confessed.

Luke took a pull of his beer. "Don't you?"

Eli answered with a bland stare. "Do you think I'd be standing around like an idiot if I did?"

"Elijah." Luke clasped Eli's shoulder, shook it slightly. "The fact you're confused and second-guessing yourself is a sure sign you're at least not immune to her. Remember how certain you were you didn't want to date Willa when she asked you out?"

He could. Easily—Willa was far too exuberant and clingy for him, Eli thought. She would only annoy him, but Luke was the kind of easygoing that wasn't phased by such a personality, and he knew his friend enjoyed her attention.

"Knowing what you don't want is sometimes easier than knowing what you do want," Eli hedged.

"Fair, but that's kind of my point. It wasn't too long ago you were irritated by the sound of Dani's name, and now you just look lost."

Eli tried to laugh, but it came out forced. "Well, I just got to kiss an attractive woman—and I can admit I find her attractive even if she doesn't return the sentiment."

"Not that again." Chuckling, Luke shook his head. "You're forgetting how much she looks at you."

"Maybe she's trying to figure out what she doesn't like about my face."

"Oh, yeah." Luke rolled his eyes. "Because women love to stare at things they find repulsive."

As Eli tried to think of a response, his line of sight was caught by Dani returning with a tray of wine glasses.

Logically, he knew Luke had a point. His mind drifted back to the night he'd met Dani at a mixer, when she'd said to Brit she had no interest in some gross frat boy. When he looked at that logically, too, he could acknowledge she hadn't actually looked at him—in fact, she'd hardly moved her head.

Chances were she hadn't even seen him, or didn't realize it was him she'd been talking about, but he'd taken it personally because he'd been stunned by her. And she didn't even notice him. Dismissed him without bothering to look.

But she'd noticed him after that, and she noticed him now.

It took him a moment to realize his eyes followed Dani as she carried the tray to the coffee table, set it down.

Luke cleared his throat, not so subtly. "You were saying?"

Eli dragged his eyes away from Dani to meet his friend's, suddenly feeling a little helpless.

Taking pity on him, Luke gave him an encouraging smile. "Dude, just talk to her."

Dani had finished handing out glasses, and taken a seat back on the couch; Bradley noticed too, and practically leaped onto the spot next to her. Clearly unamused by him, Dani crossed her arms. Before, Eli thought maybe that was her way of showing her dissatisfaction or boredom, but now he thought maybe it was a sort of protective gesture.

Dipping his head to Luke, Eli made his way to the other couch, sat down where Jason had been a few minutes before so he was across from

Dani. He was pleased to note her eyes tracked his presence, and she seemed to relax a little at the sight of him.

Before he could say anything, Brit bounded over to them, picked up the TV remote and turned on the smart TV over the mantle.

"You know what's missing from this party? Christmas music!"

Bradley frowned. "Not everyone here might appreciate that kind of atmosphere."

Brit was undeterred, opening a music app on the screen and locating a Christmas playlist. "If you mean Dani, she can wear earplugs or something."

Wide-eyed, Eli turned to Dani. "You don't like Christmas music?"

She sighed, frowning as though she were tired of hearing the question. "I like Christmas music just fine—I just don't feel the need to listen to it until after Thanksgiving. *Some* people," she mock-scowled at Brit with frustrated affection, "think my inability to play holiday songs twenty-four seven in December means I don't have enough Christmas spirit."

"Oh," Eli nodded sagely. "So Bradley was referring to himself, then."

Brit laughed while Bradley sneered at him, and Dani's lips quirked in a quiet smile she hid behind her wine glass. And as the soft sound of a jazzy "Let It Snow" began to float through the room, Eli noticed the atmosphere did indeed lift.

It lifted even more when others from the neighborhood, and some students who were still on campus, arrived, filling up the space and livening the room with chatter. Eli finished off his mulled wine as he tried to have a conversation with Dani about their respective studies—since he was studying anthropology and she to be a museum curator, they had some classes in common—but Bradley was quick to insert himself.

Brit and Jason, who were back on the couch with Eli, managed to draw Bradley into their conversation a few times, but whenever he had an opening, he focused on Dani. He would spout some snooty opinion, clearly believing—or hoping—Dani would agree with him, if the way his eyes gleamed at her was anything to go by. And inch by inch, he kept scooting closer to Dani, who in turn kept leaning farther and farther into the arm of the couch. The more he spoke, the quieter Dani became, and the more bland her expression.

Why hadn't he noticed that before? Eli wondered.

Because you didn't want to, he answered himself.

He was trying to think of a way to rescue Dani when a squeal of delight erupted from the dining room near the food table. Everyone looked in that direction, including Bradley, inadvertently causing him to move away from Dani a little.

In the dining room, Willa plucked a sprig of mistletoe from the poinsettia and pine centerpiece on the table, and Eli watched as she dangled it in front of Luke. *I knew it*, Eli thought, even as Luke's mouth widened in a grin, and he yanked Willa to him. She eagerly twined her arms around his neck, still holding up the mistletoe; to everyone's wonder and delight, Luke shifted, then dipped Willa as though they'd just ended a dance, and captured her waiting lips with aplomb.

Her elf hat fell off, but she swiped it up as he lifted her back up to a round of applause, and she plopped it back on her head before giving the room a little curtsy. Then she winked at her boyfriend, plucked off a berry from the sprig, and placed it back in the centerpiece.

With the distraction, Dani took the opportunity to stand, setting her empty wineglass on the coffee table.

"I'm going to get some food," she declared, just as Bradley opened his mouth.

As she made her way to the dining room, Eli's stomach rumbled at the mention of food—he could only be glad Dani was out of earshot, as the sound was an embarrassing garbling noise that complained of neglect. He didn't miss Bradley's superior smirk, but Eli only laughed as he stood up.

"I think that's a sign my stomach is woefully empty of Christmas cookies. If you'll excuse me," he said to Jason and Brit.

Dani looked up sharply from the plate she was loading as Eli approached the table across from her, but smiled when she saw it was him. He smiled back, picked up a Christmas-themed paper plate from the end of the table; he deliberately stayed on the other side, as the centerpiece mistletoe was still in the middle of the table, and he didn't want her to think he was angling for another kiss.

He reached for a couple frosted gingerbread cookies—one shaped like a reindeer, one shaped like an angel—noting her particular smile as he set them on his plate. He quirked a brow in question, and she opened her mouth to respond; but just as suddenly, something behind him caused the smile to drop from her face, and her eyes zeroed in on the centerpiece.

She set down her plate and snatched up the mistletoe sprig Willa had replaced, frantically glancing around her before tossing it in the direction of the cooler filled with beer, soda, and other drinks. It landed among a patch of ice, partially hidden by the cooler's edge.

Eli slowly set down his plate and blinked at her while she calmly picked up her plate and reached for a stuffed olive as though nothing had happened. His curiosity was abated when Bradley came up to the end of the table, picked up a plate, eyes skimming over the food and straight to the centerpiece.

Dani pretended not to notice him, moving to the opposite end of the table to pick up some cheese and crackers, and Eli played along, scooping a pile of puppy chow onto his plate. Bradley frowned as he reached the middle of the table, absently picking up a stuffed olive as he peered at the decorative foliage.

He huffed when he failed to find the mistletoe, practically dropping his plate and moving as though to go around to the other side of the table when he bumped into someone.

Eli had been too busy pretending not to watch Bradley to notice Pen Long had wandered over to the cooler and bent to rummage around for a drink. Now she straightened when Bradley bumped into her, confusion plain on her face as instead of a drink, she held up the mistletoe.

Right between her and Bradley.

Her almond-shaped eyes narrowed on Bradley's shocked face as they both realized what was happening. "Oh, hell no," said Pen, her straight, ink-black hair swishing as she shook her head, and Bradley's grimace turned into an affronted frown.

"My sentiments exactly," he sneered.

Pen flipped him off.

"Come on, you guys," Brit called from across the room. "It's bad luck to skip the mistletoe kiss."

"Yeah," Eli shrugged. Though he felt sorry for Pen, he had to admit he was enjoying just how thwarted Bradley was in his designs, and couldn't resist needling him. "You'll be cursed if you don't."

Pen smirked, but Bradley barely spared him a bland stare. "Cursed?" he said, disbelieving.

"Yeah, the mistletoe curse." Dani chimed in, all innocence. How she was keeping a straight face, Eli wasn't sure. "If you don't kiss someone when you're caught under mistletoe, no one will ever want to kiss you again. And a mistletoe kiss is the only way to break the curse."

"You guys are a riot." Though Bradley still wasn't amused, Pen snickered humorlessly before looking up at Bradley and sighing, resigned to her fate. "Well, at least you're not hideous."

She tipped her face up expectantly, and Bradley groaned.

"Fine," he grumbled.

Fisting his hands at his sides, Bradley squeezed his eyes shut and slowly leaned his head down to where Pen had also clamped her eyes closed, as well as her lips. At the last moment she seemed to remember she needed her lips, and pursed them just before Bradley's met hers in a chaste and placid peck.

They both tensed for a second, visibly sagging in relief when they pulled apart and opened their eyes, ignoring the hoots and claps of the room.

Luke approached Eli, arms folded across his chest and a shit-eating grin on his face. "Your girl's got a mischievous side," he said in a low voice.

"I think it was self-preservation, actually." Diverted, Eli grinned back as he relished the tortured look on Bradley's face. "And she's not my girl."

"Yet."

"You better stay away from me for the rest of this party," Pen was saying, shaking the mistletoe she still held at Bradley. "I don't want to be caught with more secret mistletoe with you around."

He scoffed. "What are you going to do, send the Japanese mafia after me?"

"I'm Chinese, you dick. But I suppose I could call in a favor from the Yakuza."

"Whatever, like I'd want to kiss you again anyway."

Pen flipped him off again, then shoved the mistletoe into his chest, grabbed a random drink from the cooler, and stomped off to find her sister.

Bradley turned to find Eli and Luke holding back laughter, and from her vantage point at the other end of the table, Dani concealed a smile behind her hand.

"What are you laughing at?" he growled, and chucked the sprig he now held at Eli. Eli fumbled with it as it hit him in the chest, but managed to catch it in one of his hands. As was his habit, his brow rose at Bradley's mocking smirk. If his intention was to embarrass him or Luke, he picked the wrong target.

Eli turned both brows on Luke in question, and, unaffected, Luke only shrugged. "My best kisses are for my girl, but I suppose I can spare you one."

Then he grabbed Eli's face in his hands, turned his head, and smacked an enthusiastic kiss to his cheek. Releasing him, Luke thumped a hand on his shoulder, humor lighting his eyes.

"I love you, man," he said.

Chuckling along with his friends and neighbors, Eli shook his head, mock-shoving his friend away. "I love you, too. Now go away before Willa gets jealous."

"Will do."

To Eli's consternation, Luke winked at Dani, then gave Bradley a two-fingered salute and sauntered away. Eli couldn't help the smirk that took over his face as he pulled two berries—one for Bradley and Pen's kiss, one for his and Luke's—off the sprig, leaving only one remaining. Grumbling, Bradley stalked out of the room.

Instead of replacing the mistletoe in the centerpiece, Eli stepped over to the cooler and dropped it back in there. Then he went back to the table

for his plate, began to load it up again. He took a bite of one of the gingerbread cookies he'd already selected, hummed in pleasure as the mixture of
spices flooded across his taste buds.

"You like the gingerbread?"

He turned his head to find Dani a couple feet away from him.

"Mm." He nodded, swallowed. "I love gingerbread, and these are
great. There's something…different about the flavor. I can't figure out
what it is."

"Orange zest," she told him. "My mom's special ingredient."

He paused, his hand still outstretched toward a toothpick of something
wrapped in bacon, and turned his attention back to her. "You made these?
I didn't know you could bake."

"Yep. The mulled wine, too—that's actually Anita, our housekeeper's,
recipe. I help her make it every Christmas, and I used to make the cookies
with my mom. My brother was too young, but he would watch."

He put the bacon thing on his plate, straightened as he pondered her.
The way she spoke, he thought she was implying her housekeeper was
like another mother to her, and the sentiment surprised him. Though
perhaps it shouldn't, if the woman had always been in her life, and had
been there when Dani lost her parents.

"Where is your brother?" he asked.

"With our cousins," she said, smiling a little. "I'll join them in a few
days for Christmas. Anita went to visit her children and grandchildren."

"Why aren't you with your family now? You could have gone home
for break."

"I wanted to be here."

Her eyes met his, and he could've sworn his heart just tried to do a
kick flip and face-planted instead. Words he didn't even know he thought
left his mouth before he realized what he was saying.

"I'm glad."

Her smile crinkled her eyes before she turned to spoon some fruit
salad onto her plate. As she replaced the spoon in the fruit bowl, she stiffened, and Eli tracked her gaze across the room to where Gia stood
talking with Leah, Brit, and Jason. Gia had been watching him and Dani,
but glanced away when they spotted her, a distant frown marring her
face.

Meanwhile, Dani kept looking in Gia's direction with such undis-
guised longing Eli felt the sting in his own heart. Again he felt the urge to
ask, but didn't want to poke into her concerns.

But they both looked so unhappy.

He took a breath, leaned a little closer to Dani. "Do you want to talk
about it?" He murmured lowly.

Her head whipped up, eyes shifting over his face before swiveling away again. "I don't know what you're talking about."

"Dani." He laid a hand over hers on the table, gently so as not to spook her. "I know it's not my business, but you look miserable, and so does Gia. So if you need to talk about it, I promise I'm a good listener."

Her eyes welled, and for a fleeting moment he thought he'd royally screwed up, but she held the tears back.

"We used to be friends," she confessed.

He kept his voice gentle and reassuring as he removed his hand. "Can I ask what happened?"

Dani sniffled, swiped at her eyes with the sleeve of her sweater before steadying her voice. "She came out in high school, and nothing changed between us. But last year she told me she had feelings for me. I thought maybe she was just telling me because she thought I deserved to know, but she asked if I'd be willing to give us a chance."

"And you said no."

A quiet sigh escaped her as she nodded, her eyes downcast and heavy. "And I said no. I'm not gay, and she knew that. But she didn't feel we could remain friends after that."

Again she looked so sad, it nearly broke his heart; and with the guilt he felt for misinterpreting what little Gia had said about her relationship with Dani, he was reeling. On the surface Dani appeared distant and moody, but he'd seen the depths of her start to shimmer through the cracks. His natural curiosity would have been enough, but the connection he felt forming between them made him want to pry the cracks open.

Though the answer was obvious to him, he felt his next question should be asked anyway. "Do you miss her?"

Her eyes snapped back up to his, softening as she swallowed.

"Yes. And not just…" she looked away, toward Gia. "Because it's hard for me to make friends, but because Gia and I were inseparable growing up. It's been strange not talking to her, or hearing from her."

"Maybe she's waiting to hear from you," he suggested.

"I…I didn't think she'd want to hear from me."

"No way to know if you don't try. She may not know how to reach out to you either."

If possible, she looked even more despondent. "I never thought of it that way."

Glancing back at Gia, he tapped his fingers against the table as he determined what to do. Then he looked at Dani, who was watching him curiously.

"Wait here," he instructed.

She blinked, opened her mouth to question him, but he'd already started walking away. As he joined his cousin, his friend, and their respective partners, Gia's eyes narrowed on him. He deliberately put a cheery smile on his face.

"Hey, Eli," Jason beamed. "Enjoying the party?"

"I am. You? You've managed to avoid the mistletoe so far."

"Oh, well…"

"Ooh!" Brit piped up as Bing Crosby began to croon about a white Christmas. "Dance with me, Jase!"

"Alright." Jason colored, but let Brit tug him toward some empty space by the tree to sway to the music. It wouldn't have surprised Eli if there were any mistletoe on that tree.

"You and Dani seem to be hitting it off." Leah brought Eli's attention back to the mission at hand, suspicion lacing her tone.

"You know, I think we are," he agreed. "At least, enough for her to open up to me about a certain friend of hers."

He intentionally let his gaze land on Gia's face, and continued. "You should talk to her."

Gia lifted her chin. "She doesn't want to talk to me."

"She does." He gave her a stern look. "She looks like she's going to cry every time she looks at you, and you don't fare much better. *Talk* to each other."

And suddenly, Gia sighed, slumping as though she'd just set down a heavy box and finally looking back at Dani, who was still at the table watching them, fingers nervously twiddling her hair.

"Yeah, okay," she said softly, then turned to Leah. "I'll be right back."

Leah slanted a look at Eli as Gia approached Dani, hesitation stilting her movements. The hesitation melted when Dani simply turned to her, wrapped her in a fierce hug.

"I feel like I should be jealous." Leah cocked her head as she watched the reunited friends pull apart and begin to speak.

"But you're not."

"No, I'm not." She gave him an assessing look. "I've been trying to get Gia to talk to her, but she wouldn't budge. I think she was afraid of being rejected again."

"Dani, too." He draped an arm over Leah's shoulder, and she leaned into him, her thick ponytail of Gardiner hair—oak brown like his, as he got his hair from his mother—swinging as she gave his shoulder an affectionate head butt.

"Want me to scheme to get you and Dani under the mistletoe?" She wiggled her eyebrows at him.

The side of his mouth curved up. "We already got caught under the mistletoe."

"What?" She straightened and pulled back to get a better look at his face. "When?"

"When I got here."

"And I missed it? Damn." She grinned at him. "So how was it?"

Flustered, he cleared his throat as he glanced back toward Dani and Gia. "It was…um…"

He felt the back of Leah's hand thwack him lightly in the sternum. "That good, huh?"

She crowed with laughter when his eyes narrowed at her, puzzlement plain on his face.

"Eli, you should see your face. When you look at Dani, it's like you're undressing her with your eyes."

"What?"

"Seriously, though." She laughed again. "You've got it bad. So did she like it when you kissed her?"

"Well, I didn't think she'd want to kiss me at all, but she kissed me back." He shrugged, shook his head as he felt the tips of his ears burn. "And…Brit said it was hot."

"Oh, really? Guess I'll have to ask Brit about it then."

She would do it, too, he knew. He was about to ask her not to when he noticed Dani and Gia making their way back to them, a plate of food in both Dani's hands.

Smiling, she held one out to him when they reached them. "You forgot this," she said.

"Oh, thanks." He took it, picked up his partially eaten cookie and bit in, chewed cheerfully.

"Your mom's gingerbread is the best," Gia told Dani wistfully, then looped her arm through Leah's, turned a teasing eye back to Dani. "She taught you well, *Danica*. Nothing I bake ever comes out right."

Dani rolled her eyes, but smiled. "You don't have the patience for baking, *Georgia*."

Eli blinked. "Your name is Danica? Why didn't I know that?"

Bemused, Dani shrugged. "Only a handful of people call me that, I guess. Anyway, I have to restock the food supply; some of the dishes are getting low."

"Shouldn't Brit be doing that?" Leah asked.

"You think Brit's been paying attention?" Dani's smile filled with mirth as she spotted her friend dancing with Jason, and they all snickered knowingly at her insinuation. "I'll talk to you later."

As she headed off toward the kitchen, nibbling on the cheese and crackers from her plate as she went, Leah nudged Eli with her elbow. He turned his head to see she and Gia were staring at him, amusement clear on their faces.

"What?" he asked, though he had a feeling they could see right through him.

But instead, Gia said, "Thank you, Eli. We both needed a little kick in the ass."

"Happy to help."

It was the truth—he'd hated seeing the miserable look on Dani's face, and he'd only wanted to see her happy again. The smiling, teasing version of her was the woman he was coming to like quite a bit.

Alright, he already liked her quite a bit.

"And Eli?" As if reading his mind, Gia winked at him. "Go get her."

THE NEXT HOUR of the party was just as eventful as the first.

There were plenty more mistletoe kisses, including a shy but delighted one between Becca and Harrison after they'd discovered some behind a pillow on the couch they were sitting on. And as Eli had surmised, there was indeed a sprig hidden among the branches of the Christmas tree— only it was Steven Goulding and Amy Long who'd found it, thereby making Steven's dreams come true.

Eli hadn't managed to get close to Dani after she'd refilled the table food, as Bradley did his best to commandeer her time; or if Bradley was occupied by something else, Dani spent her time talking to Gia and Leah.

The latter he couldn't blame her for. She wanted to catch up with her friend, and she didn't owe him her time.

There was no rush, he reminded himself. They would talk eventually —maybe his time would be better utilized figuring out what to say to her. He wasn't sure he should declare feelings that were still brewing, but he could get to know her better, maybe even ask her out.

Did he want to ask her out?

See, he told himself. He should figure that out first.

Jason nudged him from his reverie, and he blinked at his friend, realizing Brit was no longer standing with them.

"Sorry, I spaced out. Where'd Brit go?"

"Bathroom." Jason eyed him skeptically, which wasn't an expression he was used to seeing on Jason's face. "What's up with you? You don't usually space at a party."

"Just something on my mind."

"Or someone."

He shouldn't have been surprised. Everyone who knew him well was grilling him about her tonight. "That obvious?"

Jason shrugged. "It is to me. And I admit I'm curious what you'll do next, because I think you've changed your mind about her. I think you like her."

"I do like her," Eli admitted. "And I'm itching to talk to her, but I don't want to force it."

"Maybe if everyone else here had witnessed your mistletoe kiss, they'd clear the way for you."

Eli quirked a brow at his friend's small smile. "Et tu, Brute? I didn't expect *you* to rib me about this."

"I've gotta give it back to you at least sometimes," Jason chuckled. "Plus, you might get some curious glances—a handful of people over-heard Leah asking Brit about your kiss with Dani."

Eli groaned. He knew he shouldn't have told Leah about that. "Great."

"Since when do you care about gossip?"

"I don't, but I don't want Dani to be embarrassed."

Jason shook his head as he gestured to where Dani was happily chatting with Gia, Leah, Denny, and Ryan. "She's fine, man."

"Yeah, I guess she is," Eli nodded. Then, his humor restored, he side-eyed his friend. "So what about you, then? I think Brit's pretty disap-pointed none of her mistletoe plots have caught you yet."

A bit of pink flushed up the back of Jason's neck. "I know. I just…I don't think I could handle the spectacle."

Nodding again, he slapped Jason's back in a show of encouragement. "I know, man. It'll all work out."

Even as he said it, Dani broke off from her group and wandered over to them.

"I'll leave you to it," Jason said quietly, giving Dani a smile as he walked away, headed toward the food table.

"You know, Elijah, if I didn't know better," Dani said as she stopped in front of Eli, "I'd say he wanted to give us the opportunity to talk alone."

Her smile turned cheeky at the use of his full name, and he couldn't resist smiling back, recalling how Gia had teased Dani in a similar manner earlier—a teasing that spoke of intimacy and affection. "But we're not really alone, are we, Danica?"

"Hm," she hummed, her eyes drifting down to his empty hands. "Do you want a beer?"

The abrupt change of subject threw him off. "Uh…sure?"

Her smile brightened. "Come with me."

Intrigued and willing, he followed her, his curiosity only growing when, instead of going to the cooler, she veered off out of the dining room and into the hall, away from the party. He kept pace behind her, the sounds of the party fading away; they passed by a table decorated with a nativity display, a darkened hallway, and a couple doors, before she finally turned into the kitchen.

It was a space filled with light and warmth, and the scents of Christmas baking, likely remnants of when she'd made the gingerbread cookies.

It was also large, with tall cream-colored cabinets, sleek butcher block countertops, and lots of stainless steel. Four high-backed stools flanked one side of the large island in the middle of the room where the countertop overflowed. A large lidded pot sat on the quiet stove, and Eli assumed it was the mulled wine; a peek inside and a sniff of the fragrant steam that rose confirmed it.

He watched silently as she pulled two beers from the fridge, eyes tracking over the profile of her face—her expression was decidedly calm, and it reminded him something of the practiced serenity Jason often projected. And in Dani's case, Eli knew there was at least a little bit of emotional turmoil swirling around in her mind—perhaps she needed a quiet space for a moment to clear it.

He wondered if she was enjoying the party as she straightened a little, turned from the fridge with the necks of two bottles clamped in her fingers; and when she gave him a self-deprecating shrug, he realized he'd posed the question aloud.

"I don't mind parties so much when I'm not the center of attention," she said, handing him one of the bottles. "By now the novelty of my family's wealth has pretty much worn off on everyone here, and I'm just a person again."

"Ah." Eli felt his face scrunching together. "I suppose I should apologize then."

Her brows formed a slight V. "For what?"

"For…" He paused, cleared his throat. "Well, you just said you don't like being the center of attention, and my arrival drew quite a bit of attention to you."

"Oh." Her face relaxed in humor. "Well I won't deny I wish we didn't have an audience, but that audience was pretty small. And you know as well as I do Brit's shenanigans are to blame."

"Shenanigans. There's a word."

"Right? Every time you say it, an etymologist gets its wings."

A laugh burst out of him, sudden and strong, before it trailed off in a quiet chuckle. He shook his head, and his eyes, still brimming with merriment, met her own laughing green orbs. After a moment, she pulled at her bottom lip with her teeth; though her smile remained, she looked down, fiddling with her bottle, and he suddenly recalled her words from before their kiss.

I promise I won't bite.

But he could imagine it—her teeth nibbling at his lips, or his ear. At this point he wasn't even surprised by how much he wanted that.

"Hey, um," she was saying, and he refocused his thoughts. "I wanted to thank you, you know, for your advice. For pushing me to talk to Gia."

"You're welcome."

"No, really. I...I get so stuck inside my head, sometimes I forget other people might be just as uncomfortable as I am. You reminded me how fragile the human ego can be, especially my own. And Gia has always had a confidence I lack."

"You lack confidence?" He probed. "Are you sure?"

"Quite."

"Doesn't seem that way to me. I am sorry if having to kiss me made you uncomfortable, though. I know I tease you, but I don't actually want to cause you discomfort." He didn't know where the words came from, but as he said them he realized they were true. Even when he'd thought he didn't like her, he hadn't wanted to hurt her.

"I never thought you did." She angled her head, smiling and curious. "I thought you were trying to draw me out. And you didn't make me uncomfortable. In fact, you seem to be one of the few people I'm comfortable around."

The bewilderment must have been clear on his face, because she blew out air on a soft laugh.

"There are only a handful of people I've ever felt like I can be myself around," she explained, playing with a strand of her hair. "And the more I get to know you, the more I...find my defenses crumbling."

His heart echoed that sentiment entirely. But before he could respond she took a deep breath and met his eyes.

"I like you, Eli. Quite a lot, actually."

He released his own breath—in relief or disbelief he wasn't sure. "You do?"

"You really didn't know?"

He hesitated, then shook his head. He really had been in denial, hadn't he? For someone who wanted to study human society as a career, he hadn't done a very good job of reading her—though in fairness, he wasn't studying psychology.

Her half-laugh brought him back to reality.

"And I was worried I was too obvious." She still twirled her hair, coiling the ends of it around a finger now. Almost mindlessly, he reached out to still her hand, his own fingers tugging gently on the strand.

Her hair was so soft.

"Um." She cleared her throat, dropped her hand, causing his own to fall back to his side, and he wondered why she was suddenly nervous after such a bold confession. But then, he hadn't actually said he liked her back, so maybe she was scrambling to make things less awkward. "Anyway, let me get the bottle cap thing for these beers…"

She set down her bottle on the countertop as she pulled open the island's wide kitchen drawer, picking out the bottle opener, but when she went to close it, she stilled. Then her shoulders relaxed, and she released a quiet snort through pressed lips as she set down the tool.

"You've got to be kidding me."

"What?" He set his beer on the island next to hers, glanced down to look in the drawer just as she picked up a small sprig of mistletoe dotted with small white berries, and closed the drawer.

She held it up, pinched between her thumb and forefinger, tilting her head and raising her brows as if to say, *"would you look at that?"* He choked out a laugh.

"Wow, when Brit said everywhere, she really meant it."

"Indeed," she agreed, her eyes catching his. Holding.

There was no one around this time if they decided to forego the kiss. But she had just admitted she liked him; this felt like an invitation. Or a challenge. This time he would know she meant it; and if he chose to accept the invitation, he would be admitting he liked her, too, wouldn't he?

Perhaps he should test the waters a bit first.

His lips quirked, eyes sparkling with mischief. "Does it count if it's not hanging over our heads?"

"Hm, fair point. Here." She held the sprig out to him, smiling pertly when his brows furrowed. "You're taller than me."

Now his brows lifted slowly as understanding lit his face, mouth slowly turning up in a grin as flutters zigzagged from his stomach to his chest. His fingers brushed hers when he took the sprig, and he stepped closer as he raised his arm to hold it over their heads, dangling it between them like a dare.

"Is this better?" he murmured, his voice low and teasing.

She didn't even bother looking up at the sprig; instead her eyes had stayed on his, watching and tempting at the same time. Though her answering smile was seductive, she didn't waste time with pleasantries—an attitude that fit her, Eli thought, as she simply trailed her palms up his chest.

When her fingers curled lightly on the back of his neck, making his skin tingle, he nearly gave in and jerked her to him. But he wanted Dani to move first. He wanted to see what she would do.

He didn't have to wait long to find out.

"It's perfect," she said, rising onto her toes. And the fingers cupped at his neck propelled his head down, gentle but insistent, until his mouth met hers.

This time he was prepared, but only slightly more so. Before, he'd been the one trying to bait her, but she was taking the reins here. Before, they'd been testing each other, but now they knew the taste of each other and were going back for more.

She didn't hesitate to press herself against him, deepening the kiss, and now he did wrap his free arm around her waist, holding her as close as possible. She hummed against his mouth, inclined her head to nip at his bottom lip. When she brought her lips fully to his again, her tongue flicked out, a clear demand.

On a groan, Eli gave up the pretense of holding the mistletoe, flinging it back over his shoulder. Once freed, his fingers wound their way into her long waves, gripping the bottom of her scalp. He felt her laugh in the subtle shake of her shoulders and the curve of her lips as they parted under his.

Her arms came around his neck, somehow tugging him even closer, and she released a quiet whimper when his tongue finally swept out to seek hers. She met him stroke for teasing stroke; she was a more eager kisser than he'd anticipated, but he wasn't complaining.

Although, things might get a bit awkward if they kept this up.

She seemed to sense this too, because she slowed the kiss, releasing her arms to rest her hands on his shoulders and nibble at his lip again. He moved his own hands to rest on her waist, thumbs gently grazing back and forth.

"I think that mistletoe got more than it bargained for." Dani bit her lip with a coy smile, nuzzled his nose with hers much like he had before their first kiss.

Eli chuckled. "That was probably enough kisses to pull off all the berries."

"Hmm…" She tilted her head side to side in mock consideration. "No, I think we missed a few."

He grinned. "On second thought, I think you're right," he agreed, and took her mouth again. The hands at her waist slid to her lower back, and her own arms slinked around him, fingers splaying up his back.

He meant to keep this one slow, but the feel of her already had his control fraying. His tongue had found its way to mingle with hers again, their kisses deep and heated. A number of images flashed through his brain—all the things he'd held back from imagining doing with her before —and felt himself begin to harden.

"Dani," he mumbled against her lips, pulling away just a hair's breadth.

Her eyes drifted open almost sleepily, green mists swirling. "Hm?"

"Unless you want me to to drag you to the nearest private location and have my way with you, we need to stop."

Her eyes flashed up to his in awe. Then slowly, a sly smirk played on her lips—the kind that had his lower extremity twitching. He knew she felt it because she glanced down, smirk widening.

"Good to know I'm not the only one getting..." She cleared her throat, raised her eyes back to his. "Excited."

Now it was his eyebrow that twitched as a pretty blush spread across her cheeks. "Is that so?"

"Eli." She sounded almost exasperated, clenching her legs together and squirming, almost as if she had to go to the bathroom. "I'm wetter than the freaking ocean. In the middle of a storm."

Well, that did it. He was definitely hard now.

Though the thought she might have to use the bathroom had had him settling for an instant, the comment that followed had his stomach dropping. He stared at her a moment before finally blinking, and said the first thing that popped into his lust-hazed brain.

"Fuck."

She must have been thinking the same thing, because when he crushed his lips back to hers, she was right there with him. He wanted to devour her, and it seemed like she wanted to devour him; it was easy to forget where they were. A dangerous combination, given there was a party still going on.

But her lips were so intoxicating, and he could still taste mulled wine on her tongue, and the moan that escaped her mouth when his hands cradled her head and curled in her hair made his insides hum with pleasure.

She kissed him back so hard he wondered if his lips would bruise.

"Oh boy, now I'm definitely jealous."

Eli and Dani jolted, pulling apart, but not away from each other. Dani kept her arms around his waist, so he slid his hands back down to her waist as he turned just slightly, craning his neck over his shoulder to see Brit bending down to pick up the mistletoe from the floor where it had landed when he'd discarded it.

Grinning suggestively, Brit waggled her eyebrows as she waved the wayward sprig. "This mistletoe really did its job, huh?"

He knew his ears were probably a little red, but he grinned back at her, unashamed. When he glanced at Dani, she was blushing, too, but laughter danced in her eyes as she considered her friend.

"The utensil, drawer, B?" she asked. "You don't cook."

Brit shrugged. "Hey, you never know. If I happened to be in here with Jason, you can bet your ass I'd want some on hand."

"Brit, you know you don't need mistletoe to kiss Jason," Eli pointed out. "If you kiss him, he will happily kiss you back."

"Really?" Brit looked at the mistletoe in her hand doubtfully. "I feel like he's been avoiding me all night, especially around mistletoe."

"He's just shy," he assured her. "He wants to kiss you, but he'd much rather do it in private."

"Oh." Brit's eyes widened hopefully, and Eli couldn't help but think her answering smile was a little mischievous. "I might just do that, then. And take this with me," she said, pocketing the mistletoe.

He was surprised she didn't have some in there already.

"Well, I'll just get out of your hair, then," Brit continued, winking at them as she turned to go, and pausing just before the doorway.

"Oh, Eli," she smirked, pointing to her lips and tapping them, "You've got a little something…"

He lifted a finger to his lips, and saw a light smear of cheerful red when he drew it back to look. Brit's laugh faded as she left the room, and Dani's shoulders shook as she laughed quietly, leaning her forehead against his chest.

When she glanced back up at him, he could see her lipstick was a little smudged, though not as much as he thought it'd be. Funny how he hadn't noticed it sooner.

"I guess not even super stay lipstick can hold out against super intense kissing," she said wryly.

Snickering, he gave her one more quick peck before reaching for a paper towel; she stopped him by taking his hand in hers.

"There's another powder room down the hall," she said as she tugged him out of the kitchen. He lifted his brows but let her lead him without question, rather enjoying how her hand felt clasped in his. When they reached the little half bath next to the laundry room, she dropped his hand and turned on the light.

"Wait here. I'll be right back."

He thought about asking her where she was going, but she clearly had a plan, so again he didn't question it. Instead he stepped into the powder room, a little shocked by the image that faced him in the mirror. It wasn't as bad as he'd assumed, but the random splotches of dark red swiped across his mouth still gave him a jolt, the deep blue pools that were his eyes rounding at the sight.

He pulled a tissue from the box on the counter and wiped it across his face, confused when it came away a little red, but his face looked exactly the same. Shrugging to himself, he wetted the tissue a little, wiped again.

And again, barely anything was removed.

"What the...?" He frowned at his reflection. He couldn't go back out to the party like this. Maybe he could look around for a washcloth or something.

He was still frowning at the useless tissue when Dani returned, amusement dancing over her features as she took him in, leaning against the door jam.

Well she was one to laugh—her lipstick was still smudged, and her glorious espresso tresses were a bit mussed, as was his own hair. He found he was relieved she hadn't fixed either, though, as it was the first time he'd really seen her look less than perfect.

He tossed the tissue in the wastebasket. "This stuff won't come off. How is that even possible?"

"Witchcraft." Then she brandished a tube of chapstick, waving her wrist as though she were holding a wand, held it out to him. "Luckily, I know a few spells of my own. Put some of this on."

He took the chapstick from her, did as he was told as she explained, "Let that sit a little bit, then wipe it off. The lipstick should come off more easily then. It might take a few rounds, but it does the job. I put some on on my way down."

To demonstrate, she grabbed a tissue, wiped roughly along her lips, and sure enough, her tissue came away dark red—though her lips appeared to be even more smudged.

He snorted. "Witchcraft indeed."

"It gets worse before it gets better," she shrugged, then held out her hand for the chapstick, reapplying some as he tried again to wipe off his mouth.

This time, to his relief, he got nearly all of it. One more round of her chapstick trick ought to do it.

It took her a couple more applications to get all hers off, and then she applied one last coat just to soothe her lips, which were still tinted slightly and looked perfectly pink, even with the lipstick gone.

He wanted to kiss her again.

Eli shook his head at the pile of crimson-smeared tissues in the wastebasket as she stepped out of the powder room.

"That's a lot of work for magic lipstick."

She nodded as he turned off the light. "That's why I only wear it on special occasions."

They headed back toward the kitchen, her shoulder bumping against his arm as they turned the corner; whether she did it on purpose or not, the fact she was comfortable being so close to him when she seemed to shy away from everyone else was a wonder to him.

He nearly bumped into her full on when she suddenly halted in the middle of the hallway, cocked her head at an ajar door a few feet away.

"Why is the garage light on?" she murmured, moving to the door. Curious, Eli moved behind her, peeking over her shoulder as she used a finger to push it open wider, and poked her head out into the cooler air.

And they saw Brit and Jason standing together near the freezer, lips locked in a fierce embrace with their arms wound tightly around each other. They pulled apart at the sound of the door creaking; warmth flooded Jason's cheeks, and Brit ginned widely.

"I see you completed your mission." Dani's brows quirked as she goaded her friend, and Eli gave Jason a similar look. Jason, contrary to his usual shyness, stood his ground and arched a brow at Eli right back.

"I conned him into helping me restock the cooler," Brit explained.

The cooler from the dining room sat a few feet away, ice and drink supply still dwindled down. Dani eyed the half-full boxes of beer and soda organized on top of the freezer, bit the inside of her cheek.

"Oh, then we'll just get out of your hair," she said saucily as she edged back into the hall, shutting the door firmly with a definite *click.*

"Well, I don't know about you, but I'm not surprised in the slightest." The smile she sent Eli was one he could only call conspiratorial.

"Definitely not the most surprising thing to happen tonight," he agreed, then mused aloud, "What are the chances no one will ask us where we've been?"

"Pretty slim," she speculated, side-eyeing him with a playful smirk. "Bet you ten bucks Bradley asks first."

"I am surprised he hasn't come looking for you." Eli nudged her shoulder with his own, grinning. "But my bet's on Luke. He's been watching us like hawk because he was convinced you had a crush on me."

"Your friend is very observant."

"He is."

When they reached the kitchen, Eli let out a short laugh—the beers they'd pulled out were still on the island, along with the bottle opener.

"I can't believe we forgot about these. They're probably warm now," he said as he went to pick one up.

Dani picked up the other, noted the condensation on the outside of the bottles. "We could put them back, but I think they're still pretty cold."

In response, he picked up the bottle opener, popped the top off hers, then his. When he'd set down the tool, he held out his bottle for a toast.

She gave him an arch look as she clinked the neck of her bottle against his, her lips curving wryly as she took a sip, met his eyes over the rim.

"Shall we?" she asked.

His mind went blank as he looked down at her lips. "Shall we what?"

Her face brightened with laughter. "Get back to the party?"

"Right. Yes. We should…do that."

Shoulders quaking, she sent him a look of pure affection, and he took a swig of beer to keep from kissing her again—he had a feeling his expression matched hers, and if the events of tonight were any indication, there would be other times for that.

They took their beers and wound their way down the hall toward the dining room; this time it was Eli who halted when he heard a shuffling noise. When Dani turned an inquiring gaze on him, he held up a finger, and after a moment there was a quiet thud, followed by a muffled grunt.

Dani's eyes widened, and they approached the curve in the hall where it veered off before the stairs and led to rooms like the den, a bathroom, and the library; just up ahead, adjacent to the hall, was the opening to the dining room, and beyond that, the one for the living room, and Eli could hear the music and the chatter loud and clear. But from where they were standing, he and Dani could just make out the slight moans someone wasn't making much effort to conceal.

He sidled up to the edge of the wall, peered cautiously around the corner—and muffled a laugh with his fist. At his reaction, Dani put a hand on his shoulder and stood on her toes to see, and he bent to give her a better view.

Her eyes flared, and her mouth dropped open in stupefied humor as, in the dim light from the hall, they both saw Bradley pressing Pen up against the wall, his mouth fused to hers as she gripped the collar of his slightly open shirt. His thigh was between her legs, and her hands swept up into his hair, yanked him closer on another moan.

Pressing her lips together, Dani crept back, and began to tiptoe toward the dining room entryway. Evidently, she'd decided it was better not to interrupt, and Eli followed her lead, feeling a bit like a child trying to sneak down the stairs to get a glimpse of Santa Claus.

Once they'd passed the hall, their steps returned to normal, and they turned into the dining room, rejoining the party. There was a little bit of dancing going on near the tree, but many were gathered on the furniture, deep in conversations that spurred laughter, while others stood around with plates of food.

Luke and Willa were back in the big wingback chair, and Luke was the first one to notice them as they neared the couches. Eli took a sip of his beer to avoid his friend's discerning eyes, but failed to hide a smile.

"Hey, where have you two been?" Luke asked, a smug suspicion glinting in his gaze.

Eli lowered his beer, turned his head to give Dani a victorious eyebrow raise and a grin.

"Yeah, yeah." Rolling her eyes, she pulled her phone from her pocket, flipped open the case, and took out a ten dollar bill. She slapped it into his hand as she tucked her phone away, and he pocketed his prize.

"I won a bet," he explained to Luke, who'd been scrutinizing the exchange with both gratification and utter confusion.

"What the hell kind of bet?" he asked.

When Eli elaborated, Luke and Willa burst out laughing.

"Bradley was a good guess, though," Luke said as his laughter subsided. Then he grinned at Eli. "But, hey, since I'm the reason you won, maybe I should get half your winnings."

"No can do, man." Eli shook his head. "I'm gonna use it to take my woman out for ice-cream."

He felt Dani's eyes on him as Luke's eyebrows shot up over the rim of his glasses.

Willa giggled. "Your woman?"

And Dani's hand slipped into his, squeezed; when he looked down at her, her smile was soft and hopeful.

"Yes," she answered Willa.

Some people on the couch next to them got up to go dance, and Eli was quick to take a seat on the end, setting his beer on the coffee table. He expected Dani to sit next to him, but instead, after setting her bottle next to his, she slid onto his lap, hanging her arms loosely around his neck, her lower back against the arm of the couch.

"So," she murmured. "You're taking me out for ice-cream, huh?"

"What's wrong with ice-cream?"

"Ice-cream is never wrong. I just wasn't expecting it, considering the cold weather."

"Well, as you said, ice-cream is never wrong."

She grinned. "When are we going on this ice-cream outing?"

"How about before you go visit your family?"

Her voice vibrated against his ear as she whispered lowly. "I like the sound of that."

The tip of his nose bumped against hers as he turned his head to smile at her, and he found himself mesmerized just as before. Funny how much had changed in only a few hours.

Maybe he was the one who'd been acting the Grinch—his heart had certainly grown, had opened, and it was all because of her.

And maybe a little bit because of mistletoe.

Her eyes, so deep and green, held his, promising him more kisses, more laughs, more moments—just more. He hoped his eyes were telling her he wanted all of it.

Their tacit conversation was interrupted when Brit tapped Dani on the shoulder, held out the mistletoe she'd been carrying around for her own purposes.

"You look like you need this," she smirked.

Coloring a little, but smiling contentedly, Dani shook her head, gently swatting Brit's hand away. "We don't need it."

Eli's arms tightened around her waist as she turned her face back to his, stroked her fingers across his jaw. "Do we?" she asked.

In answer, he leaned in and kissed her.

MIDNIGHT MACHINATIONS

WHEN ONE HAS both the means and the opportunity to throw the party of the century, one typically spares no expense to ensure guests are appropriately awed.

If that wasn't a universally acknowledged truth, thought Elizabeth Bennet, perhaps it should be.

The enormous, open concept Netherfield penthouse on Lake Shore Drive was exquisitely decorated with the typical silver, gold, and black that denoted the occasion, sparkling with light and elegance, with nary a streamer or party popper in sight.

It was the fanciest New Year's Eve party she'd ever been to, that was for sure. So fancy, in fact, the hostess, Caroline Bingley, insisted on calling it a gala.

A New Year's Eve *Gala*.

Because that wasn't pretentious at all, Elizabeth thought. And neither was the ice sculpture of Aphrodite, or the black tie dress code. Or the *hors d'oeuvres*.

The chocolate fondue fountain was cool, though. No one could find fault with that.

Except maybe Darcy.

He seemed like the kind of person who could find fault with anything if he tried. Especially her. He certainly stared at her a lot, cataloguing her faults based on some unrealistic standards of which she was unaware.

It was infuriating, really, how he held his tall frame above everyone else, quite literally looking down on them with calculating blue eyes, only intensified by his dark navy suit. With his onyx hair swept up—and not one out of place—he presented a suave, yet unapproachable, picture.

Unconsciously, Elizabeth tugged at the end of her dress, a shimmering dark gold number that flared a double-layered skirt at the waist, down to her mid-thigh. The top half was held up with spaghetti straps and formed a slight V above her breasts; thin ruffles scooped loosely across her upper arms where sleeves might have been, but kept her shoulders exposed.

It was shinier than she usually went for, but it felt right for the occasion. Plus, she looked damn good in it; it fit her just right, and the gold color brought out the amber in her hazel eyes. Her sister Jane had styled her corduroy brown locks in a curled updo, with little tendrils framing her face just so, and done her makeup with a light but effective touch, including a pop of ruby red color to her lips. She'd worn her favorite necklace, some simple gold earrings, and a gold bracelet with little ruby stones her grandmother had given her.

Eat your heart out, Will Darcy. She silently dared him to call her *tolerable* to her face.

Jane herself looked resplendent in a silver, sequined dress with an intricate black belt, her strawberry blonde hair twisted up in a perfect bun.

Their family had almost immediately split up upon arrival, just after seven; spotting her close friend Charlotte over at the open bar that had been set up in the dining room, Elizabeth went to join her there. According to the party's invitation, cocktail hour began at eight p.m., and dancing would begin at nine, music provided by a jazz ensemble.

Charlotte had spotted her as well, and had another glass of wine ordered and waiting for her friend by the time Elizabeth made it to her side.

"Perfect timing," Charlotte quipped.

"It's a talent," Elizabeth grinned before taking a sip of what she discovered was a lovely moscato. "You look great, Char."

Charlotte, who's pale blue eyes popped against the royal blue velvet of her wrap dress and copper curls, perked up at the compliment.

"Thanks." She smiled wide before gesturing to Elizabeth's outfit. "You look like you're trying to make a certain Mr. Tall, Dark, and Handsome eat his words."

Elizabeth's smile dropped. "Really? Do you think it's too much?"

"No, Lizzy." Charlotte poked her friend in the arm. "I think you look stunning, and Will Darcy would be an idiot not to notice."

"I don't particularly care if he notices or not."

"Liar." Charlotte only lifted a brow. "But regardless, he will notice, considering how often he stares at you."

They'd had this conversation before, and Elizabeth wasn't taking the bait this time. Instead, she only quirked a brow back at her friend and took another sip of her wine.

Jane had found Charles and Caroline Bingley and was conversing with them, so Elizabeth and Charlotte meandered from the bar over to the refreshment table, where they both picked up a cake pop, dipped it in the chocolate fountain, and hummed with pleasure at the decadent taste.

"I'm going to have to pace myself over here," Charlotte mumbled, her mouth still full of cake pop.

Elizabeth nodded wholeheartedly. "Me, too."

They spent most of the next hour wandering the room, chatting with their neighbors, nibbling on confections, and avoiding the attention of their mothers.

One could only avoid something for so long, however. As the dancing hour neared, Mrs. Bennet caught them unawares—with the loathsome Bill Collins, dressed in a tuxedo with a tailcoat, in tow.

Collins was the son of an old acquaintance of Mr. Bennet's, who'd made himself known to their family by showing up on their doorstep and stating he wanted to 'heal the breach' between their families. It didn't take long for them to realize this involved winning the heart of one of Mr. Bennet's daughters—whether they liked it or not.

Mrs. Bennet was the only one who thought this an excellent idea, and had contrived to throw her next-eldest (as Charles Bingley was for Jane) and least favorite daughter (Lydia was too good for Mr. Collins) together with Bill Collins as often as possible.

It either escaped her notice or didn't concern her that Elizabeth was very put off by the man. With a slight frame, neatly trimmed, silvery blonde hair, and pool green eyes, his appearance was not unappealing. However, Elizabeth found him to be condescending, self-absorbed, pompous, and completely obsessed with his haberdashery's investor, Catherine De Bourgh.

Not to mention he disregarded almost everything Elizabeth said, and routinely doused himself in a vile cologne that made her nostrils sting.

"Hello, girls." Mrs. Bennet smiled in a way that put Elizabeth on edge. "Charlotte, don't you look nice."

"Thanks, Mrs. B. You, too." Though she could probably hear the disappointment in Mrs. Bennet's voice, Charlotte remained gracious.

"Indeed, the ladies look quite lovely," Collins asserted. Elizabeth could have sworn he was about to lick his lips as he raked his eyes down her body.

"You know, the dancing's about to start, Lizzy." Mrs. Bennet turned her I'm-up-to-something smile on her second-eldest daughter. "Charles has already asked Jane to dance. Do you have a partner?"

Elizabeth met her mother's gaze with an unflinching expression. "No, but I'd rather not dance right now."

"Oh, pish." Her mother waved the comment away.

"Your natural modesty does you credit, Elizabeth." Collins smiled at her and gave a slight bow. He was always going on about female modesty. "It is one of the reasons I will give you the honor of the first dance."

He'd *give* her the honor?

She was about to tell him where he could shove his so-called honor when Mrs. Bennet inserted herself.

"Of course, Lizzy would be delighted to dance with you, Mr. Collins."

"Wonderful!" Collins clapped his hands together. "I shall return to collect you at nine o'clock precisely, Elizabeth."

Without waiting for a response, he turned and sauntered off toward the open bar.

It was eight fifty-five.

Hopefully he'd be too distracted to come back for her.

She turned to her mother, her mouth a thin line, eyes narrowed. "Mom, why did you do that?"

"Do what?"

"Answer for me. I don't want to dance with Mr. Collins."

Mrs. Bennet patted her daughter's arm as if Elizabeth didn't comprehend the situation. "Now, now, Lizzy, give the man a chance. You wouldn't want to hurt his feelings."

Why not? All he does is offend mine, she thought. But that wouldn't go over well, so instead she said, "What about my feelings?"

She knew there was no point trying to explain why she wasn't obligated to 'give him a chance,' so more than anything it was a somewhat desperate, if futile, attempt to point out to her mother how off her matchmaking ideas were—one that went right over Mrs. Bennet's head.

"Oh, don't you worry, Lizzy dear," she said with a patronizing smile. "Mr. Collins has no intention of hurting your feelings."

Elizabeth couldn't suppress a grimace, one made up of her frustration, bewilderment, and despair. She could only imagine what she must look like, as her expression sent her mother all aflutter; if Mrs. Bennet had a handkerchief, Elizabeth was sure she'd be waving it about.

"Lizzy! You'd better hurry and smile, or you'll chase him away! Quick —he's coming back."

She didn't bother to wait for Elizabeth to smile, just took her daughter by the shoulders and turned her around; sure enough, Collins was heading back her way, not noticing when he bumped into anyone in his haste to reach her, and nearly spilling the wine in his glass.

When he was a few steps away, the conductor announced that dancing was about to start, and launched right into a song.

Collins quickened his pace, and Elizabeth felt a little shove on her shoulders as her mother literally pushed her at him.

When he reached her, Collins looked flabbergasted by the half-full glass still in his hand, and even though she hadn't moved, said, "There you are! It's time for our dance!"

Clearly flustered, he thrust the glass at Charlotte, who took it with obvious amusement. Then he swung out an arm and grasped Elizabeth's wrist.

She stumbled a couple steps when he yanked on her arm, managing to find her balance as he practically dragged her across the room to the dance floor. They were one of the first couples to reach it, and Elizabeth breathed a quiet sigh of relief when he let go of her, rubbing her wrist where his hand had clamped around it.

Her relief was short-lived, however, as he wasted no time placing a hand dangerously low on her backside and clasping the hand of the wrist she was soothing in his other. He stepped in and pulled her right up against him; she had to suppress a shudder at the unwanted contact, and held her breath to keep from breathing in the overwhelming scent of his cologne.

She placed her free hand on his shoulder and pushed until there were a few inches between them, and thankfully he didn't notice because he had immediately begun to sway back and forth—completely off rhythm from the upbeat pace of the song.

"I can't tell you how much I've been looking forward to this dance, Elizabeth." Collins beamed at her. "I'm sure you've anticipated it as much as I have."

Luckily, he seemed not to notice her lack of response; her eyes tracked around the room, searching for someone that could rescue her.

She saw Jane dancing with Charles, perfectly in sync; they even looked perfect, as Charles wore a slim black suit with a silver bowtie that matched Jane's dress and complimented his bark brown hair. She dared not catch Jane's eye, as she didn't want to interrupt them. Lydia was bouncing around with Peter Denny and wouldn't notice Elizabeth's silent plea for help. She saw her mother glancing between her and Collins and Jane and Charles with a satisfied look on her face, but no sign of her father. And unfortunately Charlotte was no longer standing with Mrs. Bennet, and Elizabeth couldn't find her.

Even more unfortunately, she noticed Caroline smirking at her from the edge of the room. And next to her was Darcy, countenance stoic as he observed them, face grim. Caroline's smirk widened into one of superiority when Collins stepped on Elizabeth's foot, causing her to wince. Inwardly, she cringed that Darcy should witness her mortification.

Collins was, of course, oblivious to his blunder, continuing to babble on about nonsense and swing her around with no real concept of his movements. He nearly ran them into another couple more than once, and Elizabeth did her best to redirect him.

"I flatter myself that the lesson I took was sufficient to teach me the intricacies of dancing with the female sex," he was saying.

"Lesson—as in one?" She was reluctant to ask, but the absurdity of the statement had piqued her sense of the ridiculous.

"Of course! Catherine De Bourgh insists that one should learn to dance, but to take more than one lesson would be a waste of time and money."

When she looked up at him, not bothering to hide her consternation, she saw his smile was pitying, as though she with her *female modesty* wouldn't understand such things; this irked her so much it took her a moment to realize his eyes weren't on her face, but her chest. The hand at her back dipped lower, over her tailbone.

Her eyes narrowed, and she was about to give him a warning when he spoke.

"Have I told you how lovely you look this evening, Elizabeth?"

"Yes," she said, as bland and unwelcoming as possible.

He continued, oblivious as ever, "I have many more compliments where that came from. I believe I have perfected the art of commendation, if I do say so myself."

He emphasized this statement by sliding his hand even lower, skimming the top of her butt. Elizabeth didn't bother with a warning now; she just whipped her free hand back and, gripping his arm, moved it up to the middle of her back—and closer to her side than her spine for good measure.

She shouldn't have been surprised by his contrary response to this, but an eyebrow-waggle was the opposite of what she expected.

"How modest you are," he said, nearly giggling.

"Modesty has nothing to do with it." Though she did nothing to soften her displeasure, in either expression or tone of voice, he still looked at her like he thought she was teasing him. "I don't want your hand there. It's neither appropriate, nor welcome. Do I make myself clear?"

"Modesty is an admirable trait in a woman." It was like he hadn't heard her. "Do not underestimate your charms, my dear Elizabeth, for I find you immensely charming."

How any man could take a woman's obvious discomfort as charming modesty she didn't want to dwell on—that would undoubtedly only lead to frustration. Instead, she decided she'd had enough; she didn't care if she seemed rude, or if her mother would disapprove. Avoiding those things wasn't worth putting up with Collins's condescending company.

She'd even prefer Darcy's company to this. He, at least, would never blatantly try to feel her up without her consent, or in public—regardless of what she thought of him, she knew he was a gentleman.

"It is my intention," Collins continued, "to remain close to you tonight."

She tugged her hand out of his grasp and stepped back from him—and none too soon, because his other hand had begun to sneak over her backside again.

Thankfully, the song came to an end, which meant she wouldn't be causing a scene.

Without a word, she turned on her heel, and immediately power-walked toward Jane and Charles, hoping they could act as a buffer. To her relief, they were leaving the dance floor and headed toward the refreshment table; she pivoted to follow them, the sound of the next song starting trailing behind her.

But again, relief was fleeting, as she noted her mother move to intercept them. Mrs. Bennet reached Jane and Charles only a few moments after Elizabeth did.

"Oh, Charles," she gushed. "Watching you and Jane dance was simply *divine*. You're very fortunate in your choice of partner."

On that, Elizabeth could agree.

"Thank you, Mrs. Bennet," Charles grinned, and Jane blushed at their mother's lack of subtlety. Charles didn't seem to mind, though. He turned his grin on Elizabeth.

"I'm hoping Lizzy will agree to dance with me, next."

"I'd like that," Elizabeth grinned back.

When she noticed Collins had followed her, and was now pushing his way through the dancers, she kept the grin in place and said, "Until then, I think that chocolate fountain is calling my name."

But her mother must have noticed Collins too, as she grabbed hold of Elizabeth's elbow to keep her from moving away.

"Hold on, now, Lizzy. Mr. Collins may want to ask for another dance."

She opened her mouth to protest, but Collins reached them before she could. He stopped next to her, a little out of breath.

"My, Elizabeth, you are quick." He lifted a hand to place it on her waist, but she sidestepped him, twisting out of her mother's grip, and slapped his arm away. "If you'd like some refreshment, I can get some for you."

"I'd rather do that myself," she stated firmly.

"Nonsense," he waved a hand. "I know what refreshments ladies prefer, as Catherine De Bourgh instilled in me what hors d'oeuvres are appropriate for women to eat."

Jane's eyes widened at this pronouncement, and Charles looked at Collins like his head was on backward. Even Mrs. Bennet seemed flustered, but didn't contradict him.

"Not every woman prefers the same thing," Elizabeth pointed out.

Collins only blinked at her.

"Well," Charles intervened. "I think the next dance will start soon. Lizzy?"

Even as he held out his hand, Collins threw up his hands with a dramatic flair, causing him to drop it. "Oh! How remiss of me to forget. I hoped to elicit the dance just before midnight from you, Elizabeth."

He bowed slightly as he did the dumb eyebrow-waggling thing again. "For it is the most anticipated dance of the evening."

Elizabeth's revulsion must have shown on her face, because Mrs. Bennet took it upon herself to answer for Elizabeth—again.

"Oh, Mr. Collins, Lizzy would be absolutely flattered!"

Though she frowned, Elizabeth wisely said nothing—and instantly resolved to be nowhere near Mr. Collins come midnight. In fact, if she could contrive to leave the party well before then, even better.

She still glared at her mother, who was either as oblivious as Collins, or was choosing to ignore her daughter's ire.

"Marvelous," exclaimed Collins. He looked like he wanted to say something further, but the current song came to an end, and noting Elizabeth's displeasure, Charles once again held out his hand.

"Lizzy?" he said again.

She took the lifeline without hesitation and let him lead her back to the dance floor. Unlike Collins, Charles was a good dancer, and he led her with the effortlessness Collins had lacked.

"Thank you," she said to him, knowing he knew what she meant.

"Anytime," he said, his mien more serious than usual. "Are you really going to dance with him at midnight?"

"Hell no," she scoffed. "Any suggestions as to where I can hide?"

He smiled humorlessly. "I could escort you to a private room."

"I might just take you up on that."

"Want me to warn him off?"

She shrugged, touched by his concern. "Thank you, but something tells me he wouldn't take you seriously. I can handle it."

He still looked concerned, but nodded to indicate he was letting it go. They enjoyed the rest of their dance talking about more pleasant things— namely Jane. It brightened Elizabeth's mood to see how far gone he was for her sister.

When they returned to the refreshment table, Collins and Mrs. Bennet were gone, but Jane was still there, speaking with Charlotte. Charles solicited a dance from Charlotte next, leaving the two sisters to commiserate over their mother's antics in peace.

"I'm sorry, Lizzy." Jane's soft brown doe-eyes crinkled with second-hand misery. "I know she thinks she means well…"

"Which is exactly the problem," Elizabeth agreed, picking up a clear glass plate. "And it's not your fault; she doesn't listen to anyone."

She piled a handful of cheese and crackers onto her plate, a spoonful of olives next to that, and settled on a crostini spread before stopping at the chocolate fountain.

Jane followed, filling her own plate; Elizabeth noted she'd spread some of her crackers with caviar, which Elizabeth had automatically skipped over.

The spread for the chocolate fountain was laid out in big, clear glass bowls: strawberries, marshmallows, sliced plum, cherries, peanut butter balls, orange slices, graham crackers, shortbread cookies, the cake pops, and various other fruits and delicacies.

Elizabeth picked up several of the small skewers, loading them up with whatever struck her fancy, and running each one under the waterfall of warm, dark chocolate. When Jane had followed suit, they took their plates to one of the free standing tables. The most recent dance having ended once they reached the table, it wasn't long before Charlotte and Charles joined them with their own plates.

Conversation flowed companionably as they ate to their hearts' content, so much so that it was a few minutes before they noticed they had nothing to drink. Charles offered to fetch them all something, and went to the bar while the three friends remained.

Elizabeth was laughing at something Charlotte had said when she caught sight of Darcy for the first time since her dance with Collins. He wore his usual blank expression, but he was staring at their table, and walked with the sort of determination that told her he had a purpose. Charlotte noticed this as well, and sent Elizabeth a discerning look.

And Caroline Bingley chose that moment to approach them, looking sleek in her black, floor-length cocktail dress, which clung to her curves and dipped open in the back. Her sneering gaze honed in on Elizabeth, who noted with a surprising ripple of disappointment that Darcy changed direction the moment Caroline stopped in front of them. She was suddenly glad for Jane's foresight in making her lipstick a super-stay, because it meant she still looked awesome no matter what Caroline, who had a habit of mocking her appearance, said.

"Well, Eliza, your dance with Bill Collins was quite *interesting*." She pursed her lips in a superior smile. "He certainly seems to like you in particular."

No, he just likes the way I look, Elizabeth thought. Fortunately for her equilibrium, her annoyance with Caroline was lessened by the knowledge Darcy was deliberately avoiding her.

"Seems that way," Elizabeth acknowledged in a disinterested tone, biting into a chocolate covered strawberry.

"Well, I for one am pleased for you." Caroline tossed her glossy, impeccably highlighted blonde hair, which was perfectly straightened for the evening's festivities. "I'd be so *embarrassed* if I didn't have anyone to kiss at midnight."

Elizabeth merely tilted her head, a small smile playing on her lips. "I'm sorry you feel that way. Personally, I wouldn't mind not kissing anyone at all, but you do you."

Caroline's face scrunched up in an unpleasant mixture of disdain and confusion. "I will," she said with a forced confidence, and spun around, her hair whipping behind her as she strolled away.

Elizabeth and Charlotte snickered while Jane frowned, both unable to laugh at Caroline or scold her sister.

"She had no idea how to take that," Charlotte cackled. "We all know exactly who she wants to kiss at midnight, and you might've just made her doubt she'll get her wish."

"What do you want to bet she's going to go stalk Darcy all night?" asked Elizabeth.

"Lizzy," Jane admonished.

"Speaking of Darcy," Charlotte smirked. "He was on his way over here before he made a beeline for wherever Caroline wasn't."

Elizabeth's heart rate kicked up, but she shrugged. "He probably wanted to ask where Charles went."

"Or," Charlotte suggested with an emphasis that said the reason she was about to give was the correct one, "He was going to ask you to dance."

"Yeah, right."

Charlotte wagged a finger at her. "Mark my words, Lizzy Bennet. Will Darcy has a crush on you."

"A crush?" Elizabeth rolled her eyes. "What is this, high school?"

"I agree with Charlotte," Jane piped up. "And Charles thinks so, too."

"What do I think?"

Charles had returned to the table as Jane spoke, each of his hands cupping two wine glasses.

"That Will likes Lizzy," Jane answered as he set the glasses on the table and picked up his own.

"Oh, yeah." Charles grinned conspiratorially at Lizzy. "He definitely has a thing for you, Lizzy. I overheard him telling Caroline he thinks you have 'beautiful eyes.'"

Elizabeth paused with her glass halfway to her lips, her heart having lurched to a stop, then picked back up rapidly enough to echo in her ears. "Really? When was this?"

Charles scratched the back of his head. "At the Lucas' potluck I think."

Which was about a month ago, Elizabeth recalled. If Darcy had thought that all this time, why hadn't he said anything to her? She could easily brush off Charlotte's conjectures, but it was harder to write off the word of a friend who knew Darcy well.

"Well, if he has a thing for me, he has a funny way of showing it," she finally said.

"Yeah." Charles dragged out the word, frowned slightly. "He told me the arguments he had with you were debates, but I don't get it. But Will doesn't really flirt, so what do I know?"

"Maybe he thinks those debates were foreplay," Charlotte grinned slyly.

"Charlotte!" Elizabeth's cheeks pinked. "They were not."

"Whatever you say."

Elizabeth decided it was the opportune time to take a gulp of her wine, and thankfully the subject of Darcy was dropped.

COMPARED to the first hour of the party, the next few hours were uneventful. Elizabeth managed to avoid Collins and her mother entirely, which was a blessing, and she danced with a few of her neighbors, again with Charles, and even once with her father.

She followed her father to the game room, where a lot of his friends were gathered, to take a break from the crowd by playing a game of billiards with him. Halfway through the game, she noticed Darcy in the small crowd, watching her, and thought again of what Charles had told her before being distracted once more by the game. By the time the game was over, Darcy was gone.

Most of her time was spent with Charlotte, as Jane was occupied with Charles and vice versa. They had pleasant conversations with the Long sisters, the Gouldings, and Charlotte's siblings. Ian Forster pulled Charlotte away to dance more than once, and Elizabeth didn't tease her friend about possibly dancing with him at midnight—too much.

Darcy once again intruded on her notice when she was waiting at the bar; her skin prickled when she realized he was staring at her again, and their eyes met. He pushed off the wall he was leaning against like he was about to walk over to her, but was stopped by an undetected Caroline, who clutched at his arm and flipped her hair over her shoulder. When Darcy glowered and looked away from Elizabeth, she was torn between amusement and pity for him—and again that sense of disappointment for herself.

The only damper on the evening since the Collins debacle was her younger sister. For some reason Lydia decided to start a game of tag with Peter, wine sloshing out of her glass as she ran carelessly around the room, barely managing to dodge the people in her way.

Luckily she didn't splash anyone with wine, but a server had been summoned to clean up the spills, and people were definitely annoyed. Jane had managed to replace Lydia's wine with some of the sparkling grape juice meant for the under-twenty-one crowd to toast with at midnight and convince her it was champagne, and Peter sheepishly lead Lydia to the refreshment table to counteract some of the alcohol.

Elizabeth wondered vaguely if this was what Lydia was like at the college parties she frequented.

Neither of her parents were around to see or control Lydia's display, but of course Darcy had been one of the people Lydia nearly dunked with wine.

Why did he seem to be everywhere?

Finally, she and Charlotte stood with a small crowd gathering around the television in the living space, watching the city's live New Year's Eve proceedings and keeping an eye on the countdown. They managed to snag an open spot on the sofa—it felt blessedly good to sit—but Elizabeth watched the TV without seeing anything on the screen.

Her eyes were a bit droopy, and she was a little emotionally drained. Perhaps it was time to make good on her resolve to leave the party. It was only a matter of time before Collins found her again; it was a miracle she'd been able to escape him for so long.

As if reading her friend's thoughts, Charlotte nudged her shoulder.

"Incoming," she warned. "Mr. Cologne has spotted you."

She looked in the direction Charlotte indicated, and saw Collins stumbling his way through the crowd toward her.

"Crap." She glanced at her watch. "I lost track of time. There's only ten minutes left before midnight."

Charlotte smiled knowingly. "I'll tell him you went to the bathroom."

"Thank you."

And with that, Elizabeth rushed off toward the bathroom. But when she tried the handle, it only jiggled.

"Double crap." Why did it have to be occupied? Glancing around, she spotted the darkened hallway leading to rooms like the library, the game room, and—

Wait—the library!

She scurried past the game room, the sound of billiard balls clacking behind her as she nearly sprinted down the hall and around the corner. As her eyes adjusted, she zeroed in on the library door. A giggle threatened its way up her throat, but she held it back. She felt ridiculous and clever at the same time; while Collins could still come look for her in the library, for the moment he'd probably think whoever was currently in the bathroom was her.

With any luck, they'd distract him for a while.

She slipped inside, and with the quiet click of the door closing, pressed her back up against the door, closing her eyes. Reveling in the dense silence of the room, distant, muffled voices on the other side of the door—

literally closed off from her—she stayed like that a moment, letting out a relieved breath.

But the stillness was just as quickly disrupted by a shuffling noise from the other end of the room. Her eyes shot open to see a figure, no more than a shadow, rising from the sofa, and before she could ask who was there—though part of her just *knew*—the shadow bent toward a lamp on the end table. A soft *click* and the corner of the room glowed with dim light, illuminating the face of Will Darcy.

Heart in her throat, Elizabeth pushed off the door as he straightened, merely tilted his head as if waiting for her to explain herself.

Well, she didn't owe him an explanation.

"Why were you sitting in the dark?" she asked.

His expression remained blank. "The light coming through the window was sufficient."

"That doesn't really answer my question. Or, it only answers part of it."

"I wanted a reprieve from the crowd." He stepped away from the sofa, moved toward her with slow, languid steps as he considered her. "Same as you, I suppose."

Instinct made her want to back up into the door again, as there was something primal about the way he moved. But she stayed where she was, the darkness of his eyes becoming more blue the closer he got. And he kept his eyes on hers, a chain being pulled, until he stopped a few feet from her, roamed his eyes over all of her before centering on her face again.

Why was her throat dry?

She swallowed. "Made an escape from Collins, mostly. He's been tailing me, not-so-subtly suggesting he'd like to be *close* to me at midnight."

His gaze darkened. "So he's still pestering you? I witnessed your dance myself, but Charles told me some of what else happened."

Blowing out a breath, she shrugged helplessly. "The man needs no encouragement. Or rather, he has the encouragement of my mother, and apparently that matters more than the opinion of the object of his desire."

If possible, his expression darkened more. "Why is she pushing you at him?"

He had no idea how literal that statement was, she thought.

But what was with all the questions? Why was sullen, silent Will Darcy suddenly so talkative and interested?

Shrugging again, she wandered toward the window to look out over the city, alive with light and celebration. She wasn't sure why she felt inclined to answer his question, but Charles's words again rang in her ear. Maybe she should test the theory.

"Because Jane was taken, because I'm the next oldest, and maybe because she thinks he's the best I can do."

"It hasn't occurred to her you're not suited at all?"

She whipped around to stare at him, eyes narrowed. "Why do you care?"

She meant for it to sound a little scathing, but instead she noted she sounded a little flustered and unsure under the bite.

"I…" He paused, his mouth a thin line as he considered her question. "I beg your pardon. You're right, I shouldn't have pried."

"That's not what I said."

When he only lifted his eyes, stared into hers with an expression that seemed deliberately disinterested, she cocked her hip and folded her arms. Jutting out her chin, she raised a customary brow in challenge.

"You've never taken an interest in me or my family before," she pointed out. "So why the sudden inquisition?"

He blinked, and guffawed—actually *guffawed*—his eyes widening just a little.

"Never taken an interest?" His tone heightened slightly. "You're one of the few people here I can manage to talk to without wanting to Van Gogh my ears. If anything, I thought I'd taken too much interest."

"Real flattering opinion you have of our neighbors," she ground out.

His shoulders hunched. "I didn't mean it that way. I'm just uncomfortable with small talk and crowds, especially with people I don't know. But you're easy to talk to."

"I am? I kind of thought I was provoking you."

"Provoking me to speak more than usual, perhaps." Something resembling a smile lifted his face from brooding to contemplative. "If you were trying to annoy me, you chose the wrong tactic—you should have used Caroline as your role model."

She couldn't help it: She snorted. *Snorted* in front of Darcy, and let out a disbelieving laugh. "I take it she's included in the ear-gouging category?"

"She's the worst offender." Darcy cringed, and Elizabeth could only presume he was thinking of how Caroline had cornered him earlier. "She's been hinting all night she'd like me to ask her to dance—thankfully, since she expects me to ask, she won't ask me herself—but I've mostly managed to avoid her."

Elizabeth barely managed to resist rolling her eyes. "She and Collins would make a great pair. C squared."

Miracle of miracles, the comment had Darcy's mouth turning up in something not just resembling a smile, but actually affecting one—it was a wide grin full of amusement, and Elizabeth had to remind herself not to stare.

Good God, that smile. It changed his entire demeanor.

Her astonishment must have been clear, because the grin became a smirk as he asked, "What? Do I have something on my face?"

"Yes," she replied honestly, and mimicked his smirk. "You're *smiling*. Are you sick or something?"

His brow scrunched in confusion. "I smile."

"Like a full-on smile, not just a smirk?" She shook her head. "This is the first I've seen it."

She was sorry to see the smile fade, but relieved he didn't go back to frowning. Instead, he just seemed pensive.

He bowed his head. "Do you want to dance?"

The question came so far out of left field she wasn't sure she heard him right. "What?"

"Do you want to dance?" he repeated. "See, it's almost midnight, and I think we could help each other out. If we dance with each other, Collins can't hound you, and Caroline can't harangue me."

"Or we could keep hiding in here."

"Unless they come looking for us."

Ugh, Elizabeth thought, and couldn't help the grimace. "Yeah, I wouldn't put it past Collins to look in every room."

"We could lock the door, of course," Darcy continued, shrugging as he slipped his hands into his pockets. "But if someone figures out we're in here, or sees us leave together, they might make some...particular assumptions."

When it hit Elizabeth what he was implying, her cheeks warmed—she was sure she was red to the roots of her hair.

"No one would think that," she said tightly. "Everyone thinks we can't stand each other. Which is also why we'd shock the entire room if we did dance. Especially at midnight."

He cocked a brow, and the smirk from earlier made another appearance. "Is that what they think? Interesting."

"Well, what else would they think?" Not sure where the conversation was heading, Elizabeth spread her hands. "We haven't exactly been getting along."

"That doesn't mean we couldn't." Darcy withdrew his hands from his pockets, crossing the room to join her at the window.

"I don't know—we're both pretty stubborn and opinionated."

"Let me prove you wrong." He held out a hand. "Please, Elizabeth. Dance with me."

She didn't really know what made her do it, but as his eyes held hers and a flutter got caught in her throat, she thought maybe it would be quite nice to dance with Darcy. Plus, there was no way it'd be worse than dancing with Collins.

"Alright."

Even though they were still alone, she put her hand in his. He surprised her by raising it to his lips, placing a light kiss to her fingers.

"Thank you," he murmured lowly.

She knew she was blushing again, but gave him a small smile, then glanced at the clock. "We'd better go if we don't want to miss it. There's only a few minutes to midnight."

He nodded, giving her hand a squeeze before dropping it. "I'll get the light."

He waited for her to open the door, then switched off the lamp and crossed back to her. Her eyes had to adjust a little, but the light and noise from the party guided their way down the hall.

Elizabeth braced herself for stares and questions, or for Collins to pop out of nowhere; she slowed her steps without realizing it, and Darcy stepped back into the room ahead of her. He paused to wait for her, an action she thought would give them away, but no one was paying them any attention.

Internally, she breathed a sigh of relief.

And they were just in time—only a few moments after they'd approached the dance floor, the jazz band began a new song. Without hesitating, Darcy drew Elizabeth to him with one hand on her waist, the other lifting one of her hands. Though her opposite hand automatically placed itself on his shoulder, and her eyes lifted to meet his gaze, her mind had gone somewhat blank.

His touch was light, but firm enough she could feel the warmth of his hand on her waist through her dress. If he was an iron, she was fabric, heating everywhere her body pressed to his. In her heels, her eyes were level with his chin, she noted, and when she darted her eyes up, his gaze was already locked on her face.

It was a vastly different experience from her dance with Collins.

Darcy's eyes never left hers. It wasn't an understatement to say she was mesmerized, if not intoxicated by the way he was looking at her. They didn't speak, just kept watching each other, moving to the sway of the music, a sweet, seductive number interspersed with long, drawn out notes from the saxophone and twinkling trills from the piano.

And then Collins did one of the things he did best—pop out of nowhere.

Their dance halted as he tapped Darcy on the shoulder. He bowed ever-so-slightly as he said, "May I cut in?"

Elizabeth fought to control her features, which would surely reveal absolute horror otherwise. Then she had to fight the urge not to laugh when Darcy merely flicked Collins a glance and offered a curt *no* in reply.

"But…" Collins stuttered. "I promised this dance to Elizabeth."

Darcy spared him another glance, then looked back at Elizabeth with a hint of mischief lightening his features. "Did Mr. Collins ask you to save your midnight dance for him, Elizabeth?"

"No," Elizabeth said, and it was the truth. Collins had implied many things, but never outright asked her, and she certainly hadn't dignified any of his insinuations with a response. "You're the only one who's *asked* me for this dance."

"Dear Elizabeth," Collins protested, his words slurring a bit. "I was told you'd be flattered to dance this particular dance with me."

People were starting to notice the commotion, including Jane and Charles, who were dancing only a few feet away. Both looked delighted she and Darcy were dancing, but worried about the situation.

"Yes," Elizabeth acknowledged, wondering just how much wine Collins had had. "By my mother, but not by me. I never said I would dance with you. Now if you don't mind, you're interrupting my dance with Will."

She surprised herself when his name rolled off her tongue. She'd only ever thought of him as Darcy, but all of a sudden he was just *Will*. As he smiled at her and began to move her away from Collins, she realized just how right it felt.

Collins stepped after them and blubbered, "But this is the midnight dance! You can't dance with Fitzwilliam Darcy, he's intended for—"

"I beg to differ, since I'm the one who asked her," Will growled. His arm came around her waist, and he turned her slightly away from Collins in a gesture she realized was protective. "Go sit down, Collins, or I'll have you thrown out."

He need not have issued the warning, for Collins had begun to look a little pale. As Will finished speaking, Collins clamped a hand over his mouth and scurried in the direction of the bathroom.

For the servers' sake, Elizabeth hoped he made it there in time.

"Now, where were we?" Will's protective grip loosened, and they picked up their dance as though they hadn't stopped. Anyone who'd been trying to catch a glimpse of the action went about their own activities— though when she and Darcy looked over at Jane and Charles, Jane was beaming at them, while Charles sent them a wink.

Elizabeth heard Will chuckle low in his throat.

"You know, for someone who dislikes dancing, you're very smooth," she said, her tone now arch and flirtatious.

"I can enjoy dancing, when I'm comfortable with my partner." He gave her a soft smile, one that told her she'd only scratched the surface of this man's depths. Then the smile turned self-conscious.

"Elizabeth, I have a confession to make."

"Oh?"

"I didn't just ask you to dance to put off C squared. I also just wanted to dance with you."

Curious, she drew back a little to look up into his face. "Why didn't you just say so?"

"Would you still have said yes?" He arched a brow. "You've rejected my offer to dance twice before; I guess I just wanted to make sure you'd agree."

She thought of the Lucas' potluck, when he'd asked her to dance after Charlotte's father had suggested he do so, and of her and Jane's time at Netherfield, during which Will had indirectly indicated he would like to dance with her.

"Honestly?" She gave him a sheepish smile. "I didn't think you were serious either time."

"Then I will clarify for you: I don't do anything I'm not inclined to do."

"I know that now."

"Good." His smile was soft and affectionate. "Let there be no more misunderstandings."

She nodded. "Speaking of—what was Collins saying, when he said you're 'intended for' something?"

"Ah." Will's mouth flattened, and he rolled his eyes in a way that reminded Elizabeth of herself. "Catherine De Bourgh must have told him her fantasy about me marrying her daughter. Since she's an old acquaintance of my mother's, she's been trying to tell me my mom promoted the match, but my mom never said anything to me. Anne and I are nothing more than friends—and actually, I think she has a thing for my cousin."

"Good to know," Elizabeth said without thinking.

"Is it?" Will's brows rose as he grinned that disarming grin. "Happy to hear I'm single?"

She knew she was blushing again, but couldn't bring herself to admit she *was* glad. This whole evening had her feeling topsy turvy.

Will must have noticed her embarrassment, because he asked, "What about you?"

"Hm?"

"I know you have no interest in Collins, but are you seeing anyone else?"

"Oh." She bit her lip. "No. Your ex-buddy George asked me out, and I almost said yes, but something about him just seemed…insincere."

Will had stiffened at the mention of George Wickham, but loosened up as she continued. Now his gaze was full of admiration and relief.

"You're one of the few people I know who hasn't been charmed by him. Usually that's something people discover too late. May I ask how you came to that conclusion?"

Her answering smile was secretive, and she shook her head. "A story for another day. I don't think it's a topic for this lovely dance."

"Alright."

They moved in silence for several moments, but neither felt pressed to speak. At one point he twirled her, rather elegantly, if she did say so herself. It made her laugh, which got a satisfied smile out of him.

She knew there couldn't be much time left before the song ended and the clock struck midnight. She felt a little like Cinderella; perhaps it was silly to think of the evening as a fairytale, but the sense of whimsy it provided added to her enjoyment.

The only question was, would the night end with true love's kiss?

Hm.

Okay, maybe calling it 'true love's kiss' was taking it too far. She'd leave that sentiment to Jane.

The music began to wind down, and the vocalist addressed the room, letting the crowd know the new year was only ten seconds away by starting to count down. Elizabeth looked up at Will, and held in a gasp when she realized his eyes were staring rather intently at her lips.

She swallowed, but found she had enough wherewithal to tease him. "What? Do I have something on my face?" She deliberately wet her lips a little with her tongue, catching her lower lip between her teeth.

Six, five…

Will inhaled sharply. "Yes," he croaked out, his arm snaking around her waist to hold her more closely.

Three, two…

She merely tilted her face up expectantly.

Ecstatic, and in some cases, drunken, cries of *Happy New Year!* broke out among the crowd. Despite the lack of party poppers provided, some mischievous soul had snuck in a substantial number of noisemakers; but Elizabeth barely registered the high-pitched clown wheezing emitted from the little plastic annoyance machines.

There was both an infinite amount of time and no time at all before Will's lips took hers, soft but assured, in a heart-pounding, toe-curling kiss. The hand that still held hers let go to cup her face instead and deepen the kiss; her own hands gripped the lapels of his jacket, holding him in place just a few more seconds when it seemed he would pull away. The flick of his tongue teasing hers for a fraction of a second sent her heartbeat into overdrive.

But they had to pull apart, or they'd be bordering on overzealous PDA. He pressed one more kiss to her cheek.

"Lizzy." His breath caressed her lips. "I have another confession to make."

"What's that?" Good Lord, was she breathless?

"When I saw Collins trying to grope you, I wanted to throttle him."

She released her breath on a laugh. "So did I. And when I saw Caroline climbing on you, I wanted to bitch slap her."

His chuckle was low and approving, but whatever he was going to say was replaced by a sigh and a frown. "Speak of the devil," he said instead.

Elizabeth finally looked at the crowd around her. Servers were milling about, handing out champagne, and most people were preoccupied with their own celebrations. She had to hold back a chuckle when she noticed her parents standing by the bar—her mother was practically gaping at her, while her father merely wore his typical sardonic smirk. Next to them, surprisingly, was Collins, having apparently recovered somewhat, his jaw slack with disbelief.

She spotted Charlotte, hand in hand with Ian, each holding champagne as they picked their way toward her and Will. She hadn't seen Jane and Charles yet, but as Will had, she saw Caroline stomping toward them, her expression a furious contortion.

And Lydia chose that moment to do what Lydia did best—cause a ruckus.

"Ooh, more champagne!" she squealed, grasping at one of the flutes on a tray as a server passed by her. As she snatched it up, however, she miscalculated her movements and nearly tripped over her own feet. She was saved from tumbling over by Peter, who had hold of her arm, but in an effort to correct her balance herself, Lydia waved her free arm about, sending the bubbly liquid in the glass she held flying.

Right as Caroline marched into its path.

A gurgled gasp left Caroline's throat as champagne hit the side of her neck and shoulder. Lydia didn't even notice, as Peter quite deliberately dragged her toward her parents, mouthing an abashed 'sorry' to Caroline. For her part, Caroline could only glare open-mouthed at Lydia.

Then she turned her rage-soaked expression on Elizabeth; biting back a laugh, Elizabeth imagined the champagne evaporating in the form of steam rising from Caroline's skin. Apparently thinking better of entering a confrontation covered in sticky liquid, Caroline stalked out of the room.

Elizabeth blinked. "I don't think I've ever been more grateful for Lydia's immaturity."

Will let out a startled laugh, just as Charlotte and Ian reached them. "This is the part where I say 'I told you so,'" Charlotte smirked, and winked at Darcy.

Elizabeth gave her friend an affectionate eye-roll. "Yes, you did."

The music was starting back up, so they moved off the dance floor, and were met by Jane and Charles, who held out a couple extra flutes of champagne to Will and Elizabeth.

"Party's not over until we toast to the new year," Charles said cheerfully.

Elizabeth took in her sister's expression, flushed with pleasure, and was assured Jane's evening had been as fairytale-esque as her own—and perhaps Charlotte's had as well.

The six couples raised their glasses, clinked them together.

As the sweet, bubbly wine slid down her throat and settled pleasantly in her stomach, Will wrapped an arm around her waist. A little surprised, she turned her head to find him gazing at her intently. She slid her own arm around him and smiled; it was all the motivation he needed to lean his head down and capture her mouth for a sweet, affectionate peck.

"Happy New Year, Lizzy," he murmured, eyes shining with possibilities.

He had beautiful eyes, too, she thought, and smiled brighter. "Happy New Year, Will."

ACKNOWLEDGMENTS

This has been such a whirlwind, I don't even know where to begin. Sometimes I look back and wonder how I did all this, and I still don't know the answer.

But I do know it feels good to write these stories, and I wouldn't have had the courage to do this alone.

So, first and foremost, thank you to my family—for giving me books, encouraging my dreams of writing, and also for reading all the weird stories and Kitty Comics about my cat Beanie Babies I wrote when I was a kid. Shout outs to my mom for giving me the P&P short story collection Yuletide for Christmas a couple years ago, which started me down the whole JAFF reading rabbit-hole (and thus, inspired my own JAFF writing), and my partner in crime, my brother, for partaking in my imaginative flights of fancy growing up.

Thank you to my college professors and mentors for giving me the tools to craft a story, proofread, edit, keep going, keep learning, and get over myself and just write.

HUGE thank you to my friends—for supporting me, encouraging me in this endeavor, and giving me input. Oh, and for assuring me that writing random Pride and Prejudice stories and self-publishing them isn't dumb and is actually super cool and I can write what I want gosh darn it.

And finally, thank you to my own Mr. Darcy—for being my calm and my quiet, for easing my anxiety without even trying, for loving me without reservation, and for not rolling your eyes every time you come home to find me watching a Pride and Prejudice adaptation of some kind and say, "Again?" In return, I do not roll my eyes when you watch the same YouTube videos repeatedly. Such is love.

MORE BY MCKINLEY JAMES

Snowed In

In the Stacks

Down the Heart

P&P Mashup Series:

A Pride & Prejudice Story

ABOUT THE AUTHOR

Of all Austen's characters, McKinley James identifies most with the quiet, socially awkward, and introverted Darcy. Pride and Prejudice is an old friend, and upon discovering the vast and fascinating world of Jane Austen Fan Fiction (and subsequently journeying down a year-long JAFF reading rabbit-hole) she decided to toss her own P&P stories into the fray. McKinley has a bachelor's degree in Creative Writing and, in her other life, works at a library. She lives in Chicago.

www.mckinleyjameswrites.com